Rough Passage to London

Elisha Ely Morgan. Charles Robert Leslie, R.A., 1847.

Rough Passage to London

A Sea Captain's Tale, A Novel

Robin Lloyd

SHERIDAN HOUSE

Published by Sheridan House
4501 Forbes Boulevard, Suite 200, Lanham, Maryland 20706
www.rowman.com

10 Thornbury Road, Plymouth PL6 7PP, United Kingdom

Distributed by National Book Network

British Library Cataloguing in Publication Information Available

Library of Congress Cataloging-in-Publication Data

Lloyd, Robin, 1950–
Rough passage to London : a sea captain's tale, a novel / Robin Lloyd.
pages cm
ISBN 978-1-57409-320-9 (cloth : alk. paper) — ISBN 978-1-57409-321-6 (electronic)
1. Sea stories. I. Title.
PS3612.L69R68 2013
813'.6—dc23

2013013851

™ The paper used in this publication meets the minimum requirements of American National Standard for Information Sciences—Permanence of Paper for Printed Library Materials, ANSI/NISO Z39.48-1992.

Printed in the United States of America

For Marisa and Samantha Lloyd,
great-great-great-great-granddaughters
of Elisha Ely Morgan

"Wouldst thou,"—so the helmsman answered,
"Learn the secret of the sea?
Only those who brave its dangers
Comprehend its mystery!"

—Henry Wadsworth Longfellow, "The Secret of the Sea"

Preface

This is a novel about the seafaring life of Elisha Ely Morgan. Although Morgan was a historical figure, most of the book's characters and situations are invented. That being said, a great deal of effort has been made to accurately depict the world of the American transatlantic packet ships in the early to mid-nineteenth century. The packet ships mentioned in this book are the actual vessels Morgan sailed on and commanded. Morgan made over one hundred voyages across the Atlantic in nearly thirty years at sea. As far as could be determined by this author, he left behind no detailed records of what transpired on these passages.

Elisha Ely Morgan is my direct ancestor. This story is the way I have imagined him based on what is known about his life and personality from family records and extracts in books and articles. As a child, I often looked at his portrait hanging in the living room of my grandmother's house. A faint hint of a smile on his lips implied a touch of whimsy. I was told simply that he was a famous ship captain who sailed to London and was a close friend of Charles Dickens. Much later, when I began researching his history, I learned that Dickens had written a short story where the central character was closely modeled after Morgan. The story was called "A Message from the Sea." I was motivated to find out more. I hope that this ancestor of mine, who entertained Dickens and many others in London with his seafaring yarns, has passed down to me some of his storytelling ability.

PART I

You must know your road well to travel among these shoals on such a night as this.

—James Fenimore Cooper, *The Pilot*

1

April 7, 1814

Darkness descended as the British sailors leaned their backs into the rowing. Weathered faces grimaced as they pulled in unison. Four heavy rowing barges weighted down with men, and weapons, and two lighter rowing pinnaces pulled away from the dimly lit Royal Navy warships anchored in Long Island Sound. It was ten o'clock in the evening. They headed toward the mouth of the Connecticut River, passing the sandy bar that protected the town of Saybrook. Loaded aboard were lightweight cannons, bayoneted rifles, gunpowder, boarding lines, and grappling hooks.

The young British officer in charge kept his eyes peeled on the shadowy banks looming ahead, looking for any signs of movement. He had 136 men on this expedition. His informants ashore had assured him they would face no resistance, but he was taking no chances. Some five miles of hard rowing lay ahead until they reached their target, the town of Potapoug, home to one of the biggest shipbuilding yards on the Connecticut River. The British had spied on the shipyard for weeks and seen how many armed vessels were being built there. Five of those American gunships would soon head to sea to attack British supply ships unless this raid was successful. The captain knew there was a lot at stake, particularly as British forces had already suffered too many losses in the nearly two years of war.

Fortified against the nighttime chill by an additional tot of rum, the sailors were keen on rowing. The men were eager for action after months of frustrating duty where nimble Yankee schooners continued to dodge and weave their way through the British blockade. Ever since the war began in 1812, American privately owned armed ships, or privateers, had wreaked havoc on British supply vessels.

❁

As the British forces slowly rowed up the river, passing the open fields and pastures of outer Lyme, they were unaware that they were being watched. It was about three o'clock, and the night was so black that hardly anything could be seen more than twenty feet away. Two boys crouched in the muddy reeds alongside the river, too frightened to move. One of them was only eight years old, a wiry, skinny boy who was small for his age. His older brother was almost thirteen and was already stocky and muscular. They both had covered their curly hair with small, dark caps. Their linen shirts and coarse overalls were now covered with river mud. They were farm boys from Lyme who had escaped from home on a nighttime dare. They had just poled and rowed their way over to the northern tip of Nott Island in a small, flat-bottom skiff, when they heard noises coming from the middle of the river.

"What's that, Abraham?" whispered Ely to his older brother, his voice cracking nervously. "Sounds like a boat." The young boy's biggest fear was that he'd be caught by his father, who, he well knew, had little tolerance for misbehavior. Ely Morgan had felt the wrath of his father's whipping belt too many times for what seemed like the smallest of infractions.

Abraham listened intently but said nothing. The creaking of oars and the muffled voices of men were now easily heard floating across the water, making them sound much closer than they were.

"That ain't Pa coming to get us, is it, Abraham?"

"Ely, if it is, I reckon he's bringing the whole Lyme militia with him," murmured Abraham with a nervous half chuckle. "There's a pack of boats under weigh out there, and from all that grunting and whispering and them rowing without a light, I'll warrant they don't want to be found out."

With that, the boys quietly hid their shallow-draft rowing boat behind some shoreline bushes and a stand of willows in the soggy marsh. They climbed an old solitary maple tree, scrambling to hide behind some of the larger branches. For weeks now these two boys had gone over the details of this nighttime adventure. Their plan had been to cross the river and board the newly built brig, which would soon be equipped with eighteen guns and was at anchor off the town of Potapoug, just across the river from their farm. It was no secret that Captain Hayden's newest ship was ready to go to sea with plans to seize British ships, but there was still no crew so the ship was empty. They thought a nighttime visit would surely go unnoticed. They waited until their whole family was asleep before they crawled out their window and slipped away into the night. The two boys wanted bragging rights that they had trod the decks of the newest American privateer built at the famous Hayden yard.

They could now hear the gruff voices of dozens of men and more splashes of oars breaking the surface of the water. The boys clutched the coarse bark of the tree as they tried to melt into the branches. That's when they heard a man's voice call out.

"Pull hard, men! Pull hard! Almost there. Soon we'll give these Yankees a taste of their own medicine."

The dim shape of four heavy rowing barges filled with men and weapons and two smaller rowing vessels slowly emerged from the darkness down river as they came near the shore. To the horror of the boys, a man with a black tricorn hat gave orders for the small flotilla to pull into shore, just fifty yards from where they were hiding. The six rowing boats slid in among the reeds, one of them landing with a muffled thud just feet from where they'd hidden their boat.

"Take a rest here, men. We are close. Our target lies just across the river, less than a quarter of a mile from here."

He then turned to the man next to him.

"Mr. Stryker, give the men another tot of rum each, for tonight their labors have just begun, and light that lantern. No one will see us on this island."

"Aye, aye, Captain."

With the glow of the lantern, the two boys could just make out the shadowy faces of the huddled men, and the dull gleam of the bayonets on the rifles. These weren't the blue-coated Connecticut militia. These men were English redcoats, the enemy, and there was no question what the purpose of their trip was, a raid on the town of Potapoug. Ely felt a cold shiver crawl down his spine as he looked at all of these armed men. There were so many. There were scores of redcoats, all clutching their rifles. The ones who were manning the oars wore no uniforms, but they all had knives, axes, and pistols. He supposed they were the sailors. He gulped, and struggled to take a deep breath. He watched wide-eyed and petrified as the officer with his high black boots stepped ashore and addressed both the sailors and armed marines clumped together in the barges.

"Men, all ships we find are to be torched. That's our main objective here. Every ship in the harbor must be destroyed. I will land with the marines to seize and commandeer the town. Once the town has been secured, we will burn their ships, even those being built on the yards. Sailors, prepare your hooks and your torches!"

The men, who had been resting on their oars, looked up at their commanding officer with a mixture of fear and patriotic fervor in their eyes, and then responded with a muffled chant, calling out, "God bless the King! God bless England!" like devout members of a church congregation. Ely Morgan looked over at his brother in desperation. He couldn't make out Abraham's expression in the darkness, but he knew they must stay absolutely quiet.

The British officer then turned to the sailors in his own boat and the young midshipman who was acting as coxswain.

"Mr. Stryker, you will stay here with your pinnace. You are to make sure that no boats come by here. If one does, you will shoot to kill. We want no informants."

On hearing that order, Ely hugged the tree where he was hiding more tightly. The British officer then began to chuckle to himself.

"And Mr. Stryker, when you see the harbor lit up like two dozen torches, you'll know we are celebrating Guy Fawkes early this year. Then you must come and join us."

"Aye, sir," Stryker responded, a wide, careless grin breaking out across his clean-shaven face.

With those firm orders, the five other rowing boats pulled away into the night. The darkness momentarily revealed the wake of the small fleet in the open river, but the ripples from the oars soon faded, and the water's surface returned to glass. The man called Stryker and his men watched silently from the shore. He ordered the marines to take up scouting positions at the tip of the marshy island. Ely held his breath as two of the British redcoats, their rifles ready, walked directly underneath the tree where they were hiding before disappearing into the bush. Two other shadowy figures moved slowly toward them, and sat down almost directly under their tree. They lit a small lantern and placed it on the ground between them. Ely could just make out their faces. He was surprised at how young they seemed, maybe just a few years older than Abraham, he thought to himself. He could barely hear them. One of them whose name was Bill had a bushy head of hair. The other had curly red hair. They both spoke with an English accent that Ely found hard to understand.

Just then the smudgy gray of predawn was pierced by the loud thud of cannons and peppery musket fire. It was much closer than Ely had expected. There was a flickering of lights across the river like tiny jack-o'-lanterns followed by faint shouts and shrieks.

"Abraham," whispered Ely. "What should we do?"

"Hush up and stay quiet," Abraham breathed out in a hoarse whisper. "There ain't nothin' we can do."

"I don't hear a call to arms, Abraham. No bells. You suppose they killed everybody?"

"Quiet, Ely. You'll get us caught."

Then there was silence from across the river. Moments later, the boys watched as the first of the ships in the harbor went up in flames. Soon this was followed by another ship exploding, and crackling in the gray light. The tightly furled sails on the yards ignited first followed by the masts, which were swallowed up in a ball of yellow fire like giant torches. White smoke billowed upward, and with each new fireball the harbor and the village houses were lit up more brightly. Ely's heart was pounding and beating so fast he thought for sure the British sailors below would notice, but their faces, dimly lit by the flames, remained firmly locked on this fiery inferno across the river. He looked over at his brother, whose face was frozen in shock.

Ely could see the silhouette of the British barges moving from ship to ship, the nimble sailors clambering aboard with their grappling hooks and lines and then moments later, another explosion of flames. The crackle of wood and the crash of timbers filled the air along with the sooty smell of burning ships. The noisy spectacle was so dramatic Ely momentarily lost his grip and almost fell out of the tree, catching himself at the last minute, his gasp snapping Abraham out of his trance.

"We've got to make a run for it. Daylight's coming soon and they'll spot us up here."

To the southeast, the sky was already a lighter shade of gray. Ely noticed that the redcoated marines were now walking back to their barge. The two sailors beneath them stood upright, looked to the right and left, and then swept their gaze out to the river. The diffused light revealed the wooden stock of a gun and the handle of a pistol. As soon as the pinnace filled with marines and sailors pulled out from shore, Abraham and Ely slid down from the tree and crawled over to where their rowing boat was hidden. Carefully, they pushed it out from behind the reeds and bushes into the current and gave it a shove, pulling themselves on board at the same time. By now the British pinnace was working its way toward the burning ships, the oarsmen pulling hard into the current. In the faint dawn, Ely could now see their faces more clearly. Both boys began to row furiously upstream to round the northern tip of Nott Island and head east into the safety of the marshes near Lord's Cove on the other side of the river.

"They've spotted us!" Ely yelled.

He could see commotion in the pinnace, arms pointing and men yelling.

In a desperate panic, the two boys rowed unevenly, their oars wildly slapping and splashing the surface of the water. Their small boat soon ran aground in a shallow, muddy area. Abraham jumped up, grabbed the pole, and began frantically pushing the small flat-bottom boat forward.

"You keep rowing, Ely. Let me know when they stand up to fire," yelled Abraham, "or if they turn around and come at us, hammer and tongs."

Shots rang out, but Ely was too intent with his rowing to pay any attention to how good the marksmanship was. Then there were more shots. This time Ely could see the bullets hit the water around them.

"Get down, Abraham!" he yelled as he threw himself into the bottom of the boat. Ely hugged the wet floor planks, anticipating that he would soon be shot. He was imagining the painful sensation of a lead bullet tearing through his skin when a spectacular burst of sunshine rose over the surrounding marshes. The blinding early morning sun sent sparkles across the surface of the water like a scattering of tiny diamonds. Ely peeked over the side of the boat, and he could now clearly see the Englishmen with their rifles, the vibrant red of their coats glistening in the brilliant sunlight. Strangely, they had put their rifles down. They were cupping their hands over their eyes, and were looking due east, directly at them. Ely was confused, but Abraham understood what had happened.

"Row, Ely! Row! They can't see us anymore!"

The low-lying sun was shining directly into the eyes of the British riflemen, allowing the boys to grab their oars and begin rowing away. As they put their backs into the rowing, Ely looked across the river to the west and sighed with relief as he saw the British pinnace splashing its way in the other direction, toward the harbor. Their flat-bottom boat soon slipped into the marshes along the muddy banks of the river, and they jumped out and pulled it into the reeds. Ely wiped his brow with the back of his hand as he realized how narrow their escape had been. Across the river less than half a mile away, he could see flames from burning boats and black smoke billowing high above the harbor. He wondered if the British were torching the village as well as the ships.

2

1822

A lone figure carrying a canvas bag walked down the dark wharf toward a small schooner tied up at the pier. His wide-brimmed hat was pulled down tightly over his head, his step, deliberate. It was six o'clock in the morning, and the air was cold for October. Roosters were already crowing, telling the Lyme townspeople it was time to wake up. Some wharf rats clad in dark overcoats were loading the small sailing ship with barrels of newly picked golden sweets and crates filled with the famed Connecticut peaches and pipes of freshly squeezed cider.

The captain was a Block Island man with a loud voice, a thick head of silver curly hair, deep-set eyes, and a bony, whiskery face. He was telling them to hurry up as the tide was falling. He turned to face the young man who had walked up to the boat's gangway and stood beside him. He sized him up quickly like a farmer does a hog. He was younger than he'd thought, a good-looking boy, medium size in stature but athletic in build, with light hazel green eyes under dark eyebrows, a smooth and square forehead, a well-rounded chin. His reddish hair hung uncombed from a broad-brimmed canvas hat. He wore stitched and patched overalls and a dark woolen jacket. Definitely a farm boy, he thought to himself.

"What did you say your name was, boy?"

"Ely, Ely Morgan."

"Pleased to have you aboard, Morgan. The name is Captain Foster."

The man extended a large, calloused hand to help Morgan aboard and with the other took the three dimes that Ely gave him for the fare. He then turned back to the men loading the boat.

"Hurry up, you villains, or I'll put the boot to you! The tide's ebbin' now and the current is strong."

So it was on that cool October day, with the first taste of fall in the air, that Ely Morgan left home on a coastal schooner to take up his new life as an ocean sailor. He was sixteen years old. It had taken him months of working at a nearby farm on Sunday afternoons to save the money for the fare. He reached into his pocket and rubbed the remaining quarter. That was all he had. Captain Henry Champlin, a well-known ship captain from the Connecticut River, who worked with the John Griswold firm out of New York, had promised him a berth on his new ship being built on the East River. Champlin told him to come to the firm's offices at 68 South Street on the corner of Pine and ask for him once he got there.

To avoid anyone recognizing him, Ely had picked a small, unknown schooner named the *Angelita* that worked the Connecticut coastline bringing fresh produce and vegetables to New York. Moments after he arrived, the lines were cast off, the sails hoisted, and the heavily laden schooner, riding low in the water, began to run down the swiftly moving Connecticut River. The dark gray sky over the river was decorated with several formations of Canada geese moving in tandem, honking their warning that winter was coming as they flew south from Middletown over old Potapoug. The small river town that the British had attacked years ago was now known as Essex. The townspeople had only recently changed its name as a way to forget the painful memories of that fateful raid.

Ely looked out at the swirls and ripples in the river. He thought back to that night of the Good Friday Blaze, and the danger that he and Abraham had faced. The charred remains of some of the American ships that were burned by the British were still visible at low tide. Twenty-seven American ships were torched, vessels capable of carrying more than 130 cannons. The town of Potapoug was spared because the surprised villagers agreed not to resist if the British would not burn their homes. Many on the river were embarrassed by this defeat at the hands of the British. Even worse, the raiding party escaped with few casualties, only two dead and two wounded. The whole incident was a major blow to the pride of the Connecticut River militia, but for Abraham and Ely, it was their special bond, their secret adventure that was never discovered by their father.

Six years had gone by since his brother Abraham had left home to become a sailor, following in the footsteps of their older brother, William. They both had left shortly after the war ended. For a restless younger generation, not content with the ways of the past, a berth on an ocean-bound brig was like a siren call. Their departure had made life difficult at home, but it was the arrival of that fateful letter during the summer of 1816 that had changed the Morgan family forever. Like a cold winter's wind, it had swept away hopes and dreams. A dark cloud had settled over the family, leaving his mother with no trace of her once familiar warm smile.

Ely's mind drifted back to that day when he and his brother Josiah had raced home with the letter. The entire family had gathered around Sally Morgan as she broke the wax seal and unfolded the small letter. It was from New York and the date July 12, 1816, was stamped on it. Ely was squirming with anticipation at what he was sure would be exciting news from one of his brothers. The older girls—Asenath, Sarah, and Nancy—each picked up the two younger children, Maria Louisa and Jesse, so they could see what was happening. Abraham Morgan looked over his wife's shoulder as she unfolded the letter written on a plain sheet of paper. The older man's gaunt face was glowering. In his mind, his two older sons had abandoned their obligations by going off to sea. They are "the Devil's own," he would say. "No doubt they do their worshiping in a grogshop."

"It's from a John Taylor," Sally Morgan said slowly with surprise and a sudden note of doubt and hesitation in her voice. "Do we know a John Taylor?" No one answered. Ely watched his mother mouth the words as she slowly read the letter to herself. It was her face and the way it suddenly aged before his eyes that told the story. He watched as the letter fell from her hands onto the floor like a leaf from a tree. Her shoulders went limp and she began trembling and shuddering like an injured bird with broken wings.

"What is it, mother?" one of the girls asked.

In a weak voice that cracked into a faint whisper, she said, "They're gone. Dear God, they're gone." With that she left the room, her head down and her body shaking. It was the older sister, Asenath, who picked up the letter from the floor and began reading it to all her siblings. Like a chiseled carving on a granite boulder, those words remained etched in Ely's memory. Each time he recited them he felt a burning inside.

> *Dear Madam,*
> *This is to inform you of all that I can concerning your sons. William sailed on the second day of June bound to Canton in the ship John S. Williams. Captain Depyster and I have not heard of her since.*
> *And as for Abraham, my Bosom friend and Brother, I am much afraid that we cannot meet in this troublesome World. But Let us Still Cherish the hope that we will all meet in that country where Sorrow and Sighing is done away. Where the wicked cease from troubling and Where the Weary be at Rest. So my Dear Madam, all the News of your Sons I Will send to you. I have Nothing Worth adding at present.*

Despite the promise in the letter of more news, none came. Nothing was ever heard from John Taylor again. Several weeks after receiving the letter, the family knew that William had died because the sinking of the *John S. Williams* was reported in one of the New York shipping papers, but Abraham's fate remained a mystery. The dimly lit dinner table at the Morgan house was often filled with awkward silences. The crackling of the fire in the kitchen and the flickering of the candles in the drafty house only accentuated the long gaps in conversation. His mother, whose face had grown drawn and tired, had refused to acknowledge his death. "He's out there somewhere," she said. She even refused to give away his clothes and some of his treasured pennywhistles.

Ely watched as an osprey lifted off into the air with its morning catch squirming in its curved beak. The memory of that letter never failed to make him teary-eyed. He wiped his eyes with the back of his hand as he looked up the river and thought about its long journey. The Connecticut traveled all the way from Canada to the Long Island Sound. It was open ocean after that. The Algonquian Indians called it the "long tidal river." For years Ely thought that its name should be "the river with no escape" because he felt that it held him prisoner. When he was younger, he had stood on the high ground and gazed longingly down at the river.

Occasionally he would see the tall masts of an oceangoing brig coasting downriver with the outgoing tide, the sailors' songs filling the air as the men aloft set the ship's square sails. Even as he hitched up a makeshift dragging cart to one of the plough horses, Ely used to imagine himself on one of those big ships.

He now watched as the first orange rays of sunlight shone through the trees on the banks of the river. Small sloops and schooners carrying freight and passengers tacked back and forth. A flat-bottomed scow powered by long sweeping oars was carrying a full load of Jersey cows across the river. He looked off to the left and saw the rooftop of the Morgan barn framed by the first tint of red and yellow leaves on the oak trees. His family would be getting up soon to start picking the last of the delicious Golden Sweets and the first of the Greenings and Russets. His brother Josiah would be carting the apples over to the neighbor's cider mill where they would be thrown into a circular trough, crushed into a pomace, and then squeezed in a heavy screw press.

He would miss that family ritual, the first cup of cider. He would miss Josiah. His brother was the one who had made the arrangement with the schooner's captain. He was the only one in the family he had confided in. Josiah had tried to dissuade him, but he had shook his head. The whippings that his father used to give him were now replaced with fists and slaps and shouting. It seemed like old Abraham had donned the sackcloth of the prophet Jeremiah, even as he saw his willful son as a sinner who needed to repent.

A freshening northwesterly breeze filled out the sails, and within an hour, the small schooner was clearing the Saybrook Bar headed into Long Island Sound toward the entrance to the East River at Throgs Neck. Ely looked back at the low-lying coastline, barren and empty of trees. The sun was now shining brightly over the leeward side of the boat. He felt a knot in his throat and a tightening in his stomach as he thought about what he was doing. He felt nervous, guilty, anxious, and excited, all at the same time. It was a confusing mix of emotions and sensations that overwhelmed him as he looked back at the fading entrance to the Connecticut River.

His mother would be heartbroken when she read the letter he'd left behind, but there was nothing to be done. He could no longer work under his father's thumb. The old man's anger and rage had only intensified after the tragic news about William and Abraham. Josiah got along with his father, and so did the girls, at least those who remained at home. Asenath had married a church deacon named Talcott from the small inland town of Gilead, but neither Sarah nor Nancy showed any signs of leaving Lyme. Then there were the two younger girls, Maria Louisa and Jesse. They would all find a way to keep the farm working, he told himself. Then again, he knew the pain he would cause his mother, and he felt the knot in his throat return.

After William and Abraham had left home, Sally Morgan was determined that her younger son get a good education. She was friendly with Margaret Carpenter, one of the local deacons' wives, who was well read and had a small library and a piano. She persuaded her that Ely was the scholarly one in her family and asked if she could teach her young son about the Bible's lessons and also introduce him to some of the classics like Shakespeare's *Hamlet* or Cervantes's *Don Quixote*. Part of Ely's mother's hopes was that her religious friend would instill in her young son an ambition to become a deacon or even a pastor at the Lyme Congregationalist Church. Margaret Carpenter's father had been a ship merchant, and she had traveled with him when she was younger to Paris and London. France had left a strong impression on her. At church meetings, she'd described the Parisians as poor, misguided heathens who worshiped statues of naked men and women and who cared about nothing but gratifying the carnal mind and feasting their lowest senses. In England, she said, the food was awful and the people boring.

Sally Morgan had thought these negative views of the ways of the Old World might persuade her son to give up his wayward dreams of going to sea. Paradoxically, the reverse happened. Young Ely Morgan found Margaret Carpenter's descriptions of her early life at sea to be the most interesting part of their Sunday-afternoon reading sessions. She had spoken to him of the beauty of the sea at dawn, and showed him one of her sketchbooks with watercolors and drawings of the ship's deck with ocean birds flying alongside. All of these stories only served to fire up the boy's imagination.

Ely again thought of the note he had left for his mother in the kitchen. He had simply written that he had to leave home to find Abraham and he did not know when he would return. He thought back to the words he had used, and wondered if his letter would give his mother any comfort.

"You must kiss all my sisters, Mother. I am sorry I had to leave without saying good-bye. I hope you will understand my decision one day. With love and respect, I remain your son, Ely."

With the wind picking up and the choppy seas splashing on the deck, the captain could see he was shorthanded. He only had two sailors and a cook on board. The winds were piping up sharply now. The headsails were thrashing about wildly, the lines all tangled together. The two men on the foredeck, inexperienced and dim-witted, were having a hard time wrestling with the halyards. Something must have gotten snagged. With no one else available, he turned to Morgan and looked down at him with a hawkish stare.

"Can you steer, son?"

Morgan nodded, gulping slightly. He was already feeling a little uncertain about what he was doing.

"That's good, 'cause we're headed into a blow," said the captain as he stroked his thinning whiskers. "You just hold the tiller on this course and don't let go."

Captain Foster pointed at the black thunderclouds moving in from the west, indicating with his other hand the course he wanted Ely to steer. He handed the tiller over to Morgan and clambered out on top of the cabin house to help two other sailors trying to lower the flapping main gaff topsail. Morgan grabbed the tiller, his fingers wrapping around a well-worn, twisted, rope-covered grip. At first, he was thrilled that he was steering a ship, but then he began to be frightened. He couldn't believe how much the four-foot-long tiller pulled at his arms. It was like trying to rein in a team of horses on the run. He braced himself with his feet against a wooden block on the deck, and pulled with all his might. Like most farm boys, the only boats he was familiar with were scows, small gaff-rigged sloops, and rowing skiffs. For that matter, he had never been in rough weather before, and as the ship began to pitch and heave, a strange feeling started to come over him.

The seas had started to build and the water was swashing over the decks. He was feeling dizzy and suddenly sick to his stomach. His head was spinning. He'd never been sick like this before. The ship was heeled over at an alarming angle, and pretty soon Ely let go of the tiller as he threw his upper body over the side in a reckless effort to rid himself of this sudden misery. It felt like the whole upper portion of his body was turning inside out. The acrid taste of bile filled his mouth. He paused for breath, and then the whole paralyzing process began all over again.

Free of a steadying hand at the tiller, the schooner swung into the wind, sails flapping wildly, thrashing about, the masts and rigging shaking and trembling. Ely was too far gone to even care, and with no one to tend it, the tiller now swung wildly back and forth, causing the boat to lose momentum. The captain rushed back to take the helm even as the schooner now swung through the wind onto a different tack and headed for the dangerous Long Island shoals. As he passed the prostrate form of the boy he'd left in command of his ship, he landed a kick in Ely's backside and cursed him loudly.

"Hoist up the centerboard!" yelled the captain to one of the other men, panicked that his heavily loaded ship would run aground with a small fortune of cargo lost. One of the sailors down below in the cabin frantically pulled on the tackle to lift the centerboard. The captain looked over the side and cursed some more as he realized how shallow the water was. The boat scraped bottom, the bow leaping upward and then crashing down again. The next instant waves lifted up the stern, propelling the boat forward, and then with a fearful thud she struck bottom again. The bow was lifted up by waves, once again falling and scraping the bottom. By this time, the storm had struck with high winds and pelting rain. Waves hit the boat broadside and water started filling the cabin. The flashes of lightning and the roaring of the wind only made Morgan feel more like he was facing the end of the world.

Fortunately, the schooner soon plowed and scraped through the narrow Long Island shoals, making its way safely into deep water. The crew immediately set about to pump and bail, and by the early afternoon, the water was out of the hold. That night they threw the anchor down just off Throgs Neck at a pretty little anchorage in full view of an old farmhouse. After a pannikin of rum and the assurance that his cargo was safe, the captain soon regained his composure, and turned his attention to his quiet, sickly passenger.

"Have you ever been to sea before?" he asked with a knowing smile on his face as he gave each member of the crew a stiff glass of rum.

Morgan didn't say anything. The captain handed him a plate of hard sea bread and salty codfish. Morgan's face turned green as he felt he would have to vomit again. He turned away and looked down at his feet.

"Guess I know the answer to that," the captain said. "We already guessed that you were a runaway. Might as well tell us your true story."

Captain Foster looked over at the leering faces of the two sailors and the cook, then filled Morgan's glass with a generous shot of rum. He'd come across many runaway boys in his thirty years at sea. "Rackety youngsters sowing a considerable crop of wild oats" was what he called them. He thought most of them were no better than chicken thieves and liars.

"Tell us all about yourself, lad. That story your brother told about you going to visit your widowed aunt is nothing but a bunch of palaver. Don't bother telling us that."

The only light came from a hanging lantern overhead. It shone directly in Ely's eyes and made him feel weak and vulnerable. To try to appear like one of the crew, he took a sip of the rum and immediately regretted it. He made a face but swallowed it anyway. There was no point in trying to keep a secret. First he told them about his two older brothers, the dream they shared of going to sea, the special bond he'd had with Abraham, and how the letter they'd received had devastated his family.

Ely took another sip of rum and felt the alcohol burn the insides of his throat. He told the captain and his crew how he had given up his dream of shipping out to sea. How he'd resigned himself to a life on the farm, but then he'd run into an old sailor down at the docks in Essex who had surprising news about his brother Abraham. When he heard this man's story it changed everything.

Morgan took another sip and began his story.

"His name was William Marshall. I thought he was just a drunken sailor looking for a free tot of rum. He introduced himself, and explained he was in a boarding house now waiting for a new Griswold ship to come off the yards. He was one of them Maine boys from the Penobscot, a little place called Camden where there's not much of anything, just a few houses scattered about where the mountains meet the sea."

"Get to the point, boy," shouted Captain Foster, picking up the rum bottle and pouring out another generous glassful for himself. "There's hundreds of no-good sailors like that. What did he tell you about your brother?"

"He caught me by surprise when he said, 'Are ye Ely Morgan? Brother of Abraham Morgan?'"

"Go on," said the Captain abruptly.

"He said he sailed with my brother and his friend John Taylor. They were two young pups, he said, as green as the first shoots of grass in April. They were sailing from Montevideo with a cargo of jerked beef when one of them hurricanes struck about four hundred miles south of Cuba. He told me it's a wonder that the ship wasn't dashed to pieces on some shore. Anyway, they put into Barbados, the crew all the time pumping and bailing. He said the ship was so badly damaged the captain dry-docked her, and after looking at the worm-eaten planking in the hull, sold her directly. The captain thought she was a cursed ship. Then he told me that the last he saw of Abraham and Taylor was the sight of them disappearing on a fast British ship. It looked as if they didn't have much choice. A couple of the mates on board were beating on them with belaying pins and ropes."

Foster piped in, interrupting Morgan. "Sounds like they were shanghaied by John Bull."

Morgan nodded. "That's what the old tar told me. He never laid eyes on my brother again, but he'd seen Taylor three years later in one of them grog shops on Cherry Street. He described him as a much-changed man, old beyond his young years. Said Taylor looked like he'd seen the Devil himself. He was fired up pretty well with the grog."

Morgan had a rapt audience at this point, with Captain Foster and his men settling into the small cabin for a night of storytelling. The air was moldy and the wooden cabin sole was still wet from all the seawater that had poured in through the hatchway. They had no fire to warm themselves so the men kept passing the rum bottle.

"Did that old tar ask Taylor about your brother?" Foster inquired.

"He did," Morgan replied. "He said he flat out asked Taylor whatever became of Abraham."

"So . . ."

"Marshall told me that when he asked about Abraham, Taylor got all scared and shaky and started to whisper, 'I ain't supposed to tell, but I tell ye what, it was foul play of the worst kind, the Devil's own mischief.' Marshall said Taylor kept holding his hands over his ears and talking about the voices he was hearing, voices from hell he called them. He said something about how Jonah should have been cast forth into the sea."

Morgan pulled his coat more tightly around him.

"Sadly, that's all I know," he said shaking his head despondently before continuing with his tale. "I know I need to find out more. Abraham would have wanted that. Whether my brother's dead or alive, I need to get some answers. And if by some miracle he's alive, I need to go find him and bring him back home."

"Where you reckon you're going to find him, boy? The world is a mighty big place."

Morgan was silent. He looked down at his feet, and then his jaw tightened and his face took on a more determined look. "I don't rightly know how I will find him, but make no mistake, I will. I got me a berth on a John Griswold ship going to London."

The captain shook his head, spitting a squishy wad of tobacco out a porthole into the water. "Sounds like one of them new American ocean packet ships. You know about them packets, don't you, boy?"

Morgan felt intimidated, but managed to stammer a response.

"They're mail boats, ain't they?"

"That's right, but these new ships are full rigged with three masts. Square-riggers on a schedule, that's what they call 'em. The Black Ball Line is sailing regular each month with fixed dates from New York to Liverpool these past few years. They're carrying cargo and passengers as well as the mail. I seen the letter bags with the packet's name on it hanging down by the Tontine Coffee House. No serious man of business is relying on those slow British brigs to deliver the mail anymore. The smart merchants are sending their packets of mail on ships flying the stars and stripes."

Morgan had no idea about any of this, but he nodded knowingly.

The man paused and looked at him with a bemused expression on his face. "Speaking truthfully boy, if I was you, I'd turn around and go back where you come from. Your brother, he's probably long ago dead. That's just my cogitations, mind you. You rackety youngsters always do as you please."

Morgan shook his head. "What if my brother is out there? He could still be alive. Maybe he's hurt? Maybe a prisoner somewhere? Or he could be sick? Ain't that right, Captain?"

The Block Island captain paused in thought as he ran a calloused hand through his bushy head of silver hair, then turned to Morgan with a smile. "You might be lucky, boy. Who knows? You might find that critter John

Taylor down in them quim houses along Cherry Street in New York, or the alehouses on the East End of London. I venture to say sailors and sewer rats never stray too far from those two hellholes, no matter how much they roll and tumble around the world."

After that bit of sage advice, the captain punctuated it with another stream of tobacco juice he squirted, into a spittoon this time. He then hitched up his pants and picked up the rum bottle, giving all hands another round. The next day, with the wind dead aft, the coastal schooner sailed with the tide into the East River. For Ely, who had only gone as far as New London and Hartford, the great booming port of New York was a wonder. The masts of ships were stacked up like a leafless forest. Hogsheads of sugar, chests of tea, and bales of cotton, wool, and merchandise were strewn all around the wharves. Swarthy stevedores pushed squeaky wheelbarrows loaded with outbound barrels of flour and corn. He could hear the shouts of wagon drivers blending in with the noisy clatter of horses' hooves on cobblestones. He began to despair. How could he possibly hope to find any trace of John Taylor in the midst of all of this confusion?

At Peck's Slip, Captain Foster hired two wharf rats for five cents each to help unload the cargo. Ely swung his duffel over his shoulder as he said good-bye to the captain and his crew and stepped ashore. When he looked back to wave, Foster gave him one last word of advice.

"Remember what I told you, son: life shipboard ain't near as nice as what it looks like from shore."

Nearby at the new fish market on Fulton Street, a vendor yelled at him: "Heh boy, you want a job scalin' fish?"

Morgan looked at the grinning face of the grizzly fish salesman and then down at the scaly table filled with fish heads. Flies were buzzing around the vendor. The lifeless eyes of one large, dull, gray codfish seemed to be staring at him. The fetid smell of the old fish overwhelmed him and he gagged. He quickly turned away. His destination was 68 South Street, the new address of the offices of Griswold & Coates. There at the corner of Pine Street, he was to meet Captain Henry Champlin, his new employer. For one awful moment he wondered what would happen to him if Champlin wasn't there. He had no place to go and only a quarter in his pocket. He put that unpleasant thought out of his mind. His eyes scanned the docks, gazing at the long line of ships with their graceful bowsprits pointed upward over the walkways. There were so many ships he couldn't even count them.

He wondered if Abraham's ship had docked here before it left for South America. He began to reminisce about his brother. The truth was he still missed him. They were five years apart, but unlike the other brothers, they had enjoyed a special friendship. Ely was small for his age, smart and quick with his studies, and the bigger boys at school had constantly picked on him. They pushed and shoved him and called him names. Feisty and strong willed, he'd return their taunts. It was Abraham who had always stepped in to protect him. In return, Ely had frequently helped his older brother with spelling and punctuation, which Abraham hated. But it was their mutual fascination with the sea and the oceangoing sailors that had bonded the two boys; that, and the harsh treatment they had both received from their father, had served to pull them together. They saw each other as kindred spirits with a shared destiny.

Ely looked at a group of burly men heaving and hauling thick lines as they pulled their ship into dock. Maybe one of those men knew John Taylor. He ran up to one of them to ask if he'd ever heard of Abraham Morgan or John Taylor.

The bearded sailor, who towered over Ely, looked down at him with a scornful expression.

"Can't say that I have, son. No, no Taylors or Morgans on this ship, boy." Just then the man paused and started stroking his beard.

"Now hold on a minute, you say Taylor?"

"Yes, yes. John Taylor," Morgan said excitedly.

"Why don't you try over there," the man said, pointing to an adjacent ship. "I hear tell they got a Taylor on board."

Ely's heart was beating rapidly as he rushed over to the ship. He couldn't believe his good fortune. Maybe Abraham was alive after all. Taylor would know. The letter to his mother had been so cryptic, its words so puzzling. Now the mystery would be solved.

Those few moments of euphoria were soon cut short by the awful sound of deep belly laughter coming from behind him. He stopped and looked back at his helpful informant, who was now laughing and joking with his shipmate, pointing in Ely's direction as he made fun of "that stupid country bumpkin boy yonder."

"Need some stichin', do you?" the man asked. "That why you lookin' for a tailor?"

"Where's your mother, boy?"

Ely turned away, suddenly feeling small and alone.

PART II

We were again set to work, and I had a vile commission to clean out the chicken coops, and make up the beds of the pigs in the long-boat. Miserable dog's life is this of the sea! commanded like a slave, and set to work like an ass!

—Herman Melville, *Redburn: His First Voyage*

3

On a cold, drizzly November morning, Ely took the first tentative steps onto the gangway of the *Hudson* with great trepidation. Like many landlubbers, he was nervous and worried. The newly built 360-ton ship was sailing to London that same day on its inaugural voyage, and the seriousness of what he was about to do was just beginning to dawn on him. He looked around as he clambered aboard, awestruck at the smooth decks and the hundreds of feet of heavy lines that extended upward like intricate cobwebs. The ship was 106 feet long, about four times as long as it was wide. There were several hatches that led down below, but otherwise the decks were open spaces framed by the green bulwarks on the sides of the ship and the sweeping curve of the rails at the stern. The nine passengers in cabin class, all finely dressed, had already arrived with their crates and boxes. They were clustered together on the quarterdeck. Bundled-up stevedores wearing stained and patched woolen sweaters were loading barrels of apples and hogsheads of turpentine into the cargo hold at the center of the ship.

There were ten other sailors who came aboard at the same time he did. Some of them were dandied up, wearing tarpaulin hats with long black ribbons streaming behind them. Others had uncombed hair with untrimmed beards. They wore an assortment of stained woolen jackets and dirty canvas trousers that looked and smelled slept in. Morgan swung his small duffel over his shoulder. He suddenly had the urge to turn and run as fast as he could. But then he thought, he had no place to go. That sobering thought kept his feet anchored to the deck.

At that moment, he saw the wavy black hair of Captain Champlin emerge from below decks. He remembered how frightened he had been at Fickett's shipyard on that first day in New York. He had been told to go there by a man at 68 South Street. He had waited for hours standing by the sawpits, watching men with two-handed saws slice through huge oak beams. Showers of sawdust filled the air. He had asked several workers if they knew Captain Champlin, but no one paid much attention to him. He was about to give up when he felt a firm hand on his shoulder. He had turned around quickly, almost jumping out of his pants at the sight of a big-headed man with a black top hat, bushy, arched eyebrows, and a large, protruding jaw. For one frightening second he had thought Champlin was his father and he had come to take him home. Instead, he'd reassured him that he was a lucky sailor to be going out on the maiden voyage of John Griswold's newest ship.

"You know the difference, Morgan, between this here ship up on the ways and a transient ship?"

Ely had shaken his head.

"Quick voyages with no delays in port. That's the difference between this ocean packet and a transient ship. Sailing on a schedule, that's what people want now, son, no matter what the weather or the season."

Morgan had smiled weakly.

Champlin had patted him on the back as he pointed to the large looming sides of the ship up on the ways. The hull, made of live oak, had just been painted; some of the workers were now varnishing a strip that ran across the middle, from bow to stern. Riggers were busy installing the three masts.

"No shipping firm is providing regular packet service yet from New York to London, and Mr. Griswold aims to do just that. This will be his flagship. Imagine that son, we'll be haulin' the mailbags from New York to London and back again with all the important correspondence and all the news! I reckon we're like a stagecoach on the Atlantic highway. A floating bridge from New York to London, you might say."

Morgan had nodded as Champlin laughed and slapped him on the back. With the lecture over, he had then sent Ely over to the sawpits. For the next month until the ship was launched, he had worked at the shipyard, sleeping on the floor of a temporary work shed along with many of the workers, and some of the sailors who would soon be his close companions.

All that flashed before him as he saw the captain greet his cabin passengers with a ready smile and a handshake. As Ely surveyed the flushed deck of the *Hudson*, he turned to look at some of his new shipmates. He already knew some of them from the yard. Most of them were Americans from New England. Some of the men near him were laughing about a girl named Molly. Most of the sailors loved to talk about the grog shops they'd been to, the quantity of spirits they'd drunk, and the saucy women they'd encountered ashore.

"Like a cat that's ketched a mouse, that g'hal can't help thievin', but this time I fooled her," said a snub-nosed, red-faced man.

"How so?" asked a bald-headed sailor, whom the others called Curly Jim. "Why, I hid my money in my boots. I didn't give her any opportunities."

"That so," said Curly Jim as he pulled out a quid of tobacco. "I reckon she gave you plenty more than just opportunities."

"What do you mean by that?" replied the leering sailor.

"A case of the French pox."

The men laughed and hit one another, continuing their banter and carousing. Morgan's unease grew with every step he took onto the ship's deck. He could see his shipmates were a hardened, tough group of men, most of whom were still drunk from shore leave. He jumped suddenly at the sound of some commotion behind him. Crouching up against the bulwark, trying to make himself as small as possible in case there was a fight, he watched as two sailors started to push and shove each other.

"You stole it! That's where you got the money, you hornswoggling scalawag."

"I ain't stole nothin'."

A short, muscular man with eyes that gleamed like black river stones was accusing another with a pockmarked face of being a thief. Pretty soon the two men were exchanging blows, and the surly sailors were cheering on the fight. A curly haired man wearing a blue jacket and a black leather porkpie hat, who was checking off the sailors' names by the foremast, quickly stepped in to break up the scuffle. He lunged at the men, beating them with a belaying pin, and kicking them after they fell down. Morgan remained crunched up against the bulwarks, terrified by this display of raw brutality.

"Go forward, you two no-account rum-holers," the man with the pork-pie hat said as he kicked the two men again. "You two nancy boys can kiss up in the fo'c'sle."

The other men all laughed at this homosexual reference, and the curly haired man continued his lecture as he squirted tobacco juice on the two men's shoulders. This was Morgan's introduction to the ship's second officer, Jack Brown. He was a short, stocky man with a red face framed by black whiskers. He had piercing gray-black eyes that darted about the deck. His broad frame, long arms, and hairy chest made him look like more of an animal than a man.

Brown's lips turned up slightly at the edges, giving his mouth a cruel expression. His lips were stained with tobacco juice that trickled down his stubbly chin.

"I want no more scuffling, men. If you have a mind to make trouble, I've a right to flog anyone I've a mind to. Now throw your bundles in the fo'c'sle. This packet sails with the tide. Remember tide and time wait for no drunken sailor."

With that vivid demonstration, Mr. Brown squirted another stream of tobacco juice, this time in Morgan's direction, narrowly missing his head as the squishy, brown gob flew over the side of the ship. Morgan caught the man looking at him with a predatory stare that seemed to hold little hope of good tidings to come. He cast his eyes downward, as he could already tell that Mr. Brown was the kind of man who expected others to submit to his will. He thought of his father at that moment. He followed behind the sailors as they walked to the front of the ship. Morgan watched as the men heaved their wooden chests and duffels into the dark hole in the deck, which was the entrance to the fo'c'sle. It was too late to run now.

Cautiously he stepped down the steep ladder, his hands gripping the man rope tightly until his feet finally touched the floorboards. He groped his way forward into the darkness. He felt clammy and uncomfortable, overwhelmed by the smell of old ropes and tar, mixed with the musty odors of unwashed men and alcohol. Someone lit a lantern. Finally he could see where he was going. Amid the boxes, duffels, and bundles of bedding, the old hands greeted one another with bursts of laughter, slaps on the back, and gruff calls. Someone else tried to light another lantern, even as another silhouetted figure bumped his head, cursing at the darkness. Morgan put his hand into a black corner of his new sleeping quarters, reaching out until he found a bunk with no mattress. He started to throw his canvas bag onto the simple wooden bunk when a voice cried out.

"Don't you put your bundle thar', you worthless critter. Move away!"

Startled, Morgan jumped back. The unseen voice continued.

"You better pull foot out of here now or I'll slash the hide off you."

Morgan stammered an apology. "I'm sorry. I couldn't see anything."

The light from another passing lantern revealed a boy his age, or slightly younger, who was stretched out on the wooden planks. He had auburn hair, freckles, a round face, and a snub nose with a few stubs of hair growing from his dimpled chin and over his upper lip. In the flickering light, he was glowering at Morgan as his hand clutched a piece of wood.

"This here bunk is mine," he said defiantly, lifting up his makeshift club.

"Where can I throw my duffel?" Morgan asked, backing away quickly.

The boy shrugged with cold indifference, and then pointed upward at the stacked bunk above him.

"Just stay out of my way, you hear. You can't be too careful in a ship's fo'c'sle. Some of these old tars are a bunch of sodomite codfish and there's nothing they like better than to land a young mackerel."

Morgan quickly dismissed this as an exaggeration and decided he would try to be friendly even if this gesture wasn't reciprocated. He clambered up into the upper bunk. Right over his head was a piece of glass inserted into the deck to provide light. He thought to himself that at least he might be able to read on sunny days. He had brought along a tattered copy of William Cowper's poetry which included his favorite, the comic ballad *John Gilpin*. The book had been given to him by his old tutor, Margaret Carpenter, a year earlier. He looked down at his new bunkmate.

"What's your name?" he asked.

"Smith," was the curt reply. "Hiram Smith."

Morgan nodded to himself. "My name is Morgan, Ely Morgan."

The next frightening encounter Morgan had was with the first mate, a big man with a powerful chest, arms like tree trunks, a squashed nose broken down the middle, and a prominent beard covering most of his face. His name was Tim Toothacher, a Connecticut man from Middletown who had sailed since the age of thirteen to China with the old-timers. He was a firm believer in young sailors learning the hard way, or as he would say, "coming in through the hawse holes and not through the cabin doors."

It was Toothacher, with his chest thrown out in a disciplined military manner, who addressed the entire crew once they'd all come aboard. He and the second mate, Mr. Brown, divided the men into watches that first day. At the end of the selection process, Morgan was alone on the deck, a solitary figure and last to be chosen. He suddenly felt the unfriendly stares of his new shipmates. Who would have him? The first mate or the second mate? Did he care?

"What's your name, boy?" the burly first officer asked. "I don't think I know you."

"Morgan, sir, Ely Morgan."

"Morgan, Morgan." He paused with a smile on his face. "Or did you say Organ?" At that, he began to laugh at his own joke, and most of the sailors joined in. "What do you say, my hearties? From now on we're calling this young bumpkin over here monkey, the organ boy. Maybe I'll just baptize ye monkey boy for short."

Morgan's face was petrified by this humiliation, but there was more to come. The second mate with the black porkpie hat strode over to him with a hostile swagger and began picking at his clothes with his large hands, his breath smelling of rum.

"Lookee here," said the second officer with a gleeful smirk, "a piece of straw." He picked it up and looked at it closely. "It appears like this yokel brought a bit of the farm with him on his duds."

Mr. Brown walked around Morgan, inspecting him like he would a farm animal or a Negro slave. "Nobody wants you, it seems, boy." He spit out a wad of tobacco juice over the side, then turned to his fellow officer in what seemed like a rehearsed bit of choreography. "I reckon I'll do you a favor, Mr. Toothacher. I'll take the young pup this time, but I don't mind saying I don't like his name. From now on I'm going to call him Hayseed."

Morgan's last memory of his former life was looking back at the fading outline of Staten Island as the ship coasted by the highlands of the New Jersey shore. He gazed ahead of him at the sandy strip of land called Sandy Hook and then out toward the wide ocean that lay beyond. He could see angry whitecaps and what looked like some rough seas ahead.

During those first few days, Morgan was sick as a dog. The water swashed over the decks and over him. The second mate amused himself by tormenting him, forcing him to walk on the deck as the ship was rolling. Morgan staggered like a drunk man, falling down on the slanted deck repeatedly. Mr. Brown beat him with the end of a rope and told him to stand. When he couldn't get up, the mate threw buckets of cold water over him. Morgan was desperate for someone to save him. He looked over at the first mate, who was watching them as he walked by. Morgan thought for sure that Mr. Toothacher would put a stop to this abuse, but he just looked the other way.

The shipboard cruelty wasn't just confined to the mates. Some of the veterans jeered at him, but one old sailor kindly offered to give him a remedy for seasickness. Morgan was sent to the center of the ship where the farm animals were kept and came back with the sailor's medicine, a pail of fresh sheep dung. The old veteran told Morgan to wipe this all over his face, and if he did that, he would never get sick again. Morgan did as he was told, and soon the entire ship was laughing at him, holding their noses as they avoided getting too close to him.

A few days into the voyage, some of the sailors were muttering that heavy weather was coming. He remembered gray clouds and green seas.

The ship had fallen into a deep valley between two ridges, hiding the horizon. Just then came the order from the second mate to shorten sail.

"All hands aloft! Reef the topgallants! Reef the topsails! That means you, Hayseed!" Brown lunged at him and pushed him up the ratlines.

Morgan clambered up the shrouds as best he could, squirreling his way through the lubber's hole, the less risky way to climb to the topmast platform. The captain was driving the ship hard with all sails and gear taut and straining. Morgan looked around him at the hundreds of feet of heavy rope lines that wove their way through the masts like a spiderweb, and wondered how he would ever learn their names. The *Hudson* had more than fifteen sails, most of which were fastened onto the stout yards. Each of the three masts was divided into three sections. At the deck level was the lower mast, to which was fastened the topmast, which in turn supported the topgallant mast. That much he already understood. However, he knew nothing about the pulleys and blocks that ran to other blocks on the mast, and then further down to a row of belaying pins around the foot of the mast and extending out to the bulwarks.

He continued crawling upward, slowly and awkwardly, his hands clutching the shrouds, his feet treading on the ratlines. He couldn't look down. It was too frightening. The wind felt much stronger now, and the roll of the ship was quite pronounced. His heart was pounding. He could hear the second mate yelling at him. He stepped out onto a rope slung under the yard, gingerly pulling himself out onto the swaying topgallant yard eighty feet or so above the deck. His arms were wrapped around the yard so tightly he could feel the pain from the pressure on his biceps. He had a knot in his stomach when he heard another order.

"Ease the sheets! Haul on the buntlines and furl!"

All this was a foreign language to Morgan. He watched as another sailor on the adjacent mast started gathering in the sail. He had never even helped furl a square sail before, much less one eighty to ninety feet above the deck, but he set about his task as best as he could. He clumped together the sail, pulling at the heavy canvas from all directions. Suddenly, the first mate's voice was directed at him.

"Hayseed, gather the bunt up onto the center of the yard."

Morgan had no idea what the bunt was. He looked around and below to see if anyone would help him. There was no offer of assistance. Hiram was sent aloft to show him how to furl a topgallant. Reluctantly, his bunkmate took on the role as his teacher. Hiram showed Morgan how the buntlines and the clewlines were used for hauling up the foot of a square sail, and how, once the sail was furled, a gasket was used to tie it in place. Despite the helpful instruction, Hiram offered no sympathy.

"I reckon the second mate's gonna beat you when you get down on deck. I'm glad I'm not in your shoes."

When Morgan landed on deck, Mr. Brown boxed him in the ears and set him to work cleaning off tobacco stains on the decks. On that first voyage as the new cabin boy, Morgan was already getting used to being kicked and cuffed by every bully on board, particularly the second mate. Sailors held the belief that the more punishment they gave a cabin boy, the better sailor he'd become.

The worst job he was given was to clean up after the farm animals on board. Day after day, Mr. Brown chose him for this lowly task. Most of the packets had an outdoor area on deck in the middle of the ship where they kept a cow for milk. The sheep, pigs, ducks and hens were all destined to end up on the table for the cabin passengers. Morgan mostly showed deference to Mr. Brown, but one day he made a big mistake of talking back when the mate took away the small wooden shovel he had been using to scoop up the manure.

"I need a shovel to do that job," Morgan said with some conviction, his fists clenching. "At home on the farm we do this kind of work with shovels."

Brown locked eyes with Morgan and Ely noticed that they were twitching.

"Is that so, Hayseed? You hear that men? Hayseed here is making demands."

Brown grabbed Morgan by the ear with one of his large, calloused hands.

"What do you think this is, Hayseed? Your ma's flower garden? We're here on a ship. We don't use shovels to clean the pigpens. We use our hands. That's why we need a farm boy like you. So start cleaning up the pig shit. Then you can move on to the sheep dung, which we know you like to wipe all over your face."

He laughed and pushed Morgan into the pen, knocking him down onto a mound of wet, oozy manure. As he heard laughter from the men nearby, Morgan's spirits sank even lower.

4

Shivering with the November cold and wet as he helped reef the main topsail, Morgan wondered what he was doing in the middle of the Atlantic. The bell had just struck as it did every half hour. He still had several hours to go before the end of the first watch at midnight. The mast swayed from one side to the other while he hauled out the reef tackles for the topsails. He climbed higher out onto the more challenging and dangerous topgallant yards, resting for a moment on the crosstrees before climbing higher to tend to the royals. He was slightly more comfortable climbing the ratlines and wrestling with the sails now, but it still terrified him to look down.

He was now in his second week at sea, and he had gotten to know his way around the 106-foot-long ship. The lower hold below the waterline was where the heaviest freight was stored. Above that was the upper hold area, where fine freight and the low-paying steerage passengers went. He had already been sent below to the bleak steerage compartment to distribute wooden buckets to the seasick passengers. It was a dank, windowless, enclosed space some twenty by forty feet with stacked, narrow, wooden bunks made of rough, unplaned boards. He remembered the distressed faces. The smell was putrid, making him want to vomit. He had quickly dropped the empty buckets, scrambled up the ladder to get on deck, throwing his head over the bulwarks as he emptied his stomach into the ocean.

One time he had peeked through a glass skylight into the passenger cabin below the quarterdeck at the stern of the ship. The captain was lounging over a decanter of wine. This area was called the saloon. There through the skylight he had seen finely carved mahogany pillars, polished tables, and sofas. One of the stateroom's ventilated doors opened out onto the dark saloon area, and he could see a small berth with shiny silk curtains, a washbasin, and some drawers. A woman's figure disappeared into another cabin, a forbidden territory for sailors. Only the captain and occasionally the first mate mingled with the first-class passengers. Mr. Brown had yelled at him before he could see much of anything else.

The ship's masts were now swaying back and forth, making him dizzy and sick. To keep himself from falling, he grabbed hold of one of the lee braces for support. With his other hand, he pulled his pea jacket tighter around him even as he shuddered in the cold wind. The winds had switched to the north and it had started to sleet. The yard he was perched on was already icy and slippery. Down below him on the frozen, ice-covered decks, he could see men slipping and falling as they tried to make their way forward. He thought of his mother and the warmth of the kitchen fireplace, the reassuring smells of freshly baked bread and roast turkey, his three older sisters giggling as they ladled a creamy filling into a pie crust. This work aloft in the rigging was frightening enough in calm seas, but in stormy weather it was deadly.

Morgan wondered if this was what could have happened to Abraham so many years ago, falling, falling. He looked down some eighty feet to the deck below, then to the ship's plunging bowsprit, diving, slicing the water like an axe splitting a log in two. Suddenly, he felt as if an unknown force was pulling him downward. He clung to the slippery, cold jackstay, his feet resting precariously on the foot rope slung under the yard. A destructive urge seemed to be pulling him downward and telling him to let go.

Morgan shook his head, calmed himself with deep breaths, and followed the example of some of the old veterans who controlled their nerves by singing. He would conquer this wave of fear, he told himself. He thought of the terror he'd experienced when those British Navy sailors had fired on him and Abraham. He thought of the angry, scowling face of his father. For some reason, his mind flashed back to that first year after Abraham left home. He and Abraham had always gotten into trouble, letting out the neighbors' pigs, or scaring the girls next door by pretending to be Indians on the warpath. With Abraham gone, the pranks seemed less fun and he had gotten into fights. After one of those scraps in the center of town, one of the deacons, Squire Ridley, had come out of the meetinghouse to break up the fight. News of that shameful rebuke made its way back to the Morgan farm and Ely was given a thrashing by his father. The old man had met him with his whipping belt in hand. He marched him into the barn where he was forced to drop his pants and lean over. He whipped him until the skin was raw and he cried for mercy.

"Maybe that will beat the freewheeling nature out of you," he had yelled. The memory of that beating and how it had stiffened his defiance of his father strengthened him now. He started to climb down the ratlines, more confident than before. If he couldn't control his fears, he told himself, the only alternative was to return to the Connecticut River Valley to work as a farmer. That image of a life shackled to a horse-drawn plow helped him overlook the new hardships he was enduring at sea.

On that first voyage, Morgan soon got used to a sparse diet of salt beef or pork and weevily sea bread. In fact, the *Hudson*'s cook, whose name was Scuttles, was the first to befriend him. He told him that if he ate a pound of cold salt beef he wouldn't get sick. Scuttles had escaped from a Maryland plantation when he was eight years old. He'd then found a life with the small Negro community living on Staten Island. When he got older he realized that there were few good opportunities for him in New York. Like so many colored men, he'd ended up choosing the sea as a way to escape the severe discrimination he faced ashore. Generally speaking, the sailors accepted most everybody once they were on ship, though when they didn't like the food, some of the sailors called him "that no-good Guinea nigger-cook."

Morgan had never come into close contact with a black man before, so with food as the primary incentive but curiosity a close second, he befriended Scuttles, whose real name was Samuel Cuttlefish. Hiram had the same idea. As a result, the ship's galley and pantry became a meeting place for the two boys, a refuge from the mates and the constant abuse they received from many of the other sailors. It was there as they ate their burgoo porridge after their four-hour watch, among scattered pots and pans, that Morgan and Scuttles heard how Hiram came to be on the *Hudson*.

"Is this your first voyage with Captain Champlin?" Morgan asked as he took a spoonful of the thick oatmeal mush covered with molasses, which the sailors called long-tail sugar. Hiram shook his head. He was a Penobscot boy from Thomaston, Maine. He confessed that he had left home when he was only fourteen years old. His mother had remarried and his stepfather used to beat him. One day down at the docks in Thomaston, he had spotted a small trading schooner that was sailing to New York. He decided to sneak on board where he hid in a dark corner in the bow of the ship. They never found him until they were well out to sea. Once they arrived in New York, they booted him ashore.

"I didn't know where to go," Hiram said. "I had not a cent in my pocket and no clothes neither."

"What did you do?" asked Morgan.

"Spent a couple of nights sleeping in a fish vendor's cart down by Pine Street. That fishmonger discovered me when he came to hitch up his horse. He kicked me from here to kingdom come. Some sailors came and yanked me away. Took me to see Captain Champlin, and when he found out I was a New England boy, he put me to work on board the *Cincinattus*. He says New England boys work harder. That's why he hired me. That was two years ago, and now I'm on this new ship."

Morgan told Hiram his own story, about how he had met Captain Champlin. His parents had gone upriver to Middletown to a baptism, and he had slipped away and taken the ferry over to Great Meadow. A new ship was being launched at Hayden's Yard. Champlin had singled him out from a group of boys, and offered him a berth if he could get to New York. Then he told his new friend about the cryptic letter from John Taylor.

"The letter didn't even say for sure that my brother was dead or how he died." Morgan hesitated. "Something strange there, don't you think?"

Hiram shrugged as he wiped his mouth with the back of his hand.

"Could be, but then maybe not. What sailors do and what they say don't always make sense. Your brother could be lying senseless in a street somewhere. Maybe he's shipwrecked somewhere off the coast of Africa. You'll probably never know, but if there was foul dealing, I understand you need to find out who done it."

Those conversations helped create a tie between the two cabin boys. Morgan even confessed to Hiram his love of reading and produced the book of poetry that Mrs. Carpenter had given to him. He hid the book under his mattress. If any of the other sailors saw him reading, he knew it would create an ugly scene, not just name calling, but possibly a fight.

That was another reason why the friendship with Hiram was so important. Morgan sensed he had found a new ally who could help him learn the ropes, and he sorely needed one. The tobacco-chewing second officer was always looking for him to clean the farm area or to lower him from the catheads over the side of the ship to chip rust from the anchor.

When Mr. Brown first ordered Morgan to slush down the masts, he replied he didn't know what that meant. The mate flew into a rage, hitting him with the belaying pin. Morgan felt his hands drawing into fists as he thought about fighting back. Then he heard Hiram's voice cautioning him, and he thought of how Josiah had always counseled him never to cry out when their father was in one of his rages. Mr. Brown handed him a heavy two-gallon bucket filled with thick gravy, which Scuttles had prepared from the remnants of the boiled salt beef. He then ordered him up the rigging.

"If one drop falls, Morgan, you'll be licking it off the deck. I want the masts to be thoroughly greased so the topsails, topgallants, and royal yards can be hoisted up and down easily."

Biting his lip in humiliation, Morgan held onto a rope attached to the pail with one hand, twisting it around his wrist. It was so heavy he felt like his hand would separate from his arm. With the other hand he pulled himself up the ratlines, squeezing through the narrow lubber's hole, hauling up the heavy bucket behind him. The slush-filled pail scraped against the mast, tipping back and forth, its foul-smelling contents almost spilling over the edge. Gritting his teeth, Morgan pulled the bucket up the shrouds. His heart pounded as he kept climbing past the topgallant yards up into the royals, refusing to look down. The higher he climbed up the swaying mast the colder he felt. He held on tightly to the shrouds from his precarious perch, more than eighty feet above the deck on the three-foot-wide crosstrees. There he was able to set down the slush pail and gather his strength.

Mr. Brown sent Hiram up to help him. The two cabin boys were busy slathering the masts with the thick grease when they first heard a commotion below them on deck. It sounded like a fight. They had worked their way down the mast so that they were now perched just below the upper topsail yard, about fifty feet from the deck. They could hear stomping and an angry voice shouting, "I'll give you the toe of my boot and knock you all the way into the middle of next week."

"What's going on, Hiram?"

"Sounds like Mr. Brown is having a frolic with one of the sailors," Hiram replied dryly. Morgan looked down through the spiderweb of the rigging until he spied the blue pea jacket and the black leather hat of the second mate, hurling abuse at a big sailor and shouting into his face.

"Answer me, you great white monkey!" he yelled as he rained blow after blow on the big man's back with the belaying pin. Morgan could recognize the sailor by his yellow hair tied back in a ponytail. He was a great hulk of a man with wide and broad shoulders, a big square face with thin whiskers, pale blue eyes, and thin lips that rarely smiled. His name was Olaf Rasmussen. Everyone just called him Icelander because that's where he was supposedly from. The story was he'd gone to sea because he'd killed a man, or at least that's what some of the crew whispered behind his back.

Morgan watched, mesmerized as the shipboard drama unfolded directly underneath him. Another sailor came to Icelander's defense, a small dark-haired man who spoke little English named Luis Ochoa. He was known as the Spaniard. He was a man near thirty, thin and bronze-skinned with a drooping black moustache and heavily tattooed arms. Morgan had already heard about his reputation of being quick with a knife. Some of the other sailors claimed he had once been a pirate sailing out of Havana. The ship's officers didn't like these two foreigners. Some of the river men took a special dislike to sailors who weren't from New England.

The second mate was striking both men now. Morgan could see the flat top of his hat and the thrashing motion of the belaying pin. Suddenly, the Spaniard drew his sheath knife and was about to lunge at Mr. Brown. Morgan held his breath and began to panic as he felt the rope holding the slush bucket slipping out of his grasp. Hiram had warned him that this could happen. He tried in vain to wrap it around his wrist, but his hands and arms were thick with grease and the rope kept slipping. He knew he couldn't hold it any longer.

"Hiram, help me!" Morgan cried out. "It's slipping! The bucket, it's falling!"

Hiram was on the other side of the mast, but he was quick to react as he saw the impending disaster unfolding. He stepped over to Morgan's side and sidled toward him, being careful to keep one hand on the shrouds. Morgan reached for the rope with his other hand, but he lost his balance, and started to fall backward. Hiram was close enough to grab him by his belt while he held onto the rigging with the other hand. Morgan was now precariously hanging in the air, his hands frantically trying to grab the shrouds, his feet barely touching the ratlines. By this time, the bucket with its foul and greasy contents was in free fall. The slobbery mess landed on top of the unsuspecting second mate's head like generous dollops of pig fat on a skillet. The bucket hit the mate squarely on the shoulder. The blow was enough to knock him down onto the deck.

Hiram called out for help. His hand on Morgan's belt was beginning to slip.

"Hurry!" Hiram yelled. "I can't hold on much longer."

Like a nimble monkey, the wiry Spaniard was the first up the mast, climbing around the futtock shrouds for speed and then up the rope ladder to the topsail area where the boys were dangling. The taller Icelander was right behind him, carrying a thick hemp rope. Morgan's head was now facing downward, his hands clutching at thin air. He was attempting to grip the ratlines with his feet and legs, but to no avail. The Spaniard climbed up above the two boys, wrapped his legs around the topsail yard's foot rope, and then like a monkey swung upside down to grab one of Morgan's feet with both his hands, allowing Hiram to let go of his belt. At the same time, Icelander tied a bowline at one end of the rope and tossed the knotted loop to Morgan's outstretched hands. He then passed the other end of the rope over the topsail yard and wrapped the line two or three times around the mast to secure it.

"Put both your hands through the loop and hold," he yelled. Morgan did as he was told and wrapped his wrist in and around the loop, grabbing the area above the bulging bowline knot. At a signal from Icelander, the Spaniard let go of his hold on Morgan's foot, and his body catapulted downward toward the deck. His free fall was quickly arrested by the rope, leaving him dangling, swinging back and forth, hanging by his wrists and hands, but safe. Icelander slowly lowered him to the safety of the deck to the cheers of the onlookers down below.

Captain Champlin came over to check on the condition of his second officer. Jack Brown's pride was the gravest injury. He made sure that Morgan not only holystoned the decks but scrubbed the pigpen. This punishment went on for days until Brown's wrath was eventually redirected to another greenhand.

Because of Morgan's miraculous escape from almost certain death, some of the more superstitious men now saw him as a lucky sailor. Sighting a pod of dolphins was considered a harbinger of good fortune. A black cat on board ship was good luck, and now young Morgan was finding himself accepted as a member of the crew because he was viewed as a good omen.

Days later, Ely and Hiram were down on their knees, holystoning the cold decks late one morning when the cry came out from aloft that land was in sight. Earlier they'd already seen some black-and-white seabirds, their stiff wingtips dipping from one side to another as they skimmed the water in search of schools of herring or other small fish. They had been twenty-five days at sea.

"Can't be long now to Mizen Head," cried out one old sailor who was pointing to the northeast. The man was tall and skinny, his bony shoulders drooping like the broken wings of a bird. Morgan couldn't see anything but a white haze on the horizon. He looked at the man's craggy features. His long, gray beard hung down like strands of Spanish moss from the limbs of a tree. The scarred and furrowed face and well-defined crow's-feet at the corners of his light blue eyes were all a testament to a man who had been at sea for most of his life. His name was Jeremiah Watkins. Most of the sailors just called him Old Jeremiah. He was one of the veteran sailors on board who was both superstitious and religious. In his youth, he had attained the rank of a harpooner on one of the Nantucket whalers. He had traveled as far as China and Bombay. At night, when some of the men were off watch and spinning yarn in the forecastle, he would tell tales about the East India trade and "them Oriental monkeys in Bombay who don't wear no togs, nothing but a white bandana around their privates." Because of his knowledge of Scripture and legends, good and bad omens, the sailors on board the *Hudson* looked to him for guidance.

"Why do you say we are close to Mizen Head?" Morgan asked respectfully.

"See those black-and-white birds darting about?"

Morgan nodded as he followed the direction of the sailor's long extended arm and pointed finger.

"Those are shearwaters, and they're the first to welcome us across. They nest on the rocky cliffs of Ireland. That's how I know we're getting close to Mizen Head."

Jeremiah's voice was hoarse with the cold weather, and Morgan detected that his breath was tainted with the smell of rum.

"The Scripture contains considerable amount of teachings, but so do the old legends. Both harrow up important truths out here in the open sea. Who's to say why storm petrels are said to protect sailors? Some believe these birds carry the souls of drowned sailors. Some say any sailor who kills one of them birds will die. Who's to say?"

The old sailor pointed again at one of the shearwaters, which twirled to one side, exposing its white underside, while its wings were rigid and unmoving.

"You see, the shearwater looks like a flying cross, calling on all sinful sailors to repent."

Morgan's eyes followed the bird as it flew out of sight, thinking how much he had to learn. He wasn't superstitious by nature, or overly mystical, but he had enough respect for old sailors and their beliefs not to discount anything.

As the *Hudson* began to heel sharply with a sudden gust of wind, Mr. Brown sent the two cabin boys aloft to check on some of the buntlines and clewlines. There, dangling from the stirrup with his arms draped over the topgallant yards on the main mast, Morgan looked down at the well-dressed cabin passengers gathered in the quarterdeck. The men sported their black top hats, their long overcoats, and their finely polished boots. There were only two women, both seated, bundled up with blankets pulled tightly around their shoulders. A steward was passing refreshments. It looked like hot cups of tea and a platter of small sandwiches. Captain Champlin was looking through his spyglass. He said something to one of the male passengers, and suddenly they were all gesturing wildly, pointing off to the northeast.

Morgan swiveled around and in the far distance he caught his first sight of the cliffs of Mizen Head, the southwesternmost tip of Ireland. He looked across a meadow of whitecaps to the dark, windswept cliffs, and the tufts of green beyond. It had taken them over three weeks to cross the Atlantic, and the intensity of this moment left him without words. With an easterly wind, they were forced to tack back and forth along the south coast of Ireland, passing Glandore Harbor and Galley Head in the Celtic Sea. In the distance, they could see another prominent point of land with a lighthouse. He watched as Old Jeremiah poured a tot of rum over the side and asked Hiram what the sailor was doing.

"That's an offering to Neptune," Hiram replied curtly. "Just six months ago one of the Black Ball packet ships, the *Albion*, went up on the rocks off this coast here in a terrible storm. Twenty persons were clinging to the wreck until finally the ship broke apart and the sea claimed her. The captain was lost along with almost all the crew and the passengers. They say the heavy surf and waves pounded the ship to pieces."

Morgan stared out at the inhospitable coastline and the rolling waves of the Atlantic crashing onto shore, the white foam of the sea swirling in whirlpools around the rocks. He thought of William, whose ship had gone down at sea and was never heard of again. His mind turned to the mystery of Abraham's death, which he was determined to solve. It was too hard for him to accept that both his older brothers had been called away early from this life. Abraham must be alive. He thought of his smile, his cheery optimism, and some of his quirks, like his passion for collecting sailors' pennywhistles. He pulled out a small one made of lead that his brother had given him before he left home, and fingered its smooth surface for good luck.

"Why don't you ask Jeremiah Watkins about it yourself," Hiram said. "He's heard the tale of the *Albion*."

Just then the mate called out to mind the braces. Morgan could feel the big ship veer off the wind. They were now on a southwesterly course toward the western edge of the Scilly Islands.

A day later Morgan took Hiram's advice. He walked over to Old Jeremiah and began first asking him about the wreck, and then decided to confide in the old sailor and tell him all about his quest to find his brother, and what he had heard about how Abraham had been a victim of "foul play of the worst kind, the Devil's own mischief."

Jeremiah Watkins, his smoky blue eyes suddenly intense, looked down at Morgan.

"It ain't for me, an old sailor, to describe the ways of the Devil. He takes a grip on all of us and has many disguises. They say when a shark follows a ship someone on board will die. When rats leave a ship that's a definite sign you have to look sharp because the Devil will have you afore morning."

Morgan persisted.

"But this old salt who found me spoke with the sailor who sailed with my brother. He told me that this John Taylor quoted scripture, something from Jonah."

Old Jeremiah stroked the long strands of his gray beard. He said nothing as he continued to look out at the sea, his thin nostrils moving, sniffing the breeze like a dog.

"Now that's a different pannikin of wine altogether. There's the Devil's mischief in those hogsheads. Do you know what a Jonah is, son?"

Morgan shook his head.

"A Jonah is a sailor who brings bad luck. Sometimes the only way to overcome that misfortune is to sacrifice that sailor."

5

1824

Morgan looked around the darkness of the forecastle. The wet sailors dressed in their damp oilskins were silent, gathered in small groups under the glow of a single gimbaled lantern. The ship was pitching and heaving. The summer storm had pushed them far off course into the Bay of Biscay, and as a result the mood was grim. As he scanned the weathered faces of the men in the gloom of the dark forecastle, Morgan's mind wandered back. Two years had passed since he first had stepped on board the *Hudson*. After eight voyages across the Atlantic, he was now an apprentice sailor. He was strong and nimble as a squirrel in the rigging. The bristly stubble on his face and the thickness of his neck were testament to his growth from boy to man. His muscular arms and shoulders were tattooed, a compass rose on his left shoulder and an anchor on his right. Two signs of hope, he had told Hiram. His friend had scoffed at him and proudly showed off the big-breasted mermaids he had tattooed on his two shoulders. "These doxies are all the hope I need," he said. Like many of the sailors, they both chewed tobacco now, regularly sharing each other's quids as a sign of their friendship.

In the flickering yellow light of the forecastle, all eyes, including Morgan's, were now on Jeremiah, who was talking like a biblical prophet. The old tar's deeply creased face looked like a badly rutted country road.

A thin white scar ran across the bridge of his nose, crisscrossing the deep fissures that traveled across his forehead. On his head he wore a headband and a leather hat. His stone blue eyes were sunken into his head, and in that yellow light, with his imposing gray beard, he seemed to Morgan to be a man possessed.

"The storm petrels done come alongside the ship and are riding the wind with us," he muttered. "I reckon they're warning us about this here storm."

The lantern's light reflected onto Jeremiah's face, as he ominously held up a small dark bird with white plumage on its tail. Its head was bloody, its eyes still and lifeless. He paused for a few moments as if for dramatic effect.

"I 'ave found one of them petrels lying on the deck. It's dead."

The men stared at the lifeless bird. They had just come off watch. A heavy rain had driven them into the safety of the damp forecastle. Most of them were still in their dripping oilskins. They were wet and hungry. Within minutes, most of them were reaching into their hiding places and pulling out the rum bottles that were forbidden on board ship. The forecastle was filled with the gray haze of tobacco smoke, adding to a sense of foreboding.

"It's no good that dead bird ain't," Jeremiah intoned. "I'll warrant it means considerable misfortune. Any of you men know of any dead sailors who had something troubling their souls?"

Instead of the swearing and coughing that usually filled this damp, dark underworld, there was a strange silence. Morgan thought how cursed this voyage had been. They had been becalmed for days in the English Channel. The ground swell and the pull of the tide had carried them into the Sea of Iroise near the coast of France. They had almost run up on the rocks off the deadly coast of Brittany near the islands of Ouessant and Molène. Now a bad sea had kicked up, and it was clear to all aboard that a big storm was brewing. The captain had tried to reach across the English Channel toward the Scilly Islands, but the winds and the waves had knocked them down to the south, forcing them far off course into the Bay of Biscay. It was as if the Devil himself didn't want them to complete this voyage.

This passage had started well under fair skies and freshening wind just one week ago on the first of July. The *Hudson* had floated down the Thames, the stars and stripes fluttering over the mizzen peak, colorful pennants streaming from her masts and rigging. It was the official inaugural voyage of the new London Line, a loose-knit business partnership between Grinnell and Minturn's Red Swallowtail Line and John Griswold's company, the Black X Line. The X was for express, signifying fast, dependable delivery of the mailbags, passengers, and cargo across the Atlantic between London and New York. Along with the Red Swallowtail Line, the Black X Line now joined the other American packet lines to England—the Red Star, the Blue Swallowtail, and the Black Ball. There were other American ships, of course, that traveled to Liverpool and London, but they were freighters, not packets. Morgan had felt a surge of pride run through him.

Now as he sat in the forecastle listening to Jeremiah speak about strange superstitions and ominous signs of misfortune on the sea, he felt a cold sensation crawl up the back of his neck, giving him goose bumps. He started to shiver. It was almost as if they had fallen under a sorcerer's spell. A large wave slammed into the midsection and thundered over the bow. He could hear loud cracks. The hull's crossbeams shook and trembled in protest. The seas crashing on the deck and the waves on either side of the ship mingled together in a frightening roar.

Morgan could hear the wailing and moaning of the emigrants over the howl of the wind. They had about thirty people in the adjacent steerage compartment. He had been told that most of them were simple cottagers from the Salisbury Plains area of southern England. A few others were tenant farmers from Ireland. None of them had ever been on a ship before, and so not surprisingly they were terrified by stormy weather. The ship's carpenter had hammered shut their hatchway to keep the compartment watertight. There was no way for any of them to reach the open air, no escape if the ship went down. He imagined them piled together: men, women, and children, clutching the wooden bunk beds in desperation in the total darkness of the upper hold, their boxes and chests hurtling from one end of the ship to the other.

Morgan put aside for the moment his empathy for the steerage passengers and looked around the forecastle, slowly retreating behind most of the other men. Not a smile offered, and not a word spoken. He had learned to keep his mouth shut in these cramped quarters. Some of these tough men did things to one another that were best not talked about. They were quick to anger, and once angered hard to control. Resentments among sailors on board became permanent shackles. He knew the dangers of drawing attention to himself.

Old Jeremiah was looking for someone to blame for the bad weather. Several new sailors had come aboard in London. The suspicious eyes darting around eventually landed on these newcomers. Morgan looked at the turned heads, the reluctant glances, and the downcast eyes. Even the old hands had something to hide, he thought to himself. They all had something they didn't want the others to know. After moments of silence where only the howling wind could be heard outside, Jeremiah lifted his bearded chin as he raised his voice to a higher pitch.

"Men, I fear that no-account Irishman who we cast off in Ouessant is not our sole source of misfortune. There is another problem," he declared with solemn authority.

"What might that be?" Curly Jim asked as he stroked his bald head. "Is there someone else who we should cast off the ship?"

Morgan thought of the man they'd left behind on the French island of Ouessant, an Irish emigrant by the name of Peter Corrigan. The sailors had forced the captain to run him ashore. He had kicked the ship's cat overboard, a sure sign of bad luck. Sure enough, shortly afterward the wind had died. Some had muttered that the ship was cursed on account of that black cat being drowned. Someone was to blame for this strange weather, they said. It's the emigrant's fault, they had whispered to one another. He needs to go. Corrigan had cried, begging them to let him stay on board because his entire savings had been spent to purchase the fare to America. Morgan remembered as the *Hudson* set sail, seeing the man standing on the treeless, rocky bluffs of Ouessant looking out at the ship, his red hair waving in the wind. The small, forlorn figure on the cliffs had been as still as a statue, his arms hanging at his sides.

Now Jeremiah told the men that the curse was still with them. The dead bird was a bad omen, he warned as he stood up, and began walking around the cramped forecastle, pulling and stroking his beard. A haunting silence hung in the air. No one spoke. Morgan noticed one of the new sailors who seemed to be frozen in fear. The man moved to the back of the room further into the shadows as Jeremiah raised his voice again, his pale blue eyes, now big and staring, bulging out of their red-rimmed sockets.

"We have a Jonah in our midst, men. I am loath to tell you this, but tell you I will. I am as certain of this as I am about the Scripture. Unless we find him, misfortune is going to find us. So it is written in the Book of Jonah."

The forecastle was filled with a flurry of urgent angry cries to find the Jonah and remove the curse. The noise increased. There was a sense of frenzy in the air.

"A life for a life," Jeremiah shouted. "So says the Bible."

Morgan kept his eyes on that one sailor. In the light from the hanging lantern, he could see him clearly. He was a tall man, hollow cheeked with a weak jaw that fell inward toward his long thin neck. His dark eyes had an inward gaze of someone lost in thought. The dark shadows under his eyes gave him a haunted, gaunt appearance. He looked to be just a few years older than he was. His name was John Dobbs. He had shipped on board at the last minute. He told the mates that his normal vessel had left port without him and he needed to get to New York. The officers had welcomed him aboard as they always needed an extra hand. He was an odd sort. He mostly kept to himself, but in the sailors' lonely world that was not that strange. People just left him alone.

A stony silence now pervaded the cramped forecastle. Old Jeremiah had delivered his sermon and the men had much to think about as they took careful measure of their situation and of one another. The ship was pitching and heaving more heavily now, and the sailors retreated to their bunks. Morgan made his way through the narrow aisles past the hanging bundles of dripping wet clothes and gear. He decided to escape from the madness that surrounded him. Lying in his bunk, he took out the last letter he had received from home and began reading it again in the dim candlelight. It was a letter from his brother Josiah, who was the only one who wrote him. The words were a comfort, a link to the life he had left behind.

"My dear brother, For now, all is well on the farm, although with your absence we have had to cut back on the number of hogs and cows. We've been growing less barley too, as it is too hard to harvest. The apple trees are thriving."

Morgan tried to imagine the farm as the ship pitched and heaved.

"Our sister Asenath is well," wrote Josiah. "She says that she has never enjoyed such good health as she has since she married. Young Jesse and Maria Louisa are growing up quickly and are a big help to mother with the farm chores, even though Maria Louisa likes to torment the dog."

Morgan thought of his sisters and smiled. He wished at that moment that he was together with them and his mother, watching them all making dinner in the warmth of the kitchen. He resumed his reading.

"Rest assured brother, all of us, especially our dear mother, want to hear how you're faring. It's just father who vents his gall by cursing all sailors. Sadly, he says he wants to hear no news from any who have chosen the life of the sea. He has forbidden mother or any of us to write to you, and I am sad to say he tears up your letters if he intercepts them before we do."

Reading those words again left a bittersweet taste in his mouth like biting into a tart green apple. He loved reading about the family, but the news of his father only tied his stomach in knots. The thought of his father's glowering face with his bushy silver eyebrows just made him more determined than ever to find out what had happened to Abraham.

As he clutched his letter and thought of home, Morgan could feel the wind pick up sharply. It was midnight, time for the watch to change. The gale was intensifying and soon the mates were banging on the forecastle hatch, delivering the captain's orders to shorten sail. Morgan was actually glad for the excuse to go aloft and escape the fearful atmosphere in the forecastle.

"All hands reef topsails," came the shout from Mr. Toothacher.

The forecastle emptied out and nearly all the sailors on board the *Hudson* were soon aloft in the dark, clambering out on the yards, manhandling the canvas sails and securing them with gaskets. With the ship beginning a more pronounced pitch and roll, Morgan struggled to hold his balance as he leaned out on his stomach on the yard. The wind was whistling through the rigging, the masts creaking as the ship strained to meet the rush of wind and sea. He looked down to see the ship's lee rail disappear under surging black water and white foam. He held on as tightly as he could. The *Hudson* was now heeling sharply to one side.

Suddenly, the sheets and braces were eased to save the masts from splintering, and he found himself dangling out on a swinging yard. If he hadn't secured himself on the jackstay, he might have hurtled overboard. As it was, he would have fallen if several sailors hadn't pulled tight the loose brace and secured the yard. Then came the order: "All hands on deck!" Morgan swung out from the topsail yard, dropped down to the mast doublings, grabbed the backstay, and slid down to the deck, all in a matter of seconds. This was relatively easy for him to do on the windward side when the packet was heeled over with the tips of the masts tilting toward the sea.

"Stand by to come about," cried out Mr. Toothacher using a trumpet so that he could be heard above the wind noise.

Along with several others, Morgan was hard at work on deck unfastening sheets and braces on the starboard side. The yards for the main swung around, the blocks clattering, the canvas thrashing. He could see Ochoa and Icelander fastening the braces on the port side.

"Release foresail!"

Morgan let go of the foresail to help the bluff bow of the *Hudson* swing across the wind. He watched as Ochoa wrestled with the thrashing lines as he adjusted and trimmed the sails. On the new tack, the packet was now pointed on a northerly heading toward Greenland, what some sailors called the uphill road. The storm had blown them way to the south, some six hundred miles off the coast of Ireland. At this rate, with the wind and the waves on their nose, the best they could hope for would be to make thirty to forty miles a day. Just then, Morgan felt the hot breath of someone standing closely behind him. He turned abruptly, and jumped back, as Mr. Brown thrust his bushy black whiskers into his face, his beady eyes glistening with malice.

"You're on my watch tonight, Morgan."

"Aye, aye, sir," replied a startled Morgan.

"Where's Smith?"

"Don't know, sir."

"You tell that two-bit nancy boy to report to me, ye hear!"

"Aye, aye, sir."

That night Morgan and Hiram were ordered to report to the pump station just forward of the mainmast. All night long, they pumped ship, their hands moving back and forth in unison as the bilge water from the belly of the ship spewed out into the ocean.

6

On that rough westward passage, Morgan often thought of Old Jeremiah's warnings. He took more notice of John Dobbs, the hollow-cheeked man with the droopy jaw. It wasn't just the worry in his eyes and the unsmiling face. Dobbs kept looking over at Morgan as if he wanted to tell him something, but when Morgan returned his gaze the man would look away. One morning, Morgan was walking the deck on his watch when he spotted Dobbs looking over the side, his clothes hanging loose on his body like baggy old sails. The man seemed to be in a trance as he looked forlornly at the jagged landscape of whitecaps before him.

Without warning, Dobbs grabbed hold of one of the topsail halyards and climbed up onto the waist-high bulwark on the side of the ship. Morgan began to move toward the sailor to try to say something, but the foaming seawater sweeping the decks prevented him. A tremendous wave crashed over the side with a thundering roar. All he could do was to catch a proper handhold and brace himself for the impact of the next wave. To his horror, Dobbs looked back at him with eyes flat and expressionless and then, zombie-like, he leaped over the side without making a sound. It took Morgan several seconds to realize that John Dobbs had jumped into the ocean.

He shouted in desperation, "Man overboard!" Morgan quickly turned to go aft to man the falls of the quarter boat, the waves sweeping him down the decks with such force he could barely keep his footing.

The helmsman turned the wheel sharply. "Bring the ship's head round!" the first mate yelled out. Slowly the *Hudson* turned back into the wind, pitching and heaving as the vessel hove to. By this time, several sailors had come to Morgan's assistance, lowering the quarter boat so that it was hanging just above the surging sea. The clouds of flying spindrift made it difficult to see. Several men finally spotted the man's head floating above water, rapidly coming toward them in the waves. Morgan positioned himself with both feet squarely in the middle of the boat and threw a rope at the bobbing head approaching.

"Catch it, man. Catch it!"

The rope had reached its mark, but Dobbs seemed unable or unwilling to grab it. Morgan could see his head and his fear-stricken eyes disappear below the waves and then pop up again. Dobbs floated by and Morgan swung the rope again and this time the man grabbed it. He called on him to hold on.

"He's got it," yelled Morgan as he started to pull Dobbs in. Hand over hand, he pulled the frightened sailor through the water until he could haul him onto the edge of the quarter boat. At that point, Morgan yelled, "Man the falls! Pull us up!"

Slowly the quarter boat was lifted upward toward the bulwarks. Morgan kept pulling underneath the limp shoulders of the gasping man until most of his body was safely inside. Finally, as the quarter boat was raised even with the deck, Morgan succeeded in hauling the shivering man into the boat. He spotted Captain Champlin and the cluster of cabin passengers that stood behind him. He caught a glimpse of the cold, hostile eyes of Jeremiah and Curly Jim. Dobbs was pulled onto the deck of the *Hudson*, wrapped in warm woolen blankets, and taken into the cook's quarters, where Scuttles tried to pour hot soup into him.

Morgan stayed with the cook to help keep the man warm. Dobbs was in shock, shaking and shivering uncontrollably. Morgan and Scuttles started to undress the emaciated man, stripping him of his shirt, and it was then that Morgan saw something unexpected. There on Dobbs's bare back, framed by his two protruding shoulder bones, was a large tattoo with two anchors intertwined. Beneath it was written something oddly familiar: "Bosom friend and Brother."

Morgan looked at these words on the man's back, letting them slowly resonate in his mouth. Scuttles tried to feed him more pea soup with a spoon, but the man vomited it up. The cook made him drink some water and he fell back onto the table. He tried to speak, but he opened his mouth and no words came out. Dobbs's skin was a deathly blue. Morgan couldn't take his eyes off his back. How strange that he knew those words. Something connected him with this man. What was it? At that moment, the first officer came down below to check on the nearly drowned man and told Morgan to go and get his clothes in the forecastle. Scuttles volunteered his observations.

"Ain't no way about it, Mister Toothacher. Sir, from the looks of Dobbs, he'll have to bunk here in the sick bay. If we put him back in the forecastle, he'll either die on his own or they'll do it for him."

Above decks, the ship was rolling and pitching, the winds gusting over thirty knots. Morgan was met in the foredeck by the ugly, threatening stares of Old Jeremiah and Curly Jim. They seemed to be the ringleaders, but there was a motley group who stood right behind them. Morgan had been around these sailors long enough to know that the mood of the crew was in a dangerous state.

"You the Devil, ain't ye," cried out Curly Jim with an ominous tone in his voice. "You saved Jonah, the sinner. He should have drowned in the sea."

Morgan didn't answer. He jumped down into the dark forecastle and walked toward the area where Dobbs kept his clothes. The same group of six sailors who'd met him at the foredeck followed closely behind. They stood there holding two lanterns as he collected the small bundles of clothes and personal effects around Dobbs's bunk. He saw a letter that he had been writing and decided to put it in his pocket. He could feel the men's cold, hostile stares, and knew that trouble was ahead.

It was Old Jeremiah who spoke first.

"The man needs to be thrown into the sea."

"If you won't do it, we will," another cried out.

Old Jeremiah then continued, his voice sounding like a prophet. "Jonah fled from the Lord. He must pay the price. Those are the Bible's teachings. It is the Lord's will."

A low murmur reverberated in the gloom.

"Aye, aye, 'tis the Lord's will."

Morgan looked at the weathered faces of these older men who were his shipmates, the scruffy beards and the sagging, haggard cheeks. Despite oil skins and boots, they were soaked, their faces and beards streaked with water. The anger and fear in their bloodshot eyes told the story. Morgan had no weapon. For a brief moment, he thought of trying to run through this gauntlet of men. Instead he spoke up in a stronger, more authoritative voice than he thought possible.

"Maybe this man is a Jonah," Morgan said, looking Curly Jim squarely in the eye. "That's not for me to say. It's the first mate who wants Dobbs's possessions and I'm here to collect 'em. Now I mean to do what I was ordered to do. If you have a quarrel with that I reckon you will want to take that up with Mr. Toothacher."

Morgan put his shoulders down and stepped into the press of men, who now seemed intent on seizing him. They moved forward, arms outstretched like a lynching mob. It was the huge form of Icelander who emerged to pry him away from the clawing clutches of this small mob. At six foot four, he towered over most of the other sailors. They all knew that his calm, cool demeanor masked a powerful anger that they were all afraid of.

At that moment, a trumpet sounded and a cry went out from above deck. "Icebergs ahead! All men on deck!" The sailors sprang from their berths, buttoned their pants, grabbed their caps, struggled into their jackets, and bolted up the stairs of the forecastle companionway. As suddenly as that, Morgan and the Jonah were forgotten. He scrambled up on deck with the rest of the men, only instead of going aloft he dropped off Dobbs's possessions below decks in the galley area and made his way back to the chaos on the foredeck.

The crew had been battling heavy winds for days now, but no one had bargained on anything like this. On its northwesterly course, the ship had sailed into a field of icebergs. They were now north of 40 degrees latitude but still far enough away from the Grand Banks off Newfoundland and the Labrador current so as not to expect to encounter the southerly drift of ice fields. All around them they could see these large mountains of ice, some two hundred to three hundred feet high, rising out of the water like white cathedrals. Most were still half a mile away. The danger was clear, but eager to make up lost time, Champlin pressed ahead, ordering Mr. Brown to station lookouts aloft as well as on deck.

That night Morgan was placed on the foredeck watch. The Pleiades were still visible on the eastern horizon and the Dipper beckoned to the north. He looked back at Icelander, who was on the opposite side of the ship, a thin speck of light from the lantern highlighting his face. Watchful and mute, he stood there in the dark, his jacket flapping and fluttering in the wind. Over the years he'd gotten to know more about this mysterious man of so few words. Icelander, or Olaf, had grown up as a fisherman's son. His father had drowned in a storm, leaving only him and his mother. When she eventually remarried, her new husband constantly beat her. One evening when his stepfather raised his fist, young Olaf came to his mother's defense. The fight ended with his stepfather falling backward, hitting his head on a ship's anchor with a fatal thud. That was not only the end of his stepfather but also the end of Olaf's life in Iceland. His mother told him to leave home and never come back. He never understood why she didn't want him to intervene. He eventually found his way to Denmark and finally to London, where he'd shipped on board one of the Griswold ships.

Morgan looked at the square pale face of the melancholy sailor with the thin lips and the strange, white eyelashes. He wondered about his own family. His decision to go to sea left him isolated like Olaf Rasmussen, a wandering sailor who, like a piece of driftwood, never comes farther inland than the shoreline.

As the early morning sky lightened on the horizon, Morgan had run up the ratlines to help with the foremast topgallant sail. The air was strangely filled with the smell of mountain lake water, not the salty smell of just the day before. All around the ship were white mountaintops peeking out of the ocean waves like frozen pyramids. It was from his high perch that he spotted something enormous and bluish. It was just a vague shape concealed in one of the black cresting waves. At first he thought it was a shark or a whale. He rubbed his eyes with his fist. It was still there, a pale, translucent blue object coming directly at them. He didn't want to believe what he was seeing. One of the bluish edges of the object broke the surface. It was sharp and jagged, and then he knew for sure what it was. Morgan sounded the alarm, which was echoed back to the mate. The helmsman spun the wheel around so that the ship narrowly missed the sunken block of ice, its uneven edges scraping up against the ship's sides with a wrenching sound. Had it occurred an hour before in the dark of the night, nothing could have saved the *Hudson*. The underwater iceberg would have punctured a hole in the bottom of the ship's hull. Champlin approached him later and personally thanked him. It was the first time that had ever happened. The captain had actually spoken to him and congratulated him, something he rarely did with the younger, less experienced sailors.

"What do you think, Morgan, does prayer bring good luck?"

"I don't know, Captain," he replied, somewhat surprised by his question.

Champlin pushed his hand through his disheveled head of hair as he looked out at the cold blue ocean. He seemed strangely shaken.

"One thing's certain about this life, Morgan. It comes to an end. Out here in the ocean, the Creator reminds me of that fairly regular. Thank you for your vigilance."

With that comment, he walked away.

The next day dawned with bright sunlight and light air. Looking back to the north, there were no signs of the lethal icebergs. The forecastle was alive with storytelling and chanteys. The dark tension of the past few days seemed to have lifted, and Morgan joined a small group of sailors on deck who began singing "Fire Down Below." He watched as Ochoa pulled out his guitar and began playing, his calloused, ring-covered fingers strumming the chords lightly and quickly. Along with Hiram and Icelander, Ochoa had become one of his closest friends on the ship. He supposed the common bond they shared was that they were all the favored targets of the second mate's rages. They had banded together to help one another. He didn't know much at first about Ochoa, but then when he realized that the Spaniard understood and spoke more English than he let on, he came to hear the man's tragic story. When he was only ten years old, his family traveled from Cadiz to Cuba. Their ship was only one day away from reaching Havana when a pirate ship boarded them. All aboard were shot or hung. He had watched as his parents were killed, shot at close range while they were on their knees. His sisters were taken by a few of the men on board the prize ship and he was forced to join the pirates. He never forgot their fear-stricken faces just before they were pushed down the companionway into the hold.

It was then, amidst much foot stomping, singing, and yelling from the sailors, that Morgan remembered the letter that he had stuffed into his pocket. He'd asked earlier about Dobbs, the jumper, and he'd been told by another sailor that the sick man was still talking incoherently in a semiconscious state. He went off to a dark corner on the other side of the livestock shed and sat down to read the letter he'd picked up from the man's bunk area. He was always happy when he could slip away and read in seclusion, and this was one of his hideouts. There was no way to describe the extent of his astonishment as he unfolded the piece of paper. The handwriting was shaky and jagged, the lettering uncertain, a sign of the writer's weak and trembling hand. Dobbs had not finished it, but that wasn't what left Morgan speechless.

Dear Morgan,
When I first Spied you high up in the yards after we cleared Margate and headed into the North Sea, I thought I had seen a Ghost. I thought it was Abraham as your appearances are similar. Then when I heard your name spoken, I realized you must be his Brother. It was then that I knew the heavy hand of Fate had directed me to this Ship for a purpose. It was my Time. I know that I failed to fulfill my Promise to write your Mother, and now I embrace this Opportunity to inform you. Your brother deserved better from me, his friend John Taylor. I find myself unable to easily relate to you what happened, but I must try to make you understand. I did all I could . . .

Morgan sat stunned at what he was reading. He turned the page back and forth, but found nothing more there. His mind raced ahead. The two anchors and the words tattooed on the man's back, "Bosom friend and Brother"; it suddenly came to him. Those were the words John Taylor had used to describe Abraham in the letter he had sent. Even the odd use of capital letters was the same. How could he have forgotten that? Each sentence was imprinted in his mind like a phrase from the Bible.

Now it was clear. Dobbs was Taylor, the man he'd been searching for. Here he was lying in a bunk below him. He allowed himself to think that perhaps Abraham was alive. Taylor had not mentioned any details, only that his brother had been surrounded by wickedness, and that they would not see each other again. He must keep this man alive. The mates had told him that he now had a recurring fever with severe chills and sudden sweating. Scuttles thought it was one of the African fevers.

Days later, Morgan was draped over the fore topsail yard tying off the gasket to secure the sail to the yard when he spotted the line on the horizon several miles to the northward of them. At long last, they'd arrived across the Atlantic. They passed one of the emigrant ships carrying a full boatload of three hundred passengers. Two or three outward-bound ships with their cathedral-like towers of white sails were heading south en route to the Caribbean, South America, or even further to China. By afternoon, he could hear the faint booming of the surf even before he could see the white line of breakers rolling onto the sandy shoreline of Long Island. The voyage had taken a punishing six weeks. Most of the steerage passengers had pale and hollow looks. He looked down at a small group of them who had gathered on deck near the barnyard area to sing a hymn of thanks, their voices drifting upward, blending in with the murmur of the breakers in the distance. The melodic singing made him think of home and the Sunday service at the Lyme meetinghouse. He wondered if he would ever see his mother again. He clenched his teeth to fight back a muted sob, shook his head and looked out to sea. Soon he spotted the narrow spit of land called Sandy Hook that marked the entrance to New York harbor, and the first mate gave the order to back the yards. From his perch in the topsail area, he could see the pilot boat and the speedy news schooners sailing quickly toward them, black-backed gulls riding the air currents around the hulls.

As one of them came closer, Captain Champlin shouted out, "What's the news?"

A man at the bow of the boat shouted back that General Marquis de Lafayette had arrived safely.

"He's back! He's here in America."

It was August 15, 1824.

The sixty-seven-year-old Lafayette had come back to the United States for the first time since the revolution. The next day New York's streets were filled with the sounds of patriotic Yankee Doodle marching bands and men dressed in military uniforms on prancing white horses. With the sight of Lafayette waving at the adoring crowds from his horse-drawn carriage, Morgan and Hiram carried the semiconscious John Taylor off the ship and put him on a cart. The captain had told them to get the man off his ship. He never wanted to see him again, and he didn't care what they did with him. At the sight of a sick man, the crowds parted, giving them plenty of space. They took him to a sailor's boarding house where a doctor eventually confirmed that Taylor had come down with a recurrent form of malaria. The doctor treated him with quinine, and over the next two days Taylor improved considerably. By the time Morgan came to see him, just before the ship sailed for London, Taylor was conscious, although extremely weak.

At the sight of Morgan walking through the door into his room, the sick man began shivering uncontrollably. His eyes opened wide with fear.

"No, Abraham," he shouted. "Have mercy! Have you come for me?"

Morgan didn't reply. He shook the man strongly and slapped his face.

"Pull yourself together, man. I'm not Abraham. For God's sake, tell me what has happened to my brother. Is he alive or dead?"

The bedridden man was taken aback by this sudden attack.

"Why did you sail under a false name?" Morgan continued with his interrogation. "What have you got to hide?"

The sick man looked up at him, his eyes only half open. "It was the Englishman who did it. It wasn't me. It was the Englishman, William Blackwood, that's his name, the captain on that blood boat. He and his curly red-haired mate, Tom Edgars. Big Red, they called him, but it was Blackwood who done it. He hated and resented Abraham, and now he wants me dead."

"What blood boat?"

"The *Charon*," he replied with fear in his eyes. "That's the English ship that conscripted us. The Devil's own ferry, that one." Old memories of the British raid up the Connecticut River suddenly resurfaced in Morgan's mind. His childhood fear and anger toward the British Royal Navy rose up like unwanted phlegm in his throat.

"Why does he want you dead?"

"I know too much about them and their foul dealings."

"What foul dealings? Where do I find this Blackwood?"

The bedridden man paused for some time before he answered, and then he mumbled, "The East End of London." He said something else, which Morgan couldn't hear well. He shook him again, but the shivering sailor didn't respond. His eyelids flickered and closed, his body starting to shake as he slipped back into unconsciousness.

PART III

And the muddy tide of the Thames, reflecting nothing, and hiding a million of unclean secrets within its breast, — a sort of guilty conscience, as it were, unwholesome with the rivulets of sin that constantly flow into it, — is just the dismal stream to glide by such a city.

—Nathaniel Hawthorne, *Our Old Home*

7

1826

An early summer wind was blowing hard from the direction of Staten Island that June morning, pulling the *Hudson*'s anchor chains taut like the strings on a fiddle. Morgan stood by the windlass on the ship's foredeck, ready for the order to weigh anchor. He was chewing a quid of tobacco, enjoying the bitter taste and the way it sharpened his mind. A couple of steam tugboats were puffing around the harbor. The jib sheets were pulled tight and the crew at the stern of the ship was busy raising the spanker. He could hear some of the sailors singing the "Sally Racket" chantey.

"Oh Sally Racket, pawned my peak jacket, hi-oh!"

Just then, the big, square-shouldered first mate strode forward from the quarterdeck with his rigid, military-like posture.

"Heave up the anchor, let's get it aweigh," yelled Mr. Toothacher gruffly.

Morgan and Hiram joined in the singing as they took their places along with the rest of the crew heaving on the windlass, their bodies' movements matching the rhythm of the chantey song. They were now considered full-fledged seamen, or "jacks of all trades" as the sailors liked to say. After four years at sea, the tasks on ship strangely soothed Morgan like the monotony of the ocean on a calm day. He could toss the lead from the forechains, tie a cuckold's knot around a spar, or take the helm during the night. All were as familiar to him as combing his hair or trimming his thickening reddish whiskers. He was twenty years old, but he felt much older.

Morgan looked over at Hiram, whose bearded face was now aglow in the morning sun. His teeth flashed. His eyes sparkled. He was stripped to the waist, revealing a sinewy white torso that gleamed and shimmered as he strained and heaved away. He now looked like a Yankee tar, a true foredeck sailor. His muscular arms and shoulders, tattooed with his busty mermaids and a trident-holding Neptune, flexed and tightened as he sang the chantey with the rest of the sailors. Icelander and the Spaniard, along with several of the Connecticut River men, were still visibly feeling the effects of taking too big of a "swig at the halyards" the last few nights of shore leave. Morgan noticed that they were having a hard time keeping up with the rhythm of the song as they heaved against the wooden capstan bars.

There were many new men in the crew. Old Jeremiah had left after the Jonah voyage, vowing that "he wouldn't sail no more on no cursed ship." Many of the other old-timers like Curly Jim had gone as well. Morgan had been glad to see most of those troublesome sailors leave. In their place, the captain had hired on some Cape Horn veterans from Salem and Newburyport, a couple of river men from Connecticut, and a colored man from New Orleans who'd been working on coastal packets.

Sailors were now on the yards bracing around the topsails of the foremast and the mainmast. The anchor was up, and the foredeck sailors were securing it to the cat head, ready for the next order. One of the men started singing "New York Girls," and soon the yards and the foredeck were filled with song. All around were other transatlantic packets getting ready to weigh anchor, some already leaving New York harbor under full sail.

"Ely, look over there."

Morgan's head snapped up from the cat head. He watched as a small transatlantic packet fought its way toward the East River.

"Look Ely, it's the old *Cadmus*. Remember two years ago when that Havre packet brought in General Lafayette?"

Morgan nodded. Hiram was right. It indeed was the *Cadmus*, a smallish snub-nosed packet on the Havre–New York run flying the tricolor. She must have just arrived from France. The sailors were high up on the yards furling the topsails. The sight of the old *Cadmus* brought back poignant memories for Morgan. He began thinking of Old Jeremiah, black cats, and that fateful voyage two years ago that had seemed cursed from beginning to end. He thought of his traumatic encounter with John Taylor. Immediately after that voyage he had written his brother to tell him the good news that he had found Taylor, but then four months later when he had returned from London he found that the man had vanished from the boarding house where he had been delivered.

His mind wandered back to that boarding house. He had walked up Cherry Street, noisy with drunken, rowdy sailors spilling out into the snow-covered cobblestone street. It was freezing cold and the snow was crunching underneath his boots. He had found number 39 easily enough, a wooden two-storied building, with a nondescript blue door. The boarding house lady, a harried middle-aged woman with her hair tied up in the back, had poked her head out the door. At first, she had threatened to have her husband pummel him if he didn't leave, but then she recognized him when he pulled his woolen cap off and invited him inside.

"Take off your coat, sailor, and come over here by the fire. I am right surprised you came back. Your Mr. Taylor disappeared soon after you left."

Morgan had raised his eyebrows in surprise.

"What happened? Where did he go?"

"Can't say," the woman replied as she looked at him expectantly.

"As soon as he was strong enough to walk, he just left. Look'd to me like he were a man who didn't care much for himself," she said simply as she offered him a piece of pound cake and then poured him a cup of tea.

"He a relative of yours?" she had asked inquiringly.

"No, ma'am," Morgan had responded matter-of-factly. "Just a fellow mariner, that's all."

Then he remembered how her face had become animated, her eyes widening. "I ask ye 'cause I'm curious. A big English fellow came looking for him just after he disappeared," she had said. "Scary-looking fellow with tattoos and puffy eyes. He said Taylor was his brother, but I knew that weren't the case."

Morgan asked her for his name.

"He gave no name," she had replied, "and no address neither, but he was an Englishman."

She had paused and looked at him again inquisitively. "You sound like you might know him? Friend of yours, sailor?"

Morgan shook his head, thanked the woman, and left, disheartened and preoccupied by what he had just heard. It sounded to him like an English bloodhound with no kind intentions was hot on Taylor's trail. He wondered if this Englishman could be connected to Abraham.

Those thoughts were passing through his mind when the first mate yelled out, "All hands aloft." As Morgan climbed the ratlines of the main mast, he looked back toward the East River and could just barely make out the tips of the masts of the fast new Swallowtail packet, the *York* and the *Canada* of the Black Ball Line still loading freight and passengers. Morgan was busy unfastening and unfurling the topgallants from the yards when he heard the order for more sails. He looked down from the yard on which he was perched and noticed that the new cabin boy, Dalrymple, was already down on his knees, holystoning the decks. The second mate, Mr. Brown, was yelling in his face.

"Look at me boy when I talk to you," the mate shouted derisively, his face scowling underneath his black leather hat. "Stop skylarking and clean the decks, boy, so they're as smooth as your little pup's face."

Out of the corner of his eye, Mr. Brown caught Morgan's glance and saw him staring down at him from the yard. Morgan quickly looked away, but not before he noticed the mate's lips curl with an expression of malice. At first he thought that Brown was looking at him, but then he noticed that his churlish face was turned in his friend's direction. Hiram was on the royals yard just above him.

That night, the winds began to pick up sharply. Morgan was on watch aloft, squatting in the crosstrees and holding on to one of the stays for support. He had grown to like sitting high above the deck at night. The tangy smell of the sea and the freshening breeze filled his lungs and invigorated him. He looked up into the blackness around him and marveled at the immensity of the star-filled skies. The tip of the mast swayed from side to side as the ship's bow plunged into the waves. The melancholy whistle of the wind caused his mind to wander. He reached his hand out into the blackness as he pretended to pluck one of the brighter stars out of the sky. It reminded him of picking apples. He thought of home at that moment and felt a sudden sadness. Just then, a sharp gust of wind caused the ship to heel over sharply. He grabbed onto the mast to steady himself.

His eyes searched for Hiram, but he was nowhere to be found. Lately his friend had been slipping away, mysteriously disappearing. The mates were always looking for him, particularly Mr. Brown.

As his glance fell to the deck, he noticed the shadowy figure of the second mate climbing over the futtock shrouds heading up the mast toward him, and he braced himself for the worst. Moments later, Brown had climbed up the ratlines and thrust his face inches from Morgan's nose, his foul-smelling breath almost making him gag.

"Where's your chum, Morgan?" asked the second mate, his voice growling with hostility. The reflected light off the white canvas sails revealed the man's yellow teeth and shiny black eyes. Morgan thought he knew the answer. On one of the voyages a year ago, Ochoa had taken him and Hiram down into the dark corners of the main hold and shown them where the rum barrels were kept. This was the black belly of the ship, where rats scurried over crates and barrels and the cross beams creaked and cracked with the ship's movement. To Morgan, the place seemed like a musty tomb with the smells of rank bilge water filling his nostrils, but despite the unattractive surroundings, trips to the rum barrels soon became a welcome diversion for him and Hiram.

Ochoa taught them the sailors' trick of sucking the rum directly from the barrels with long quills. Once the novelty had passed, Morgan still enjoyed numerous forays into the rum barrel area on each passage, but he noticed that Hiram was always pushing to go again. He was probably down there now. His friend was fond of the grog, no matter what the risks of being caught, no matter how stormy the weather.

"So where is he, Morgan?" Mr. Brown asked again in an even more menacing tone.

"I reckon he's out on the jib boom tending to the sails," Morgan lied, in as convincing a voice as he could muster. As a sailor, he had learned how to lie with a straight face and a forthright voice. That answer seemed to partially satisfy the second mate. Brown had already caught Morgan and Hiram below decks around the rum barrels before on an earlier trip. They had been busy sucking the rum out of one of the barrels with quills when they heard footsteps. The second mate had been snuffing around below decks when he heard voices and saw the glow of their lantern. When he yelled out, they'd been quick to come out of the shadows with a story about how Scuttles had sent them down there to look for more flour. The cook was making biscuits and didn't have enough, they'd said. Mr. Brown had been suspicious, but fortunately for them Scuttles had backed up their story.

Like many in the crew, Morgan tried to stay away from Brown. The man was edgier than usual on this trip. No one seemed to know much about his history. It was rumored that he had gone to sea at an early age because of a crime he committed, but no one knew where he came from or what the crime was. He clearly enjoyed inflicting pain on any sailor who crossed him or failed to do his job. Morgan had also heard other unsavory things about Mr. Brown and some of his activities when he was on shore leave.

On that early summer passage, the *Hudson* had taken a more southerly route to stay clear of possible ice fields. One of the Black X packet ships on the London to New York run had never arrived in port and was presumed lost. The *Crisis* had not been heard of now for more than two months. The talk on board ship was that the captain had been given orders to look for any signs of wreckage.

For the first one thousand miles they sailed along the North American mainland, leaving the dangerous Nantucket Shoals to the west, and passing over the Great South Channel. They endured several days of stormy weather with heavy rains, thunder, and lightning. Despite more vigilance than normal, there was no sign of a shipwreck. The *Crisis*, with its twelve passengers and two dozen sailors, had disappeared without a trace. The Black X Line now only had one other remaining ship besides the *Hudson*. Morgan once again thought of Abraham and looked out at the sea from high atop the masthead, where he was tightening one of the stays. For a moment, he imagined that he was looking at a battlefield cemetery, the foaming whitecaps extending to the horizon like luminescent marble gravestones. He felt humbled, and he thought of the captain's words about the reminders of death out on the ocean. He looked up at the stormy, black sky crackling with lightning and listened to the roll of the thunder. He murmured a small prayer.

Among the cabin passengers on board was the famous American author James Fenimore Cooper, who was traveling to England with his wife and five young children. Cooper was already well known as a successful and widely read author after publishing *The Pioneers*. Some even referred to him as America's Sir Walter Scott. He was headed for Europe on an extended stay to give his young children the benefit of learning French and Italian. He was also trying to secure English rights for his books.

For Morgan, that June voyage was memorable because Captain Champlin brought him back to the quarterdeck to take the helm. Like all the sailors, Morgan was required to take his turn at the wheel, but usually he was given the early morning or night watch. This time his watch occurred in the late afternoon, when the cabin passengers were being served tea and refreshments in the quarterdeck area. A dense fog had rolled in, and the air was cold.

Morgan walked back to the stern of the ship, shifting his weight effortlessly from one foot to the other. The repetitive motion of the waves, the slant of the deck, and the wind on his face all spoke to him now in a wordless language. He waited respectfully until the captain signaled him to replace the man at the wheel.

"Your turn at the helm, Morgan."

"Aye, aye, Cap'n."

Morgan stepped up to the wheel and wrapped his fingers around the well-worn, braided twine on each of the spokes. He looked over at the man standing next to the captain. He had unruly dark hair and a high forehead with deep-set eyes. His squared-off jaw hinted at a proud, determined character. His formal dress, a white cravat and a dark jacket, made him appear to be a landed gentleman, but the way he stood with his legs straddled wide for balance, caused Morgan to think he was a seafaring man.

He stood silently at the helm, first looking up at the trim of the sails, then glancing down at the binnacle to check on his course, north-northeast. The fog was thickening and the wind was strengthening. He could feel the tug of the rudder as the ship began to heel over more sharply. The two men were studying the performance of the ship, and he could feel their eyes on him. He kept waiting for a critical comment, but none came. Champlin was boasting that two new ships were being built for the Black X Line. They would soon have four ships, which would help make the London Line more competitive with the Liverpool shipping lines. Morgan soon realized that it was James Fenimore Cooper. He was quite familiar with Cooper's work as Scuttles had given him a copy of *The Pioneers* from the ship's library, as well as Cooper's highly successful seafaring novel, *The Pilot*.

At one point, the topic of conversation switched to the *Crisis*, and the author began asking questions about what could have happened to the Black X packet. Morgan watched as Champlin's mood darkened even as he shuffled his feet on the deck defensively.

"Most likely she ran into a floating iceberg at night." Champlin replied sadly. "Being as you were once a sailor and a midshipman in the United States Navy, Mr. Cooper, you well know the ocean gives and she takes. She is both kind and cruel."

Cooper nodded soberly. Sensing the captain's discomfort, he changed the topic to ask about the fast-growing packet trade with England and France. It was well known that American packet ships were now carrying over not just the mail, but ninety percent of the freight going both ways, as well as most of the passengers. There were now four sailings a month from New York to Liverpool, two to Havre, and one to London.

"Some of my shipping friends in New York say steamships are the future on the Atlantic. What do you think of that notion, Captain?"

Champlin laughed.

"Those stinkpots?" he snorted in disgust. "I venture to say that if I were a passenger, I would not risk my life crossing the stormy Atlantic on one of those smoky tinder boxes."

After the two men tired of talking about ships, Champlin left the quarterdeck to go below and tend to some of his more demanding passengers. Morgan remained quiet, feeling awkward with so important a man as Cooper standing next to him. He looked over at the flush-cheeked author, who was clearly enjoying the motion of the ship and the cool, misty fog on his face. Finally he broke the silence and told Mr. Cooper that he had enjoyed reading his sea novel.

Clearly surprised by this sudden remark from the quiet young sailor at the helm, Cooper smiled at Morgan skeptically.

"A keen-eyed critic of the sea, are you?"

"Yes sir. I liked the part about them escaping through the Devil's Grip, and I greatly admired Mr. Gray, the pilot. Reminded me of some of the American privateering captains who fought the British in the last war."

Cooper's dark eyebrows lifted slowly as he studied Morgan's face more closely.

"You seem a little young, sailor, to know much about that war. What did you say your name was?"

"Morgan, sir. Ely Morgan. I was a farm boy from the Connecticut River, a little town called Lyme, during the war. My brother and I, we were there when the English torched our fleet in old Potapoug. We saw those redcoats close up. We were fortunate we didn't get killed."

Cooper's smile broadened as he listened. He wanted to know more about this young sailor's life. Morgan told him about his search for Abraham. He told him about John Taylor. He didn't know why he divulged all of this, but the author's deep-set eyes, although stern and inquiring, seemed trusting. Perhaps he just needed someone to confide in.

Cooper's interest was piqued at the mention of the mysterious Englishman named William Blackwood.

"What will you do if you find this man, Blackwood, Mr. Morgan, what then?" asked Cooper provocatively.

"I will make him tell me what happened to Abraham," Morgan replied with conviction.

"And what if this Englishman tells you he killed your brother?"

"Why then, I . . ." Morgan bit on his lip, looked up at the sails, and didn't say anything. At that point, Morgan was leaning against the wheel, concentrating on Cooper and not the ship's progress. He hadn't noticed a sudden shift in the wind. Champlin emerged from below decks and looked up at the fluttering sails that were snapping back and forth in the gray fog.

"Fall off, boy, damn you, the fore-topgallant is luffing."

When his watch was over at eight o'clock, Morgan rushed to tell Hiram that he had met the famous author James Fenimore Cooper. He found his friend spinning yarn in the forecastle with some of the other sailors. The sailors, half undressed, were reclining on their sea chests or sitting on their bunks smoking their small half pipes and chewing wads of tobacco. They were listening to one of the old-timers, who was in the middle of a tale. Hiram didn't even know who Cooper was. His eyes were bugged out of his head, his face red and splotched, and his breath was hot like a panting dog. He was in a blurred stupor that Morgan recognized only too well. He pulled his friend out of the smoky, steamy forecastle into the cool, foggy night air. They walked over to the far forward section of the bow where they could talk in private.

"You been quilling rum again?" Morgan asked under his breath.

Hiram nodded with a satisfied smile, and then started to speak in a hoarse, slurred whisper.

"Yeah, I've been quilling that sweet Jamaican grog fairly regular on this passage. You won't believe what I seen down there in the hold last night. I thought I was all alone with them rats scurrying all around me. I had just put the quill through the gimlet hole in the head of the barrel when I heard some commotion in and around the crates. At first, I thought it was just the rats, but then I started hearing rustling noises, and some heavy breathing. I never been so frightened, I thought it might be a ghost or something. I started to run back through the dark, bumping my head on the stores hanging from the heavy timbers. I was dodging and weaving through the maze of crates. I almost made it to the ladder, but I tripped on a coil of rope. Then I seen this lantern light swinging toward me in the darkness. I couldn't see nothing more than that light running at me like a horse coming at me full gallop. Then I heard a voice yell out, 'Who's there? Who's there, damn ye!'"

"Who was it?" Morgan asked excitedly, wondering if there was a stowaway on board.

Hiram raised his eyebrows and leaned closer to Morgan to whisper in his ear, "It was Mr. Brown."

Morgan drew back in surprise.

"I tripped and fell. Then that critter was on me. He bent down and put that light in my face, and asked if I'd been quilling rum. That's when I recognized the mate. I could see his rotten teeth and smell his foul-smelling breath. I lied and told him Scuttles had sent me down there, but he wasn't convinced. He asked me in a real threatening voice what I'd heard. 'Tell me now, Smith, or I will beat it out of you.' I told him I just heard rats and ran because I was scared. Mr. Brown looked like he was going to kill me right there."

"Go on," Morgan urged. He was now beginning to understand why the second mate was paying so much attention to Hiram.

"This is the worst part," Hiram recounted with a worried frown. "Then I seen that new cabin boy named Dalrymple holding up a lantern. Why, he came out of the shadows and calls out all scared-like to Mr. Brown, and the mate, he whirled around and yells at him to get back on the foredeck. . . ." Hiram paused for a moment, and then spoke in almost a whisper, a twisted smile on his face. "I reckon the second mate, when he gets out at sea, he feels certain needs."

It took several seconds for the reality of what Hiram was saying to register. Morgan had wondered why the second mate was always snuffing around the freight hold, and why he always wanted to know where Hiram was. Now he knew. Brown was afraid he would be discovered by Hiram in his secret lair. Jack Brown was just making sure that no one else was down there in the guts of the ship.

"Man alive! Then what happened?" Morgan asked in a more serious tone.

"Brown grabbed me by my shirt and shoved that lantern in my face and then said, 'Whatever you heard, Smith, you better keep to yerself or you'll find yerself climbing up Jacob's ladder and not climbing down.'"

Morgan said nothing for a moment, and then turned to Hiram, shaking his head. He pulled the quid of tobacco he'd been chewing out of his mouth and handed it to his friend.

8

By the twentieth day with all sails set, they spotted Bishop's Rock, the southern outpost of the Isles of Scilly, which seamen call the graveyard of the North Atlantic due to the hidden underwater ledges. Morgan was relieved. He thought it unlikely that Brown would create an incident now. He had seen the mate's eyes, glaring at Hiram, burning with hate, and he had warned his friend to keep his distance. They had just passed the *Don Quixote*, the Havre packet, which left New York just ahead of them on the same day three weeks ago. Three thousand miles of ocean, and amazingly the two ships had come together again. The ship labored against the wind and rising seas, battering her way eastward toward the French coast. Morgan was just climbing down the ratlines after furling and fastening the fore-royals and topgallants. The wind had picked up and the seas threw a flood of water onto the deck. To the north, he could see the looming rocky cliffs of Lands End, and the breakers in the distance. The *Hudson* veered northward past the dangerous rocks at the Lizard, then headed northeasterly, skirting the wild Cornish coast as it made its way up the English Channel.

A day later, Morgan was high up in the fore-royals, his feet balanced squarely on the footropes, when he noticed the rocky cliffs of St. Aldhelm's Head jutting out into the Channel. To the north, he could just make out the tips of the one-hundred-foot jagged white rocks of the Needles. He shouted down to Hiram, who was freeing a snagged buntline, that they had arrived. For Morgan, the first sighting of St. Aldhelm's Head and the Needles was a sign that the voyage was almost over. They would be at anchor within hours. With a fair tide, the Black X packet coasted through the five-mile-wide Solent without tacking. The *Hudson* ran in under clewed-up main and fore topsails, dropping anchor at Spithead within sight of the rooftops of Portsmouth, near the town of Ryde, as was customary. Most of the cabin passengers preferred to get off at Portsmouth and take a bumpy carriage ride into London than spend two more days on a slanted deck.

Morgan remembered thinking at the time how unusual it was that Mr. Brown escorted the cabin passengers into Portsmouth. Normally, the second mate stayed aboard ship with the crew. Brown had told the captain that he had a few personal matters to attend to, and Champlin had granted him a few hours of shore leave. Hours later, with Jack Brown once again aboard ship, the *Hudson* weighed anchor and headed up the Channel toward Dungeness and then into the chop and swell of the North Sea.

Two days later, as they rounded the point at Margate in the predawn darkness of early morning and coasted into the muddy swirl at the mouth of the Thames, the weather started to change. They had timed their arrival to the first rush of the flood tide. Morgan stared at the dark, gray sky, but he saw nothing. The fog came in from the North Sea, like floating mists, thinning and then inexplicably thickening so that they had little to no visibility. There was a sudden air of mystery sailing into the river. The lookouts blew on trumpets every few minutes as a warning to any incoming ship. There was only a boat length of visibility, if that.

Morgan was standing on the port forechains, throwing the lead forward of the slowly moving ship, calling out the depths methodically. The tallow on the bottom of the lead sinker was still pulling up some gravel, not all mud. They were feeling their way from one brightly colored buoy to the next. He caught glimpses of barges stuck in the thick mud along the shore. The low-lying riverbanks were disappearing and then reappearing, the blanket of cold fog occasionally revealing a lonely wooden jetty along the banks or, in the distance, the tip of a church spire.

Even before they reached Sheerness, Luis Ochoa was pulling at his moustache, a sign he was getting nervous. The pilot boat they normally would have encountered was nowhere to be seen. Some of the old hands also showed signs of uneasiness. The sailors aloft were frenetically signaling with their hands. Morgan looked where they were pointing but could see nothing through the fog. After speaking with Mr. Toothacher, the captain surfaced from his cabin with two pistols in either hand while the mates started handing out kitchen knives to the sailors. Morgan had no idea what was going on. He wondered if there was a mutiny brewing. He looked around the deck, but there was no sign of any commotion.

"Tómate este cuchillo," Ochoa murmured to Morgan as he motioned for him to come inboard on deck. "Mejor para matar a estos hijos de puta." Morgan didn't understand exactly what he said, but he took the knife Ochoa handed to him. Something was about to happen as the first mate was ordering lookouts to the port and the starboard. He sent several more sailors up into the yards.

"What's going on?" Morgan anxiously asked the Spaniard.

"Son los piratas del río."

Morgan shook his head, still not understanding.

"Thieves," replied Ochoa with a hushed voice. "River thieves." At the mention of this word, the Spaniard's dark eyes became still and cold, deadly as an iceberg floating underwater. Morgan had always heard tales about ships entering the Thames being attacked by river pirates. They were called scuffle hunters. He had always assumed it was just talk from some of the old sailors as he had never heard of any packet ships being attacked. Still, there were many stories of robberies and murder on the banks of the Thames, and the serious threat of river piracy had led to the formation of the Marine Police years earlier.

Morgan could hear the sound of oars breaking the water's surface, but he couldn't see anything through the shifting fog. A shiver went down his spine. They were about to be attacked. He held the knife that Ochoa had given him. It felt awkward in his hands. He wasn't certain if he could use it against another man. A wave of panic swept over him, just like when he first came on the ship years ago as a cabin boy. He found himself looking at Mr. Brown with his black hat. He seemed alert, but strangely relaxed. The second mate caught his glance, and Morgan looked away. Just then, a distinctly English voice broke through the gloom.

"Stand by to be boarded or we'll bring ar guns to bear on ye."

The fog was so thick Morgan hadn't noticed that Mr. Toothacher had mounted two four pounders on the quarterdeck. Some of the old-timers from the river rammed them full of grapeshot and langrage. As soon as they heard the voice, Toothacher began shouting.

"Fire when ready!"

With that there were two loud explosions, one after another, but the pirates had planned this well. There were no cries for mercy, no screams of pain, only a deathly silence followed the roar of the cannons. Toothacher looked surprised and puzzled as he stared out into the gray, foggy mist off the side of the boat. Morgan clutched the knife's handle more tightly and held it in front of his chest. Only the Spaniard seemed to know what was going on. He motioned to Icelander and grabbed Morgan, pointing toward the stern of the boat. Then he yelled out, "Es un truco! Llegan del otro lado a estribor!"

Some of the sailors understood a few words of Spanish so at least they had turned toward the starboard side of the ship where the Spaniard had warned them of danger. There was a loud bump and a thud. The next moment the *Hudson* was grappled and boarded. Morgan watched in horror as the first of the scuffle hunters surfaced over the bulwarks. A dozen men armed with knives, cutlasses, and pistols emerged over the sides of the ship, calling for the *Hudson* crew to surrender. One or two had pistols, and they opened fire. Morgan watched as Mr. Toothacher grimaced in pain as he reached for his shoulder. More shots rang out. The scrape of metal against metal could be heard above the shouting. Morgan could see that two more of the *Hudson*'s sailors had been hit. Captain Champlin, his wavy, silvery black hair all askew, fired one pistol and then the other.

Morgan was about to join the fray when the Spaniard and Icelander pulled him along, running to the stern of the ship to begin lowering the jolly boat over the transom.

"Where are we going?" Morgan shouted. "We can't leave the ship."

"Don't worry," Icelander told him. "Ochoa has a plan."

Morgan quickly looked at the Spaniard, whose face was burning with intensity and hatred. He took one last look back. He spotted a short, stout man with a pea jacket and a black hat in amidst men with belts and scabbards. He wasn't sure because of the foggy mist, but it looked like it was Mr. Brown. Instead of fighting, the second mate was talking to one of their attackers. Morgan watched astonished as Mr. Brown motioned to another group of these river thieves with his long arms. Morgan looked over to where he had appeared to signal. He saw Hiram amidships just forward of the quarterdeck. Without thinking, he yelled at him to watch out.

Hiram looked over to the port side of the ship where Morgan was pointing. Two men were running toward him with knives in their hands. He reached into one of the quarter boats on the starboard side and pulled out one of the oars. He grabbed the long wooden oar, holding it with both hands in the center, striking one pirate in the jaw with a left hand jab of the blade, and then with a lunge, jammed the handle side into the other man's stomach.

Pausing only for a second to observe the pain he had inflicted, Hiram ran back to the stern of the ship. He followed Morgan over the stern rail into the jolly boat, as Icelander and the Spaniard began rowing away, disappearing almost immediately into the fog. Morgan still had no idea what the plan was or what they were doing. Ochoa signaled the other three to be silent although the noisy chaos of fighting above them muffled any noise their oars could have made.

Within minutes, they came upon the boarding vessel, a Thames river hoy. The heavy sailing barge, about half the length of the *Hudson*, was attached to the looming sides of the packet with the grappling lines. They quietly tied up at the boat's stern with the jolly boat's painter, and without saying a word, the Spaniard clambered up the sides of the barge with his long knife in his hand. He had a fierce look on his face as if he felt he had a score to settle. The large form of Icelander followed closely behind, clutching a heavy, eight-inch-long capstan bar firmly with both hands.

Ochoa cut the grappling hook lines so the sailing barge now slowly drifted away from the packet. Both he and Icelander disappeared into the cabin house. Moments later through the gray mist, Morgan heard a man scream out in surprise, and then a gasp. This was followed by another man cursing loudly, and then the sound of a blow, a groan, and then silence. Morgan and Hiram looked at each other through the fog as they realized what they had just witnessed and heard.

Emerging from behind the cabin house, the Spaniard, his eyes glimmering with adrenaline, revealed his plan of action to the other three. They searched the ship and found the combustibles and gunpowder that they had expected to find. These river pirates were apparently planning to board the ship, and then burn it once they'd retrieved the more valuable cargo. Within five minutes, the Spaniard had lit a fire in the hold of the boat, and then jumped off into the *Hudson*'s jolly boat where the other three were waiting. They'd salvaged some guns, but everything else on board was now up in flames. The exploding fire on the barge lit up the water like a torch, creating an eerie glow through the fog.

It looked as though the *Hudson*'s sailors were holding off their attackers with a mixture of knives, kitchen cleavers, and belaying pins. The Spaniard's plan soon became evident. The explosives on board the pirate's barge went off in what sounded like dozens of cannons firing simultaneously. The two masts and the barge's furled sails shot up in flames. The fighting on the deck of the *Hudson* stopped immediately, and the pirates, confused by the noise and the hypnotic sight of their burning vessel, momentarily seemed to lose the will to fight.

Sensing the tactical advantage, the captain ordered them to put their weapons down. The packet's sailors easily outnumbered their attackers two to one, and they now formed a tight circle around them. The two sides were now just ten feet apart, and they seemed poised for a bloody close-in battle of stabbing and slashing. At that moment, a final huge explosion went off, and what remained of the fiery barge disappeared into the water, restoring a gray stillness to the fog-shrouded river.

"Put your weapons down," Champlin reiterated. "Thrown 'em down or you will have breathed your last."

One by one, the river thieves threw down their weapons.

When Morgan got back on board ship, the quarterdeck was a shocking sight, the white decks covered with blood, some of the *Hudson*'s crew nursing knife wounds. Three of the scuffle hunters were sprawled motionless on the blood-splattered deck. It looked like they were dead. Another three were down on their knees or squatting, clutching their wounds, grimacing in pain. Captain Champlin had received a blow on the head. The first officer's shoulder was soaked in blood. All around him, Morgan could hear the cursing, the groaning, and the cries of pain. Scuttles emerged from the companionway with a bowl of hot water and an armful of bandages and began tending to the captain. Morgan eyed Mr. Brown briefly, but he was careful not to reveal any of his dark suspicions about the mate. Amazingly none of the *Hudson*'s sailors had been killed. The six men from the raiding party who were still standing were manacled and led forward into the steerage area, which was empty on this leg of the journey. Morgan and Icelander were ordered by the first mate to stand watch over them for the remainder of the trip up the Thames to London.

Under the flickering light of a lantern hung from the beams, Morgan studied his prisoners, who were squatting and clumped together in the center of the steerage compartment. Three of them were cut and bruised and needed medical attention. They were a rough group dressed in old trousers and patched shirts, their pale, haggard faces downcast. Morgan had seen this type before on the London docks. They looked like old, run-down sailors who had arrived at the end of the road and had nothing to lose.

"Why did you attack us?" Morgan angrily asked one of the pirates who seemed to be looking in his direction.

At first there was no response, and then the man grunted a reply.

"Cos yer bloody Yankees, that's why."

"What do you mean by that?" asked Morgan.

"We workin' English got to stand up agin' ye Yankees. We got nothink, no money, no bed, no job. We're 'ard up we are. Yer ship is in England now, and as yer in English waters, it's fine and proper that yer should share yer wealth with poor Englishmen like us."

At that point, the man turned to his compatriots for support, and they nodded their heads in agreement. Morgan tried to get more information from them about how they chose the *Hudson*, but they weren't talking. He had his suspicions. He had heard of spies in Portsmouth on the lookout for cargo ships that they could later plunder on the slow-moving run up the Thames. But who would have been their informant in Portsmouth?

An obliging steamer came and threw them a line, and they began the twenty-five-mile journey upriver to London. Morgan came up for air from the dank steerage just as the ship wound its way past a shipyard near Tilbury. They passed barges stranded in the mud, and he could see the tips of masts reaching over the rooftops of warehouses. He stood by the bulwarks, gazing out to some waterside stairs that emerged from the foggy gloom. He was lost in his troubling thoughts as the ship wound its way toward the Isle of Dogs. The haunting sight of Brown in the midst of the fighting stayed with him.

By afternoon, they had reached the busy section of the river. A parade of small boats followed them in and around the constant flow of barge traffic. Word had gotten out on the Thames that a Yankee packet had been attacked by some scuffle hunters. Just a few miles south of Blackwall, he returned to his guard duty, relieving Icelander. He was left alone with his half-dozen prisoners. He looked at one man with a pigtail hanging down his back, and yellow and blue gewgaws dangling down the sides of his curly hair. His left eye was closed shut from a blow he'd received. His shirt was open, revealing tattoos running across his chest and down to his arms. On his hands, swollen knuckles; a silver-colored skull ring on one, and a deep scar from a burn on another. Morgan's eyes paused suddenly. The tattoo of a scaly red serpent spiraling down one of the man's white arms caught his attention. Not expecting any reply, Morgan threw out the question he'd been asking around the London docks for months now.

"Ever heard of William Blackwood?"

"What if I 'ave? What's it to ye, Yank?"

"I heard he was looking for sailors," Morgan replied quickly, too stunned to say anything more.

"Why yer asking about Blackwood," another man asked suddenly, clearly suspicious. "'Ow's it yer know about my old China Bill? Ye be a copper's nark?"

"What's a copper's nark?" Morgan asked innocently.

"A Blue Bottle's blower? Is that what ye are, Yank?"

The man with the pigtail glowered at Morgan with undisguised disdain. His one good eye seemed clearer, a sharper, more intelligent tool than moments before, as if suddenly it had spotted an opportunity.

"If 'e's in London you might find 'im down by Wapping Old Stairs," the man volunteered with a malevolent grin. "'E's got some ale'ouses there 'e frequents. One of them is called the Frying Pan Tavern on Vinegar Lane just north of the 'ighway in Shadwell."

9

The drizzle was now a drenching rain. Lightning flashed to the west over Tower Hill, illuminating London's skyline off in the distance. Morgan watched from the sodden foredeck as several burly constables with the Marine Police kicked and shoved their prisoners off the ship onto the London docks. The river pirates who could walk slinked and shambled in the steady rain past the stern of the ship, their heads down and their hands manacled. The other three were thrown into a small wagon and carted away. Morgan spotted the man with the pigtail who had told him where he might find Blackwood. He whispered softly as he went by, "Say 'ello to Bill for me when ye find 'im."

A horse-drawn wagon waited to carry them away to what some of the sailors said would be a dark hole in a watch house, probably in Whitechapel or Bethnal Green. Morgan had heard about these places, narrow dungeons with dirt and gravel floors steaming with stagnant air reeking of human feces. Poor wretches, Morgan thought to himself, even as he recognized them for what they were, mean and squalid creatures from London's unforgiving streets.

Morgan knew well enough that these crime-ridden places surrounding the docks were haunts where sailors sometimes disappeared forever. Still, he fully intended to go there to follow this latest lead. Before that, he wanted to talk to Hiram about his suspicions. He hadn't had a chance to talk with his friend since the attack on the ship. He watched the wagon loaded with the prisoners lurch and rattle its way out of the well-guarded dock area into the streets, the heavy-set truck horses straining at their leather harness. Once it had disappeared, and the heavy, creaking iron gates had closed behind them, he found Hiram and told him what he'd seen during the attack.

Hiram wanted to confront Brown and report him to the captain, but Morgan convinced him that he wouldn't get justice that way. "The captain would never believe you," he told Hiram, "and besides, Brown would just deny it." They decided to confide in a few other sailors. The Spaniard, once he was given a translation of what Morgan had seen, wanted to slit the mate's throat, "Cortarle el cuello come el cochino, hijo de puta que es." Icelander wanted to keelhaul him or string him up in the yardarms. It was Whipple, the ship's carpenter, who gave Morgan the idea of what to do.

Henry Whipple was a Connecticut River man, an old sea dog who had been on many deepwater voyages and was full of just as many stories as the days he'd spent at sea. He had a simple face overloaded with a wild, unkempt growth of graying whiskers, a dull, gauzy shade of blue in his eyes, and a wide sloping forehead, cracked and uneven like a New England stone wall. His hair was thinning at the top of his head, so he'd drawn it back in a Chinaman's pigtail. After the suddenness of the river attack, Captain Champlin had told Whipple he wanted a way to hear what was happening on deck in the privacy of his cabin. Whipple mentioned this casually by way of making conversation. A group of sailors were drinking water at the ship's scuttlebutt when Whipple volunteered the latest task he was doing for the captain.

"He's got me building a speaking tube contraption with one end in his cabin and the other end coming out by the cabin house at the stern of the ship," Whipple said dolefully as if he were making a confession.

"That so," one of the sailors replied. "What's that for?"

Whipple explained that his hollow tube would allow the captain to hear everything going on at the helm area, and if necessary, make his voice heard from his cabin if the sails were shaking or luffing. It was also a good protection against a mutiny or a surprise attack by river pirates.

Whipple's uneven brow furrowed as he realized that he was talking too much.

"The cap'n didn't want me to tell a soul, so don't let on you know anything about it," he said anxiously, his voice noticeably distressed.

When Morgan heard what Whipple was doing, the outlines of a scheme to get rid of the second mate slowly began to take shape in his mind. The plan was set in motion days later when the captain returned and Mr. Toothacher left the ship. Whipple had finished installing the new speaking tube. That night Champlin retired to his cabin after dinner as was his custom, and Morgan and his cohorts gathered on the quarterdeck. Morgan and Hiram weren't the only ones who wanted to get rid of the second mate.

At eleven o'clock, Morgan began his preparations. He picked a spot right next to the helm where he could speak into one end of the hollow tube, the other end of which was right next to the captain's berth, just several feet away from his head. Morgan and Hiram then began speaking in a hoarse whisper, knowing that their voices would be sufficiently loud enough for the captain's benefit.

In a dramatic hushed tone, Hiram described the unspeakable horrors he'd seen down in the rum barrels, sparing no details, adding a few revealing sounds he hadn't actually heard. Morgan played along as if he'd never heard this salacious story before. He also piped in with his own story of foul dealing about Brown. He told how the mate had contacted the scuffle hunters in Portsmouth, striking a deal with them, and then, once they'd boarded the ship, directed them toward Hiram, their intended victim. This was part fact, part guesswork, and pure theatrics.

Soon other sailors joined in on the discussion. A mock fight ensued as the sailors pretended to argue about what they should do to Brown. At that point, down in his cabin, the captain would have heard muffled shouts, the stomping of feet on deck and a plethora of cursing. All this was being done for his benefit. In actual fact, there were now about six or seven sailors who were pretending to have a fight, all in the interest of luring the volatile mate back to the helm area. Right on cue, Mr. Brown showed up wielding his favorite weapon, a belaying pin, and began hitting and striking any and all of the sailors involved in the fighting.

"Mr. Brown!" Morgan shouted directly into the hollow tube above the din of the shipboard brawl. "Why is it that you didn't fight like this when the scuffle hunters came over the side of the ship? One of them told me it was you who invited them on board."

An irate Brown lunged at Morgan with his long, powerful arms raining him with blows of the belaying pin. As Morgan raised up his elbows to fend off the blows, Hiram started shouting into the hollow tube again.

"What is it that you did down in the darkness of the hold, Mr. Brown? Did I hear what I thought I heard amongst them rum barrels?"

Brown's face became beet red, and he flew into an even more intense rage, wheeling and turning on Hiram like a wild animal, growling and snarling. He had Hiram by the throat with his head up against the helm. He was strangling him when the captain, dressed in his silk pajamas with his head still bandaged, emerged from the companionway wielding his two pistols.

"What's the meaning of this?" Champlin shouted as he rushed into the melee. His eyes fell on Morgan and he demanded an explanation.

"Is this a mutiny, Mr. Morgan?"

"No, Cap'n, there is no mutiny. Just a difference of opinion with the second officer."

"What might that be, Mr. Morgan?" the captain asked sharply.

"There are certain of us who believe that Mr. Brown had something to do with the scuffle hunters that boarded us."

The captain looked around at some of the other sailors from Connecticut whom he trusted, Horace Nyles and Ezra Pratt, two of the more experienced seamen from the river. They were nodding at him, acknowledging that they agreed with Morgan. He turned to his second mate and addressed him directly.

"Mr. Brown, what explanation is there for these libelous statements?"

Brown had by now released his hold on Hiram's throat and was standing over him like a cat with a mouse, his explosive anger still red hot.

"It's nothing but malicious gossip, Captain," the mate said with an authoritative voice, his restless eyes moving about the deck. "Pure tattle and obloquy." He gestured angrily toward Hiram and Morgan saying, "These sailors should be cobbed and then manacled below decks. They deserve a proper floggin', sir."

Morgan held his breath. It looked like the plan had failed.

Champlin paused, his two pistols still at the ready. He'd heard all the accusations through the hollow tube into his cabin, but it was very difficult for a captain to rebuke one of his own mates in front of the men, and these accusations were severe. At that point, he might have backed down if it hadn't been for the sudden surprise appearance of Dalrymple. The new cabin boy stepped into the light of the lantern at the helm, immediately drawing the eyes of all the others. The boy's pasty-white face was stricken with fear. A silence suddenly fell on the quarterdeck. No one expected what happened next. Dalrymple spoke clearly and in a straightforward fashion.

"All of that is true, Cap'n."

"What's that, boy?" Champlin asked with astonishment.

"It is true," the boy repeated in a quiet, restrained voice. "I was made to be an accomplice to Mr. Brown. When the ship was off of Ramsgate on that last night before we sailed into the Thames, Mr. Brown ordered me back aft to send a signal with the lantern on the port side of the ship. He told me to tell no one, but some men would board the ship in the morning and they would take care of things."

Champlin pulled on his earlobe, rubbed his nose, and then fired off a question to his second mate.

"Mr. Brown, why did you have the boy send a signal, and who were you sending it to anyway?"

Clearly flustered, his face reddening, Brown stammered a response as he stepped away from Hiram.

"I was just signaling other ships in the area, Cap'n," he stammered. "The fog was so thick. I was just trying to avoid a collision."

Champlin's eyes passed from the smooth, hairless face of this blond-haired boy to the scruffy, weather-beaten face of his second mate. He looked at the silent faces of his crewmembers. Justice was never easy to determine on board a ship, where truth was a frequent casualty. As a veteran shipmaster, he couldn't always tell when a man was lying, but he had learned to sense fear and guilt in a man. He saw both of those emotions in the weaselly black eyes of his second mate. He turned to Nyles and Pratt.

"Put Mr. Brown in irons and bring him down below."

Brown tried to make a run for it, but a dozen tattooed arms restrained him and forced him facedown onto the deck. Icelander and the Spaniard helped manacle the second mate and bring the enraged man down below.

"Put him in one of the passengers' suites for now," Champlin said. "Mr. Morgan, you and Mr. Smith will stay here on the quarterdeck. I think we have some matters to discuss."

The next morning the American consul came on board with a number of soldiers and, after a long conversation with Captain Champlin, a manacled Jack Brown was led off the ship for the last time. The crew was told later that Brown would be shipped back to New York, where he would stand trial for mutiny and attempted murder. No mention was ever made of the rum barrel incident. That was one of the secrets that stayed on board ship. Champlin did not want to run the risk of a scandalous story like that becoming known. His ship's reputation was at stake.

During those last days in port, stevedores were busy loading cargo onto the *Hudson*, everything from Kendall cottons to blankets to bundles of pans and spades. The sailors attended to more last-minute repairs, fixing the rigging and mending the sails. At dusk, on one of the last days in port, Morgan and a small group from the packet walked out of the garrisoned London Docks to the freedom and danger of the city's crime-infested East End. Morgan persuaded them to head for the Shadwell area, where sailors liked to say there was a whore for every twelve men. He was determined to get to the Frying Pan Tavern, even though he realized they were now walking through the roughest part of London.

Once they'd done several twists and turns through squalid riverside streets and crumbling stone archways, they found themselves in the alleyways near Prince's Square, not too far from Wellclose Square. Morgan watched as men, women, and children lined up to pump water into pails close by the common privy, its foul-smelling contents spilling into the streets. A woman dressed in rags lay in a heap on the street, her baby crying and screaming. A thief was picking through the pockets of a drunken man lying unconscious at the foot of some stairs. Morgan yelled at the robber, shaking his belaying pin, which he had brought along for protection. A good-looking middle-aged woman hung out a second story window in a suggestive, revealing way and laughed at him derisively.

"Ain't you the gentleman now sailor boy. Ye be my knight in shinin' armor, my own sweet prince," she cried out in a throaty voice. Then she leaned further out the window, her face breaking out into a lurid smile. "Come up 'ere and I'll make ye a king."

Her laughter echoed into the small courtyard. A few blocks later there were more women, standing by doorways, calling out to these men like seductive sirens. One by one, the sailors disappeared; even Hiram left him when two young buxom women with dark seductive eyes approached them, their loose-fitting, wide-necked blouses leaving little to the imagination. It was too much for Hiram to resist.

"I'm sorry, Ely," he said as he walked off with a grin, the two women laughing on either side of him. "These two beauties have given me a glimpse of paradise."

Morgan walked on, exhaling deeply, fighting his own temptations. He was alone by the time he reached Vinegar Lane and spotted the sign for the tavern, which was hanging outside the ground floor of a blackened brick building with a dark green door. Underneath the sign, a drunken sailor was belting out a lover's ballad, his sonorous baritone voice rising above the noisy din around him. Across the street there were various lodging houses and brothels where he could hear the sounds of raucous laughter, but a few others seemed to attract a more dignified clientele seeking anonymity amid the squalor. These were small hotels for the toffers who catered to the amorous needs of discreet gentlemen from the West End. He looked up at one of the two-storied houses and caught the eye of a striking young brunette looking down at him, his starved eyes transfixed as he paused for a moment to look at her.

With his mind still on the pretty woman in the window, Morgan stepped inside the tavern and began to assess the kind of place he'd walked into. The air was stagnant and stale, not unlike the ship's moldy forecastle. The bar was lined with sailors, each with their hands squarely around a mug of ale. Several dusty lamps swung overhead. The smoky blue walls were filled with sailors' drawings of ships and mermaids, sea chanteys and poems. Sailors were belting out lusty ale songs as they stared dumb-eyed and dim-witted into the blousy, loose tops of the bar maidens delivering them ale swipes.

"I put me arm around her waist
Sez she, young man, yer in great haste!
I put me hand upon her thigh,
Sez she, young man, yer rather high!"

Morgan soon found the owner of the establishment, a portly man by the name of Stillwell, who was behind the bar. His puffy red face and piggish eyes told the story of a tavern owner who patronized his own grog far too generously. Morgan introduced himself as an American sailor off a New York packet.

"What will ye 'ave?" he asked.

"A tankard of swipes," Morgan replied.

"Not that often that we get Yanks in 'ere," said Stillwell. "What brings ye to this part of London?"

Morgan asked if he knew an English sailor named William Blackwood, and Stillwell put his hand to his bulldog jaw and double chin as if he was thinking, and then nodded his head slowly.

"Sure, I know of 'im. Bill, yeah I know 'im. 'E comes in 'ere from time to time. A right fine sailor is Bill."

"Where do I find him?" Morgan asked abruptly.

Stillwell seemed to ignore the question as he reached for a bottle off the shelf.

"Not that often that I get to serve a Yankee tar. 'Ave some of our own grog, our own special recipe. This one 'ere is on the 'ouse."

He poured the clear liquid into a cup and handed it to Morgan. Ely drank it down in one gulp. It had the flavor of musty gin with a bitter lemon taste. He didn't like it much, but he asked for another anyway. Normally he would have shown more caution, but he convinced himself that he needed to get on the bartender's good side. He saw the man beckon one of the girls over and whisper something into her ear.

"How do I find him?" Morgan asked again, his speech now strangely slurred.

"Well now, I was just talking to pretty Susana 'ere and she says yer friend Blackwood may be in the 'ouse. She can take you to 'im. You might be in luck."

Morgan followed the young woman up a rickety staircase to a long hallway lit by tall brass candlesticks that emitted a thin thread of smoke rising to the ceiling. The old wooden boards groaned and creaked as he took the first steps down the narrow hallway. Susana beckoned him to follow her. She pointed to a room at the end of the smoky hallway and said he should go in there. Morgan hesitated before stepping inside, a chill penetrating his clothes, his head starting to swim, his vision beginning to blur. Something was happening to him. He shook his head and slapped his face, but he still felt like he was sailing into a North Sea fog. With little to no ventilation, the stagnant air hung heavy in the room. A petite young woman sat on the bed with a candle flame flickering on the table beside her. She was stark naked, motionless and voluptuous.

Morgan stood staring at her long neck, firm breasts, and the curve of her hips and suddenly found himself overcome with desire. He hesitated even as he felt the blood pounding in his ears. His heart beat rapidly. At that moment, this was everything he ever wanted, beckoning him. The room was misty now, much like a hazy dream. He had no sense if he had been in that room for hours or even days. She smiled at him as he walked toward her, his arms reaching out to touch her like long sinewy tree limbs. Suddenly he sensed more than saw a figure coming up from behind him, grabbing both of his arms, and then he felt an excruciating pain in his head. Through the dizzying blur, he could see the shape of a large man looming over him. A set of narrow eyes looked down at him from their setting of fleshy eyelids.

A man's voice asked, "Do yer know this 'ere man, Bill?"

"Never seen 'im before," a gruff voice replied.

And then everything went black.

The next thing he remembered he awoke in a damp cobblestone alleyway where the smell of urine and filth made him cough and wretch. Everything was a blur. His head throbbed with intense pain. His ribs felt like a wagon wheel had run over him. His eyelids only partially opened. His mind was filled with shapes, colors, and vivid dreams when suddenly a few faces and figures came into view. A young woman was dabbing his head with a wet cloth as she came in and out of focus. It was a different woman than the one in the room, he thought. She was so familiar. How did he know her? The dawn's first light was streaking through her brown hair, and all he could think of was that she was like an angel with green eyes.

"'Elp me get 'im into the house," she said.

Two arms pulled him up from behind as two other arms lifted his feet. The pain in his head was so sharp he wanted to scream. He felt like he would soon lose consciousness. He looked at the woman who was leaning over him. He suddenly recognized her. She was the pretty woman in the window.

"Whar ye want to put 'im, Laura?" asked someone.

"Just put 'im in my room fer now," came the reply.

PART IV

Of all men, sailors shake the most hands, and wave the most hats. They are here and then they are there; ever shifting themselves, they shift among the shifting: and like rootless sea-weed, are tossed to and fro.

—Herman Melville, *Redburn: His First Voyage*

10

1829

Dressed in his pea jacket with his woolen hat pulled tightly over his head, Morgan stood by the helm in the grayish black light just before dawn. Watchful and mute, he rolled his first fresh cigar of the night. This had become a habit for him now that he was the first mate. He had given up chewing tobacco. A cigar helped calm and clear his mind, and he felt it gave him a look of authority. First ship's officer, he thought to himself. It was hard for him to fathom that he was now in charge of the ship's navigation, the setting of the sails, and the discipline of the crew. He was only twenty-three years old.

Cold and damp, he put his hands in his pockets. It looked like it might rain or sleet. The ship was heeled over sharply under a stiffening late November breeze. He could see the vague figures of the sailors on watch forward of the waist of the ship. He stepped to the windward side and looked down at the shadowy water, and then upward to check the sails, which were now barely visible. One of the topsails was flapping, probably on the foremast. He looked over at Ochoa, who was at the helm. Without a word spoken, the Spaniard corrected the ship's course, and the protesting canvas quieted down. Morgan once again fell back into his thoughts.

He smiled as he thought about Laura Hawthorne. She had nursed him back to health. If it hadn't been for her, he felt sure he would have never made it out of that alleyway. She had kept him in her room, bandaged him, and made sure that he got back to the ship. He still had no idea what had happened to him. It was all a hazy dream. He thought he had been drugged. That pig-faced bartender must have put laudanum in his drink. He had heard that this was how some men were shanghaied off the docks in London. He wondered if that was why he'd been drugged, but that didn't explain why they dumped him in the alleyway. He had so little memory of what had happened. From the bloody gash on his head, he knew that he had been bludgeoned with some kind of blunt object. The bruises and swelling on his rib cage and face implied that he had been kicked and then presumably dragged out into the street. What he did remember was a man with fleshy eyelids. He was leaning over him, a man whose name might have been Bill.

His mind shifted back to Laura. She was somewhat of a mystery to him. He wasn't sure how she found him there in that alleyway, or why she took the trouble to care for him. He knew very little about her except that her mother had died when she was twelve years old. Her father had taken to drink shortly afterward, abandoning the family. She and her older sister had been left without a home. Her sister had married a tavern keeper and she had taken the maid's job at a boarding house as her best option. She was a good-looking woman with high cheekbones and piercing green eyes. Morgan found her physically attractive, but he was not emotionally attached. It was certainly not love. Their relationship could best be described as a sailor's romance, born of necessity and nurtured more by practicality than love. Many of the other sailors had similar loosely defined ties with women in London.

Morgan and Laura would sometimes spend an afternoon together walking along the Thames as far as the London and Southwark Bridges. She was always full of questions about his family and his home. She wanted to know all about why he went to sea, and why he chose to sail with the London Line. He told her about his brother Abraham and his quest to find out what had happened to him. She always seemed interested and wanted to hear more. He revealed to her the puzzling information he had received from John Taylor, and how he was looking for one English sailor in particular, named William Blackwood. She'd said she would ask around the taverns and the boarding houses to see if any of the girls had heard of Blackwood or a ship called the *Charon*.

Morgan was thinking about this as he stood by the helm looking into the darkness, puffing on his cigar. A sudden gust of wind caused him to reach for one of the windward stays to keep his balance. Sea spray splashed his face and his thoughts abruptly shifted to his own career. The last two years had brought so much change in his life. He remembered when he first got the news that he was to be promoted. It was in the summer of 1827. They'd just arrived off Sandy Hook. The captain had given the order to square the yards. One of those fast newspaper schooners had come alongside, the reporter shouting the startling headline that slavery had been legally abolished in New York on July 4, Independence Day. That same afternoon, Captain Champlin gave him the good news that he would be promoting him to second mate. He was turning the *Hudson* over to his brother, Christopher, and Morgan would be serving as one of his new ship's officers. It had all happened so quickly.

He thought back to Henry Champlin's last words to him as he stepped off the *Hudson* in New York.

"I suppose you wonder why I decided to promote you, Morgan."

"Yes, sir."

"I can tell you that Mr. Griswold thought you were too young. So did my brother."

"Yes, sir," Morgan replied glumly as he watched Champlin fold his arms over his chest.

"But I told them I'd observed that you had a watchful eye and a keen desire to know the reason why of anything, two important and desirable traits out on the open Atlantic highway. You were a good sailor man, I told them, with a ready smile no matter the weather, and if we didn't promote you soon we might lose you to another line."

Champlin paused to take in a deep breath, then straightened his back and adopted an air of frigid dignity. He looked around to make sure that no one was listening, and then began speaking in a more serious tone of voice.

"But that's not why I wanted you as a ship's officer, Morgan. No, the real reason I wanted to promote you is over the years I saw some rare leadership skills in you, most particularly in the way you handled Jack Brown. You showed me then that you were a sailor at your best when the weather was at its worst."

Morgan's eyebrows now arched upward in surprised astonishment.

Champlin paused and took his top hat off, running his hands through his thick, silvery hair.

"I never would have believed it about Brown if you had just come to me with that story. I would have just kicked the sorry lot of you off my ship. As it was, I was so startled by what I learned, I came close to putting you in manacles. But later I got to thinking how I underestimated you. Brown was a wicked storm coming in your direction, and like a sailor choosing to ride out the waves with no more than a double-reefed topsail, you found a way to stay clear of him. You showed me what I didn't want to see about Brown, and you let him reveal his dark side. That's what I told Mr. Griswold. I told him you had the quick thinking and resourcefulness needed to be a ship's officer. And he agreed."

Champlin then looked at him with a skeptical frown, and then a sort of curiosity in his probing eyes, like he was trying to figure out something that puzzled him.

"But I don't mind telling you, Morgan, you've got your fair share of flaws as well."

Morgan didn't reply as he shuffled his feet and cast his eyes down.

"From what I've heard about your wanderings in those dark alleyways around the London Docks, you're more foolhardy than I would have expected. I would be careful where you put your feet, Morgan. Like a chance meeting with a snake that crosses your path, you have to know where to step. The world is like a snake, Morgan, whether you're shipboard or on land. Make no mistake, it will bite you if you give it the opportunity."

☸

With that parting remark, Captain Henry Champlin had walked out of his life. Those were words he would always remember. Mr. Toothacher and some of the more experienced sailors had left with Champlin. Morgan had watched the old sea dog walk down the gangway and slowly saunter off to the offices of the Black X Line at 68 South Street. He thought to himself how much their relationship had changed since he had first come aboard ship as a cabin boy. That seemed like a couple of lifetimes ago. Champlin had been so stern at first, and then become almost like a distant father, but one who seemed to understand him. He would miss sailing with him.

Ochoa interrupted his thoughts.

"Ya llegamos. Allí está Irlanda."

There in the distance off to the port side, Morgan could see the faint outline of the Cape Clear lighthouse on the bleak, barren southern tip of Ireland. They steered the ship so as to pass some three miles from the lighthouse and then headed toward the Cornwall coast at the southwestern tip of England. The long vigil of being on watch afforded him plenty of time to think about things, not just his life aboard ship and his time in London, but also his family. The first ray of sunlight had now peeked above the horizon, and the darkness began lifting like a slow-moving curtain revealing a rolling seascape with frothy whitecaps.

Normally the London-bound packet ships traveled well to the south of Ireland so they could clear the western edge of the Scilly Islands. But the favorable northwesterly winds had convinced Morgan to hug the Irish coastline before bearing off and running before the wind.

"Plenty of sheep in the meadow today, Ochoa. We should make good time to the Scillies."

Ochoa nodded. Frozen drops of rain and hail began to pelt the ship's decks, and the sound made him think of falling chestnuts dropping onto the barn roof back home. He wondered if he would ever get home again. He had been at sea for seven long years now. The last letter from his brother had made it sound like his father no longer wanted to see him ever again. It seemed that he and Icelander had something in common. They were outcasts who had left the unrest of the land to embrace the risks of the sea. Maybe all sailors were that way, with no place to call home.

"Home," he murmured softly to himself under his breath. "Home." He wondered if his long journey to find Abraham was no different than chasing a mirage. He thought of reading *Don Quixote* and smiled as he remembered his tutoring sessions with Margaret Carpenter so long ago. A wave of melancholy overwhelmed him. "Home," he whispered again.

Ochoa, who was just six feet away from him, turned in his direction.

"¿Que cosa? ¿Me dijo algo?"

Suddenly embarrassed that he had been talking to himself, he responded with the little bit of broken Spanish that he knew.

"No, no es nada, Ochoa. Pensando. Just thinking, that's all."

He smiled at the Spaniard and then began walking toward the bow on the leeward side, holding onto the bulwarks, looking down at the green, blue color of the sea. The changing colors of the water never ceased to amaze him, from the clear, welcoming turquoise of the Gulf Stream to the dark, somber blue of the mid-Atlantic. The cresting whitecaps with their splashes of foam and froth made the ocean seem to him like a painter's canvas. He fell back into his reverie. Where is home? he asked himself. Maybe it was the sea and the ship. Maybe home is internal, ever changing, rooted to the past and memories, but connected at the same time to the people in the present who surround him. He didn't know. All he knew was that at that moment he missed his family. He missed the apple orchards, the smell of summer by the river, the laughter of his sisters, the jokes with Josiah, the quiet presence of his mother, . . . but at the thought of his father's scowling face his mind jolted back to the duties at hand. He shook his head and whispered to himself that he would stay true to his goal. He would find Abraham.

The wind was coming up quickly from the north, bringing with it a gray stampede of squalls. Foul weather, he thought to himself, unpleasant, but good packet sailing weather. The sun was now hidden behind the incoming storm clouds. Morgan buttoned up his pea jacket and pulled his woolen hat down firmly over his head. He might have to reef sails sooner than he thought. He walked past the slanted stretch of the ship's main deck where the animals were kept, acknowledging the sailor on watch as he walked over to the windward side, feeling the cold north wind on his cheeks. The rain and the gusts were now stirring up the ocean. They only had a few passengers in steerage on this trip, twelve people in the saloon, and a cargo of tobacco, beeswax, and hides. He flexed his knees and moved his body forward and backward, feeling at one with the seesaw motion of the ship. He breathed in deeply as he cast away his doubts and felt a surge of self-confidence. This was his first trip as first mate. Even though he knew the captain of the ship would be coming up on deck soon, for the moment he was the commander and the ship was under his watch.

The coast of Ireland was now well behind them and Morgan was surprised as he calculated that the ship had probably covered over a hundred miles in the last eight hours. Moments later, Captain Christopher Champlin surfaced from below and looked up at the men in the yards. He was a man much like his brother, medium height with a head of thick, wavy hair, and dark, perceptive eyes. He was frugal with his compliments and quick to express his disfavor.

"Mr. Morgan, get those men up on the royals and the topgallants. Trim those sails."

Morgan picked up the trumpet and started shouting.

"Reef the foresail, men. And set the main topgallant close-reefed!"

"Main topsail haul!"

Ochoa signaled to Morgan that he might have a problem. One of the big bucko Irish sailors on board, a six-foot-tall brute named Callaghan, didn't move but stood there defiantly refusing to obey orders. He had also bullied several others not to lift a finger. Morgan had never liked this surly man with his sneering face, bald head, and strangely pale blue eyes. He was a rule breaker who never stopped cursing. He was always the last out when the men were mustered. Taciturn and disdainful, he was always looking for an excuse to dodge the work on a dark night. Now he was cursing at his fellow sailors, urging them to blow the man down.

Champlin's face was beet red.

"Mr. Morgan," he said sternly. "Go knock some discipline into that miserable Irish devil's head."

Some mates enjoy exercising their power over men as the ship's enforcers, but Morgan did not. He preferred to use common logic as a persuader instead of pain from a belaying pin. When that didn't work, he would think of innovative punishments that didn't involve flogging. He had already put one belligerent sailor into a large canvas bag and hoisted him up the mast. He left him there all curled up in a ball, swinging back and forth in that bag for several hours. He came down panic stricken and gasping for breath. As far as Morgan was concerned, the job of first mate was all about gaining and earning the respect of the crew rather than beating them into submission. Christopher Champlin, on the other hand, preferred a bully mate with an iron fist and a voice of doom to spread the fear of God into the sailors.

Morgan walked over, but before he could lay a hand on the man, the sailor rushed at him. If it weren't for Icelander and Hiram, Morgan's authority on deck might have been seriously challenged as he had not been prepared for a violent attack. The two sailors, who had stood by Morgan whenever there was a flare-up, knocked the Irishman onto the deck and presented him to the first mate for punishment. Instead of beating the man, Morgan ordered him out to the isolation of the jib boom, which sailors called the widow maker. He was ordered to stay there at the tip of the thirty-foot-long bowsprit for the next twenty-four hours.

"Try your hand alone, Mr. Callaghan," Morgan said to him with compressed lips. "Test your courage and endurance with Old Man Neptune. Maybe by tomorrow you will have learned the value of a ship's company all working together."

Morgan watched as the frightened but still defiant man pulled himself along the pole out to the very tip. Just then, the *Hudson*'s bow plunged into a deep trough, sending the jib boom and the man below the surface. Moments later, the bowsprit emerged from the waves and the man, drenched and shivering, was still clinging on. He had lost his hat, and his stringy wet hair dangled over his fear-stricken eyes like a wet mop. His shoes had been washed away. A long day and night awaited him, dwarfed as he was by the immense waves washing over him. Just before nightfall, Morgan took pity on the man clinging to the jib boom and ordered Callaghan to be pulled back on deck, where he was put to work holystoning the icy-cold decks.

Four days later, a drizzle was falling on the deck. The *Hudson* had completed the journey up the Channel and into the Thames. A pilot boarded the ship near Sheerness and a small steamer threw them a line. As the ship rounded Cuckold's Point and passed the busy London Docks, the sailors spotted the buoys and the lock chamber that marked the entrance into their new destination, St. Katherine's Docks, nestled underneath the Tower of London. The ancient fortress's reputation for torture and death seemed dark and imposing from the vantage point of the river. The old turrets and towers stood in sharp contrast to the newly built St. Katherine's with its mortared walls and long, massive brick warehouses that lined the quays. These smaller docks were designed to handle as many as 120 ships. As the packet pulled into the sheltered waters, the dockmaster was there waiting to review the ship's manifest. Once they were tied up and the ship secured, he stood by overseeing the unloading of the cargo, a process that usually took one to two days.

On one of the first evenings ashore after that cold November voyage, Morgan met Laura at a tavern in Change Alley. It was in the middle of a busy commercial section of London bounded by Lombard Street, Cornhill, and Birchin Lane. This narrow alleyway was filled with lively coffee shops, fine-quality ship chandlers, and goldsmiths from Lombardy. It was a perfect place for a sailor to take a young woman he wanted to impress. On their way there, he had been surprised when a well-dressed stranger, some English dandy from the fashionable West End, tipped his top hat to Laura, saying something in French he didn't understand. "Mon plaisir, mademoiselle. I trust I will see you on Thursday, comme d'habitude." Morgan had asked who he was. She had looked flustered and said that she didn't know. Morgan wanted to believe her, but all his instincts told him she was lying. He kept his doubts to himself. He knew it was best for him not to rush to any sudden judgments.

"I 'ave something to tell ye, Ely, that I know will interest ye," she told him coyly that evening as they walked down one of the shadowy alleyways adjacent to Lombard Street.

Morgan looked at her inquiringly, wondering if she was going to reveal something personal about herself.

"The man ye were asking about, William Blackwood, 'e's here in London."

"How do you know that?" he asked incredulously.

"'E's been seeing a girl I know named Mary. She works upstairs in the tavern my sister runs. You know, the White Bull Tavern. She says 'is ship is tied up in the West India Docks. It 'as just been repaired at a nearby yard."

"The *Charon* is here in London?" Morgan was taken aback by this startling news.

"Yes, but Mary says 'e won't be 'ere long. His ship 'as been replanked and caulked and is ready to set sail. That's why I was so anxious for yer ship to arrive. I thought ye would never get here. Blackwood told Mary 'e's leaving to go to India and China for several years. He says he's exporting Bengali opium to Whampoa."

"An opium trader," Morgan mumbled to himself. He smiled at Laura. Any nagging doubts about her had disappeared. All suspicions about her character and activities were now completely forgotten.

The next day Morgan told Hiram the news. They both decided that the best thing to do was to find Blackwood's ship, the *Charon*. If by some chance they found it, perhaps he could find Blackwood and confront him. He didn't know what they would discover. Between St. Katherine's Docks and the West India Docks were several miles of dangerous roads through London's East End, certainly not walking distance, so they took a hackney cab along Ratcliffe Highway and Commercial Road.

To gain access to the West India Docks, they pretended they were drunk, although in Hiram's case, this role was more real than Morgan would have liked. The guards laughed at them and let them pass. This was a far bigger dock area than the new docks at St. Katherine's. There were hundreds of ships inside the walls, loading and unloading. Morgan stared at the long rows of brick warehouses. Some of them were five stories high and filled with stacked hogsheads of sugar above ground. The vaults for rum below ground were more than a half-mile long, separated by brick firewalls to minimize the risk of fire. Like the other enclosed dock areas on the Thames, the quays were alive with men unloading hogsheads of West Indian sugar and barrels of rum. Morgan inquired where the ships being rigged up for departure were and soon they were walking briskly along the north quay.

In the distance, all the way at the end of the docks, they could see men high up in the masts of one ship that had recently been caulked and painted. She was sleek and low in the water with the looks of a raked-back brigantine. Morgan could tell that this ship was built for speed. Her hull was too low in the water to be a merchant ship or a frigate, but it was sharp in the bow with an attractive sheer back to the stern. Morgan thought that she had the look of a Baltimore-built topsail schooner. A rush of adrenalin swept over him as he realized that this ship might be the *Charon*. He and Hiram tried to get closer by telling the guards who stopped them that they were returning sailors, but this time they were turned back.

They might have given up at this point, but Morgan spotted a small gaff-rigged sailing boat tied up at the edge of the quay. They quickly pushed it off and jumped in. The oarlocks wiggled and creaked as Morgan and Hiram rowed toward the ship. It was near dusk now and the four o'clock winter sun, low on the horizon, was shining directly onto the ship they were trying to approach. When they were one hundred yards away, they raised the two small sails and tacked in close to the bow. The sun shone directly onto a sea serpent carved under the bowsprit. They let out the sail and began coasting toward the stern of the ship. That's when they were noticed.

"'Eah down there. Ye river scum in the wherry. What are yer doin' 'ere?"

A sailor with a raised pistol was looking down from high up above them.

"Just making deliveries," Morgan quickly replied.

"This 'ere ship is not taking deliveries. Clear off ye river rats or I'll fill ye full of lead."

"'Oo's thar?" another voice cried out.

"A couple of filching thieves that's all. I chased 'em off."

Any plan to board the ship or ask any more questions was quickly aborted. Hiram sheeted in the sails, Morgan looked back quickly at the stern where he could plainly see the name of the ship, the *Charon*. He felt a moment of sudden exhilaration, but then he heard a man calling out for the police. "Mudlarks!" the man cried. "Mudlarks! Police! Thar they are!" The man was running now and pointing in their direction. "They filched me boat!"

"Ely," Hiram cried out. "We better pull out of here fast. If not, we're going to end up like those scuffle hunters, being carted off to some English dungeon."

In the fading light, they headed out through the small channel leading to the wide-bodied Thames. They could hear voices muttering and feet trampling on the quays as they were now clearly being pursued. The Marine Police kept a high-profile presence there on the West India Docks. Looking back through the night gloom, Morgan could see the faint lights from a small vessel. Hiram sheeted in the sails on the leeward side as Morgan hung out over the windward rail, his left hand on the tiller. He was steering by the feel of the wind, nudging the little boat to windward as much as it would tolerate. They could hear men shouting in the distance. He couldn't tell who they were, but given the extreme darkness on the river and the cold temperatures, it was a good guess that they were not friendly. No working boat would be on this frigid river at this time of night. He guessed it was a police boat. Morgan bundled his dark, heavy peacoat around him to ward off the bone-numbing cold. Spray from the polluted Thames splattered on his face as the lee rail on the small boat tilted into the dark river water. They used the lights from some of the bulky Thames river barges to gauge where the shallows were on either side. His bare hands had lost any sense of feeling. It was no wonder, he thought, that the English referred to this time of the year as the "suicide month."

They waited for the sound of gunshots, but none came. They listened for the noise of muffled oars or the shouts of men, but the river was silent and dark. It took them most of the night to zigzag their way up the Thames, battling against the current in their small sailboat. At one point when they were close to shore, they thought they heard their pursuers, but the putrid smell told them it was just some men shoveling sewage into the river. Their boat bumped into something heavy, jarring the hull. Morgan thought it might be a piece of driftwood.

"Hiram, what the devil is that?" he cried out in a whisper.

He reached down with his right hand to clear the debris away, and jumped back in horror. There was something long and pale floating alongside the boat.

"Lawd sakes alive! It's a body, Hiram!"

The two of them looked over the side. There was just enough light to see the ghostly white, oval face of a man looking up at them. His round eyes were open and bulging like a dead fish, staring off into the darkness, his open hands clutching outward.

"Push it away, Ely!" Hiram cried out. "Push that tarnal floater away. This river is the Devil's own."

As the darkness of night receded, they hauled their stolen boat at the next convenient stop, Union Stairs, just off the London Docks. They pulled it ashore, turned it over on its side, and ran into an alleyway, hoping that no one had seen them. Morgan looked back briefly to see the oarsmen of a pinnace rowing frantically in their direction, the blades of their oars splashing in the water like a school of fish in a feeding frenzy. Without waiting any longer, he turned to follow Hiram as they both ran toward the Ratcliffe Highway on their way back to the ship and the safety of St. Katherine's Docks.

11

Morgan was half expecting a squadron of the London Marine Police to show up shipside to arrest him and Hiram the next morning, but nothing happened to break up the tedium of the day. They had walked through the opening gates at St. Katherine's that morning along with hundreds of dockworkers and scores of drunken sailors. No one knew that they had stolen a boat and been pursued on the Thames River. Morgan was already making plans to go back to the West India Docks as soon as he could.

After the decks had been thoroughly scrubbed, Morgan's stomach turned when one of the dock constables came on board ship asking to see him. It was Constable Pinkleton. The police officer was English to the core, stout-chested with ruddy cheeks and a muttonchop beard. He was a stubby man with large ears sprouting so much hair it was a wonder that he didn't try to keep them better groomed. He was usually in search of someone who had forged a signature, stolen money outright, or run off with somebody else's wife. But in many cases, he simply wanted to eyeball the ship and see if he saw something suspicious. It was Pinkleton who had told Morgan that in England they had a special name for every type of criminal. A dipper or a flimp was a pickpocket. A duffer was someone who sold stolen goods. A mughunter, a street robber. A dragsman, a highway robber. A screever, a forger. A snakesman, a specialized house burglar. A snoozer, a thief specializing in robbing hotel rooms. As far as Pinkleton was concerned, all of the above were potentially trying to flee

English justice on board American packet ships. Morgan kept his disdain for British authority as well as his own personal concerns to himself as he walked up to the officer.

"Mr. Morgan?"

"Yes, officer."

"A young lady dropped this off at this gate and said it was important."

Morgan breathed a sigh of relief when the officer had disappeared out of sight. It was a letter from Laura. She had sent him a note that she would meet him at her sister's tavern. She said Blackwood was still holed up with Mary upstairs above the bar. Her sister Molly, who ran the tavern with her husband, would help him get upstairs to see Blackwood.

It was a noisy din that evening as Morgan and the five other *Hudson* sailors walked into the White Bull Tavern. Morgan should have known something was amiss as the entire tavern of rowdy sailors went silent as soon as they walked through the door. Each of the *Hudson*'s sailors had a knife or a belaying pin tucked into the outside pocket of their woolen pea jackets. Morgan had taken the ship's pistols in case there was serious trouble. With his hands in his coat pockets, he fingered the wooden handles of the two pistols for reassurance. He looked around and spotted Molly passing drinks. She looked like an older Laura, which is how he recognized her. She was a well-built, buxom woman, about thirty he guessed, wearing an airy cotton blouse. Her hair was black, her eyes blue. She wasn't as good looking as Laura, but attractive nonetheless. The way she walked, with her feet and shoulders squared, clearly demonstrated that she wasn't afraid of anybody. He waved his hand at her, expecting that she would signal him by waving back. Instead she turned away. There wasn't even a greeting, not even a subtle acknowledgment. Maybe she didn't know who they were?

After the first few minutes of awkward silence that greeted their entrance, the small tavern slowly resumed its noisy hum. The sailors returned to their drinks and their conversations. Morgan quickly scanned the dimly lit room with its low-timbered ceiling and its chipped walls. There was only one window and a small side door leading into a narrow alleyway. He looked out the window and noticed a ladder lying on the cobblestones. He wondered what it had been used for. Inside, every bench, chair, and table was occupied by about two dozen men scattered about in various dark corners and alcoves. Morgan could feel the cold, hostile stare of eyes following them as they walked further inside toward the bar. He could see that the sailors were a particularly rough bunch even for the lowly East End, where ignorance and cruelty were close relatives.

"I don't like the looks of this, Ely," Hiram murmured under his breath. "There's an abundance of vermin and land sharks in this room."

Morgan continued to take in his noisy surroundings. Two servant girls were running about with tankards of swipes. There was no sign of Laura. Hiram walked up to the bar. Morgan could see that he was talking with a man who was serving grog and swilling down swipes. He guessed that this was Molly's husband from the description Laura had given him. Bull Bailey was his name, she had said. He was a portly man of medium size, with an oily red face and hawk eyes peering out of a balding head. Morgan could just overhear Hiram introducing himself as a friend of Laura's. Bailey nodded and then shouted a greeting so the whole tavern could hear.

"From America, are ye? Well drink up hearty, my beautiful sailors. Thar's plenty 'ere even for ye Yanks."

Ochoa and Icelander started walking toward the bar, smiling at the prospect of getting a drink. Morgan and the two other sailors looked around for chairs. Before too long there was trouble brewing. It started with a steady stream of hushed whispering that swept from table to table, but that soon led to shouting.

"Yankee dogs!" one of the drunken English sailors yelled out. His nose was squashed against his face as if it had been broken. "Too good for the king, are ye? Why don't ye go home and take all the thieving poor beggars from here that you want? They'll make good Americans!"

The insult was greeted with cruel laughter.

"Yeh, ye Yanks can 'ave all the dippers, dragsmen, and mughunters ye want!"

The two barmaids, who were making their rounds with the sailors, quickly put their trays down on the bar and left the room. To their credit, Morgan's sailors kept quiet, but the baiting continued. Morgan looked for Molly, but she was nowhere to be seen. One barrel-chested man with arms like a bear strode up to the bar where Hiram was now standing.

"Will ye be swearin' allegiance to the crown now that yer drinkin' with proper Englishmen?" asked the man.

Out of the corner of his eye, Morgan spotted the glint of a knife blade under a table, and then another glimmer of metal emerging from a man's pocket.

Bedlam broke loose. Pistols came out in the open and shots were fired. The few women who remained in the room began screaming as the British sailors charged toward the American sailors, clutching their weapons. The White Bull Tavern became a dizzying whirl of clubs and cutlasses, shaggy heads, bristly beards, and muscular tattooed arms. Morgan yelled for the *Hudson*'s sailors to head for the alley and pointed at the side door he'd spotted earlier. He could see Icelander's white head of hair moving in his direction. He was swinging his heavy capstan bar with two hands, knocking down two sailors with one blow and then hitting another in the head with a thundering crack. Morgan watched in horror as an English sailor raised his pistol to fire at Icelander, but then the man dropped face first to the floor like a tree falling in a forest. The Spaniard retrieved his knife, and smiled at Morgan as he and the others passed him and reached the door to the alleyway. To slow the onrush of their attackers, Icelander picked up one man he had just clobbered and hurled him onto the heads of his closest pursuers.

Once outside, Morgan told Ochoa and Icelander to quickly close the alley door with the wooden latch and hold it shut.

"Don't let them out!" he cried. "Hold 'em in there!"

He found the ladder he'd seen earlier. It had clearly been left there by some painters who must have been scraping and painting the façade of the building earlier that day. The dark alleyway was surrounded by a high brick wall with broken bottles stuck into the mortar. He took the ladder and propped it up on the wall. He clambered up to the top rung and pulled out his pistols. He told the rest of the sailors to run for it, and he would hold off the English. Morgan aimed his pistols, loaded with one-ounce lead balls, at the tavern's alley door. When the first sailors broke the door down, he fired at their legs. Two sailors cursed loudly, clutching their legs while the others retreated back into the tavern. Morgan pulled the ladder over the wall and jumped to the other side, making a clean escape. From the courtyard where he had landed, he could hear the angry shouts of confusion as his assailants tried to deal with their wounded and figure out which direction the Americans had gone. This commotion was followed by the pounding of feet on the cobblestones as they ran off.

It was his concern for Laura that convinced him to walk back into harm's way. Instead of running away into the maze of alleyways that surrounded him, he reloaded his pistols with lead balls and clambered back over the wall, pulling the ladder with him in case he needed to make a quick escape. Silence greeted him as he opened the tavern door and looked inside. With a pistol in each hand, he stepped inside the White Bull. The floor of the tavern was littered with the debris of broken tables and chairs. The whole place stank of stale beer. Shattered glasses, plates, and mugs were scattered across the floor. He was about to call out for Laura when he heard a woman sobbing. He turned toward the sound to see Laura's sister, Molly, and quickly walked over to where she was crouched on the floor. Beside Molly lay a still, limp body. Morgan stood there, silent and motionless, for what seemed like an hour, but was probably only a few seconds.

"All of this destruction! It's yer meddling!" she cried out, her mouth twitching in pain. "They was waiting for ye. Ye know that, don't ye?"

Morgan was speechless. There was nothing he could say.

"Who is this?"

"My 'usband, you fool. One of yer men knocked 'im on the 'ead, that big tall brute with the white ponytail."

"Is he dead?"

"No, I don't think so, but 'e's as cold as a two-day-old codfish."

Morgan bent down beside the body, grabbed the man's wrist, and found a pulse. He examined the man's balding head where he could see a bloody bruise, but there was no open wound.

"I reckon he'll live," he pronounced confidently, but with a sudden panic in his voice he asked, "Where's Laura? Is she here?"

Instead of answering, Molly continued her rant, her wet, dark eyelashes now blinking rapidly in mounting anger. Morgan could see the similarity with Laura now. If it weren't for the drooping corner of one lip and the hairy black mole on her face, she might be considered a beauty.

"The only reason they didn't get ye was it was yer other friend who stepped up to the bar. They thought he was ye."

Morgan snapped to attention.

"Hiram? Hiram Smith?" he asked with trepidation, not wanting to hear the answer. It occurred to him for the first time that he hadn't seen Hiram in the alleyway. Maybe he didn't get out? Then he remembered the man at the bar with arms like a bear.

"What happened to him? Where is my friend?"

Molly shrugged.

"And where is Laura?"

A malevolent smile came across her face, her lip drooping more visibly to one side.

"I suppose ye never suspected that she was 'ired by that brute, did ya now?" she said with contempt. "He 'ired her to find out who ye was, and why ye was looking for him. He planned to kill ye, fool."

The gleam in her dark blue eyes revealed a certain innate cruelty.

"Ye was just an opportunity for her, Yankee boy, just another opportunity."

"What do you mean by that?"

Her voice sank to a low, husky murmur. "As for yer friend, who knows what 'appened to 'im. As soon as you yelled out yer warning, the man next to my husband pulled a knife on yer friend and put it up to 'is throat."

Morgan stood silently for several moments as he allowed this information to sink in. Hiram was gone, nabbed by Blackwood's men, or even worse, lying in a urine-soaked gutter somewhere, bleeding to death. Worse still, it was his fault. What would they do once they found out Hiram wasn't him? Maybe they've already killed him. He felt drained, empty of strength. He looked over at Molly, who was pulling at her hair as she looked at her prostrate husband. Her dark mood had returned as she gazed at the destruction around her. She started yelling for the police. She grabbed a knife from her husband's pocket, cursing him as he walked out of the tavern, all the time screaming for a constable.

He walked back to the docks, grappling with his own feelings of depression, anger, disappointment, and failure. He trudged by the closed pawnshops and the foul-smelling alehouses, where a few stragglers were still stumbling out the door to relieve themselves on the wall. At that moment, he was seething with anger toward England and the English. Foul dealing, he said to himself, appears to come naturally to these people. He had been betrayed by a woman he had trusted. He had been set up. His best friend might be dead. But as bad and as miserable a place was this depraved city, he knew he had to accept the blame. It was his fault, and he was a fool. He didn't even know where to begin to look for Hiram. A faint hope that he might somehow have escaped kept him focused as he made his way back to St. Katherine's Docks.

The next day, an irate Captain Christopher Champlin ordered Morgan to report to his cabin. Fearful of what awaited him, Morgan gingerly turned the white porcelain handle and stepped inside the stateroom adjacent to the two officers' cabins. He'd never been inside the captain's quarters before, so his eyes were busy scanning the room. The only source of light was a bulkhead lamp on gimbals with a sooty flame. Champlin was standing beside one of the portholes across from his desk, his hands behind his back with his feet broadly spaced apart as if he were bracing for a storm.

"Come in, Mr. Morgan, and shut the door behind you. Sit down over there, if you please."

"Yes, sir, Captain."

He pointed to the only wooden chair in the room across from him. Morgan took his seat and waited for the storm to follow the silence that pervaded the room. Champlin at last cleared his throat and began to speak in a slow, ominous voice.

"My brother told me you might be trouble, Morgan, but I never expected this. I reckon you got some explaining to do. My pistols have been stolen. Four of my men have been banged up right fine in a tight scratch with some drunken English sailors and river scum. The tavern owner wants to be compensated. One of my best men, Hiram Smith, has been kidnapped or dead, and it looks as if my first mate is the one who brought these sailors into harm's way."

Champlin paused, his eyes boring into Morgan's face.

"I ought to have you put in irons."

A humbled Morgan handed over the pistols, and speaking in a subdued voice, began telling Champlin about his quest to find out what had happened to his brother.

"I thought I'd found the man who did harm to my brother, Captain. It was something I needed to do, and the men wanted to help me. Hiram is my friend. There isn't anyone who feels more deeply troubled about him than me."

Champlin listened quietly, and then paced around the room, his voice steadily rising as his anger mounted.

"Listen up, Morgan. I'll only tell you this once. You're the first officer on my packet ship, and that's all I care about. I've got a ship to run, I've got a schedule to keep, cargo to load, and passengers to look after. I don't give a donkey's ass about your ill-founded quest for your brother. That's your business. If you want to go looking for trouble down in the East End, go ahead, all-possessed, limber and lively as the Devil, you go ahead, but not from my ship. Have you got that, Mr. Morgan?"

Morgan nodded.

"From now on, those whoremongering taverns in the East End and quim-filled boarding houses are off limits for you. When we're in London you're confined to the ship."

"But what about Hiram, sir? He might be in danger. I've got to find him."

"I reckon Smith is either dead with his throat slit or in the fo'c'sle of a British merchant ship headed for Calcutta. Either way there's not much you can do for him."

A chastened Ely Morgan turned to leave Champlin's cabin with a heavy step when Champlin called him back.

"I need to know, Mr. Morgan, that nothing like this will happen again."

Morgan paused as he shuffled his feet. He didn't say anything.

"I need to know, Morgan, do you hear?" he said emphatically. "I need that guarantee!" He stood up with his red face inches from Morgan's nose. "If you don't have the answer by the time we back our sails off Sandy Hook, then I reckon you'll be looking for work on another ship."

On that cold January voyage back to New York, Morgan went about his duties like a man in a trance. He felt guilty that he had left London without looking for Hiram. He could have chosen to leave the ship and stay in London to look for him, but he hadn't. What kind of friend was that? But then what could he have done? He didn't know where to begin to look. For all he knew, like the captain said, Hiram had been crimped and dumped aboard another ship bound for a distant port. It was Icelander who talked him through his problems during one late-night watch. They were somewhere east of Newfoundland. The weather had turned cold and miserable with the winds blowing from the west and forcing them to double-reef the topsails. Morgan had put several men on watch up in the bow of the ship. The rigging and the ratlines were lined with a sheath of ice, and the decks were covered with a thin coating of freshly fallen snow.

Morgan was smoking a cigar amidships on the lee side as he thought about whether to give the order to tack to the south. He felt the bitter cold bite into his skin, but he didn't care. After nearly three weeks at sea, his face was unshaven, his hair covered with salt, and his canvas trousers stained with tar and grease. He leaned up against the bulwarks and looked down in the blackness, where he could hear but not see the rush of the waves against the side of the ship. His mood was as dark and as bitter as the cold night wind. In between his weighing the decision whether or not to change course, he was also thinking about whether he should quit the trade. His despair was real even if his thinking was filled with uncertainty. His life had been filled with conflict. He had always met challenges that confronted him head-on, but this was something different. This time the conflict was within himself as he struggled to grapple with an enemy inside. He had always believed in himself, in his own strength, but now he was facing crippling self-doubts. Perhaps he should return to Lyme and seek penance from his father. He wondered if it was too late for that. What did he want to do with his life? Maybe his father was right after all. A life at sea can only lead to tragic loss, pain, and suffering. He thought of his mother, her drawn face, so empty and so tired, and he wondered if he was risking his life in the cruelest way.

Just then, a familiar voice penetrated the darkness and interrupted his thoughts.

"These are perilous conditions, Mr. Morgan, and if we continue further to the north the weather will likely get worse."

He turned to see a large form looming over him. It was Icelander. To conform to the ship's rules governing the relationship between sailors and ship's officers, he now called his old shipmate Mister, but it was a formality. The two men had close bonds after so many years sailing together. Morgan didn't say anything, continuing to smoke his Havana.

"Icelander, wait for the end of the watch when we have all men on deck and we'll tack southward as you suggest."

The quiet giant nodded, his white eyelashes blinking quickly. He started to move away when Morgan asked him a question, uncharacteristically using the man's real name, perhaps as a way to show him mutual respect.

"What do you do, Mr. Rasmussen, when fate deals you a sharp blow?" Icelander was surprised by this unexpected, probing question and didn't answer. Morgan continued with a follow-up question. "What do you do when your actions have caused terrible consequences for others? What do you do when someone you thought you cared for betrays you?"

An awkward silence followed. Morgan was one of the few sailors that Icelander had confided with about his own personal trauma that had sent him into painful exile. After a few more minutes of silence he finally spoke, his thin lips barely moving.

"There are always detours on a man's road which may seem to take him in a direction he doesn't want to go," he said.

"Pray tell, what is that supposed to mean, Rasmussen?" asked Morgan impatiently. "Stop speaking in riddles, man."

Icelander lowered his voice to a whisper, an indication that this was intended as a private conversation.

"You've told me what Captain Champlin said to you. It may be that you don't want to listen to him. That's understandable. He's only interested in his ship. I suppose what I am trying to say is, if one day you were to become captain, Ely, then you wouldn't have so many detours. You could do pretty much as you pleased."

Morgan didn't say anything, so it was Icelander who finished the conversation.

"What I mean to say, Ely, as someone who has worked beside you for many years, in many storms, on many rough passages, is that your road in life lies on the Atlantic highway. You are drawn to it. Just like some men are rooted in the earth, you are a creature of the sea. That's my way of thinking anyhow. That's what your brother would have wanted you to do. He would not have wanted to see you quit. Maybe he's somewhere up there looking down on you wishing he could do what you're doing right now. Maybe he's still alive and he needs your help. Did you ever reflect, Ely, on what your brother might want you to do?"

Morgan said nothing, but continued puffing on his Havana, looking down over the leeward side of the ship into the cold dark river of rushing water several feet from his face.

PART V

The captain, in the first place, is lord paramount. He stands no watch, comes and goes as he pleases, and is accountable to no one, and must be obeyed in everything, without a question even from his chief officer.

—Richard Henry Dana, *Two Years Before the Mast*

12

1831

Morgan looked out at the murky molasses-colored East River and the harbor beyond. He spotted the *Hudson* among a fleet of towering ships, the Black X flag flying from the main mast. It hardly seemed possible to him that he was now the *Hudson*'s commander. He was the master of his own ship at the young age of twenty-five, a rare accomplishment in the packet trade. He pushed his way past anxious hotelkeepers trying to quickly settle accounts while newspaper boys shouted out the headlines of the latest edition. A cacophony of tearful farewells, hysterical sobbing, and nervous laughter surrounded him. The cool April air was alive with men yelling, horn blasts, and whistles from ships. That morning, New York's South Street docks were filled with rushed arrivals and hurried departures as mule-drawn wagons and pull carts crossed paths with finely varnished carriages.

The clatter of wheels and clop of hooves echoed in his ears. Coachmen helped finely dressed ladies with their colorful bonnets and shawls step out onto the cobblestone streets. Many of them were bound for Europe in search of the latest spring fashions. Morgan had been told his ship was full. Not only did he have a main cabin of twenty passengers, but the ship was loaded with nearly one hundred tons of cargo. He was carrying everything from casks of hides and horn tips, to several hundred hogsheads of flaxseed, to more than a hundred bales of cotton. They would be riding low on the water this trip, his first voyage as captain.

The *Hudson*'s departure had been delayed now for days because the winds had been easterly. Now that they'd come round to the southwest, he hoped to be off soon. All this delay due to the unfavorable winds created more chaos down at the docks. There were many ships ready to sail outward bound, some more anxious than others. The Havre packet *Francois I* was berthed near Old Slip; the Black Ball Line's new ship, the *Hibernia,* at the foot of Beekman Street; and the Blue Swallowtail Liner the *Napoleon* had just pulled into Peck's Slip. All were tied up at their docks loading freight and passengers, and would be ready to depart soon for England and France. New York's shipyards were building ten new packet ships that spring, all bigger and faster than the old *Hudson.*

Morgan squeezed his way among carts and wagons filled with luggage until he reached the small steamer that would take him out to the ship. He took a deep breath of ocean air. For the first time in his life, he actually could look forward to earning several thousand dollars a year. He had never thought of himself as overly ambitious, but after his run-in with Captain Champlin and the stern warning he had received, he had made up his mind to be a shipmaster and become his own boss. A cold wind gusted in from the East River, causing him to tighten up his jacket. He wondered if his family in Lyme were getting this same weather. Josiah had written, "Word around here is that you're going to go master pretty soon and have your own ship. Everyone in town is congratulating father. He doesn't say anything. Mother is so proud." He suddenly felt lonely as he thought about how much he missed his family.

Josiah had written him that he was intending to buy his own farm, and he had his eye on some land owned by Judge Noyes overlooking the river. He was waiting to see if the judge would sell at a more favorable price than forty dollars an acre. He'd gotten married a few years back to Amanda Maynard, and Morgan had already written him back that he would help with the purchase of the land. Now that he was a captain he could afford to do so. As first mate he had been making forty dollars a month, but as captain he was entitled to five percent of all freight earnings, twenty-five percent of cabin passenger fares, and whatever was received from carrying any mail. At two cents a letter, that usually amounted to about one hundred dollars a voyage.

He looked out across the East River to Brooklyn and then out to the harbor. Two incoming ships from China carrying the blue-and-white checkered flag of Nathaniel and George Griswold at their mastheads were waiting to dock. A tug, clouds of black soot spouting out of its smokestack, was on its way to tow one of them into the docking area. Several coastal packets from New Orleans and Savannah were also in line to unload their cargoes of cotton by the slip at the foot of Wall Street.

He picked out Christopher Champlin's new ship, the *Sovereign*, just in from London, already tied up at the Pine Street docking area. The *Sovereign* was twenty feet longer than the *Hudson* and slightly wider. Morgan had heard that her posh interior with polished mahogany tables, brass and mahogany railings, and carpeted floors was a far cry from the *Hudson*'s more spartan cabin area.

He spotted the familiar figure of Captain Christopher Champlin now walking down the gangway as he headed for the offices at 68 South Street. He remembered what Champlin had told him the day he'd given him the surprising news that he was turning the *Hudson* over to him.

"Mr. Morgan," he said, "in my mind, you need a good deal more seasoning, but my brother and the other owners have decided to make you a captain. I've been overruled. With the ownership shares my brother has in almost all the ships, he has more clout than I do. I will say that you have a lot yet to learn. You'll soon find out that a packet shipmaster's job is as much about people as it is about the wind and the waves. I reckon that's why the owners picked you from all the others. You have a way with people and they think the cabin passengers will like you. Maybe so, but I venture to say after a few voyages you may prefer to stay above deck than face the stormy complaints from the passengers down below. You will be serving a good many of the English on your voyages. Can you handle that Morgan?"

Then he'd laughed and patted him on the back.

"Who knows, Morgan? Maybe now that you've abandoned that foolhardy mission of yours to find your brother, you've developed the sound judgment to be captain. We'll see. I'll be keeping my eye on you."

Morgan had thanked him, never mentioning that he hadn't forgotten his mission. To do so in his mind would have made him a quitter. He'd merely become more discreet in his search. In fact he was still more determined than ever to find Blackwood, but the man had disappeared, leaving no trace. It was as if he'd dreamed the whole chain of events leading up to the attack at the White Bull. He'd tried to find Hiram, but he had come up empty-handed.

Several months after the incident, he'd gone back to the tavern disguised as a fish porter from Billingsgate Market. He wore a stiff flat leather hat with an upturned brim pulled down tightly over his face, and a coat that smelled like ripe haddock. The smell alone served to deflect any overly inquiring glances. He sat for hours alone in a dark corner drinking swipes, looking for any of the men who had attacked them. From this shadowy corner, he watched as the tavern's customers stumbled out onto the street. He waited until Molly left with the servant girls and then walked over to the bar, where a perspiring, oily-faced Bull Bailey was wiping the bar counter. He grabbed the portly, bald-headed man by the shirt and pressed the tip of a knife blade into his rib cage.

"Start talking, Bull. Tell me what happened to my shipmate. Where did they take him?"

Dazed and disoriented, Bailey just shook his head. Then he recognized Morgan and his confusion turned to fear.

"There was nothin' we could do. That man Blackwood said 'e'd kill us all if we didn't help 'im find some Yankee boy. 'E offered us money, real sovereign coins. We had no choice."

"What did he do with the man he grabbed? Where's my shipmate?"

"I don't know. They took 'im away, maybe to the *Charon*. That's Blackwood's ship."

"Who is this Blackwood?"

"Can't say."

Morgan tightened his grip on the knife handle and leaned in toward Bailey until the man squealed with pain.

"Enough. Enough. Some say 'e's an opium trader. All I know is when 'e comes 'ere to the tavern, his pockets are always full o' money."

"What does he look like?"

"Big, tall, powerful bludger with curly black hair, square face with strange squinty eyes, almost like a Chinaman. That's why they call him China Bill."

That conversation was on his mind as he stepped on board the smelly, sooty steamer that would shuttle him to the *Hudson* anchored in the middle of the East River. He wondered if he would ever see Hiram again. He spotted the ship's new steward surrounded by a storehouse of supplies and crates of chickens and geese.

"How are you, Mr. Lowery?"

"Fine and dandy, Captain."

Morgan's eyebrows rose in surprise. It was the first time that anyone had called him captain. It took him a moment to recover.

"You and Mr. Scuttles making sure we won't starve on this trip?"

"Yes, sir, Captain Morgan. We'll be sailing with full stomachs all the way. Plenty of belly timber on board from smoked Virginia hams to pickled oysters and barrels of potatoes and turnips."

Caiphus Lowery was a colored freedman from New Orleans, a tall, handsome-looking man with gray eyes and a bushy head of curly black hair that tumbled over his forehead and ears. Morgan had met him at Peck's Slip one day when he was playing the bones alongside a couple of fiddlers. He was the steward for one of the other London packets with the Red Swallowtail Line. Morgan had heard that the man knew how to cook finely seasoned French dishes, New Orleans style. He thought that those culinary skills might come in handy in the cabin to supplement the generally bad food that Scuttles cooked. So he offered him the job of steward and was surprised when the man accepted.

Soon the steamer was crowded with passengers and their mountains of chests, trunks, and bags. The small ferry chugged and puffed up to the sides of the packet. Morgan was first on the ship, climbing the fifteen feet up the rope ladder to the top of the bulwarks. He looked around him, surveying the decks of the ship on which he'd sailed so many voyages. There was an awkward moment of silence as he stepped on deck. He felt the eyes of the sailors turn in his direction.

Two men who were lounging by the fife rail jumped up like rabbits and began swabbing the decks. Another man bending over the scuttlebutt looked up like a startled deer, his face dripping with water. Still another quickly hid his small bottle of rum in the folds of a greasy rag. Some of the sailors, particularly the newcomers, showed him deference by taking their hats off. Others glanced away with downcast eyes or glared at him with a defiant look. By the foremast, a few sat together with crossed arms.

Many of these foredeck hands were new to him, but some of his old shipmates had stayed with him, including Icelander, the Spaniard, Scuttles the cook, and Whipple the carpenter. His ship's officers, Horace Nyles and Ezra Pratt, the two old-timers from the river, met him at the gangway.

With his gray, whiskery face and large, smoky eyes revealing nothing, Nyles welcomed Captain Morgan aboard the ship. Morgan knew that the man must resent him, as he had been passed over for shipmaster time and time again.

"Good to have you aboard, Cap'n," echoed the smaller, bearded Pratt with a note of insincerity in his hoarse voice. Morgan again felt awkward.

"Muster the men, Mr. Nyles," he ordered with a slightly uncertain voice. As the chief mate read out the names, each sailor muttered, "Here" or "Yes, sir," and shuffled forward. Morgan sized up the two dozen men who would serve under him, taking a good look at each face. Sullen, solitary faces, weathered and unsmiling, others with friendly broad grins and whiskery beards, young and old. These were the sailors under his command, a mixture of men, several stooped-shouldered newcomers and deep-chested veterans, their leathery faces, taciturn and defiant, chewing their quids of tobacco. These hardened packet ship men could outsail any others, but Morgan well knew that they were hard to discipline.

As the twenty passengers came on board he was introduced to them one by one as they emerged above the bulwarks. Most of them clambered up the ladder on the ship's steep sides as he had done, but some of the ladies had to be lifted on board, their long dresses billowing up to reveal their ruffled undergarments in a moment of temporary embarrassment. They were the usual mixture of well-dressed men and women, many of whom traveled with servants. Just by their puckered expressions and the stiffness in their step, he could pick out the Englishmen. Most of them were in America seeing to their investments in the cotton industry and the canals. A few even came over on hunting trips for moose and bear in the woods of Maine.

A stout, red-haired man of imposing height who gave his name as George Wilberton, the third Earl of Nanvers, introduced himself as if an important event had just occurred. Dressed in a mustard-colored vest, cream-colored pants, and a green coat, he strutted on board like a proud peacock. He was traveling alone on business, he told Morgan, and was now anxious to get home to "good Old England." There were only a few

Americans: a minister, his wife, and daughter from Philadelphia and a salesman from Baltimore. One loquacious, middle-aged English woman by the name of Mrs. Elizabeth Bullfinch, who had come to America on a business trip with her much older husband, was complaining that the crates containing her delicate porcelain china plates and tea set were still on deck. The center of the ship was already cluttered with human beings, baggage, and animals.

"Captain, what will happen to my porcelain?" Mrs. Bullfinch cried out. Morgan looked at this formidable picture of English femininity. She was a short, stocky woman with broad shoulders and ample hips. A prominent jaw jutted from her face like a ship's bowsprit. Flustered, annoyed, and distracted by all the confusion on deck, Morgan answered in his own plainspoken way.

"All in good time, ma'am. As soon as we hoist the cow up and the pigs, we'll be able to get your porcelain down the hatchway."

"What!" she wailed, her voice turning into a more pronounced whine.

To escape this annoying woman, Morgan retreated to the stern and stood by the helmsman. There he sought refuge until the ship was fully loaded, the hatches closed, and the cabin passengers comfortably situated down below in the saloon.

"All hands, man the windlass!" Morgan shouted out to the first mate in the midsection of the ship.

"Heave away there forward," yelled Mr. Nyles to the foredeck.

The crew began heaving at the windlass and breaking into a chorus of "Sally Brown." Tattooed arms and calloused hands moved in unison in a blur of soggy ropes and gristly beards.

"Sheet home, the foretop's'l," Morgan yelled as the breeze fanned his cheek. The bow of the ship now tugged at its anchor chain as it slowly fell off to the starboard side, anxious to be back at sea. Even before the sailors cleared the heavy, unwieldy anchor out of the water, the *Hudson* was already underway. Morgan could feel the ship shudder and then take off in a sudden surge as the hull heeled to port and the big sails filled out. He looked around him with a critical eye, his feet wide apart, his hands fondling his cigar. Even as first mate, he always looked for any weak links in the ship's rigging, any signs of chafing or wear. He carefully examined all the hemp lines used to trim and shape the sails, and then moved to the shrouds and stays that supported the masts to keep them stable in heavy winds. He walked forward toward the mainmast, his eye following some of the heavy lines descending onto the deck leading to the pin rails and the fife rails.

"Keep the sails full and drawing, Mr. Nyles."

"Good full, sir," came the reply.

Morgan continued taking stock of the ship. In the center of the boat the animals were all secured. The waist-high bulwarks had a fresh coat of green paint. The bleached decks leading up to the cargo hatches were scrubbed and cleaned. The first mate was shouting out orders as the men pulled up and released the sails, the foredeck men hauling in the sheets. He looked up as more and more sails were set and began to fill as the ship slowly spread her white wings. Like other captains, he wanted his ship to stand out in New York harbor. That wasn't easy as the nearly ten-year-old *Hudson* was now one of the older and smaller of the transatlantic packets.

The packet was soon flying toward the sloping hills of Staten Island. Morgan looked over the leeward rail with satisfaction, the water flowing by the hull, hissing and gurgling. Just ahead was the Red Star packet called the *John Jay* that had the reputation of being one of the slowest packets. A chorus of competing chanteys filled the air from the different ships. The banging of the yards and the clatter of the sails dropping and filling made Morgan feel glad to be alive, even though he could feel butterflies fluttering inside of him. He looked out at the hazy highlands of Navesink, where the remnants of an old fort from the last war with England could still be seen on top of a cliff. He took out his spyglass and spotted some goats gazing out to sea as if they were still on watch for any sign of a British man o' war. Departure and landfall, he thought to himself, the two bookends of his life. Departure usually brought sadness in leaving the comforts of shore, but on this voyage Morgan walked the deck with a springy yet nervous step. Following his instructions to the mate, he turned from his above-deck duties to his new untried and unknown responsibilities below deck.

Most of the passengers were sick those first nights out as they encountered stormy weather off Long Island and New England. Morgan was

now accustomed to walking down the thirty-foot-long saloon used by all the passengers, listening to the plaintive cries from one stateroom after another. All their cabins opened out onto the saloon, in effect, a long narrow common room only fourteen feet in width with finely polished wooden sides. A mahogany table ran down the center. Passengers in their own way lamented about the misery of sea travel. Morgan could hear Champlin's voice warning him to keep "his salty opinions to himself and be packet-polite to the cabin passengers."

Lowery, dressed in a checked shirt and white apron, rushed from one stateroom to the next even as the ship plunged, lurched, and climbed. The steward's head and bushy hair were wrapped with a red bandanna, and he walked like a man comfortable at sea, his feet squarely apart, his body leaning forward. He had ginger lozenges, baked apples, and slices of lemon, all three remedies for seasickness, on a tray in one hand. Wet towels and fresh blankets were in the other. Morgan thought to himself that he had made a good choice in selecting this man.

Above deck, he could hear the noisy cries of the men and the stampeding rush of their feet. He could hear the mate's call to tack the ship. Down below, he watched as the long steady heel of everything switched from one side to the other. Unfastened cabin doors on the windward side flew open while they shut with a bang on the leeward side. Inside one of the cabins, he spotted a man in a contorted position on his berth with his heels over his head. They would now be clear of land and be on a course well east of the dangerous Nantucket Shoals. Sable Island and the foggy Grand Banks lay ahead.

A hoarse voice from a stateroom cried out, "Steward, bring me the bowl again. I'm going to be sick. Hurry, steward!"

Lowery opened the varnished, maplewood-latticed door with its white handle, and through the arched entrance Morgan couldn't help but see one of the older Englishmen leaning over the wash stand in his eight-by-eight-foot stateroom, his body wrapped in bedsheets, his mottled red face revealing abject misery. The man's head was almost completely bald except for a strand of gray hair that hung limply down into the washbowl like a strand of Spanish moss from the limb of a tree. His cabin was in a dreadful mess, the floor covered with vomit. It was Mr. William Bullfinch. His wife was in the upper bunk rolling in agony. When he saw the captain, he turned to smile with his fleshy jowls and tried to make the best of his frail condition.

"I am afraid I have little self-respect remaining. Please do forgive me, Captain, as I am in the depths of despair. Sadly, my poor wife is in a similarly poor condition."

Without stepping inside, Morgan could see the white-faced Mrs. Bullfinch popping multiple ginger lozenges into her mouth. He gagged at the acrid smell emanating from the small cabin. He noticed with surprise that Lowery handed the man one of the ship's fine porcelain serving bowls from the pantry. He supposed the chamber pots were all in use. He wished the man and his wife well as he continued to make his rounds. Those stormy conditions continued for the next two days. The passengers were all in a sorry state, some moaning that the ship would soon sink to the bottom. The chairs and the furniture, which were not fastened to the cabin sole, were rolling and sliding from one end of the saloon to the other. He tried to reassure everyone he spoke with that the gale was subsiding, but his words were not very convincing. The noxious odors that filled the saloon were even enough to make him feel ill. After spending many hours of the first two days down below engaged in polite conversations with his suffering passengers, he decided to leave the nursing and the caretaking to Lowery and Scuttles. He felt like a doctor in a busy hospital ward. He knew he was neglecting his duties above deck.

That night in his cabin he wrote down the noon reading into the ship's log, something he normally did during the day.

Hudson's position at 1300, Tuesday April 23rd.

42 degrees 10' latitude by 70 degrees 55' longitude.

Course: Northeast, some 400 miles from Sable Island.

Falling barometer. High winds from the southwest accompanied by squalls, ten-foot seas. Under topsails, reefed spanker and inner jib. A regular gale of wind. Most passengers sick. All types of complaints heard from the staterooms. We are surging along, averaging almost ten knots since we passed the shoals off Nantucket.

13

By the end of the first week, Morgan was tired. He took the early morning watch for himself from four to eight, but between nursing his passengers back to health below deck and asserting his authority above deck, he spent little time in his own cabin. The lack of sleep had taken its toll. He found himself nodding off. One night he did a double watch. He was standing by the stern rail. He must have fallen asleep because he woke with a start to the sound of men yelling. He thought it was the end when a huge, dark shape emerged out of the blackness. He felt the taste of fear in his mouth as he shook himself awake, and saw a faint spark of light frantically waving back and forth from another vessel. The men from the other ship were shouting over the sound of the wind and the waves. It happened so fast he just stood there, unable to react, not certain if he was dreaming or not. The other ship flew by missing the *Hudson*'s stern by only twenty feet. He saw the shadowy, fear-stricken faces staring at him. He stood there paralyzed, waving his own lantern back and forth as the other ship disappeared into the void. He knew that the sailors were watching him now. They were whispering that the captain couldn't be trusted. He could feel their accusatory eyes. He was on trial. They were judging him, whispering behind his back, and he knew it.

But for Morgan those concerns were only half his troubles. The new unaccustomed demands below deck were far greater than he had imagined. It was only when the weather cleared once they left the stormy

Grand Banks that his two separate jobs began to merge ever so slightly. With the ocean calming, one by one the sickly passengers came up on deck to take in some fresh air. The stormy seas and the boarding waves sweeping over the decks had kept most of them below. Morgan spotted one of the packets that had left New York about the same time as they had, and the somber faces faded away. It was the *Erie*, bound for Havre. The two ships sailed side by side, sometimes in a single-reefed topsail breeze for a short while. Finally, with the winds piping up, the *Hudson* edged up closer to the wind to take a more northerly course, and all the passengers waved good-bye to the unknown passengers on board the France-bound packet.

The passengers were now promenading regularly around the ship. They had learned how to walk on a slanted, slippery deck, clutching the rails or the bulwarks to keep themselves upright. A daily routine began to settle in. Some of the more enterprising men got up early for a six o'clock bath on deck, which consisted of two buckets of cold seawater thrown over them by one of the crew. Morgan had smiled as a grim-looking Icelander had tossed bucket after bucket of icy water on several naked men, who were cursing the giant sailor as they stomped up and down on the deck. By seven o'clock, one of the sailors was milking the cow, the kettle was screeching, and the smells of hot rolls and sizzling bacon filled the cabin with the aroma of breakfast. An hour later at eight o'clock, Lowery sounded the handbell, and a full meal of broiled ham, chicken, eggs, frizzled bacon, and mutton cutlets was served. The *pots de chambre* in each stateroom were emptied while the passengers ate their breakfast. That was a moment when all the sailors moved to the windward side of the ship. Afterward, if the weather was not too rough, the shuffleboard players came out on the slanted deck to try their luck at sliding the biscuit.

Luncheon was delivered several hours later, and before the sun set around six o'clock a three-course dinner was offered, followed by a walk on the deck, a cup of coffee or tea, and a glass of port. All this socializing, eating, and drinking was new to Morgan. He wasn't used to the niceties of parlor discussions, the trivial conversation, and the rigorous rules of proper dining etiquette around the eating table. He often thought of Champlin's warning to him that his well-heeled passengers would find fault with his salty table manners. He'd already sensed the disapproval of some of the older ladies during the meals. He had heard the tut-tutting and the quiet whispering even as they stole glances in his direction. He kept wiping his face with a napkin, thinking that he must have food around his cheeks. Then he thought he may have said something inappropriate. As he had no one else to turn to, he asked Lowery what he thought. The gray-eyed, brown-skinned steward looked at him with a cryptic glance, and then told him in a hushed voice that he'd heard some of the passengers critique his eating habits.

"Excuse me, Cap'n, but those ladies say you eatin' too fast. They say you got your face in your plate, and you talk with your mouth full. I don't want to rile you, Captain, and I don't mean no disrespect, but they say you have bad table manners."

Morgan stood by quietly as his colored steward reported these overheard complaints. He was furious that he had received this embarrassing rebuke from Lowery, but he said nothing. He thought about what Lowery had told him about his early life in New Orleans. It hadn't been easy. Caiphus had grown up sleeping in the same room with his mother, except for the nights when the master came to see her and he was told to go elsewhere. It was from her that he picked up his cooking skills and basic knowledge of some African dialects. French and English were spoken around the house, so he was comfortable with both languages. His mother died when he was only fourteen. The master, a local merchant by the name of Francois Lowery, freed him at that time, and Caiphus found himself alone in New Orleans's Congo Square amidst the drums and the singing. He told Morgan it was natural for him to go shipboard because he knew he could use his cooking skills. "Tain' got too many places for a freed black man ashore, Cap'n," he'd said. "At least at sea, we all are in the same boat, black and white together. If the Lawd takes the ship down, He's takin' all of us."

After Lowery's revealing information about his table manners, Morgan made a point of following the example of the passenger seated across from him. He soon learned to keep his back straight and take small spoonfuls, never eat when someone was talking to him, and to wait until everyone was served before eating. As difficult as it was for him to learn some of these rules, Morgan did not envy his steward's job. Lowery was always being summoned.

"Hello steward, my good fellow," cried out a white-haired barrister from London. "How far from land are we now?"

"Oh, your lordship, we're closer than ever, only another two thousand miles."

Lowery didn't know the difference between an earl, a duke, or a viscount, so he just called all the Englishmen your lordship, a fact that amused Morgan, so he made no effort to correct him. He himself was just beginning to grow accustomed to these puzzling titles. As an American, he did not take them seriously, finding the whole notion of titles to be pompous and affected, but he knew if he wanted to keep his job he had to show some deference to English customs.

The litany of demands usually went on for much of the morning, and Morgan began making a habit of being on deck until lunchtime. Even there in the safety of the rigging and the sails, he couldn't escape the problems of tending to his needy passengers. One windless day in the middle of the Atlantic when the ship floundered, rolling back and forth with the sails flapping and the yards braced tightly, tempers started to flare. He watched as two of his passengers argued with each other over the rules of shuffleboard. As he walked closer he got the gist of the dispute. It seemed that they had learned different rules. The Baltimore salesman was yelling at one of the younger Englishmen on board, a thin, tall man with long, slender fingers and a flair for speaking in a dramatic tone.

"You bloody fool. You Americans always get it wrong," remarked the Englishman in a disdainful, sententious tone, standing tall and erect. "This is a game first played by Henry VIII. As I told you before," he proclaimed as he wagged his finger at the Baltimore man, "the biscuit has to land squarely within the triangle. It cannot touch any of the lines!"

The man from Baltimore, a dark-haired, medium-sized man with a drooping moustache, responded in a strident way by accusing the Englishman of cheating and making up rules.

This remark incensed the slightly effeminate Englishman, who was a traveling Shakespearean actor. His name was Peter Ward. He had left New York embittered because he had been poorly treated by what he called unappreciative and coarse audiences.

"You Americans break all the rules and standards of a civilized country," he cried out dramatically, his hands on his hips.

"What do you mean by that crude remark?" retorted the man from Baltimore angrily.

"You call yourselves the land of liberty," replied the actor, now quite unrestrained in his remarks, "yet you enslave the black man."

The Baltimore salesman, named Sam Wilkins, had his own strong opinions about that topic. It was clear that he didn't much care for the rights of the black man.

"The slaves are different. They are an exception," he declared.

"How so?" asked an indignant Mr. Ward.

"That's a matter of states' rights," replied Mr. Wilkins, his voice now full of conviction. "Slaves are property, nothing more. A nigger is a nigger just like a cow is a cow. They come in different shades and different sizes, but they're bought and sold just like all property."

"You don't say," retorted a now irate, red-faced Mr. Ward with distinct animosity. "I would say that equality means equality, and either you are for it or you are not. You say all men are equal, yet you worship those with money, no matter how ill-gotten the gains. You Americans are nothing but a bunch of devious, hypocritical hucksters."

"And you, sir, are a prune-faced, frothy Englishman. I would like to block you one!" Seething with anger, the Baltimore man drew his clenched fists to his face.

Other passengers were looking to see what the young captain would do. Morgan was about to step in when one of the other passengers intervened. It was the stout-chested Lord Nanvers. He walked right up to both men and introduced himself as an authority on the rules of shuffleboard. Morgan took stock of the well-dressed man with a large pale face and red hair slightly thinning on the top. He wore a fashionable, dark, long-skirted coat, dark cravat, and cream-colored pants with a flat-brimmed brown straw hat. He quickly mediated the dispute with his pleasant manner and calming voice. He told a few disarming anecdotes about King Henry VIII and his many wives and, surprisingly, the tensions evaporated over cigars and snuff.

Afterward, Morgan approached the English lord and personally thanked him.

"Think nothing of it, old man," replied Lord Nanvers as he took off his hat and patted Morgan on the back with his other hand. "I was glad to help. It was the least I could do to patch up the ongoing quarrel between the two transatlantic cousins. No need for more misunderstandings. Hey, hey, isn't that right, Captain?"

Lord Nanvers laughed with a self-confident chuckle and as a token symbol of friendship offered the captain some snuff. When Morgan refused, the English lord took a pinch or two for himself before speaking again.

"Tell me, Captain, please forgive any inappropriate forwardness on my part, but everyone on board ship has remarked that you seem young."

Morgan smiled but said nothing.

"Might I be so impertinent to ask if this is your first command?"

"Yes it is," Morgan testily replied, "but I have been sailing on this ship before the mast these past ten years. Rest assured, your lordship, you are in good hands."

Lord Nanvers applied another pinch of snuff to his twitching nose and replied, "I have no doubt of that, Captain. I have heard said that you are a talented sailor and a worthy navigator."

It was during one of those airless days when the sails were slack that Mrs. Bullfinch, who liked to walk the deck with her newfound sea legs, approached the captain.

"Is there an explanation as to why these hideous flies are so abundant and so difficult to be rid of? Presumably they come from that filthy cow you have on deck."

Morgan's eyes fixated on her prominent jaw, hawk eyes, and beaklike nose. She was wearing a white dress with a fully decorated straw bonnet over a frilled cap with brown curls poking out from underneath. The woman was relentless. He was thinking about telling her that the flies were probably attracted to her own fragrantly perfumed vinaigrette, but he bit his lip. He remembered Captain Champlin's advice to be packet-polite at all times.

That evening at dinner, she arrived dressed in an elegant velvet gown with pleated panels trimmed in such a way to reveal a formidable bust, her hair done in a beehive of braids and curls, and her neckline decorated with several strands of pearls. Morgan was worried that Mrs. Bullfinch would spot him using the wrong fork or spoon and would report this breach of good manners to the entire table. He was careful to watch the other passengers before he picked up the next utensil. Dinner was a three-course, two-hour affair. As Mr. Lowery served a generous meal of duck, pickled oysters, and ham, Mrs. Bullfinch held forth by critiquing American speech.

"I'm tired of hearing 'ain'ts' and 'hadn't ought to.' Have you not read, Captain Morgan, what the erudite Sydney Smith has written about America?"

Morgan shook his head. He had no idea who Sydney Smith was.

"Well, Captain, he is a fine English clergyman and a brilliant speaker, so full of wit and charm. I believe it was over ten years ago that he wrote, 'In the four corners of the globe, who reads an American book, or goes to an American play, or looks at an American statue?'"

She smiled at him knowingly. He bit his lip as he thought unpleasant thoughts about her. He was just thinking that the English, even those who were friendly, wore many faces when it came to the controversial topic of America. This was his first encounter with the socially prominent English, and he was quickly learning that despite a thin veneer of congeniality, they seemed to harbor an inherent hostility to all things American. He wondered to himself if their air of superiority masked some hidden insecurity about their own cultural identity.

Mr. Bullfinch, who was seated next to his wife, wanted to know if Morgan had read Captain Basil Hall. The older man's watery eyes, with deep dark shadows beneath them, revealed the signs of another sleepless night. He was still fighting off a persistent bout of mal de mer. Morgan politely shook his head and glared at the man. His ignorance about the writings of Smith and Hall was softened somewhat by the arrival of a platter of peas and onions. Mrs. Bullfinch looked up at the smiling brown face of Lowery as he made his rounds, and then turned back to the captain, whispering loudly.

"Why, Captain Morgan, your Negro steward is exceptionally dutiful, and I might add, so exotic in appearance. I have been meaning to ask you from the beginning of the voyage, does he have a little white blood in him?"

Morgan stiffened at this tactless question but said nothing. He noticed Lowery wincing, a clear sign that he had overheard the remark.

"Excuse me for asking this rather delicate question, Captain, but is the steward a free man? He has the same features as some of the slaves who served us during our stay in Richmond."

Lowery abruptly turned away and swiftly walked back to the pantry as if he had forgotten something. Morgan remained silent, squirming in his seat, counting the minutes until this dinner would be over. He was saved from responding by the surprise arrival of another course, a platter of simmering turtle steaks framed by mashed turnips. The turtle had been snagged with a hook and line that same morning. This unexpected delicacy was greeted with great joy by most of the table, and much raising of glasses to the captain's health. His eyes lingered on Lowery, who had emerged from the pantry and was now serving Mrs. Bullfinch scalloped potatoes from a bowl that looked disturbingly familiar. Morgan realized with sudden horror that it was one of the ship's bowls that Lowery used at the outset of the trip when the mal de mer was at its peak. It was probably Mr. Bullfinch's bowl, he thought to himself, as the Englishman was only just now convalescing. Lowery seemed unaware of his mistake, or at least was refusing to look the captain in the eye.

"Please help yurself, your ladyship," Lowery said in a melodious deferential voice, switching effortlessly into French with a languid creole accent. "C'est pommes de terre au gratin. Préparé avec crème fraîche et fromage de notre vache ici à bord."

The English woman looked up uncomfortably at the gray-eyed steward, slightly taken aback by a brown-skinned man speaking French. She smiled at Lowery, clearly not understanding a word. Morgan didn't know whether to be horrified or to laugh. He was about to stammer an apology and send the potatoes back to the cook when Mrs. Bullfinch interjected her views forcefully as she heaped a generous helping of creamy potatoes onto her plate without even looking at the suspiciously crusty edges on the side of the bowl.

"It is quite a popular book in London," she said as she now turned her attention to her plate and carefully sliced the ham.

Morgan looked at her inquiringly. He had already forgotten what book she was talking about.

"You should have it in your ship's library, Captain. It's quite revealing. Captain Hall at one point described meeting your scholar, Mr. Webster, who said something so typically American. He told Captain Hall that to stop Americans from changing the English language would be like stopping the flow of the Mississippi. Quite impossible, he said. What do you think of that, Captain?"

Morgan's mind was elsewhere. He watched with a sense of dread as Lowery made his way around the table. He was waiting for one of the passengers to sound the alarm that would reverberate far beyond the saloon of his ship. It would not be good business for the Black X Line if it were known that they served their guests dinner from uncleaned vomit bowls. He stared in fascination as the voracious Mrs. Bullfinch now swallowed a generous forkful of creamy potatoes. His initial impulse to intervene had now gone away. Somewhat to his surprise, he realized that he was enjoying the sight of this pompous woman eating large spoonfuls of vomit-seasoned potatoes with such evident relish.

He smiled mischievously, but when he realized he was starting to chuckle, he quickly looked away to the other side of the table where one of the two shuffleboard combatants was holding court. The English actor, Peter Ward, was flirting with the pretty eighteen-year-old daughter of the Philadelphia minister. Her hair was tied up in braids with an eye-catching gilded headband. Morgan had admired her, a tall, thin girl with an oval face and light, sparkling brown eyes that seemed to yearn for adventure. The man's long fingers were like swirling paintbrushes creating imaginary artwork in the air. Morgan hadn't noticed him much since the shuffleboard incident and now he got a better look at his sharply cut jaw, rigid nose, and thin, clean-shaven face that seemed to have moveable parts. Just a few days earlier he had been excoriating all Americans, but now, here he was openly flirting with one of them.

"Miss Holloway, you will certainly be pleased with the refinement and luxury in London. What will your American eyes be most desirous of feasting on? Westminster Abbey? The Tower of London?"

The young woman was clearly flattered at the Englishman's attentions. She spoke of hoping to see some Shakespeare in the London theaters, or some of the sculptures from ancient Greece.

"Let me suggest a small amateur theater near Covent Gardens where, if my memory serves, they may be performing a play about Icarus," Mr. Ward said, lifting his eyebrows and straightening his posture as he reached for another slice of bread.

Seeing Morgan looking in their direction, he attempted to bring the captain into the conversation.

"Captain, I am sure you are aware of many Greek mythological figures. Icarus, for instance, was a man who didn't follow his father's instructions, and fell from the sky as a result. Then there was Prometheus and Sisyphus, destined to their tragic fates. As a seaman you will have heard of Odysseus, naturally?"

Morgan bit his lip and nodded.

"But here is one you may not know. A nautical figure from the ancient Greeks that not many people are familiar with. Let me quote from the Aeneid."

With a shake of his head, and a florid wave of his long hand, the actor began speaking in deep, rolling tones, his eyes now looking appreciatively at Miss Holloway:

> "A sordid God down from his hairy chin
> A length of beard descends, uncombed, uncleaned;
> His eyes like hollow furnaces on fire."

"I will wager you haven't heard of Charon, have you Captain?"

At the mention of Charon, Morgan was startled and jumped out of his chair. He tried to cover up his surprise, but his head was reeling.

"Yes, yes," he said with strong conviction, his face contorting in disgust. "I have heard of Charon."

The English actor raised his eyebrows and stroked his chin, nodding with approval.

"I am indeed surprised, Captain. What have you heard?"

"Someone once told me it was a blood boat, but they never explained what they meant. Tell me, what does the name signify?"

"Why, Captain," declared Mr. Ward, still slightly puzzled by the captain's sudden interest. "Actually, Charon is the name of the boatman who carries the newly dead across the River Styx. Isn't that right, Lord Nanvers?"

"Indeed so," replied the English lord, who was now leaning in closer to hear the conversation. "All those who cross the River Styx with Charon never return."

"All except Heracles," added Mr. Ward quickly. "Remember, he was the one who slew the Hydra, the nine-headed serpent, and he tricked Charon more than once, I believe."

A violent shaking of the ship rescued the captain that evening. The plum pudding was just being served. Rough weather had struck, as it often did during a meal. Every time someone reached for a dish on the table, the ship lurched sideways and the contents spilled. Plates now slid across the table, glasses tumbled over, and the creamy pudding toppled onto Mrs. Bullfinch's lap, causing the woman to scream at Lowery that her velvet gown was ruined. Morgan heard the mate calling out to the men to get a pull on the weather braces. He heard the men singing out, and he used that moment when the sailors were hauling in the weather main braces to leave the table, just as the topic had switched to a debate about which was best, a monarchy or a republic. He could hear the last strands of the argument as Mr. Bullfinch proudly stated that as an Englishman he was quite pleased with his representation in Parliament.

"Is that so?" came a distinctly American voice. "I have heard that in England only one man in five has a vote. Do you call that a fair system of representation, Mr. Bullfinch?"

The weather was so bad by late that night that the ship could only stand double-reefed topsails and the outer jib. The packet would ride up the high mountain swells, ease off slightly at the crest, then plunge downward into the troughs, only to rise upward again. They were some 90 miles to the south of Cape Clear on a safe course to the Scilly Islands, or so he thought. Over the past week he had taken periodic midday readings with the sextant. He was confident with his arithmetic, and he thought himself to be a competent navigator, but this was the first trip he'd made where the navigation was solely his responsibility. At first he dismissed Icelander's concerns. The big sailor, who was then on night watch and was doing a turn at the helm, was worried about their position.

"Better to head further south, Captain. These winds have pushed us far to the north. Earlier today I saw far too many land birds. I think we might be closer to Ireland than we realize."

If these cautionary words had come from another sailor, he would have ignored them. He might have even rebuked the sailor, but over many years Morgan had learned to trust Rasmussen's instincts. To play it safe, he reluctantly gave the order to change course. Hours later with the sun breaking over the horizon, they were surprised to see the clifftops of the Irish coast just to the north off their port side. If they had not changed to a more southeasterly course when they did, they might have run ashore.

Morgan couldn't figure out what had happened. The past two days had been overcast, and as a result he'd been unable to take the noon sightings. But he was skilled at dead reckoning. How had he made this mistake? He thought of Hiram at that moment and his disdain for packet ship captains who spent too much time below with their passengers. It was true. He had spent too much time tending to the demanding cabin passengers. He hadn't noticed how much the strong southerly winds had pushed them to the north. That was his error, not paying attention.

As it turned out, that wasn't his only mistake. He hadn't checked his watch with the ship's chronometer. His longitude calculations had been off as well. What would Hiram have said? He was becoming a lady captain, he thought to himself, more nurse than sailor.

It was an important lesson for Morgan. He looked out at the sea and the cresting waves. He had found his calling on the ocean and it had made him what he was. It had given him work, and pride in his profession, a sense of his own strength and a belief in his abilities. And now because of his own hubris and carelessness, he had almost let it destroy him, his ship, and his passengers.

He went to his cabin to write into his log.

> Passed through a blue devil night with stormy winds. Saw several land birds. Altered course which saved us from shipwreck and a watery grave off the coast of Ireland. Wet, foggy, but a stiff breeze this morning. Ship going about ten knots. Coming on deck in the morning saw two or three ships through the fog. Scilly Islands out of sight to the southeast.

Morgan made a small offering of rum to Neptune that morning as a way of acknowledging his good fortune. The passengers below decks emerged later that day as the weather improved, knowing nothing of their narrow escape. However, some of the sailors were well aware that their young captain had almost driven them onto the rocks. As he paced the decks, Morgan could sense their eyes looking at him, distrustful and fearful. That night as he stood watch by the main mast, he thought he could hear voices. Some sailor was humming the chantey "Blow the Man Down." He pulled out a cigar and lit it. The whispering from the shadows and the humming then stopped, only to be replaced by a profound silence, broken intermittently by the sound of a creaking block, a splash of a wave, and a man snoring from the forecastle. With the glowing cigar in his teeth, Morgan stared out into the black void, his mind filled with self-doubt and broken self-confidence.

Just then the man on watch yelled out, "Light on the port bow!" It was the Lizard lighthouse in Cornwall. The ship was now well into the English Channel, and Morgan puffed on his cigar appreciably as he looked forward to landfall even more than he had savored their departure three weeks earlier. He wanted someplace to hide from the critical eyes on board ship that followed him both above and below deck. He hadn't felt so unsure of himself since those first voyages when he was a cabin boy and the vile Mr. Brown forced him up into the higher yards.

PART VI

I find the sea-life, an acquired taste, like that for tomatoes and olives. The confinement, cold, motion, noise, and odor are not to be dispensed with. The floor of your room is sloped at an angle [of] twenty or thirty degrees, and I waked every morning with the belief that some one was tipping my berth.

—Ralph Waldo Emerson, *English Traits*

14

1834

The distant bells of many churches were striking the hour as the cabriolet left St. Katherine's Docks on its way to the Old Jerusalem Coffee House in the commercial part of London known as Change Alley. The cool morning air on that sparkling June day refreshed Morgan and gave him a sense of well-being. He lit his first cigar of the day and listened to the comforting clopping of the horse's hooves on the cobblestones, still wet from an early morning rain shower. He had been a shipmaster for three years, but he still wasn't accustomed to many of the different business tasks he was expected to perform while in London. One such job was to promote his ship with shipping agents in London's Change Alley. He was dressed formally in a long-skirted blue coat, a white shirt with a dark cravat, and his polished Wellington boots. As he fondled his black top hat, he thought about how much had changed in his life. Dressed as formally as he was, it seemed as if he was overreaching his station in life. He almost didn't recognize himself. He knew he had changed, but these fine clothes he wore still seemed a mask. He reached into his coat pocket and touched Abraham's old pennywhistle, stroking the smooth lead surface. This is my compass, he said to himself softly.

As they neared Gracechurch Street, Morgan could see the tip of the lofty dome of St. Paul's Cathedral in the distance. His mind wandered back to that difficult passage three years earlier when he first became shipmaster of the old *Hudson*. He felt the same way now as he did then, awkward and strange. He smiled at his naivete, thinking about how much older he felt now, but also more experienced. It had taken time, but he had gradually won the men's respect. Even his first mate, Mr. Nyles, had a grudging admiration for his abilities now. He started calling him a lucky captain ever since they had avoided running aground two years ago by kedging their way out of a tight spot off the Irish coast with several small anchors even as a strong headwind threatened to blow them ashore. If it hadn't been for a helpful ebb tide that pulled them away from the rocks, events might have turned out differently.

Below deck, he had learned many of the skills of being packet-polite. He could now sit at the head of the table, smiling and chatting his way through multiple courses. He still had trouble giving elaborate toasts, but he'd learned to keep his well-heeled passengers entertained by telling wild sea tales and sailors' jokes and offering to play backgammon and chess. The secret of being packet-polite, he had decided, was to have a ready smile, a quick wit, a helping hand for the ladies, and a plentiful supply of port and sherry. Still, relations with some of his more arrogant English passengers posed special challenges. At times he had trouble controlling his temper. A particularly cutting remark would transport him back to that fearful night as a boy on the river. Back then he had seen the British as the enemy. Now as a captain and one of the Black X Line's ship owners, he had come to appreciate the benefits of trade and commerce with England. That thought helped him temper a dark feeling about the English that occasionally swept over him.

As he puffed on his cigar, listening to the cab driver coax his horse along, he thought about the day two years ago when his new ship, the *Philadelphia*, was launched into the East River from the Bergh shipyard on Water Street. The *Hudson* had just arrived in port, and he had left the unloading of the ship in the hands of his first mate. He wanted to see the newest ship that Henry Champlin would soon be commanding. It was a summer not easily forgotten. As he watched the 542-ton *Philadelphia* slide off the ways into the river, one of the carpenters pointed out to him the plumes of black smoke rising above the city.

"It's the cholera," the man said. "It's raging here."

Morgan looked alarmed.

"They're burning the clothes and bedding of the sick and the dead. That's what the smoke is."

During the three-week layover, Morgan had seen cartloads of bodies leaving the city and daily black plumes of smoke rise above the buildings. He'd written home telling Josiah and his mother not to worry. He mostly was staying aboard ship to keep from being contaminated. He wrote how each day he saw the somber sight of horses and wagons carrying the dead to the cemeteries. They would hear the latest from some of the newsboys each morning. People were abandoning the city by the thousands. He had never been happier to set sail and head out to the open sea. By the end of the summer more than 3,500 had died in the city of 250,000.

Clouds of tobacco smoke greeted him as he stepped into the noisy hum of the central meeting room of the Old Jerusalem. He liked to visit this coffeehouse because the latest shipping news was always posted inside. The Old Jerusalem was a favorite of ship captains from all over the world. Morgan never missed an opportunity to listen and discreetly ask questions. He always kept his eyes out for any mention of the *Charon* or the name *Blackwood*. In fact, he had specifically asked a couple of shipping agents he had just met a few weeks earlier to make some inquiries about the *Charon*, saying he thought she was an opium trader. These agents always kept track of the ships and the captains that sailed up the Thames. They had told him to come back before he left London and they might have more information.

Morgan took a few moments to adjust to the darkness of the large room. Men dressed liked him in dark coats and top hats were clustered around tables, some standing, some seated. He scanned the room to see if there was anyone he recognized. A few people were reading the morning newspaper while others were glancing at some of the bulletins posted on the wall. He looked around, but didn't see any familiar faces that morning. There was no sign of any of the shipping agents he dealt with, so he posted a promotional handbill on the wall that read simply: "Passage to America with the new packet ship *Philadelphia* of the Black X Line: experienced navigators, beds, wines, and foods are of the best description. Apply to Captain E. E.

Morgan, St. Katherine's Docks. First-class cabin fare, thirty guineas. Steerage fare, five pounds."

At this time, Morgan looked young despite his many years at sea. He was almost thirty, and his tanned, weathered, clean-shaven face had few wrinkles other than the first signs of crow's-feet on either side of his light hazel green eyes. His reddish-brown hair was combed back to reveal a smooth forehead. He laughed comfortably and walked with a light and easy step. Perhaps it was that carefree attitude and winning smile that drew a particular solicitous man to his side, or perhaps it was the way he walked, like he was still on a ship's deck.

"Mornin' to you, squire," the stranger piped up, removing his top hat to reveal a head of curly black hair. "What brings you to the Old Jerusalem? You won't find any ladybirds or high-priced toffers here, if that's what you're seeking."

At the sound of the man's voice Morgan turned and introduced himself as captain of a New York–London liner. The man who spoke was a round fellow who Morgan guessed was about forty years old. He had a large sallow-skinned face with a long, bulbous nose that pointed down to a double chin. The man was dressed with an eye-catching green vest, but otherwise he wore a conventional white shirt, black cravat, and black coat. Morgan gave him one of the handbills advertising the *Philadelphia* and began to extol the attributes of his ship as well as the merits of the shipping line. The Englishman pushed his left hand through his hair and peered at the pamphlet through his reading spectacles. He then asked with a wry smile, "I see yer name is Morgan. Are ye the Yankee captain who is lookin' for William Blackwood?"

Morgan tried to control his surprise and excitement.

"Yes, yes. Do you know him?"

"Not personally, but I know of 'im. Some of the other agents 'ere told me to keep my eye out for you. They told me ye was looking for Blackwood."

Morgan nodded.

"Where can I find him?"

"What business do ye 'av with 'im?"

"Personal business."

"I see."

The man smiled as he unbuttoned the midsection of his black coat.

"No, I haven't seen William Blackwood for some time now. Let me introduce meself, Captain. My name is Fleming, William Fleming. I am a stockjobber in sugar, spices, and tea, and a shipping agent handling all types of cargo."

Morgan knew the type. The London coffeehouses in Change Alley were full of these fast-talking traders selling their quick-rich schemes, some of them honorable, many of them not.

"Captain, ye and me are experienced men of the world, am I right? Whatever your business dealings are with William Blackwood, I can offer ye some fine trading opportunities. I know a few well-dressed gentlemen with several trading firms right 'ere in this room who may be looking for a fast Yankee ship."

The man had sharp and penetrating black eyes, which Morgan thought reminded him of a hungry crow. Mr. Fleming placed his shiny top hat on a table nearby and smiled at him in an insinuating manner that revealed a row of brown-stained teeth. Morgan was repulsed by this man, but in the interest of promoting his ship, he forced himself to inquire more about his proposal.

"What, then, are your well-dressed gentlemen looking for?" Morgan asked as he lit his cigar.

"They need to move some human cargo," was the terse reply. "And they're looking for a fast Yankee ship."

"That so," Morgan replied, thinking that the man might be posturing to try to charter his ship for the Atlantic voyage. "Well, we could carry as many as one hundred, maybe two hundred in steerage on the *Philadelphia*. Up to twenty-four passengers in the first-class cabin. We can make the westward passage to New York in twenty days or less."

"Indeed, then yer ship should be perfectly suited for the kind of work my clients are seeking."

"And what might that be?" Morgan asked, his suspicions rising.

Mr. Fleming rubbed his hand over his fleshy double chin and then looked at Morgan with a slanting, restless glance. He leaned closer and in a husky whisper said, "It is what we call 'ere in England the ebony trade. You Americans call it black ivory." He paused for a second before continuing. "Most British shipmasters won't risk eboneering anymore because of the penalties handed out by the Admiralty of one hundred pounds per slave. Think about it, Captain."

"Blackbirding?" Morgan asked in disbelief, repulsed by this proposal.

The man held his stubby index finger up to his lips and nodded.

"These men would pay well, Captain, one-eighth interest in the profits."

Still reeling in surprise by this loathsome offer, Morgan now went on the offensive after he took a step backward from Mr. Fleming.

"I thought you English had banned slave trafficking. And if I'm not mistaken, a new law goes into effect just weeks from now that will end all slavery in most of the English colonies?"

"Yer well-informed, Captain. England is close to abolishing slavery. This place is filled with talk of sugarcane rotting in the fields of Jamaica, the fear of guinea slaves rising up in anger, killing their masters and raping their wives and daughters. Remember the rebellion in Jamaica couple of years back? Twenty thousand of those blackies rose up and set fire to plantations and estates."

The man pressed his oily face and bulbous nose closer to Morgan's ear.

"For those who are clever, like ye and me, there is opportunity here."

"I don't follow your line of thinking," Morgan responded while pondering whether to abruptly walk away.

"Let me explain, Captain. The English planters in the West Indies quite rightly are fearful of the future. Many of them are of high social standing here in London. They have their landed fortunes to protect. Under the Emancipation Act, Parliament will compensate them. That much is certain. There is some talk of each planter getting twenty pounds per slave. My point, Captain, is there is money to be had. In Jamaica alone, there are over three hundred thousand slaves. Those slaveholders will be getting millions of pounds of compensation money, all thanks to Parliament. Why, there are a few notable lords, even a venerable bishop, quite respected I might add, who own slaves. Hundreds of them. Then there are some of the merchant class in Bristol, even a minister of parliament or two. No names, of course. Yes indeed, there are many people of high social standing who stand to earn a lot from the Emancipation Act. Those are just a few examples of the high price of freedom."

Morgan stepped back in disgust.

He put his hat back on, irritated that he had wasted so much time talking to this wretch. Sensing failure, Mr. Fleming straightened his back and thrust his large stomach forward. "Evidently ye have failed to comprehend my meaning, Captain," the man replied with a note of arrogance and hurt indignation in his voice.

"No, I wouldn't say that, Mr. Fleming," Morgan said as he moved away. "I comprehend your meaning only too well."

"Quite right. Quite right," Mr. Fleming replied in a subdued tone. He paused as he rubbed his nose, and then snipped at Morgan with a sarcastic rejoinder. "I guess ye blooming Yankees are the last stronghold for liberty and equality then, aren't ye?"

Morgan saved himself from making an intemperate response by ignoring this openly hostile remark. He left the Old Jerusalem biting his lip in repressed anger. Like many New Englanders he had no love of slavery, but he had no solution either. He knew the southern states would never willingly give up the institution. They were too dependent on cotton and tobacco. Many northerners, particularly recent immigrants, didn't even want the slaves to be freed for fear that their own jobs would be at risk.

As a New Englander, it hurt for him to admit it, but he had to acknowledge that this vile Englishman was right. America was as hooked and dependent on slavery as a Chinaman was on puffing the magic dragon from his opium pipe. Even the packets played a part in preserving this hateful institution. Much of the cargo going eastward to New York and then on to Europe was the steady flow of cotton from Charleston, Savannah, Mobile, and New Orleans. Cotton filled much of the Liverpool liners' cargo holds, but at least the *Philadelphia* and the other London packets carried other freight like flaxseed, flour, apples, and turpentine.

Later that same afternoon at the far end of Change Alley, Morgan posted another promotional handbill in a particularly dingy coffeehouse that smelled of rotten fish and spoiled mutton. He sat down to eat a hearty lunch of smoked sausage with several slices of headcheese. He was just lifting a mug of swipes ale to his lips when he thought he saw someone he recognized. It was the red parasol and the glimpse of her hair that caught his attention and caused a tingle of excitement to run down his spine.

He bolted out of the coffeehouse, pushing people aside and knocking pewter plates onto the floor. He ran through the crowd, all the time keeping his eyes on the woman with the parasol. She and a man in a black top hat turned the corner from Castle Court onto St. Michael's Alley and were walking quickly away from him. She was smiling and laughing just like she had always done with him. That's when he shouted out her name.

The woman turned quickly like a startled wild animal. As soon as he saw the green eyes he knew it was her. She'd spotted him as well. That much he knew by her hurried reactions. She'd jumped like she'd seen a ghost. She said something to her well-dressed consort, pulled in her parasol, and then the two of them ducked behind a building on the corner. Morgan knew the area well enough to anticipate where they were going. He ran through a courtyard adjacent to the Jamaica Coffee House, then found a small alleyway that cut diagonally over to the street where they were headed. He found them trying to hail a hackney cab.

He called out her name again, but this time she wheeled around and confronted him just as he grabbed her arm.

"Go away!" she cried. "I'm a respectable lady. Don't ye meddle with me."

Morgan seemed paralyzed at seeing her again.

"I need to talk to you, Laura."

"I have nothing to say to ye. Go away. Ye ought to be arrested, ye ought."

As if on cue, the man in the top hat next to her raised his walking cane.

"Back away, you scoundrel. You have offended the lady!" The man struck Morgan on the shoulders with his cane.

As he felt the sharp sting of the blows, he acted without thinking in a sudden rage filled with confusing emotions. He punched the man first on his jaw and then his stomach. As the man doubled over in pain, crumbling to the street, he stood there transfixed by what he had done. He regretted it. He was about to stoop down and help the man when he noticed that Laura was bolting down the street. He took off in pursuit, catching up with her after she ran onto Lombard Avenue. He pulled her over into a dark alleyway, holding both of her arms.

"Tell me it isn't true, Laura! Tell me it wasn't you!"

She gave him a long steady look, her face defiant.

"Truth is, Ely, I never promised ye anything more than what I gave ye."

"You let me walk into that trap. How could you?"

"I did what I was told."

"You know they nabbed my old shipmate. What did they do with him?"

"I don't know nothin' about that," Laura replied as she turned her head to look away. "I wasn't even there."

"You must know," Morgan said, speaking more forcefully now. "Where is Blackwood? Where is he?"

"I don't know. I got nothin' to say to ye. Now leave me be."

"Where is he? Is he here in London?"

"I told ye I don't know where he is."

"Did you tell him about Abraham?"

"Abraham? Who do you mean?"

"My brother, damn you. You know exactly."

Laura looked at him with cold, stony eyes and said nothing. Morgan shook her shoulders, his voice cracking with emotion.

"Did he know my brother?"

"I have nothing to say. Now leave me be."

Laura's unsentimental stare remained unchanged, but this time she spoke in a strident voice that had the sharp edge of a cutting knife.

"He called your brother a half-wit who got what 'e deserved."

"What do you mean by that?" Morgan cried out. "Did he say anything else?"

"No, no. He didn't say more."

She struggled to free herself.

"Let me go. I ain't done nothing wrong."

Morgan pressed his face closer to hers and tightened his grip on her arm.

"Tell me, what does he look like?"

"'E's much bigger than ye. Dark, frizzled hair and a big firm stomach, a scar across 'is forehead. A brawler with snake tattoos down 'is arms. 'Is upper eyelids . . ." She stopped and didn't finish.

"What about his upper eyelids?" Morgan asked. "Tell me!"

"'E can hardly see. 'Is eyes are like tiny slits. Almost like 'e 'ad some kind of disease."

She paused for a moment, and then hardened her voice.

"If you keep pursuing him, I believe 'e will kill you. That much I can tell ye."

Morgan never stopped looking at her. By now, he had calmed himself and put his anger aside. She seemed sincere. He had never wanted to believe that she had been party to Blackwood's scheming. Her eyes were moist and he thought he saw some feeling in her face, a touch of remorse. For the first time he thought he detected something of the young woman he had once cared for, but then he shook himself and wondered how he could be so stupid as to trust her. She had lied before and was probably lying now. He handed her a fistful of shillings and walked away without ever looking back. His stomach churned with a mixture of anger and hurt. His heart beat at a rapid rate.

He walked halfway back to the docks, collapsing on a bench in the middle of a small courtyard, and put his head in his hands. He was a fool. He felt like his search for Abraham was hopeless. A huge sadness engulfed him. He felt empty and alone. He pulled out the pennywhistle and without knowing why began practicing some of the notes in "Running Down to Cuba." It was one of the old tunes Abraham had taught him when they were boys dreaming of faraway adventures.

15

A week later, the *Philadelphia* pulled in at its scheduled stop, just off Portsmouth harbor, ready to board the first-class passengers. With the anchor down and holding, Morgan gave the order to keep the ship's topsails in their gear to make a quick departure by catching the outgoing tide. He left the quarterdeck area to walk toward the bow. As he went along, he admired the stretch of his new ship's main deck, the varnished yellow-pine topsides, and the bleached white decks. She was roomy for her length of 132 feet, but still sleek, he thought, despite her thirty feet in width. For him, this new 542-ton vessel was a rite of passage, a sign that Mr. Griswold and his associates now thought of him as a qualified packet captain. He was master of a ship that was on par with the other four packets in the Black X Line, including the newly built *Montreal* and the *President*. The old *Hudson* had been sold off as a whaler like many of the older transatlantic packets. She was now a lowly blubber boat, destined to sink in some distant harbor.

He watched from the junction of the bulwark and the main fife rail the new men he'd hired in London. They were a rough bunch dressed in dirty, ragged canvas trousers and patched-up coats. Hardened, weather-beaten, dried fish-scale faces, their heads covered with woolen caps or bandannas, their arms heavily tattooed and scarred from rope burns. They had the look of Thames scuffle hunters, many of whom had done prison time.

He didn't like the looks of them, but he'd had no choice. Only one day before leaving London, six of the crew had mysteriously come down with a severe illness that caused a high fever, vomiting, and diarrhea. Perhaps it was something they'd eaten as they'd all been ashore the night before. He'd been forced to leave them behind in the care of a doctor, and he'd had very little time to find replacements. Reluctantly, he'd instructed Icelander and Whipple to go into the East End and talk with the "Paddy West" man about getting half a dozen sailors. He'd stood on the quarter-deck and watched the new arrivals as they tramped up the gangway.

The first mate, who rarely spoke, volunteered his own comment.

"Those are sea ogres if ever I saw 'em, Cap'n. Worst kind of packet rats. They're sure to give us trouble."

"That may be, Mr. Nyles, but we need tough men who don't mind filthy weather. We don't have the time to be too picky."

Still, they'd sailed here on the two-day passage down the English coast from the mouth of the Thames and there hadn't been an incident. They'd obeyed orders even under tough conditions. He'd run up all the sails from the royals to the topgallant staysails and watched with satisfaction as these new men scrambled out on the yards, overhauling the clewlines and buntlines while sheeting in the sails.

"Passengers on the way, Captain!" shouted the whisky sodden Mr. Nyles as he handed the spyglass over to Morgan. He put the telescope up to his eye and watched a broad-beamed lugger with a fore lug and a mizzen meet the waves as the sailors manned the oars. He knew that all of these cabin passengers had taken the horse-drawn coach from London the day before. They would have spent the night in Portsmouth and would now be eager to get on their way. The sight of the well-dressed passengers in the lugger, the men in their top hats and the women in their long, billowing dresses, made him think of Charles Robert Leslie, his wife, Harriet, and their three young children. Leslie was an English painter who had traveled on the *Philadelphia* to New York last October to take a job as an art teacher at the military academy at West Point. As unlikely as it might have seemed, he and this refined English artist had become fast friends.

Morgan's mind drifted back to the voyage over with the Leslies. It had been a rough passage westward. He remembered how Harriet Leslie had gripped the long table in the ship's saloon every time the *Philadelphia* lurched or heeled over. He had laughed and told her jokingly, "Let her go, Mrs. Leslie. Let her go. You can't hold up five hundred tons of ship." She had responded with a weak smile, still clutching the table at each sudden movement.

Morgan had liked Charles Leslie immediately. He was a tall, striking man ten years his senior with a gracious, easygoing manner. He had a good-natured, boyish face with an ever-present smile that signaled his enthusiasm for life. What Morgan liked the most about him was that he was a positive thinker. The painter never complained about anything or anyone, and his friendly nature immediately brought forth smiles all around. The voyage to America had been a chance for him to reacquaint himself with his family. His parents were Americans from Cecil County in Maryland, but he had been born in England and had spent most of his life there.

As with most of his passengers, Morgan never expected to see the Leslie family again, but they had reappeared at the South Street docks six months later. They hadn't liked America much and had decided to return home to England. Harriet Leslie had been sick for most of that cold winter and Charles had missed the art world and his friends in London. They had greeted him like a long-lost relative. As much as Harriet Leslie didn't like ships or sailing, she had told Morgan as she walked across the wooden gangway onto the deck that she was never happier to see the *Philadelphia*. "Take me home to England, Captain Morgan," she had said simply. "I cannot abide the long cold winters here in America."

Fortunately, that spring passage back to London had seen ideal weather, with westerly winds allowing for a full complement of sails. Morgan had spent many hours talking with Leslie about England and America. In some ways, that was the glue in their friendship. Leslie, who understood both countries, helped him comprehend some of the British sensibilities. He explained that many of the British aristocrats still viewed Americans as unruly rebels who were uncouth and unsophisticated. They needed to be taught a lesson was the view of many in England. The Americans' directness unnerved polite society in London even as their plainspoken mannerisms offended. Leslie told him that many of his friends in London high society were delighted over Mrs. Trollope's scathing review of the lowly state of American culture. Her book *Domestic Manners of the Americans* had created quite a stir and sensation in England, particularly her vivid descriptions of all "those Americans' remorseless spitting."

Morgan smiled as he remembered one specific moment on that passage back to England. Leslie had spotted him shouting at some of the men high up in the yards, yelling at them with his hands cupped to raise the stunsails and the skysails. Sailors aloft were busy releasing buntlines and clewlines for the many different sails while others climbed from the foremast to the mainmast, sliding down the shrouds with their strong hands. Leslie had looked up in awe at the cloud of snapping, billowing canvas that now enveloped the ship and the graceful ballet movements of the sailors. He had turned back to Morgan, who was now examining his handiwork.

"I can recognize an artist when I see one, Captain. In London, you will have to come and meet my friends. Stanfield and Turner will wish to speak with you at length, I am sure. You will see that the English are more friendly than you realize. They aren't all determined to set America on fire. We will discuss the art of sailing a packet ship. How a ship captain can draw as much inspiration from the wind and the sea as any man who ever put a brush to canvas. You will see. I think you will like them."

To his surprise, shortly after the *Philadelphia* arrived in London, Morgan had received an invitation to Leslie's house on Edgware Road to attend the weekly meeting of the London Sketching Club. He had walked into the Leslies' full house around six o'clock to find a noisy group of nine painters sipping punch around the fireplace in the living room. They were all formally dressed in long dark coats, white shirts, and cravats. Morgan had dressed in the same formal attire he used when he went to Change Alley. They had been expecting him.

Leslie wasted no time in introducing him as his new friend, the American ship captain. The names and smiling faces were still a confusing whirl of bald heads, curly red hair, gray muttonchop whiskers, and bushy eyebrows. Cristall, Stump, Uwins, Stanfield, Landseer, Chalon, Bone, and Partridge were the names. Turner couldn't make it, Leslie said. He had given them the topic for the evening, "friendship," and the artists immediately sat down by their easels with charcoal and crayons to begin blocking out their versions of the subject. They had three hours to complete their watercolor sketches. Morgan watched the different styles and different interpretations: a shepherd with his dog, a boy giving a flower to a girl, a ship rescue. Then time was up and they were served a modest supper of cold roast beef, potato salad, and pudding, with brandy and cigars afterward. This was followed by a game of charades where one of the artists, a shaggy-haired man named Landseer, came grunting into the living room on all fours. Morgan recognized him as the artist who painted with a brush in each hand. Another artist with a thin face and deep-set eyes, Robert Bone, whom Leslie called Bibbitty Bob, pretended to be a farmer scrubbing a grunting hog. Morgan couldn't remember laughing as much as he had that night.

His pleasant reverie was interrupted by the growl of his first mate.

"Stand by for boarding, Cap'n."

One by one, the male passengers clambered up the sides of the ship with the tails of their long coats dangling behind them. The ladies, holding onto their bonnets, were placed in wooden bucket slings and slowly hoisted aboard ship from the small lugger by rope and tackle, a journey punctuated with shrieks and squeals of fearful delight. They were the usual mixture of well-dressed men and women, many of whom traveled with servants. Morgan greeted his passengers at the quarterdeck with his customary warm handshake for the men and a tip of his hat for the ladies. He noted with subtle interest that some of the younger women were wearing revealing low-cut dresses with tight corsets, their hair in fashionable corkscrew curls and braids. The older ladies, with their slightly rouged cheeks, wore black-print dresses with semicircular brimmed bonnets tied under their chins with colored ribbons.

One young woman caught his eye as she sprung out from the wooden bucket sling onto the deck as gracefully as a cat jumps off a chair. She had the look of someone who enjoyed adventure.

"What a lark!" she cried out as she quickly surveyed her new surroundings on board ship. "I felt like I was flying!" She strode with a confident gait across the quarterdeck, a pleated skirt accentuating her tiny corseted waist. She was a small woman, barely over five feet tall, with a thin nose and sparkling amber-colored eyes. Her high forehead and long neck led his gaze down to her bare shoulders and slender figure. Behind her was an older, square, short woman wearing a black dress and a frilled white day cap. Morgan was soon introduced to Mrs. Ruth Robinson and her daughter, Miss Eliza Robinson, from New York. The younger woman's unabashed gaze and prominent chin suggested a strong-willed, independent character. The older woman had looked at him attentively and asked if there would be storms ahead. He replied that it wasn't the season for rough, stormy weather.

He was now directed elsewhere and began talking with some of the other passengers. He shook hands with each one as he welcomed them aboard like a proud deacon greeting his parishioners at a Congregationalist Church meeting. It turned out that one of the Englishmen had traveled with him before, a smiling stout-chested man with thinning red hair, George Wilberton, the third Earl of Nanvers. After a momentary lapse, Morgan remembered the robust, cheery-faced man when the English lord mentioned the shuffleboard incident on board the *Hudson*. He introduced him to his new wife, Lady Nanvers. He was taking her to America to show her this new experiment in democracy. They were going to visit Niagara Falls before attending to some business matters in Baltimore. Morgan's gaze lingered on the flirtatious, fair-haired Lady Nanvers, whose tight-fitted waist, wide low neckline, and bare white shoulders were already attracting attention.

As the luggage was hauled aboard, he led the passengers down below into the main saloon area. He advised them to hold on to the brass handrail and watch their step as they descended the steep stairs. Morgan watched as his guests' eyes nervously scanned their new surroundings. He stood at one end of the large dining table and looked toward his passengers, who were scattered around the area.

"Welcome, ladies and gentlemen. Welcome to the New York packet ship *Philadelphia*, which I dare say is one of the finest and fastest ships to sail the Atlantic."

The men and women turned toward the captain.

"Some of those harbor reporters back in New York are calling new ships like this one floating palaces. The main cabins have been finished with a mixture of bird's-eye maple, satinwood, rosewood, and mahogany. As you can see from the fine carpets on the floor, there is every comfort.

In the adjoining dining room, the ladies have their own sitting area with a piano."

This remark produced the desired murmurs of appreciation as the entire group looked over at the adjacent lounge with its blue silk curtains, two small sofas, a cherrywood piano, and walls painted with pastoral scenes. Morgan noticed that the young woman with the amber eyes had walked over to the piano with its finely tapered legs and was gently touching the keys.

"Gentlemen, I'm afraid, are not allowed in this room unless invited by a lady, of course."

This brought forth some reserved laughter from the ladies and a few coughs and some cantankerous muttering from the men.

"The steward here, Mr. Caiphus Lowery, will show you the various staterooms. We have twelve separate suites on board, each with two stacked berths. As you can see, they offer abundant room for all purposes of toilet."

Morgan could hear the clucking behind the varnished latticed doors as the group commented on the small windows, the tiny, standing washbasin, the cramped berths too short for most tall men, all in an eight-by-eight-foot space.

"Captain, how will we bathe?" asked one older woman plaintively. "I see no bathtub in my stateroom?"

"The steward will see to that, ma'am," Morgan replied in the most courteous tone he could summon. "He will draw up a bucket or two of seawater every morning for you and place it in a small tub."

Astonishment, then silence, greeted this grim description.

After an hour of letting his cabin passengers get settled, Morgan was back on deck giving orders. He could see the steerage passengers all on deck anxiously gazing back at the shore. On this trip, they had loaded eighty emigrants. They were a mixture of country English, wild-eyed Irishmen, red-bearded Scots, and crusty quarrymen from Wales. There were a few single women, but most were married with small children clutching to their dresses. Morgan was still under instructions from Mr. Griswold to take on steerage passengers only as a last resort. The shipping line could make more money carrying fine freight like Yorkshire woolens, Lancashire linens, and Sheffield cutlery in the upper hold. Still, the London shipping agents were always looking for more ships to take across the steady stream of emigrants, and the packets increasingly were adjusting their fares to make it worthwhile.

"Mr. Nyles, back the jibs."

"Backing the jibs to starboard, Captain."

"Break out the anchor."

The massive anchor came tumbling up from the sea like a huge fish. In an instant, the sailors on the foredeck released the starboard sheets and simultaneously pulled in the sheets on the port side. The men high up in the yards, who were tending the sheets and the braces, trimmed the large square sails to make them work in conjunction with the jibs. On deck, the sailors tending the lines began to sing a departure chantey:

> Yes we're homeward bound to New York town
> With a heave oh haul.
> And it's there we'll sing and sorrow drown
> Good Morning ladies all.
> Anchor up, Captain, ship's aweigh.

The *Philadelphia* shuddered as the power of the wind took her off with a sudden surge, the hull heeling to port as the big sails in the center of the boat filled out.

"Keep her sails full and drawing, Mr. Nyles."

"Aye, aye, Captain."

☸

Even before the ship had reached Land's End a day later with the cliffs of the Lizard and the Eddystone Rocks safely behind them, Morgan could see trouble was brewing. His old veteran sailors were on edge. Whipple and the Spaniard both approached him and told him that the new crewmembers were not fitting in well. There was mutiny in the air, they said. He could hear the roar of the surf now crashing on the craggy ramparts of the southwestern tip of England. As they said farewell to the Scilly Islands, one of the more brutish-looking sailors with an oxlike neck refused to go up into the yards. Morgan had to send Icelander and Mr. Nyles up to the foredeck armed with belaying pins to make the man obey. He wished Hiram was still sailing with him. His old friend could always sniff out any trouble brewing on the foredeck. He swallowed hard as he thought about him. He wished he'd never gone into that tavern. Hiram might still be sailing with him now if it weren't for that fateful decision he'd made.

Much later that same night, after a strong run across the Celtic Sea, Morgan lay on his bunk listening for any strange noises. The westerly winds had pushed them farther to the north and closer to Ireland than he would have liked. He guessed that they must be forty miles from Galley Head south of Old Kinsale. His senses were at a fine pitch of alertness because of his concerns about the ugly mood on the foredeck. The passengers had all retired to their staterooms. The winds had died down, and the packet was now loafing along at barely three knots.

The only sound he could hear was the lapping of the water against the hull, and his concerns that trouble was afoot began to subside. His thoughts turned to the young woman who had sat next to him at dinner that night. Her full name was Eliza Ann Robinson. She was attractive, but not overly so, and he guessed she was not too far from her eighteenth birthday. With her blue silk dress and single strand of pearls, she seemed bright and lively, but he also found her to be somewhat arrogant and overly self-assured. She wanted to know if she could climb up the rigging and crawl through the lubber's hole to try to spot any whales. Persistent and willful, she wouldn't take no for an answer. Even though he politely told her that women weren't allowed up into the rigging, she persisted with her request. The more he tried to say no, the more stubborn and truculent she became. After dinner she walked away with an aggressive gait, clearly indicating her displeasure with him. She began playing the piano, her fingers flying over the keys, which brought a cluster of three men around her. He concluded she was a spoiled rich girl who was used to getting her way.

The cabin was dark after he put out his lamp. Just as he was dozing off, a sudden firm knock on the door caused him to jump out of bed.

"Who is it?" he called out in alarm.

The cabin door sprung open and there stood the first mate, Horace Nyles, his silhouette and whiskery face framed in the doorway. He had a sharp-tipped handspike in his hand. Morgan felt a cold tingle down his back.

"It's a mutiny, Captain! Mutiny! Come quick!"

"Who are they?"

"It's all those new recruits we took on in London, Cap'n."

"How many?"

"All six of them, I'm guessing. Two of them tried to nab Icelander at the helm, but he knew something was up 'cause they smelled of rum."

"Did they harm him?"

"No. They pulled a knife, but he knocked the man flat. The other critter came at Icelander from behind, but Mr. Pratt and Ochoa got to him before he could reach Rasmussen. They knocked him into the bulwarks where half his body was hanging overboard."

Morgan grabbed his two pistols and pushed his way out the door. The Spaniard, a knife clenched in his teeth, was just coming down the companionway with the two rebel sailors. Their hands were manacled behind them, their cotton shirts torn exposing their bony chests, their faces bruised.

"Aquí están Capitán. Piratas, hijos de puta que no valen mierda."

Ochoa cursed and swore as he kicked them down the last few steps, his face intense, his manner purposeful.

"¿Quiere que les mate, Capitán? Do you want me to rip them open from head to heel?"

Morgan shook his head and told Ochoa to lock them up in the ice room where the meat was kept. He watched as the Spaniard kneed the two prisoners in the back and pushed them into the cold storage room where they fell with a heavy thud. Morgan had noticed these two before. One was a tall, shaggy-haired man with a bulldog jaw and deep-set eyes that glowered under a heavily furrowed brow. The other smaller one had a pale, drawn English face with a droopy nose and eyes that blinked continuously. They reminded him of the mud-covered clammers they would pass on their way up the Thames whose upturned faces were devoid of even the faintest hope. They stood there shivering among the blocks of ice and slabs of meat. Morgan stared at them defiantly, closed the door, grabbed a board, and thrust it in between the two looped handles. He told Mr. Pratt to get their story even if he had to inflict bodily harm.

With his two pistols primed and ready to fire, he climbed up the companionway steps and ran to the stern of the ship where Icelander was still at the helm. The packet ship was headed for Cape Clear off the southern coast of Ireland. It was a dark, moonless night so the land just two miles away was invisible in the darkness. The gentle southerly winds barely moved the big ship forward. Morgan could feel the cat paws filling and emptying the sails. Icelander and the second mate quickly told him the trouble was far from over. The two captured sailors' defiant shipmates had taken over the forecastle and had tied up Whipple and many of the other sailors loyal to the Captain.

Morgan took careful measure of the situation. With his two ship's officers, Icelander, Spaniard, Lowery, and Scuttles down below, he guessed that they now faced the remaining four mutinous sailors, all armed with knives they'd taken from the others. Certainly they had the mutineers outnumbered, but there were hostages to consider. He knew the only big advantage he had were the two pistols he carried.

With Icelander and the Spaniard at his side, Morgan slowly advanced to the foredeck. He'd left Nyles to steer the ship and to guard the helm. Pratt was below with the two prisoners. He noticed that the foredeck lantern had been snuffed out. There was an eerie quiet on the slow-moving ship, the only sound, the creaking masts. He strained his ears for any suspicious noises like a footstep or a human voice. The night was so dark it was hard to see anything but the bare outline of the shrouds immediately ahead of him. Ochoa held the flickering lantern in one hand and his throwing knife in the other. Icelander had a large axe that was normally used to cut down tangled rigging and splintered masts. As they came closer to the foredeck, Morgan could hear the faint lapping of the water as the waves splashed against the starboard side.

As the trio crept forward, a large shadowy object suddenly fell from the sky to the deck, landing with a solid heavy thud just several feet from where Morgan was standing. He jumped back, frightened out of his wits, the air sucked out of his lungs, leaving him too shocked to react. It was so dark that he couldn't see what it was, but Ochoa lunged toward it, lantern in one hand, the knife in the other. The Spaniard reached into the darkness, grabbed something, and yanked it up into the flickering light, revealing the head of an unconscious man, his eyes blank. A pool of blood was spilling onto the deck. Ochoa turned him over and saw the handle of a long sheath knife protruding from the man's stomach. Morgan could see that it was one of the new recruits who had fallen from the yards onto the deck. It looked as if he'd impaled himself on his own knife.

Morgan was rattled by the sight of the dead man and the blood pooling on the deck. His gaze remained locked on the man's lifeless eyes and the knife handle sticking up out of the bloodstained shirt for what seemed like a long time. A death on his own ship! Events were quickly spiraling out of control. Just then, they heard a thudding of feet on the deck. With a banshee-like yell, the rebels charged the three men amidships. All three stood their ground. Morgan extended his arms out in preparation to fire. Just when it seemed likely that there would be a bloody clash, the three rebels stopped within twelve feet of Morgan. A glimmer of shiny metal by their fists alerted him that they had their knives drawn. In the dim yellow flame from the lantern, he couldn't see them well, but he could tell from the faint flash of their teeth, and the wide stance of their feet, that they were poised for action.

"Show your face," Morgan cried out.

"Go ahead and fire, Captain, or maybe yer scared," shouted the bushy-headed sailor, who from his manner and the way he spoke was clearly their leader.

"What are your intentions?"

"What do ye think, Cap'n? We aim to take yer ship. A dozen of your sailors are all tied up in the foc'sle. They can't 'elp ye."

The words spilled out from the darkness, slowly and steadily, hauled out of a deep inner well of bitterness and hatred.

Morgan responded, his voice projecting more confidence than he felt. "Two of your men are now in manacles locked up down below. One of your number is already dead with a knife in his belly. That leaves only the three of you scoundrels left, and with my two shots, there soon will just be one of you. What will it be, men?"

Icelander and Ochoa stood with their weapons hoisted over their heads. Morgan's palms were sweaty. He could tell that this news had changed things. He could just make out the visibly startled face of the ringleader, but then the man quickly regained his composure. A fight was about to begin when out of the gloom of the foredeck, one of the rebel sailors appeared with a knife to Whipple's throat, the blade flashing in the lantern's flickering light, the man's largely bald head and long, drooping moustache barely visible.

"Stop where you are, Captain! Unless ye want this old sailor to die," said the bald man, whom the ringleader called Enochs. "I'll kill 'im without a thought. I'se done it before, you can be sure of that."

Their leader, the bushy-haired mutineer, now spoke up.

"This old tar 'ere will die like a pig unless ye 'ave yer men ready and lower the quarter boat on the starboard side. We'll kill 'im, don't y'doubt it."

It took Morgan a moment to register that the ringleader appeared to have changed his mind or at least his tactics. The mutineers no longer wanted to try to take the ship; they wanted to escape. But the danger was far from over. The tip of the man's knife traveled across Whipple's throat. Morgan hesitated. Icelander and Ochoa were looking to him for the word to attack.

"Do it, Captain, or this man dies. So might many of the others tied up below in the fo'c'sle. We'll corpse 'em all if we can."

Morgan watched the point of the knife prick Whipple's throat and heard the ship carpenter cry out in pain as the blade's point broke the skin and slid down to the base of his neck. He saw the thin trickle of blood on his neck. He could sense the ringleader's desperation and his impatience. Morgan paused another moment as he weighed the options, finally deciding on the more cautionary alternative. He gave the orders for Icelander to go lower the boat.

The big bushy-haired sailor threw his head back with a triumphant shake, and growled in satisfaction.

"Good choice, Captain. Now bring up the two of my men ye 'ave and fetch the body of Armstrong. No tricks, mind ye. Comes a time when every tar 'as to fall off the wind in bad weather. Appears like yer makin' the right decision."

Morgan kept his eyes fixed on the man. The roughness of his manner attested to his vicious nature. For the first time, under the lantern's glow, he noticed the elaborately blue and red tattooed serpents that spiraled down his arms, the fangs extending down each finger, the green eyes on either side of his large hand. The throaty, hoarse quality of his voice seemed familiar to him somehow, almost like from a dream. He didn't know why, but it was unnerving. In the lantern's dim light, Morgan could see a white weal that ran across the man's forehead, but it was the eyes that were unforgettable. One of them had an odd slant to one side, and both of them were almost hidden behind fleshy eyelids. His pistols were ready to fire, but he did as the man said, sending Lowery down into the cabin to retrieve the captured men, who stumbled up from below decks carrying the dead sailor with them.

"Get over 'ere, Compton. Ye too, Wainwright," the ringleader barked at the two men who had been apprehended earlier. "Get Armstrong's body into the quarter boat."

The five mutineers now gathered around the quarterdeck, clustered around the wide-eyed Whipple, whose neck was still bleeding. The ringleader had brought along two of the captured sailors from the foredeck as hostages. He turned to the bald-headed man who held the knife to Whipple's throat.

"If he makes one move, Enochs, stick him like a pig."

Morgan watched as the shadowy figures of the mutineers disappeared one by one over the side, climbing down the ship's rope ladder to the quarter boat below. The winds had now died down to a flat calm so that the ship was hardly moving. Their captives, their hands still tied behind their backs, were dragged along, and thrown down next to the corpse into the bottom of the quarter boat, which was hanging from the davits just a foot above the water line. Morgan was powerless to do anything. Any move by him would have caused Whipple's death and maybe the other two as well.

"Release my men!" Morgan shouted in sudden desperation as he raised his guns to eye level. "Rest assured, I'll fire unless you free those men."

The bushy-headed sailor looked up at Morgan with a pernicious smile, his heavy-lidded eyes opening wider.

"Aye, aye, Captain. Let Neptune 'ave 'em and the Devil too."

He cut the hand ties from behind Whipple and the two other captured sailors, and then pushed them overboard as he sliced the quarter boat's painter. All this happened within seconds, so fast Morgan wasn't sure of what to do next. He watched as the shadow of the quarter boat moved away into the darkness. He could have fired, but he saw what he thought were the bobbing heads of his men, their hands and arms thrashing in the water. The mutineers were already disappearing when Morgan finally reacted. He shouted out for Icelander to drop the jolly boat at the stern to try to pick up the men who had been thrown overboard. With the lack of wind and the flat seas, the men were easy to find from the noise they made thrashing about in the frigid water.

As Morgan turned and walked toward the quarterdeck, he saw that most of the cabin passengers were now clustered around the companionway. The first mate, Mr. Nyles, held a lantern. The passengers' wide-eyed faces were filled with uncertainty and fear. He himself was trembling as he tried to reassure them that everything was fine. He spotted the normally cheery Lord Nanvers, who looked like he had seen a ghost. He was dressed in silk pajamas, a plaid flannel robe, and embroidered slippers. Morgan's eyes met the gaze of the girl with the amber eyes, and he noticed that she seemed slightly shaken, but not as unnerved as he might have expected. In fact, Miss Robinson, wrapped in a pink satin coat, seemed strangely energized by all the drama and excitement. Her cheeks were flushed and she seemed to be looking at him with renewed interest.

An hour later, the three shivering and frightened sailors were down below in the cabin wrapped in blankets, sipping some of Scuttles's warm pea soup. If it hadn't been for the calm seas, these men would have drowned. Morgan had more questions than answers. The mutineers had escaped. They were probably already safe ashore in Ireland. He wondered who they were and why they had chosen the *Philadelphia* out of all the ships in London. He thought back to their leader. He remembered Laura's description of Blackwood's eyes, and the serpent tattoos. He suddenly thought of Laura's warnings about how the man would try to kill him. Maybe she told Blackwood about their encounter in Change Alley? That throaty voice had seemed so strangely familiar. His mind went back to a distant memory, a hazy room in the Frying Pan Tavern, the naked girl and that distinctive voice of the man named Bill. "Never seen 'im before." That's what he'd said in that same guttural voice.

"Fastnet Rock ahead of us, Cap'n," Mr. Nyles yelled out from the forward section of the ship. The winds had shifted and picked up sharply, coming out of the north. Morgan pulled up the collar of his coat. He could just barely make out in the gray predawn light the black rock pointing up from the sea like a breeching fin whale. This was Ireland's most southerly point. The Irish called it the lonely rock and he could see why. Off to the starboard some four miles away, he could just make out the round stone lighthouse of Cape Clear. This would be their last sight of land until they sighted the sandy beaches of Long Island.

16

Days later, the *Philadelphia* was forging along under full sail with a fair, fresh breeze at twelve knots an hour. The attempted mutiny along with the last sight of Ireland was all but forgotten now by most of the cabin passengers, but not for Morgan. He blamed himself for not being more vigilant. If he had listened to the warnings from Ochoa and Whipple he might have prevented the mutiny. He consoled himself with the fact that no lives had been lost and his ship was still on schedule. Still, he'd let them get away. He could have fired his guns, but he'd hesitated. So many troubling questions lingered in his mind. Who was that devil sailor with the squinty eyes? He wondered again if he had finally met William Blackwood. Pratt had questioned the captured men and found that they were a couple of scrappy fishermen from the lower Thames. They said their plans were to capture and scuttle the ship off the Irish coast. All on board were supposed to die, but they didn't say the ringleader's name.

Turning away from the helmsman, he began walking toward the quarterdeck. The seas were calm and radiant, taking on a furrowed appearance like a recently plowed field, offering little resistance for the large packet ship. A noonday sun warmed the wooden deck. Morgan decided to leave the sailing to his two ship's officers while he spent time being packet-polite to his passengers. Most of them had surfaced on deck to enjoy the weather. The wind was fair and balmy and everyone seemed to be in fine spirits.

He watched as some of the men, dressed in brightly colored coats, cream-colored pants, and flat-brimmed straw hats, tried to play shuffleboard on the slanting deck with their broom-shaped paddles. They laughed good-naturedly, trying to keep their balance as the waves sent their weighted biscuits sliding off to the leeward side. A group of older women in full-sleeved white cotton dresses, shawls, and calico bonnets sat on the windward side, safe from any ocean spray, crocheting and chatting. Lowery was passing sardine and cucumber sandwiches, his agile body leaning into the slanted deck like a gimbaled compass.

Morgan continued to walk toward the noisy center of the ship where the steerage passengers were kept, absorbing the sounds and sights of the small village ahead of him. A refreshing breeze came tumbling down from the enormous cavity of the mainsail and fanned his cheeks. The steerage area was a world away from the peaceful quarterdeck. He could hear whistling, whining, sobbing, laughing, and the scraping of fiddles ahead of him. As captain, he spent little time in the steerage area, preferring to let Whipple or Pratt see to the passengers' needs and keep order. Due to the attempted mutiny, the number of sailors on board was now seriously depleted. They had been forced to continue sailing the ship shorthanded. All the sailors, including Pratt and Whipple, were needed aloft, leaving the steerage passengers mostly unattended except for the occasional visit by the first mate or Morgan himself. Mostly they wanted more water, bandages for cuts, and information about the weather and the length of the voyage.

Morgan now took stock of what the sailors referred to as their human cargo. All eighty of the steerage passengers were clustered on the deck into a fifty-by-twenty-foot area alongside the farm animals. It was a mixture of men and women. There were entire families as well. His eyes scanned the patchwork quilt of humanity that lay before him. Such a raw display of the human character, he thought to himself, their faces filled with hope and fear, cruelty and humility, ignorance and despair, deception and honesty. A group of them were lined up at the scuttlebutt, tin cans in hand, waiting for their daily allowance of water. Another small group was waiting by the deckside galley for pea soup and hot water from the kettle. They had all been checked for any signs of yellow fever or cholera, as an epidemic on board was Morgan's greatest fear. As with the other packet ships, the *Philadelphia* had no doctor on board, and there was no effective way to stop the spread of an infectious disease. Fire was another great concern.

Another group gathered around the barnlike, pine board structure on deck where the animals were kept, singing and dancing a jig. Some young children were playing hide-and-seek around their parents' legs, the girls shrieking with delight as one of the boys discovered their hiding place. A few young men wearing woolen caps and flat-rimmed hats were playfully gut-punching and shadowboxing one another by the leeward bulwarks. Morgan leaned his elbows on the cabin hatch and, as often happened when he looked at his steerage passengers, felt empathy for these people. Their accommodations below decks consisted of stacked wooden bunk beds and little else. There were no walls for privacy. Men, women, and children were crowded together with only four feet of space to move around. He knew from years of observation that the lucky ones might escape New York's scalawags and scoundrels, but most would be dealing with a hard life in the new country.

Looking over the side at the waves pushing them westward, he was reminded of the distant fields and pastures that sloped down to the Connecticut River. He turned back to the steerage section of the ship, his gaze pausing at an older man seated by the base of the foremast smoking a pipe. He reminded him of his father. He had the same nose and bushy eyebrows, but a gentler expression, rounder face, and flatter cheeks flecked with silver stubbly whiskers. Thoughts of home made him melancholy, and he wondered if he would ever see his parents again. His father would be in his late seventies now. It was hard to believe. He knew he should go home and make amends, no matter how difficult, but he also was aware that he said this every year and never did. He stepped forward to where the old man was seated. The man turned in his direction expectantly, his smoky eyes looking beyond Morgan.

"That you, Sally?" he asked with a hopeful tone in his voice.

Morgan suddenly realized that the man was almost completely blind. He introduced himself, and learned that the old man was traveling with his daughter. His name was James Cleaver, and he was from Kent. He had worked all his life on a farm not far from the village of Plucks Gutter, he said, until his eyesight completely left him about a year ago.

"I am a widderer," he told Morgan. "My wife died some years ago. That was her dream to go to America to start a new life theer'. I am going out with my gal Sally. She's over yonder, gettin' me some soup. She's my oldest. Now that I am stone blind, I depend on her fairly regular."

"How did you manage to save the money?" Morgan asked.

"It took ever so many years," he replied wearily. "With a few shillings put aside each week from our wages. It took ever so long to get enough money. Finally it was done at last."

"Where will you go?"

"Not sure 'bout that," he replied. "Sally says the Lord will direct us. America is the promised land, am I right, Cap'n? Maybe we'll head west."

Morgan remained silent as he looked into the man's milky, unseeing eyes.

"Will we be theer' soon, Cap'n? Some say America only be a short distance from Ireland."

Before Morgan could answer, he heard some shouting and his instincts told him something was wrong.

"Ballenas! Ballenas!"

It was Ochoa high atop the main mast who spotted them first. Soon that cry echoed around the ship.

"Whales! Close alongside! Thar she blows!"

One of the sailors hanging out on the jib boom spotted them directly underneath him.

"Whales, whales, swimming off the starboard bow!"

Morgan rushed back to the quarterdeck area, shouting out orders along the way.

"Sheet in the fore and main courses!" he yelled.

"Aye, aye, sir," said Mr. Nyles.

"Veer off to port to keep well clear!" he shouted to the helmsman. Normally he was not that concerned about encountering whales in the open ocean, but this pod had come extremely close to the ship.

"Tighten up the inner and outer jibs!"

The ship's sails fluttered as the crew pulled on the clewlines and buntlines. The cabin passengers, eager for a diversion, rushed toward the starboard side of the boat, followed by a stampede of steerage passengers doing the same. The whales were breaking the surface just off the starboard bow, fifty-foot giants, effortlessly diving and resurfacing minutes later. The deck was filled with excited exclamations from the passengers as one of the whales surfaced, letting out a geyserlike spout of water. Soon they were close enough to see the encrusted barnacles growing on the gray heads of the larger whales. Cautiously, Morgan ordered the helmsman to head further to port.

It was then he noticed a cluster of men in dark coats and dark cravats gathered around the young woman with the amber eyes. It was apparent that Miss Robinson had found several suitors who were avidly seeking her attention. One was a young American from Philadelphia, Buckley Norris, who had studied medicine in Europe and was returning home. Another was a middle-aged French nobleman, Count Michel d'Aubusson. And the third was Sir Charles Molesworth, an older English businessman known as a successful cotton manufacturer from Liverpool. Morgan's eyes scanned the decks and noticed the girl's mother with her full, long-sleeved day dress surveying the scene like a proud symphony orchestra conductor. From the way Miss Robinson handled this field of suitors, with a magnetic smile and sparkling eyes, he could see she was well acquainted with the whirl of high society dances and the protocol of formal luncheons and teas.

At that moment the lunch bell rang, and like a herd of milking cows answering the farmer's call, the *Philadelphia*'s cabin passengers headed below for their afternoon meal. Morgan turned to leave when he heard a flurry of feet on the deck and several shouts from some of the passengers. He turned toward Mrs. Robinson, who was looking up with shock and disbelief. He followed her gaze, and to his astonishment there was a young, slim figure climbing the ratlines to the top of the lower mainmast. It was Eliza Robinson. She'd pulled her light cotton dress up between her legs and secured it in front, revealing the lower back part of her calves and the edge of her knee-length white drawers to those on the deck, shocking most of the women even as it was pleasing to the men. She squeezed through the lubber's hole and pulled herself up onto the maintop platform. Soon she was looking down and waving at the throng of upturned faces on the quarterdeck. No one was more surprised than the captain himself. Mrs. Robinson began screaming for her daughter to come down immediately. She turned to Captain Morgan, her nostrils flaring.

"Do something, Captain! She'll fall to her death!"

Just then, Eliza spotted dolphins. Hundreds of dolphins with glossy backs surrounded the ship, diving and surfing in the *Philadelphia*'s wake. Some of the steerage passengers yelled out, "Sea pigs, sea pigs!" Most of them had never seen a dolphin before. The sailors on board weren't surprised, as whales and dolphins frequently were sighted together. Eliza looked poised and confident standing on the small platform with one hand on the shrouds. All eyes now turned to watch the frothy spectacle around them as scores of dolphins raced the ship, leaping high in the air before diving under the hull and resurfacing on the other side.

Morgan sent two sailors to help Eliza clamber down the ratlines. When she reached the last few rungs before the deck, Morgan offered his hand to her, but she refused it, squaring her shoulders.

"I will be fine, Captain, but thank you very much. I found the view to be excellent."

In an effort to be conciliatory but firm he said, "Miss Robinson, I must warn you. This is not allowed on board ship. I will not have one of my passengers getting hurt."

"Captain, I want you to know I am not a fragile piece of china to be kept safely in a cupboard."

At that, Eliza walked off with her head held high and her scowling mother marching close behind. Morgan was annoyed he had been spoken to this way in front of all the other cabin passengers. He could tell from the smirks on some of the sailors' faces that his frustrated efforts to control this strong-willed young woman had made him look foolish.

☸

They sailed two hundred miles on June 22, which turned out to be their fastest day. They were now approaching the Grand Banks. Morgan remembered that day for the fine wind, but also for the creamed potato soup, the roast pig, and the apple pie. All afternoon long the quarterdeck was filled with comforting smells of roast pork wafting up the companionway hatch. Scuttles was hard at work in the galley preparing lunch. When the lunch bell rang, Lord Nanvers was in a fine humor at the sight of the feast laid out on large platters atop the saloon's long dining table, everything from stewed chicken to boiled codfish to a fine macaroni pie. He took a seat next to Morgan. Rubbing the palms of his hands together in hungry anticipation, he remarked, "Now there's a sight for a Rubens' painting, eh Captain." He pointed to the large platter where the pig's head had been placed as the centerpiece of the table. "Nothing I like better than the smell of roast pig."

With that, the barrel-chested English lord wasted no time in spearing a large slice of roast pork and serving himself a generous amount of mashed potatoes and corned beef. He then passed the pickled oysters to his lovely young wife. Morgan allowed his gaze to wander over to Lady Nanvers, a striking blonde with large blue eyes whose tall, voluptuous body was a constant distraction for most of the men on board. Her ever-present vapid smile, Morgan suspected, cloaked a far more complex character. She had the look of a woman with a strong appetite for men and had sampled many before she chose the stout-chested English lord. She was his second wife, as his first had died in childbirth, leaving him no heirs. He was hoping that they would have a son soon. Morgan discovered all of this from another of the English passengers who'd confided in him that Lord Nanvers might not have a legal heir, but it was rumored around London that "the old devil considered himself quite the swordsman and had many illegitimate children from several different women, who were not from the gentle class."

Morgan had hardly been listening to Lord Nanvers as he looked in the direction of Eliza Robinson, who was sitting at the other end of the dining room table. Her hair was done up in the same corkscrew curls that made him admire her attractively thin neck. He had to admit she was pretty, not voluptuous like Lady Nanvers, but a head turner nonetheless. He was still miffed that she had disobeyed his orders and undermined his authority, but there had been no further incidents on the passage and he kept finding his eyes shifting in her direction. She had annoyed him at first, but now he found her spirited nature to be strangely alluring.

No sooner had he looked over at her than he noticed her stealing a glance away from her three companions, who were all loudly competing for her attention. Her eyes briefly encountered Morgan's. He looked away, a little flustered and embarrassed that he'd been so bold and blatant in revealing his interest in the young woman. The thin-faced, curly-haired French count was mentioning how much he admired America, quoting something from Lafayette in French. The young American from Philadelphia, Buckley Norris, whose demeanor Morgan found to be both dull and arrogant, was bragging about his illustrious English ancestors, and how he was descended from King Arthur.

Morgan wondered if anyone else had seen him looking at Eliza Robinson. He glanced over at Mrs. Robinson and thought she had noticed when she abruptly looked in his direction, but then she turned away and appeared engrossed in a conversation with the well-to-do Sir Charles Molesworth. Sir Charles was busy mopping his brow with a handkerchief and combing back his thinning gray hair with his hand even as he expounded on the fine quality of American cotton and the efficiency of his cotton mills.

It was at this awkward moment that Lord Nanvers surprised Morgan with an unexpected question. He was pretending to listen, but his attentions were still focused on the girl at the other end of the table.

"Captain, the mutiny was certainly a shock to all of us. How did those men get on your ship? Were they known to you?"

Morgan abruptly turned to Lord Nanvers, explaining that many of his regular sailors had mysteriously taken sick. At that point Lady Nanvers, with her silky, sultry voice, turned her attentions to the young captain. Morgan's eyes couldn't help but notice a sapphire and ruby brooch in the shape of a serpent that strategically spiraled downward so as to draw the eye to her bosom.

"Captain, we are all so appreciative of your bravery. Has this ever happened to you before?"

"I've had my share of fights and deckside brawls, but I never have had to contend with a mutiny, Lady Nanvers."

Lord Nanvers put his fork down and rubbed his chin with his right hand.

"I have always been curious, Captain, about men who decide to take on the sea as their calling. I may have asked you before, but tell me again, what made you decide to become a sailor on the New York to London run?"

Morgan was again surprised at the directness and the personal nature of the English lord's question, but he answered it as truthfully as he could. He explained about his brother Abraham and how his mysterious disappearance at sea years ago was still unsolved. He had always been drawn to the sea, he told Lord and Lady Nanvers, but when his brother went missing, he knew he had to find him. He still had hope, although it was fading, that his brother was alive somewhere.

Loud voices at the other end of the table prevented Lord Nanvers from asking another question. Morgan heard the name of Frances Trollope come up with angry protests from many of the Americans at the table, who cursed that awful English woman who wrote such dreadful lies about the Americans. The English were mostly silent, their faces smug. At that point, Lowery was clearing the plates and bringing in a dessert of apple pie and molasses gingerbread. Soon the feasting began all over again. At the other end of the table, Morgan could hear Eliza Robinson expounding on her views about slavery. She had grown up in Petersburg, Virginia, but her family had moved to New York four or five years ago. Her father was a businessman, originally from Massachusetts, and as a result had never felt at home culturally in the South. She was praising the British for their moral act of freeing the slaves in the West Indies, and explaining to her English and Continental luncheon companions that there were many Americans who favored abolition and she was one of them.

He could just make out her conversation with the French count.

"It is indeed tragic, Mademoiselle Robinson. En France, many of us now realize slavery is like a serpent. Il faut couper la tête. You must cut off its head."

The days passed by with favorable summer weather, ideal for romantic walks on deck, shuffleboard games, and decoy shooting for the gentlemen. Invariably, the sight of Eliza striding along the ship's rail with one or two suitors on either side became the talk of the ship. In the roundhouse, at the head of the companionway where the shipboard gossip gathered like rockweed on a tidal shoreline, all the ladies could talk about was which gentleman the spirited Miss Robinson would pick. Morgan often heard such conversations as he walked by groups of women crocheting and reading. He listened with interest as one woman jokingly commented that the captain should preside over a contest where the three suitors would compete for Eliza's hand.

"What are you suggesting?" another woman asked. "A boxing match or shooting competition?"

"Perhaps Miss Robinson's suitors should be made to rescue her."

Morgan stopped and pretended to monitor the work of the men aloft.

"Who do you think she should choose?" another woman questioned.

"Why, the Frenchman, of course. He has a title, and besides, did you see the way he kisses her hand every night before dinner? He's like a prince."

"I think I would choose Sir Charles. He may be older and a little round around the edges, but he would be a safe choice. My friends in London say he has plenty of money."

All of this romantic drama was also playing out in the main saloon of the *Philadelphia.* There was no doubt this was an elegant setting for romance with soft carpets and comfortable mahogany sofas and cushions. But it was the piano that made Eliza's courtship memorable. She was an accomplished pianist and often showed off her skills after dinner. There were two violinists among the passengers who would accompany her in a series of Mozart piano concertos and Bach sonatas. Morgan remembered how her three suitors applauded the loudest when the trio played from Haydn's *Lo speziale*. The evenings usually ended with much singing around the piano and each of Eliza's three suitors trying to outdo the other with their voices.

When they neared the outer tributaries of the Gulf Stream, the weather was unusually sultry. Captain Morgan ordered Lowery to bring around champagne to all the staterooms with a note saying the journey was almost over and that he predicted fair winds to New York.

One evening after dinner when Morgan was alone by the stern rail, Eliza approached him. She was dressed in a white empire-waisted dress with a gold faux buckle under her bosom. A gauzy black-laced shawl covering her shoulders fluttered in the breeze.

"May I have a word, Captain," she whispered demurely. His voice was locked in momentary paralysis and his skin began to tingle at the sight of her. She had smiled at him one time earlier that day, but then had turned away quickly when her mother approached. He wondered if he had misinterpreted that gesture.

"Well, of course, Miss Robinson," he stammered. "Pray tell, what can I do for you at this late hour?"

He wasn't sure what her intentions were. He knew he should be pleased she was there standing next to him. But he was worried someone might see the two of them together and get the wrong impression. He would rather have been confronted by a black bear than Mrs. Robinson.

"Could we go for a stroll on deck, Captain?"

Morgan nodded. "Of course, it's a fine night with a near full moon."

The sight of the red moon hanging on the horizon made Morgan feel as if he were dreaming. The wind was light and the moonlight, with its strange color, lit up the lines of foam caused by the ship moving through the water. The packet was leaning to leeward, riding the gentle swells as if she were dancing to one of the Mozart sonatas Eliza liked to play. They both discussed the voyage. Eliza spoke of how much she had enjoyed being on the ship. Then there was an awkward silence. She broke the silence by suddenly talking about the dramatic sighting of the whales and the dolphins, and they joked about her clambering up the ratlines. She apologized for her impetuous behavior. Then more silence until she blurted out a question.

"Do you always smile when you speak, Captain?"

Morgan was slightly taken aback at first, but realized this was her manner, direct and straightforward.

"No, only to the cabin passengers," he said with a playful smile.

"Is your pleasant demeanor just an act for all of your passengers then?" she asked, her eyes sparking flirtatiously. "Am I to believe your smile is just a mask? Are you really a mean sea ogre in disguise?"

Morgan laughed.

"Most assuredly, Miss Robinson. Haven't you noticed my growl when I speak to the sailors?"

"Well, I was impressed with the way you handled those mutineers, Captain," she said. She was now looking at him earnestly. Then smiling, she spoke in a more seductive tone, "I certainly saw some of the growling there. I was really quite impressed, Captain."

Morgan didn't say anything. His feelings were in a state of confusion. He wondered what he was doing. He felt her eyes fix upon him as they continued to walk around the deck.

"Do you believe in fate, Captain?" she asked with a coaxing intonation. She stopped by the mainmast shrouds, turning away from him as she looked out at the dark seascape with the moonlight dancing on the surface.

"I suppose I do, Miss Robinson. Although I suppose we all make our own luck to a certain extent."

"And what do you mean by that, Captain?"

"Well, I guess I mean to say that like an observation for longitude and latitude, if it's well calculated, it will all come right in the quotient. If it's poorly calculated, then you can expect the reverse."

"You sound like a properly strict Congregationalist, Captain. You mean to say we get what we deserve?"

"Not exactly, but I suppose there is some truth in that."

Morgan was smiling now. This girl, whom he didn't know until two weeks ago, seemed to have a greater sense of his own nature than he did. He looked directly into her amber eyes even as he tried to gain the upper hand.

"You ask so many questions, Miss Robinson. You act as a magistrate. Have I committed some crime?"

He looked at her with a fixed gaze to which she smiled faintly, lowered her eyelids, and turned her head away again. She stood still and finally said in a gentle voice, "I like your smile, Captain. Would you say you are an optimist?"

He paused. "Yes, I suppose I am. Like any sailor, I know the wind eventually comes right. What about you, Miss Robinson?"

"I prefer to think of myself as a realist, Captain, but I also enjoy taking risks. Life would be so boring if you did not take chances."

Without waiting for him to respond, she continued with her questioning.

"Some women do sail before the mast, don't they, Captain? I think I have heard of women sailors."

Bewildered, Morgan shook his head. "Not that I know of. The forecastle wouldn't be any place for a woman."

He thought of the men stripped naked in the forecastle and the jokes about whoring in London. No, he thought to himself, a woman could not join in with this group, not a gentle woman at any rate. Not a lady. A square-rigger was definitely a man's world.

"What about a captain's wife?" she asked. "Don't packet ship captains take their wives to Europe?"

He seemed taken back by her persistence and a little surprised at her interest in women aboard ships.

"That's different. The sailors don't mind if the captain brings along his wife. Nor do the ship owners. Why, this was before my time as a sailor, but the man who taught me to sail, Captain Henry Champlin, took along his wife, Amelia, on many trips to France and England."

Just then the bell was sounded for a change in the watch and the quiet they had enjoyed was interrupted by men's voices and thudding feet. Eliza used the noise to speak with a sudden urgency.

"Captain," she said with her soft-spoken voice. "I am in a most terrible predicament. I find myself with several suitors on board your ship. I'm quite prepared to marry one of them, but what shall I do? How shall I know which one to choose?"

Morgan's heart sank at this news. He felt dismayed and dispirited, but then a plan began to form in his mind.

"Miss Robinson, what if your suitors all had to compete in some way to show their chivalry as well as their bravery?"

"I would like that very much," she said. "What did you have in mind, Captain?"

"Are you a swimmer, Miss Robinson?"

"I learned to swim as a young girl. Why do you ask?"

He paused for a moment.

"Well, Miss Robinson, we're now approaching the warm Gulf Stream waters. Suppose by accident you should fall overboard? I'd have the quarter boat already lowered ready to pick you up, so there would be no real danger. You can be sure the man who truly loves you will jump in after you."

"Why, Captain, I believe that is a most splendid idea!" she replied, her face lighting up with pleasure. "When will we do this?"

"As soon as the winds have died down," he replied. "Be sure to wear a light cotton dress and your slippers."

Two days later, Morgan woke early to discover a beautiful morning without a ripple in sight. The ship was drifting along under full sail, hardly making any headway in the warm Gulf Stream waters. The ocean was a clear turquoise blue, calm and sedate, the sunlight sparkling on the surface like thousands of tiny diamonds. For most of the morning, the ship cruised along on the glassy water at a speed of less than two knots, the sails limp and lifeless. Fertile seaweed brought from the Gulf Stream filled with tiny fish and shells drifted by like floating islands. The passengers were bored and restless as they sat in the roundhouse and on the quarterdeck chairs. They listened to the sails and the yards backing and filling and complained about the fickle air and the lack of forward progress.

When Eliza came up on deck followed by her suitors, Morgan winked at her, turned his head toward the quarter boat in the midsection of the ship, and motioned for her to move in that direction. Morgan had already brought several of the sailors in on his plan, including Icelander and Whipple, who were stationed at the rope tackle to release the rowboat in seconds. Lowery had distracted the normally attentive Mrs. Robinson in the saloon with some of his New Orleans recipes so she had no idea what her daughter was up to directly above her. Eliza played her part expertly. With her three suitors following closely behind, she enticed them over to the side of the ship by flirtatiously suggesting they should all play a game. Once she reached the bulwarks, she took off her slippers, grabbed the lower shrouds at the base of the mizzenmast, and jumped out onto the chain-wale on the vessel's outer hull, where the deadeyes of the lower rigging were attached.

"Look, I'm standing in the chains!" she cried out with delight. Her light cotton dress made her seem even more youthful than she was. "This is where the leadsman stands to throw his long line into the sea to determine the depth of the water. Who will join me?"

Eliza pretended to hurl the blue pigeon as the sailors called the lead, shouting out a fictional number of fathoms. Her gentlemen friends were laughing at the courage and foolishness of this lively young woman even as they reached out to try to bring her back aboard.

"Mon Dieu!" cried the French count. "Elle est incroyable. Une femme avec le coeur d'un lion." Sir Charles Molesworth and young Mr. Norris, clearly more alarmed at the risks Eliza was taking, were struggling to pull themselves up onto the bulwarks when suddenly she let out a scream.

Her hands slipped their grip on the shrouds and her feet slid off the chain-wale as she fell backward. She hit the water with a loud splash, immediately triggering the sailors high atop the yards to give out the warning.

"Man overboard!"

There was a scramble on deck as passengers and crew rushed to the side to see what had happened. Some sixteen feet below them, Eliza's head with her calico bonnet still attached was bobbing up and down, her arms thrashing about.

"Help! Help! I can't swim!"

This was a lie, of course, but none of her suitors knew that. The French count was the first one to dive in after her, followed closely by the American. Sir Charles Molesworth clearly gave it a few seconds of thought, but seeing his competitors already swimming toward her, he took the plunge, jumping in feet first with a huge splash. Morgan looked down at this scene with great amusement while most of his passengers were caught up in the drama. Even before she jumped, he had signaled Whipple and Icelander to lower the quarter boat to retrieve Eliza. The plan seemed like an excellent idea, but there were some unexpected results.

None of the men, it turned out, were good swimmers. All three were dressed in a full suit of clothes with heavy black boots. Count D'Aubusson was soon floundering and thrashing about in the ocean. Sir Charles wasn't able to make any headway and, alarmingly, he began to sink like a stone. Mr. Norris's arms and kicking feet were whirling about, stirring up the water like a paddlewheel steamer making its way up the Mississippi River.

Icelander and Whipple first picked up Eliza and then rescued the swimmers. Sir Charles was so overweight he had to be held up on the side of the quarter boat until the sailors on deck could lift him up by block and tackle. When they were finally all safely aboard, all three of the dripping trio presented themselves on the ship's deck in front of an equally wet Eliza. She'd lost her bonnet, and her long brown hair, normally neatly drawn back, was now hanging down in stringy strands. Morgan looked into her eyes, but didn't know what to say, so he turned to the three dripping men and gave each of them a pat on the back.

"Miss Robinson should count herself a lucky woman indeed to have so many chivalrous gentlemen ready to jump to rescue her. I don't know which one of you I would commend the most."

Morgan was savoring the moment. The three suitors were a picture of misery, their fine cotton and satin clothes ruined, their boots filled with water. Eliza thanked each of them for their bravery, apologized for her clumsiness, and then quickly left for her cabin, where she stayed throughout the two-hour-long dinner. Later, she sent a message with Lowery to the captain, asking him to escort her on a stroll around the deck.

That night they walked to a shadowy corner on the leeward side of the taffrail where they could have privacy. The deck was quiet, and only a few faint voices could be heard below in the saloon. It was a dark night with not a star in the sky, no gleam on the water, just a fitful puff of wind driving the ship forward. No one had seen them, not even the helmsman.

"What am I to do now, Captain," she cried in despair. "What am I to do?" After sweeping her hand across her face to wipe her tears, she continued, "Those were not the results I expected from your little contest. You have just made things worse than they already were. How will I ever choose?"

"Ah, my dear," replied Morgan with a twinkle in his eye as he reached out to grab the varnished rail. "It is indeed a difficult decision. Those are three brave, chivalrous men, and as I said, if I were you, I don't know which one of your wet suitors I would choose. They all passed the test, and you can't marry all three."

Eliza looked at him with a repugnant stare as she angrily shook her head. She drew her shawl closely around her shoulders.

"You are a cruel man, Captain. You are mocking me. I think it is time for you to leave me in my misery."

At this point, he was having a hard time restraining his laughter at the vision of the three sodden suitors on deck.

"Each of your gentlemen friends has his respective merits, but, as I seriously ponder your dilemma, I think, if you truly want a sensible husband, why I think I would pick the dry one."

His normally deadpan face broke out in a hopeful but playful smile. Eliza stared at him in surprise, puzzled at first by this reference to the "dry one," but as his words slowly sunk in she realized the portent of what he was saying. Her frown disappeared and she smiled coquettishly.

"Why, Captain Morgan," she replied, "may I be so bold to ask if the dry one might be the master of the packet ship *Philadelphia*?"

His face became flushed at this direct question. Even in the black stillness that surrounded them, she seemed to sense his vulnerability. Whether by instinct or guesswork, she seemed to have the answer she had hoped for, and she edged closer to him.

"Well then, I think I will take the dry one," she said with a beaming smile. "I've always wanted a sensible husband."

She was now close enough that he could hear her breathing and smell the lavender in her hair. She seemed more desirable than ever before, a creature so determined and headstrong, yet so delicate and small. He looked down at this tiny powerhouse of a young woman with her finely shaped nose and high cheekbones. In the darkness of the night, he couldn't see well, but he could sense her smile. All caution seemed to abandon him. He placed his fingers on her still-wet hair, gently stroking it, and allowed his hand to fall down the back of her neck to her shoulders. Their faces grew closer and Morgan's hands moved lower down to her back as he pulled her to him. His eyes locked with hers. She moved her head upward and closed her eyes as Morgan pressed his lips against hers. She reciprocated, wrapping her arms around his neck and pulling him closer to her.

PART VII

The institution exists, perhaps, in its least repulsive and most mitigated form in such a town as this; but it is slavery; and though I was, with respect to it, an innocent man, its presence filled me with a sense of shame and self-reproach.

—Charles Dickens (commenting about slavery in Baltimore, Maryland), *American Notes*

17

Morgan turned away from the ship's busy deck where the crew was securing lines and looked down at the faces lined up on the South Street docks below him. The ship had just arrived after more than four weeks at sea. There was a phalanx of horse-drawn cabbies and hotel brokers lined up, a crush of porters and newsmen eager for business and information from the packet's passengers. The hum of voices, laughter, shouting, and yelling drifted up to the ship's deck. A blend of sausage, onions, and spices wafted up from one of the food vendors on the wharf assaulting Morgan's nose and whetting his appetite for shore leave. The baggage wagons drawn by mules were already being loaded. A newsboy was hawking the latest sensationalist headlines about the second day of rioting underway in New York. "Read all about it! Mobs target homes of abolitionists!"

The riots were supposedly triggered by an anti-American remark from an Englishman by the name of George Farren, the stage manager of the Bowery Theater. He was known to be an outspoken abolitionist and had no love for Americans. Farren was quoted as publicly saying that Americans were "a damn set of jackasses and fit to be gulled." Mobs were angered by that remark, and turned their rage on many of the nearby antislavery churches. They were dunking white abolitionists in hogsheads of black ink and targeting anyone of color. They'd stormed the Bowery Theater and demanded an apology from Farren.

Morgan handed the newspaper to Lowery and said to his steward, "Better stay aboard, Mr. Lowery. With this thuggery going on you're a good deal safer in the London docklands than you are here in New York."

Lowery excitedly showed the newspaper to Scuttles and another colored sailor, Ben Sheets, who had recently signed on board as a foredeck sailor. Morgan watched Lowery run off clutching the newspaper tightly in his hand. In London, he'd seen his steward dressed in a fancy suit with a good-looking English woman holding on to his arm, his head held high. This wasn't possible in New York. If he tried to do that here, he would have been beaten by a mob.

As the passengers lined up at the gangway ready to disembark, Morgan stood ready to shake their hands. Lord Nanvers was dressed in a long-skirted coat with an eye-catching red vest. He escorted the swaying Lady Nanvers to the gangway, where he thanked Morgan for the safe voyage, assuring him that they would travel aboard the *Philadelphia* again. They were off to Baltimore, he said, to attend to some business and see some of the fine, fast clippers being built there. When the time came for Eliza and her mother to leave the ship, Morgan knew all was not well. He and Eliza had been discreet by staying apart from each other during the last few days of the voyage, exchanging warm glances but little else. Eliza had kept her suitors at arm's length by spending more time with her mother on deck and in their cabin. He'd assumed she'd told her mother about their romance and that Mrs. Robinson would approve. After all, he was a packet ship captain with a London liner and Eliza's mother had seemed to enjoy his company.

Instead, Mrs. Robinson, stern-faced and unsmiling, had studiously avoided his glance as she stepped off the ship onto the busy Pine Street wharf, holding Eliza's hand tightly. Eliza had gazed back at him with a panicked look as she and her mother disappeared into the crowded docks. Morgan watched from the top of the gangway as mobs of people swallowed them like a swarming hive of bees. He wondered what could have happened to make Mrs. Robinson so unfriendly. They had shared warm recollections about Connecticut as he had discovered late in the voyage that she had grown up in the town of Durham, twenty miles to the west of Lyme. He told himself that maybe she was just eager to get on land after the long passage.

Taking a wife had never seemed practical to him. He was more connected to the sea than the land. He knew he would be spending most of his life on board a ship. But he had been lonely and Eliza seemed a perfect match. She loved the ocean and she was fearless. Even the mutiny did not appear to have fazed her. He was certain this young woman had captured his heart. When he looked at her, he forgot where he was. He couldn't stop hearing her feisty voice, her infectious laugh, so willful and irreverent, the smell of lavender in her hair, her bare neck, her tiny hands in his grasp, so warm, so real. All of that had awakened his sensations. Hours after she and her mother left the ship, Eliza's sparkling, amber-colored eyes were still with him, as was the memory of the light touch of her lips. The very next day a lovesick Morgan sent her a letter, professing his devotion to her, asking when they could see each other again. Each morning for the next few days, he waited shipside for the mailman to deliver a reply, but none came. He began to despair. At first he was puzzled, as she had seemed genuinely drawn to him. Then he fell into a much darker mood. He began to wonder if she had deceived him like Laura. He cursed himself for being so gullible. He was such a fool. Perhaps she had simply used him to make one of her other suitors jealous? He began to suspect that all women were naturally skilled at the art of deceiving men. His mood grew darker.

Finally, three days later, a small, sealed letter in her handwriting came to him. He opened it with trepidation, his hands shaking. His heart sank as he read the blunt words telling him she wasn't sure that she loved him, but then a few lines later he found reason for hope.

> *By not responding promptly to your affectionate letter, my dear Captain, you may have thought I have forgotten you entirely. I can assure you that is not the case. Perhaps you have even questioned my sincerity? Let me affirm to you it is entirely impossible for my heart to forget our evening embrace on the deck of the Philadelphia.*

She asked him to meet her at the Battery the next day. She would find a way to free herself from her mother.

When he saw her seated on a bench looking out at the anchored ships off the Battery, she was wearing the same white empire-waisted dress she'd had on that evening on the ship's deck, the same black Spanish lace draped across her shoulders. Her hair was drawn back underneath a broad-rimmed bonnet. He grabbed her hands and looked at her reassuringly. They embraced and kissed, but he knew something was wrong. Her shoulders were tense, her face downcast, and the edges of her eyes were red. Her hands were clutching a moist handkerchief. He quickly realized he was sailing into stronger headwinds than he had anticipated. Eliza didn't know what to do. She told him how her mother had approached her on the ship with news that Sir Charles was so taken with her that he wanted to ask for her hand in marriage. Her mother was overjoyed, bubbling with excitement. She'd burst into Eliza's stateroom and blurted out the news that she had won over the old Englishman. Eliza became distraught, saying she wouldn't have him. Her mother couldn't understand why her daughter wasn't glowing about this enviable catch.

"Who is it?" she had asked breathlessly. "Is it that gracious, delightful French count? Is it that nice young man from Philadelphia?"

"None of the above, Mother. It's someone else. I love someone else."

"Who is it?" She paused and then her nostrils began to flare. "It's not . . ." She stopped midsentence. "No, it can't be. You haven't fallen for that ship captain, have you? I saw you looking at him."

Eliza's silence gave her feelings away. Her mother's face became red as she looked at her daughter with a pained expression.

"What did that ship captain do? He didn't kiss you, did he?"

"How can you say that? No, Mother."

"Tell me the truth, Eliza."

"We just walked on the deck, that's all."

"How could you, Eliza? A ship captain? There's nothing worse for any woman than a sailor. You should know that and certainly he should have spared you this. With marriage you need to be practical, dear. Consider the lives of these sailormen. They're coarse men who eventually end up at the other end of a bottle. Human driftwood, they call them, worthy of no shore. Who knows how many wicked girls that man has had in his life? Who knows how many he has right here in New York? Be sensible, Eliza."

The explosive fireworks had only continued at the Robinson home on Houston Street, with her father threatening to cut her off from any inheritance. Samuel Robinson was a self-made man who was a successful shoe and boot merchant. Now in New York, he had formed a new partnership under the name of Robinson & Olds. He was wealthy, but not excessively so. Most of his money was tied up in his growing company. Eliza was the youngest and the only one of his four daughters not yet married. He was insisting she marry Sir Charles and wanted her to commit to the English gentleman as soon as possible. Sir Charles had even paid him a visit to make his case and look favorably upon his suit. Eliza would have none of it. She said she would rather live on the street than marry that old toad of an Englishman with his fat stomach and balding head.

"He's dull as a butter knife and all he wants to talk about is his cotton mills and old English castles. I will marry Captain Morgan," Eliza had replied defiantly. "He is witty and smart and adventurous, unlike the stodgy, lecherous Sir Charles whom you are so keen about."

"Please reconsider, dear," her mother had said solicitously, even though her glowering eyes revealed a considerably less tolerant frame of mind.

Eliza just shook her head.

"Why are you so mule headed about this?" her mother demanded, mystified by her daughter's stubbornness. "Can't you see that a marriage with Sir Charles is in your best interest? A British husband with a title is the best way to win social acceptability. A duke or a marquis would be a better catch followed by an earl or a viscount naturally, but Sir Charles has a significant estate. Why can't you be reasonable?"

Her father had been emphatic and told Eliza that he had assured Sir Charles that he could sway her mind, but the standoff had continued for days with Eliza stubbornly refusing to listen to her parents' pleas. They would have locked her up if they knew she was meeting him.

"So what do I do, Captain?"

The two of them were walking on the well-groomed pathways by the Battery alongside elegantly dressed gentlemen escorting their lady friends or wives with their colorful bonnets. Just off the breakwater, a tugboat steamed out to one of the incoming three-masted ships. Morgan had listened quietly throughout but remained silent, causing Eliza to continue on in a defeated whimper.

"Sir Charles has been invited over for tea the day after tomorrow and my mother says he is going to make his formal proposal."

A steam whistle went off from the tug as it now began pulling the incoming square-rigger into port. Sailors were yelling off in the distance. Morgan tried to be as nonchalant as he could.

"As every sailor knows, when a storm's threatening it's always best to shorten sail and be prepared. I was going to wait, but given the circumstances I could, with your permission, talk to your father sooner than Sir Charles? Would you allow me to do that?" he asked with a hopeful smile.

That same day, Morgan penned a letter to Eliza's father. Eliza had told him her father was very knowledgeable with accounting and financial matters. She described him as ambitious, hardworking, a risk taker, who just recently had decided to invest a good portion of his money into building a new boot and shoe factory on Water Street. He was an optimist, she said, who tended to stress the positive. Morgan knew the Robinsons objected to him because he was a sailor. Even worse, he didn't have a place for her to live. As he wrote the letter, he thought of his own father, which helped him decide what to say. He described how he already owned a one-eighth share of the *Philadelphia* and how he wanted to invest in ownership shares in some of the other Black X ships. He talked about the growing trade between England and America. He explained his own plan, that the Black X Line would be reaping the benefits of transatlantic commerce. He spoke of his family and his part in his brother's purchase of farmland overlooking the Connecticut River. He was careful not to mention he hadn't ever seen the land, much less returned home in all the years he'd been away at sea. He decided not to mention the relatively sparse boarding house accommodations he rented just off Cherry Street. In conclusion, he wrote, he would greatly appreciate Mr. Robinson's advice on matters of business. He never once mentioned Eliza, knowing full well that Mr. Robinson was quite aware of the real reason he was writing.

The next day he waited all day at the ship, but no message arrived. He knew Sir Charles was scheduled to come for tea at the Robinson's house the following day, so he'd made up his mind he would go, message or no message. In the morning, he dressed in his best business attire, the long-skirted blue coat and matching pants, shiny black boots, a silk cravat, and his top hat. He walked up to the front door of the Robinsons' brownstone at 219 Houston Street, where he was met by an expressionless butler. He gave his name, fully anticipating that he would be turned away. He already had plans to barge in and demand a hearing with Mr. Robinson. To his surprise, the butler seemed to have been expecting him. He was escorted through the house with its walnut, wainscoted walls to Mr. Robinson's well-appointed library. There he was asked to wait outside.

After several minutes, a well-dressed man of medium height with a fine, chiseled face, neatly combed, thinning hair, and well-trimmed silver whiskers emerged from the library. He had the same prominent chin and rigid nose as Eliza, only longer. Morgan guessed he was in his late forties or early fifties. His gaze under prominent silver eyebrows was penetrating and direct, his manner taciturn and morose. He looked at Morgan with a slight note of disdain, shook his hand, and ushered him into the library toward an amply cushioned easy chair. Morgan felt like he was a cabin boy once again, being dressed down by one of the ship's officers. He remembered being reprimanded by Captain Champlin, and the sight of the angry face of his own father flashed before him. Robinson had a steely stare that was unrelenting and unsympathetic.

"I read your letter, Captain Morgan, with some interest."

"Yes, sir. Thank you, sir," Morgan managed to stammer.

"You spoke of discussing business matters. What did you have in mind?"

The man poured out a glass of sherry and handed it to Morgan.

"Well, sir, business is just one of the topics that I wanted to discuss."

The man's bushy eyebrows arched up.

"Is that so?" he replied. "Pray tell, Captain, what else did you have in mind?"

Morgan's hands were sweating and he felt short of breath. He gulped, and nervously took a sip of sherry, deciding to sail directly into the storm.

"Yes, sir," he stammered. He took a deep breath. "Mr. Robinson, I am in love with your daughter. I believe Eliza shares those same sentiments. With utmost respect and humility, I would like to ask you for her hand in marriage."

Morgan looked at Mr. Robinson with a weak smile. There was no welcoming gesture returned from the older man. Samuel Robinson got up from his chair, holding his cane, his face expressionless, and turned his back. Morgan thought he was going to leave the room, but then he stooped to pull two cigars out of a mahogany humidor.

"Will you have a cigar, Captain?" he asked in a businesslike tone as he turned back in Morgan's direction.

"Why, thank you, Mr. Robinson," Morgan responded, surprised.

"Tell me about the London Line, Captain. Is it a good business?"

Morgan explained that the Black X Line and the Red Swallowtail Line, both servicing the London–New York route, were still running ships in conjunction with each other. They were separate companies, but together they provided a fleet of ten ships traveling to London and there were future plans for an even bigger fleet.

"How much money do you make in a year, Captain?" Eliza's father asked brusquely.

Morgan gripped the wooden armrest, "With this new ship of mine I should make over five thousand dollars a year."

"And how much does your ship make for the company, Captain?"

Morgan paused as he did some quick arithmetic in his head.

"Mr. Robinson, I reckon the *Philadelphia* makes around twenty thousand dollars a year with the freight and steerage passengers she carries. With the mail, another one thousand dollars. Of course, the captain keeps most of whatever is received from carrying the mail. The cabin passengers, why that's another nine thousand dollars. The captain gets about twenty-five percent of that. Adding up freight, steerage passengers, and cabin passengers, I calculate Mr. Griswold and the shipping line make twenty five thousand dollars a year off the *Philadelphia*, give or take a few thousand."

"What about the ship's expenses?"

By now, Morgan sensed he was being tested for his business skills by a schoolmaster who was not inclined to give him a good grade.

"The firm has to pay about four thousand dollars for wages, I figure, two thousand five hundred dollars for insurance, another few thousand for food, repairs, port charges. Probably adds up to about ten thousand dollars of costs, so I suppose the owners are making upward of ten thousand dollars on each ship."

"Each year?" Mr. Robinson asked incredulously. "That's a good return. That means your share is one-eighth of that?"

"Yes sir. That would be a good estimation. Of course, that's over and above what I make as ship captain."

Mr. Robinson was silent, so Morgan continued to speak.

"As I wrote to you in my letter, this is why I hope to become a part owner of several of the ships, sir. Investing in packet ships is better than gold. Be assured, Mr. Robinson, I intend to provide well for your daughter."

Robinson stroked his chin for a moment and took a long satisfactory pull on his cigar. He watched the plumes of smoke drift upward to the high ceilings. The uplifted eyebrows and the momentary silence revealed his doubts.

"I understand there is opportunity there, Captain, but tell me, exactly how will you take care of my daughter? How can my daughter possibly look forward to a good life as the wife of a shipmaster? Where will you live, other than your ship, of course?"

To calm his nerves, Morgan puffed on his cigar, and then began to talk about how the dangers of a life at sea were greatly exaggerated. He told Mr. Robinson how Eliza would come to know the beauty of Old England, and the many attractions of London. Morgan mentioned how she would be meeting important people on his ship from both sides of the Atlantic. Then he mentioned the case of Henry Champlin's wife, Amelia, who had accompanied him on many trips across the Atlantic, and how her health had been better at sea than it was on shore.

It may have been Morgan's meeting with Samuel Robinson, or it may have been the sight of their young, headstrong daughter laughing and joking with the captain, holding his arm as she walked light as a feather through the front door of their brownstone, that changed their minds. Whatever it was, the Robinsons gave up trying to sway their stubborn youngest daughter away from what they considered to be a questionable marriage. She had steadfastly refused to marry the Englishman, and they knew her well enough to know that she would not change her mind. It was not what they had hoped for by any means. Days later, the couple reluctantly gave their blessings to the marriage.

Eliza was barely eighteen when she and Elisha Ely Morgan were married at Trinity Church in Manhattan on July 28. It was a simple service with only Eliza's parents and a few friends of the Robinson family there.

Morgan hadn't had time to contact his brother or notify his parents before the wedding. He wrote his brother a quick note before boarding the *Philadelphia*, promising that he and his new bride would come visit over Thanksgiving. They were married at six in the morning because Morgan had to ready the ship for departure that same day. It had all happened rather suddenly, with the final decision coming just a day before the wedding. The newly married couple had rushed from the altar to South Street, where Morgan presented his new bride to the astonished sailors of the ship. He had Mr. Nyles muster the crew and announce to them that the *Philadelphia* would now have the shipmaster's wife on board, and they were to behave with better manners. One of the men picked up a fiddle, another a banjo, and they were soon playing a popular tune at the time called "Take Your Time, Miss Lucy," about a young woman pleading with her father to let her have a beau.

> Indeed my dear you're joking
> You're still too young to know;
> So take your time, Miss Lucy
> Miss Lucy, Lucy oh.

The entire crew was soon clapping their hands and stomping their feet on the deck as they all got into the spirit of the occasion. Hours later, with the passengers all aboard, the *Philadelphia* was towed out of the East River by a small steamer. Morgan turned to look at Eliza's beaming face. Her eyes were sparkling. She had taken off her bonnet and was tilting her face up toward the sun and the sails. The crew, still in high spirits, sang a saltier song as they began hauling on the halyards. The Verrazano Narrows was busy as usual with all types of ships, from incoming sailing packets to shapely coastal schooners under full sail, carving their way into New York harbor. Among the cabin passengers aboard were two Catholic priests from Ireland, Father Flannigan and Father O'Toole. They had come to New York to tend to the growing population of Irish immigrants. Morgan was comforted in having two men of the cloth on board because as he told Eliza, you never know when you might need the power of prayer. By midafternoon, the open ocean lay ahead, the Sandy Hook lighthouse just astern.

"Wind come to our port aft, Captain," reported the first mate, Mr. Nyles.

"We're under topsails, topgallant sails, and a forecourse."

With the wind freshening from the northwest, Morgan called for the full entourage of sails to be raised.

"No humbugging men, haul away!" shouted Mr. Nyles.

Morgan turned to Icelander, who was at the helm.

"Steer due east and keep the buoy off the weather side."

That night after dinner, as Lowery was passing around generous portions of shoofly pie for dessert, Eliza found good company with some of the other passengers. The melodious strains of the ship's piano accompanied by a cello and a violin soon filled the saloon. Eliza and the two other musicians were playing some of Chopin's new waltzes. Two young couples began waltzing in the main saloon while the others played cards. They were laughing as they tried to keep their balance on the moving dance floor. The ship gently swayed back and forth, obligingly pushing the dancing partners closer together. Two spinsters from Philadelphia, along with one of the Irish priests, accosted Morgan to say how distressed they were because he was allowing such vulgar and sinful dancing music to be played on his ship.

But all eyes in the saloon were riveted on the dancers and the musicians, and no one made a move to stop the revelry. Soon another couple began waltzing. The three pairs of dancers were now twirling in the saloon, clutching their partners tightly, their faces flushed with the mixture of the dancing and generous helpings from the punch bowl.

"A shocking display," one woman said loudly enough for Morgan to hear. "Why, just look at that young couple. The way he's holding her. It's coarse."

"This younger generation has no morals," declared another woman named Eleanor Howell. "What do you think of these new waltzes, Captain Morgan? Don't you think they should be banned?"

"Can't say I know the answer to that question, Mrs. Howell," Morgan replied cautiously. "I'm just a seafaring man, you know."

The older woman glowered at him.

18

Seven days later, the seas started to build and the skies darkened, a sure sign of a storm approaching. Morgan had charted a more southerly course than normal because of the danger of icebergs to the north, a threat even in July. From his last reading he calculated they were about six hundred miles southeast of the eastern tip of Newfoundland. Morgan knew they were in for a blow because the previous morning he'd seen the entire eastern sky turn a brilliant red, a warning for all sailors to expect unsettled weather. Then this morning he noticed the barometer had plummeted, losing more than three quarters of an inch of mercury. It was a troubling sign.

Eight bells struck as he walked up the companionway, marking the end of the early morning watch. With the weather worsening, he was pleased to see that Icelander would be taking over at the helm. Ominously he spotted a pair of dark brown storm petrels riding the wind alongside the ship. As he watched these birds with their splashes of white in their tail feathers weave and glide overhead, his mind flashed back to Old Jeremiah Watkins and his many superstitions. The old sailor had believed storm petrels not only signaled bad weather ahead, but carried the souls of drowned sailors. Morgan shook his head as he put that dark thought out of his mind. He turned toward some of the cabin passengers who had taken shelter in the roundhouse on the quarterdeck. The two priests dressed in long black gowns and hats with rims fingered their rosary beads and said their Hail Marys as they watched the ship crash into one wave after another. Morgan told them to go below.

"No need to worry as long as the seamen are cursing," he told Father O'Toole and Father Flannigan. "As long as you hear these men saying horrible blasphemous things, you need not apprehend any danger, but if you suddenly hear silence, then you may need to start praying."

Morgan was anxious to get the two nervous men of the cloth safely down below and out of the way. He made sure Mr. Lowery gave all the passengers generous amounts of claret along with lemons. Sucking lemons and ginger lozenges was a favorite remedy of Lowery's for seasickness. The cabin's saloon was filled with pallid faces looking for reassurance. With the ship pitching and heaving, Lowery, dressed in a checked shirt and white apron, was holding a crystal carafe of claret and a small tray of glasses. His head and shoulders were extended forward, his legs stretching far behind him. Morgan continued to be amazed at the man's balance and dexterity. As far as he could see, not a drop of claret had been spilled.

With winds now gusting over thirty knots, he gave the order to reef topsails. Lowery brought him some hot coffee, half of which spilled out of the cup before he could drink any of it. Eliza wanted to stay up topsides, but he told her she must go below with the other passengers.

"I don't see why I have to go below," she said with a sullen face.

"Believe me, Eliza, it would be better. It will be safer below."

"I want to be with you," she pleaded. "This is our honeymoon."

"I know and I am sorry, but I don't control the wind and the waves and they're threatening to produce quite a blow."

He watched as she cautiously walked toward the companionway, holding on to some of the lines to avoid falling and stumbling. He was quickly learning that his young, headstrong wife wanted to be involved in running the ship. The past few days had been pleasant ones with fair wind and calm seas. He'd been teaching her how to chart their course by using the heavy brass sextant to shoot the sun and take the noon reading.

They had laughed a great deal. He had been pleasantly surprised at the reaction aboard ship to Eliza in these first few days. Despite their rough appearance and crude manners, most of the sailors tipped their hats and wished her a good mornin' or a good day when they passed her on the quarterdeck. They called her the captain's missus. Her bustling petticoats and plucky nature must have triggered some hidden memory of good manners. Icelander had told him jokingly that "she'd be the one wearing the breeches" pretty soon.

With the storm coming on, Mr. Whipple began to secure the deadlights in the upper stern ports and batten down heavy canvas tarps over the skylights. At noon, Morgan gave the order to furl the mizzen topsails. Hours later, he sent two of the younger men aloft to bring down the fore royal and main royal yards. He left the forestaysail and one of the jibs out on the jib boom to keep the ship balanced. Down below, he could hear the sound of dishes crashing as they fell to the cabin floor. There was also a cry running through the cabin that the ship was sinking. His face wet with salt water and oilskins glistening, he poked his head down the companionway to assure his passengers there was no need for any worry. He looked for Eliza to comfort her, but he couldn't spot her. Lowery was busy picking up the broken dishes from the cabin floor as they slid from one end of the saloon to the other. Some of the men were still attempting to play card games like whist and vingt-et-un under a thick, white layer of cigar smoke that hovered over their table. Morgan finally caught a glimpse of Eliza, who was clutching one of the poles. She avoided his glance. He could see that she was staring at the swinging lanterns with great misgiving.

One of the black-robed priests looked up at him as his hand clutched the crucifix dangling from his neck. It was the older Father Flannigan.

"Are your men still swearing, Captain?"

"Yes, Father, the men are still saying terrible things, the Devil's own blasphemy up topside."

"Then the Lord be praised for it," replied a clearly relieved Father Flannigan. "We are still safe."

Soon the *Philadelphia* was battling into the midst of a gale with huge rolling seas looming up ahead of her. Sheets of rain were now lashing the ship's deck, adding to the torrents of seawater sweeping across the quarterdeck. Morgan was glad they had filled the steerage compartment with a full cargo of mahogany clock cases and boxes and crates of cheese instead of passengers on this passage. Still the ship was heavily loaded. In the lower hold they carried four hundred barrels of flour, three hundred barrels of potash, fifteen bales of wool, and fifty barrels of turpentine. Because of all that cargo, the ship was riding low in the water. Long streams of spray came off the crests of the waves, and Morgan decided to prepare for even stronger winds by setting up additional stays and preventer braces to reinforce the masts and the yards, particularly the topmasts.

The men on watch, led by Mr. Pratt, struggled up the rigging, the wind flattening them against the shrouds and the ratlines as they tried to fasten and tighten the tangled ropes. To further strengthen the masts, Morgan ordered them to catharpin the shrouds by means of capstan bars lashed just below the futtock shrouds. These were then tightened by means of blocks on lines passed through bars placed on the opposite end of the ship.

"Keep tightening, Mr. Pratt. Pull on those lines and make 'em fast. We'll need all the support we can. Looks like this is one of them hurricanes from the West Indies."

Rain was slicing down even as the winds accelerated and the skies turned black. Jagged branches of lightning could be seen in the distance. As the storm intensified in strength, the ship began to steer wildly with the rudder slamming to one side. Morgan gave the order for more men to go aloft, this time to furl almost all the sails. He yelled out to Icelander at the helm to dig his knees into the wheel box and hang on.

"Starboard! Starboard! Meet her quick! Steady! Now. Port, a spoke, port!"

"Fall off! Fall off!"

The ship was riding headfirst into a rolling wall of waves, climbing upward and upward. She soared up swiftly like a bird taking flight and then, on the downward slope, dove into another mountainous wave, the water sweeping across the decks. Morgan watched as a big roller caught the bow under the weather side and the ship lurched to leeward. It looked like she was toppling over to one side. One of the lifeboats had broken loose, crashing against the deckhouse, almost hitting Ochoa, before being swept overboard. Some of the sailors in the foredeck were knocked off their feet and were slipping to leeward, trying to clutch on to anything as they slid toward the leeward bulwarks.

Morgan struggled to stand up as he held on to the windward stays with both hands. He could feel the ship trembling under the weight of the seas toppling on the deck. The tips of the windward yardarms were now pointed upward and the tall masts were leaning over to one side, reaching out to the horizon. The barely visible Mr. Nyles standing amidships, his oilskins streaming with water, yelled something, but Morgan couldn't hear him over the terrific howl of the wind, the straining of canvas, and the rattling of blocks.

He turned to Icelander, "What did Mr. Nyles shout?"

"I believe he wants you to bear off!"

Icelander's face was now a pale blue color. Morgan pulled out a cigar and began rolling it back and forth in his mouth to calm his nerves. He ordered Rasmussen to alter their course in the direction the seas wanted to take the ship. Icelander swung the spokes of the big wheel over so the waves were lifting the *Philadelphia* from the stern and propelling her forward. The ship now moved like a wide-beamed toboggan speeding downhill over broken terrain. Their new course was southeasterly, somewhere to the south of the Azores in the direction of North Africa. It was all open ocean for hundreds of miles. The waves were rising up and cresting behind them now. The ship steadied herself, but the new danger lay in being swamped by a fast-moving wave looming up unseen over the ship's stern. He turned to the man on watch on the weather side of the poop deck and told him to hold on to the mizzen rigging and look out for pursuing seas.

Then he shouted a warning to Icelander, who was standing rigidly still, his arms moving crosswise to check and then urge the wheel's rapidly moving spokes.

"Watch yerself, Rasmussen. Don't get us pooped. We're heavy loaded with freight like a sand barge. We only have about eight feet of freeboard, and I don't want to lose you to a wall of water."

"Aye, aye, Captain."

As night fell, flashes of lightning revealed the chaotic scene. Crashing seas swept across the deck, lifting anything and everything not tied down. Morgan stood by the helm and looked ahead at the whole battered length of his ship as she propelled herself forward in a rolling rush. He could see the cabin below decks was now in total blackness and guessed that all the hanging lanterns were shattered. Breaking seas were thudding and whacking the topsides of the ship like a battering ram hitting a castle's thick doors.

He wondered what Eliza was doing. He gulped at this thought. There was nothing he could do to help her. It was all he could do to hold on and try to help Icelander steer a course. He imagined her huddled below clutching one of the iron supports, the chairs upturned, broken plates all over the cabin floor. He hoped Lowery was keeping a clear head.

The *Philadelphia* was now sailing into the darkness with just two sails, the reefed main topsail in the center of the boat and one small jib on the ship's bowsprit. Fearful sailors in their boots and oilskins clambered up the rigging to escape being swept away by immense volumes of water sweeping the decks. Others crouched by the windward rigging amidships staring upward at the swaying masts above them. Morgan held on to the wheelhouse and yelled out to Mr. Nyles to tighten the lines between the shrouds, but even he couldn't hear his own voice. Another bolt of lightning illuminated the sky. Morgan turned his face streaming with water to windward and nervously looked at a big, foaming wave climbing and rising high up over the ship's stern. It seemed at any moment the ocean would swallow the ship and all who were aboard.

The next morning the winds and the rain had slackened, but the ship was still in the midst of the gale, riding enormous waves, and flying along at thirteen knots. Morgan knew the sun had risen because the sky had turned a lighter shade of shadowy gray. He could see the drained faces of the sailors around him, ragged and beaten men looking back at him with bloodshot, sleepless eyes. He wondered if he looked like them. He felt numb and cold. He was soaked through and shaking. They had all gone without sleep or food for twenty-four hours. Many of the men were gripping rails for support. Others had lashed themselves to the rigging. They were silent, tight-lipped, awe-stricken by the ocean's power. He knew all of them dreaded any call by the mates to go high up into the yards with the masts swaying back and forth from horizon to horizon. Mr. Nyles reported to him that the jib boom on the bowsprit had broken off overnight, ripping the jib to shreds. Morgan nodded. It could have been much worse. The wind and rain had also carried away one of the yards on the foremast. Otherwise, the ship appeared to be sound. No one had been lost either off the deck or from the yard, and they had avoided a demasting.

It was shortly after Nyles gave him that largely positive report that the sailor on watch yelled out a warning. Wild, startled eyes turned toward the stern of the ship in stunned disbelief as a dark green wall of water rose up behind them like a giant curtain blocking out the light. "Grab hold and look out for yourselves," Morgan yelled. Moments later, a towering wave some thirty feet high crashed over the stern with a loud boom and swamped the boat. Morgan felt his feet give way as he fell with a bang on the deck, the water sweeping him toward the leeward bulwarks on the port side. He felt himself being carried by the rush of water. The heavy weight of tons of water plunged the ship downward to a wrenching stop. The three masts whipped back and forth, threatening to snap and break off. Morgan's head was submerged. He was powerless to help himself. He felt sure that he was going to be swept out to sea.

The ship lurched to starboard and amazingly he found himself washed backwards onto the ship's deck. He got up and struggled back toward the wheelhouse, his hands grabbing ropes to pull himself up the slanted deck. He fell again as another wave of water swept over the ship, He would have slid overboard, but someone grabbed him and helped him up. Just as he reached the poop deck, he felt something give beneath him around the sternpost. The next thing he heard was a shout from below that water was coming in. It wasn't just the normal weeping. Water was actually coming through the timbers. Leaks had sprung up everywhere, and streams of water shot into the lower cargo hold, overflowing the bilge of the ship.

With the wind screeching through the bare rigging and much confusion on deck, Morgan yelled at the first mate to start jettisoning some of the cargo to lighten the ship aft. It was important to find out where the ship was leaking. He ordered all of the remaining canvas taken down. The ship was now scudding along under bare poles carried along by fifty knot winds and a huge following sea. All this time the ship was taking in more and more water.

Morgan shouted, "All hands! Man the pumps on deck! Buckets below!"

Through it all, Icelander remained at the wheel, his knees forced in between the spokes, his feet braced in the wheel box, his thin lips twitching. Morgan went down below to warn the passengers about the leak, many of whom were lying in their staterooms, nauseated in their rolling berths and moaning in misery. He went looking for Eliza. He could hear the water splashing. The force of the wall of water had poured through the companionway into the main saloon. Everything inside had tumbled from one end of the cabin to the other. Lowery and Scuttles were huddled in a heap on the cabin sole in the galley clutching one of the fastened legs of the tables, their teeth chattering. The two Irish priests were now shaking convulsively and down on their knees praying for merciful forgiveness.

"Your men should pray with us, Captain."

Morgan ignored their entreaties and walked by quickly.

"Join us as we ask the Lord for mercy, Captain."

Morgan turned back to the two men of the cloth, and uncharacteristically addressed them in a curt manner.

"You pray, Fathers. The rest of us will pump."

Just then he spotted Eliza. She was lying on the wet cabin floor in the Ladies Cabin, her hands holding onto the legs of the piano fastened to the floor. Like the other passengers, she was sick and barely seemed to see him. Morgan helped her up to a dry spot as the cry ran through the cabin that the ship was sinking. Much of the crew had already started handing up the cargo and throwing it overboard. The expensive American clock cases were on top so they had to be thrown out first. Two hundred cases of these finely made and expensive mahogany clocks from Connecticut went to the bottom before the cheese boxes eventually followed them overboard. That allowed the sailors to access and jettison some of the heavy cargo where the real weight was. Morgan told Whipple to get rid of all the furniture in the saloon. He then gave the order to toss the piano as well. He watched as Whipple took an ax to the finely tapered legs of the five-by-three-foot piano, allowing the sailors to carry the cherrywood case up through the companionway onto the deck. Eliza only managed a hoarse whisper of protest. She lay on the wet cabin sole, the fantasy of a romantic life at sea draining out of her as fast as the seawater was seeping into the ship's cabin.

Most of the weary cabin passengers were now standing in ankle-deep water as a hastily organized bucket brigade got underway. He rushed topside to find two men already working hard at the pumping station just forward of the main mast, their hands moving the two wooden handles in unison, pumping back and forth frantically, up and down like a seesaw. Torrents of water were being sucked up from the bilge in the bottom of the ship's hull and spewed forth on the deck, seething and gurgling, as the flow of water escaped through the freeing ports into the ocean. Hours passed, and the ship was now emptied of all the cargo in the upper hold. Morgan noticed with satisfaction that the *Philadelphia* was riding higher than it was before. The pumping continued nonstop at a rate of three thousand gallons per hour. The men worked in shifts, their stringy hair matted with sea salt, black pouches under their swollen, red eyes. Knowing how tired his men were, Morgan drafted some of the more stalwart male passengers, warning them that they "had to pump or drown."

All this time, the gale and the towering, rolling waves were driving the ship southward toward the African coastline, hundreds of miles off course. Fortunately, the jettisoning of the cargo helped the ship even its trim and ride the waves better. Morgan estimated they had lightened the ship by nearly one hundred tons after a full day of pumping. Whipple was the one who found the leaking area after crawling inside the dark, rank bilge area. Most of the water was gushing in from a small hole, which they quickly packed with old sails and the passengers' blankets and then plugged the seams in the planking with oakum. Morgan thought one of the ship's ribs had cracked as well, but he hoped the emergency measures would hold until they could reach England.

The storm began to subside after another twelve hours of heavy seas. Amazingly, they had lost no one overboard, but there were several men who had injuries, including Icelander, who cut his leg. Whipple bandaged him up and then tended to some of the other injuries. Morgan ordered two men to begin replacing the jib boom and the missing yard on the foremast. Down below in the cabin, he found more serious problems. When he walked down the stairs to the wreckage, he was met by a profound silence, punctuated by groaning and sobbing coming from one of the staterooms. Accusatory eyes and pinched cheeks turned slowly to stare at him. He could hear mutterings of displeasure. He felt terrible and tried to reassure the passengers that the worst was now over. Most of the fatigued and weary cabin passengers were blaming him for endangering their lives. In his own cabin he found a teary eyed and stony-faced Eliza. "This was our honeymoon, Captain Morgan. This was our first voyage as husband and wife. It was supposed to be special. Instead, we almost died."

He moved toward her with his hand outstretched, but she turned her back on him. He had never seen her so emotionally upset. He tried to comfort her again as he reached for her hands, but she recoiled from his conciliatory gesture.

"You threw out the piano! My one pleasure on this hateful ship!" she cried out passionately, her morose and reproachful eyes glaring at him. "I heard you give the order. Why? Why did you do that?"

"Rest and quiet is what you need now," he said in an effort to reassure her, even as he covered up his uneasiness. "We all need that. We can talk later," he added with fatigue in his voice. Again he reached out to touch her, but she jerked away and walked to the other end of the cabin.

"You know what they are saying in the saloon, don't you?" she said with a note of disapproval in her voice. "They are saying you took unnecessary risks. You should have turned back to New York."

Morgan was shaken to the core. He understood why she was so upset, but all he could think of saying was how much worse it could have been. They had been lucky. He wanted to say it was amazing that the ship had withstood the force of the storm. He wanted to hug her and comfort her. Instead he said nothing, fearing he would only make her more distraught. He cursed himself for not preparing her for the worst. He should have warned her about the dangers, but he hadn't wanted to scare her away. He thought how young and inexperienced she was. He thought back to the high-spirited young woman who had climbed the ratlines to the top platform. She had seemed to love the ship and relish risk and danger. Now she seemed changed. He slumped into a chair, his body beaten and exhausted, his face in his hands. He blamed himself. He had allowed her to think that each passage would be as smooth and fine as their first together. He had deceived her.

Eliza seemed unaware of his distress as she continued to voice her own anxieties.

"And now we are headed for the desolate shores of Africa, where I have no doubt we will be shipwrecked. If this is to be the life of a shipmaster's wife, Captain Morgan, I want no part of it."

19

When the sun finally came out four days later, Morgan was able to shoot the solar meridian and make his calculations. He had carefully synchronized his watch to the ship's chronometer down to the second, a habit he had developed since that first voyage as shipmaster when he had almost wrecked the ship. The sky was clearing, but the seas were still producing rolling ocean swells. Eliza helped him do the calculations in the cabin with the ship swaying back and forth. He hadn't dared ask her if she still meant what she said.

He had inquired about how she was feeling after her ordeal of being tossed around the cabin. Was she stiff? Did she have any bruises? She had shook her head.

"I am fine. I am really a very strong woman, you know. Whatever happens you must know that."

They looked at the charts of the mid-Atlantic together, drawing latitude and longitude lines, discussing their likely location. From the calculations it looked as if the ship was several hundred miles off the African coast to the north of the Cape Verde Islands. Even without much canvas, they'd clocked close to eighteen hundred miles in less than seven days. That was when the lookout at the top of the mainmast called out that there was a ship off the starboard bow.

Morgan grabbed his spyglass and put it up to his eye. Sure enough he could see a vessel wallowing in the waves less than a mile away. She was extremely low in the water. They hadn't seen her because the waves were still high. Each time the ship's bow rose, Morgan looked for a sign of the ship. It was hard to see and keep the spyglass steady, but it looked like a ship in distress. The boat was partly dismasted. He could see the remnants of the stump of the main mast. The decks appeared to be covered with people, madly waving their hands.

Despite the high waves, Morgan was able to bear down on the doomed vessel on an emergency rescue mission. He could now make out what was happening. Men and women were clinging precariously to the rigging, hanging over the ship's sides, and crawling on their hands and knees on a slanted deck. Everyone was sliding and slithering as if they were on a pitched roof. He watched in horror as a fierce gust of wind pushed the foundering ship over on her beam ends as waves crashed over the windward rail. It was clear that ocean water was pouring through the hatches. The masts cracked and the yards snapped as a large wave hit the ship broadside, hammering the cabins. They were close enough to hear the cries of desperation, the shrieking and yelling. He could see dark men and women jumping off the ship holding onto pieces of wood. It was only then that he realized none of the passengers had any clothes on. They were naked, men and women alike, and they had heavy chains around their ankles.

"I warrant that be a slave ship, Captain," Mr. Nyles said as he looked through the spyglass. "Yup, that's a guinea ship, Cap'n. No doubt about it. That's the slave cargo we're looking at."

Morgan didn't reply. He was too horror stricken by the sight of men and women, their wrists and ankles still manacled together jumping into the water to almost certain death. He looked around for any signs of telltale fins. In these warm waters, there would be a danger for sharks. There was not much time left. In fact, they were too late to offer much assistance. The damaged ship began a slow spin downward as if it were caught in a whirlpool. The stern sank first, disappearing under the waves as the bow pointed upward. Morgan looked at the rapidly sinking bow, and then, amazed at what he saw, he raised the spyglass, again pressing it closer to his eye. It was unmistakable. There, underneath the bowsprit, was the ship's figurehead, a carving of a sea serpent. It was just like the *Charon*'s figurehead.

Parts of the sinking vessel now shot upward, broken spars, hatch covers, pieces of doors, even brown bodies burst to the surface. There were shrieks for help, all in a strange tongue Morgan couldn't understand. He could see heads tossed about in the waves, hands clutching upward momentarily, then disappearing. The ship was now swallowed up by the ocean. All that was left was floating debris, and about four dozen survivors who were clinging to pieces of the deck or hatch covers as they rose and fell amidst giant ocean swells.

Morgan gave the order to round the ship up into the high waves and wind and lower the quarter boats. The screaming had been replaced with an eerie quiet, interrupted only by faint pleas for help. He and Icelander went out with four other sailors in one of the boats and began rowing through the debris, pulling aboard the survivors who were clutching pieces of the yards and the spars. Their gaunt, anguished faces were filled with fear as they were hauled aboard. Along with the other quarter boat, they were able to save about thirty people before they gave up the search as futile and rowed back to the ship. It was one of the ship's younger sailors who spotted a board with some writing on it and snared it as they went by. It appeared to be the ship's name, *Serpente Preta*. Morgan wondered if the *Charon*'s name had been changed or maybe this was another ship owned by Blackwood. Once aboard the packet, he instructed Mr. Nyles to mark the latitude and longitude of this place.

"That will be the only marker these poor souls will ever have."

With the weather now improving, the *Philadelphia* raised half of its sails to head north toward the Canary Islands and then England. The ship's crew continued to repair the rigging so the going was slow. Morgan quickly assessed the situation. He had Whipple examine the survivors, who were sprawled out on the deck in the center of the ship. Fortunately there was no sign of disease like smallpox. Many of them had been branded like sheep with a scalding-hot iron. A large O was burned into the men's skin, and the same brand was imprinted on the women's breasts. A few of them had welts and scars on their backs. They'd been shackled in pairs, and some of them were still wearing leg irons and handcuffs.

Morgan ordered Whipple and Icelander to try to remove these shackles. He told Scuttles and Lowery to make sure that these people were clothed and fed. The still-weary cabin passengers, who had not yet recovered from the trauma of the storm, stood on the quarterdeck looking down in amazement at this surreal sight of survival at sea. Without asking anyone, Eliza helped Scuttles and Lowery bring towels and clothes to the

Africans. Morgan could see she was wiping away tears as she moved from one survivor to the next.

He was wondering what he should do with these unexpected passengers when Lowery approached him, his face tense and serious.

"I been talking to some of the survivors, Captain."

"Some of them speak English?"

"No, sir, Captain. Seems as though I can speak their language. It ain't exactly the same as what my mother taught me, but it's similar enough. She was Igbo, and these people must be from the same area. They say they are Ndi Igbo from west of the big river."

Lowery's face twisted with anger as he explained what they told him. "They were captured, their villages burned, and sold off by a rival chief to a slave trader called Cha-Cha. Then they marched ten days to the coast with yokes around their necks, gagged, put in canoes, and taken to a place called Whydah, where they were kept in a barracoon with hundreds of other Africans and then loaded onto that ship."

"How many were on that ship?" Morgan asked.

"I'm not sure, Captain. They told me 'O hiri nne.' In their language, that means 'many.' I am guessing maybe as many as three hundred. Could be more."

Morgan shook his head as he pondered this figure of lives lost.

"What happened on board, Lowery? They are without crew or captain. Do they know who the slavers were?"

"They ain't saying much, Captain, but I think they rebelled and took over the ship. Maybe when the storm rose up and the sailors were busy tending to the sails. Maybe that's when they escaped and attacked. I'm just speculating. When I asked them if there was fighting on board ship, they didn't say anything, but some of them have knife cuts and bruises. They say the captain and crew punched holes in the ship's hull before they fled in the quarter boats."

"Those slavers left them to drown on board a sinking ship?"

"I believe so, Captain. They ask if we are going to take them home. They keep saying, 'Ala Ndi Igbo.' What do I tell them, Captain? They plenty scared. They think all white people want to eat black people and make powder from their bones."

"For Lord's sake, Lowery, I hope you told them we aren't cannibals. Did you tell them they are safe now?"

"Yes, sir, Captain."

Morgan looked down at these abused and frightened people he'd saved. They were squatting on deck looking around them with fear and amazement. The two Irish priests were blessing each of them as they walked through the small huddled group of shivering survivors, who were clutching towels they'd been given. Eliza and Whipple were ladling out water into tin cups from a wooden cask as they gulped down the water. He was going to have to bring them to London. There was no other choice. His ship was in need of repairs and he had passengers to deliver and a schedule to keep. He estimated they would be arriving in London at least a week to ten days later than their schedule. The Africans were now shouting and singing and Morgan stopped walking to listen.

"Onye na nke ya!"

"O di ndu onwu ka mma!"

"Anyi na-acho ila ala anyi, ala ndi Igbo!"

"They are calling for their freedom, Captain," Lowery said. "They say to be enslaved is to be part of the living dead and they want you to take them back to their homeland."

Morgan asked Lowery to walk with him so he could talk to some of them. Thirty pairs of intense dark eyes were now trained on him and Lowery as they stepped into the steerage area. He could feel their attentive stare and sense their fears and desperation. He felt uncomfortable as he looked at the huddled naked bodies with only towels covering their waists, the recently scarred and raised flesh from the branding all too visible. For the first time in his life, he felt in a most profound way the unspeakable horror of slavery with all its indignity and cruelty.

As he walked amidst the thirty survivors, he looked down at the bent back and sharply ridged backbone of one crouched man who sat at his feet. He was a young fellow, probably no older than seventeen, tall and slim, long necked with scuffed, bony knees. Morgan took a closer look. The young man was fondling something in one hand, a talisman, perhaps. He had opened what looked like a small round sundial compass made of bronze about three inches in diameter.

"Mr. Lowery, ask that man if I can have a look at what he has in his hand," Morgan said. The African, his face suddenly mistrustful, closed his fist over the compass, shaking his head. Lowery persisted, coaxing the man in his language to let the captain see this small treasure. He promised he would give it back so the young man relented and handed it over reluctantly. Morgan's eyebrows rose as he examined the brass container. He flipped the lid open and focused on the engraved lettering on the inside cover.

"Hold on. What is this?"

He read it aloud with a clear note of anxiety in his voice.

"William Blackwood, Shipmaster, *Charon*."

"Mr. Lowery, ask this man how this container came into his possession."

The man's eyes were now wide with fright. He began to speak in the singsong tonalities of the Igbo language. Lowery translated.

"Captain, he said he found it in the room on the big ship, the prison ship, he calls it, in a room with the big sleeping bed. He said he found it after all the white men fled the ship. I think he means the captain's cabin, sir. He thinks it will give him power like the white man who owned it."

Morgan was silent as he turned to look southward toward the horizon. It was as if he somehow expected to see the longboats that had carried Blackwood from the sinking slave ship. He took in a deep breath and pulled out one of his cigars. He thought of Hiram and he became remorseful. Then his thoughts turned to Abraham and he felt a rising tide of anger sweep over him. Ever so softly he murmured to himself, "I will find you, Abraham. I will find you. At the very least, I will find out what that man did to you."

One day later, it was Ochoa who spotted a sail on the horizon.

"Where?" asked Morgan anxiously as he held the spyglass up to his eyes.

"A estribor, Capitán. Todavía lejos."

The first mate soon spotted the tiny white sail to starboard. It was nothing more than a speck on the horizon.

"On the starboard beam, sir. She's got her hull down, Cap'n."

"How's she headed?" Morgan asked.

"The same course as us, northeast."

"How far away?"

"Maybe ten miles, but she's moving up quickly."

What concerned Morgan the most in these waters was that the pursuing ship could be a British Royal Navy gunship. The British had been increasing their patrols off the West African coast in search of slaving ships ever since the Emancipation Act was approved by royal decree. He had heard of several cases where English warships had seized American merchant ships and their legitimate cargoes off the African coast. The British Navy claimed "right of search" and "right of seizure" even though the Americans didn't recognize these rights. He watched through his spyglass as the distant ship tacked once to get to the weather side of the packet and then to resume her line of pursuit. She was still miles away, but a sailor's instinct told Morgan this ship was coming up too fast to be another merchant ship.

"Mr. Nyles, I trust the necessary repairs have been made."

"Yes sir, Cap'n. What do you propose, Cap'n?" asked the first mate anxiously.

"We'll wait and see if he can outsail us. Make ready the topgallant staysails as well as the jigger topmast staysail and the jigger topgallant staysail."

Sail after sail was raised as Morgan tried to boost his ship's speed by as much as a knot. He was taking a risk as the rigging had been severely strained by the storm. He could tell that despite the extra sails, the pursuing ship was gaining ground. He climbed up into the rigging with the spyglass and looked at the triangular sails that were headed his way. An unusual ship, he thought to himself, with the elegant look of a French corvette. She had three masts and lateen-style sails that rose to the highest point, and she appeared to be moving along to windward as fast or faster than a Baltimore clipper. He turned to Mr. Nyles.

"Whoever that is, he'll be on top of us soon enough, and I warrant it's not a merchant ship."

The breeze was still relatively mild and Morgan called for more sail. He looked through his spyglass and gulped as he spotted the British colors flying off the mizzen sail.

"That's a British sloop of war, Mr. Nyles."

"Yes, sir," Nyles replied. "Lately the British navy ships seem to have a particular fondness for anything flying the stars and stripes, no matter what the cargo."

Morgan looked again through the spyglass, admiring the ship's sleek hull steadily carving her way to windward.

"What kind of sloop of war is that, Mr. Nyles? I don't recognize it."

"I reckon that's one of the Royal Navy's experimental fore and aft rigs. They call it a ballyhoo. They were named after the garfish in the West Indies, hard to spot and hard to catch. Well named I would say."

Morgan had never heard of these ships.

The three-masted sloop of war was coming up fast, heeled over sharply, the lee rail buried and the spray flying over the windward rail. He could now see that she was reasonably well armed. There was one long gun on a pivot in the ship's bow, from the looks of it a long-barreled nine pounder. He could see the shiny epaulettes on either shoulder of the captain's blue coat glittering in the morning sun. On the sides and the bow of the ship he saw the dull glare of the black cast-iron carronades mounted on slides fixed to the deck. From the looks of them, he thought there could be as many as six twelve pounders. Mr. Nyles had made the same observation. Suddenly a puff of white smoke emerged from the port bow off the British warship, followed quickly by a boom of cannon and then a splash of water one hundred yards in front of them.

"Looks like we have trouble here, Mr. Nyles."

"Yes, sir. They're firing that bow chaser. What are you aimin' to do, Captain? As you can see, as soon as they come broadsides, they got the smashers ready to fire at close range."

The sloop of war soon rounded up into the wind with her sails flapping in the light, early morning breeze like a swan's wings. Her short, smooth-bore carronades amidships were now clearly visible and pointed directly at them, the gunners ready to fire. They were twelve pounders. He knew a broadside swipe from these powerful short-range guns would reduce the starboard side of the *Philadelphia* into a rainstorm of deadly wooden splinters.

"Back the yards, Mr. Nyles!"

"Aye, aye, Cap'n."

The English captain held a trumpet and began speaking in a stiff and official voice.

"I am Captain James Stryker of His Majesty's sloop of war the *Resolve* with the West African Squadron. Stand by for boarding."

Morgan grabbed the trumpet from his first mate and stepped to the rail.

"I am Captain Elisha Morgan, and this is the American packet ship, the *Philadelphia* of the Black X Line, and we are bound for London. What is your business, Captain?"

"I am sorry to inform you that we must search your ship," Captain Stryker replied formally.

"Might I ask why, Captain?"

"Yes, you are a suspected American slaver."

Morgan had anticipated this accusation, just because the Africans were clearly visible on the *Philadelphia*'s deck, but it still infuriated him.

"Mr. Nyles. Lower the ladder. We have no choice but to allow the lion and his bloodhounds on board."

Soon enough, the six-oared boat from the sloop of war pulled alongside the *Philadelphia.* The sailors and some of the passengers were leaning over the rails to see what was happening. Morgan watched the armed English sailors wearing man-of-war caps and the captain with his blue coat and silver buttons begin climbing the ladder. He knew this was unusual for a Royal Navy captain to leave his ship. Normally the captain would delegate the boarding of another ship to the first lieutenant. Morgan wondered why he was breaking with the Royal Navy's customary procedures, but that question was left dangling as the faces of the English sailors emerged over the bulwarks.

On the quarterdeck, the two ship captains stood, each taking careful measure of the other. Stryker was a slightly older man than Morgan, but he was a handsome man with square, broad shoulders, a well-defined, chiseled face framed by curling whiskers, and black hair cut short to reveal a smooth, wide forehead. Morgan thought he was the picture of an English ship commander with his stance and poise both disciplined and haughty. He was no doubt a highly ambitious naval commander eager to carry out his orders to seize slave ships with biblical zeal. Stryker's eyes, small and restless, scanned the decks as he began to address Morgan.

"Good day to you, Captain. By orders of the Crown, we will be searching your ship. I would ask you to let me see your ship's papers."

He gave Morgan a cold stare.

Morgan was incensed, but he kept quiet. He had learned to dislike this show of force by the British Royal Navy ever since he was a boy, but he was well aware he had few options.

"I regret delaying you on your long voyage, Captain, but we have orders to pursue and seize any slaving ships, and as you well know the foul ships that carry on this illegal trade all too frequently fly the stars and stripes of your country from their masts."

As if to emphasize the point, Stryker looked up scornfully at the American flag flying off the spanker. Morgan was indignant. The cigar moved from one side of his mouth to the other as he fought to control his anger. He explained the situation as best he could, describing the sinking of the ship and their efforts to save the few survivors. He patiently showed the cocky British captain the ship's papers along with the manifest and invited the captain to interview each and every one of the passengers separately to see if his story matched theirs. After reviewing the ship's papers, searching the ship, and interviewing the passengers, Stryker examined the Africans on deck, taking note of the scars from the branding, and at last seemed satisfied. He walked up to the fife rail where Morgan was standing with Eliza by his side. Stryker tipped his hat to Eliza.

"By all rights, I should seize your ship, Captain, but it appears you are telling the truth. I will be taking these liberated Africans to Freetown in Sierra Leone."

Stryker's eyes bore into Morgan's face with an interrogator's intensity.

"What was the name of the slaver, Captain? Did you see the name?"

"It was a Portuguese name," replied Morgan.

"*Serpente Preta*?" Stryker inquired.

"Yes, that was it. Do you know the ship?"

"I am afraid we do," replied Captain Stryker. "We were waiting for her outside the Bonny River, but she tricked us by picking up these slaves further to the west at Whydah."

"Will you catch the slavers?" asked Eliza. "It appears that they fled during the storm in the ship's quarter boats."

"We will make our best effort, madam, to find and bring them to justice," Stryker replied with a smile, tipping his hat again.

Morgan took a long, hard look at the British captain. Something about his face was familiar. It seemed like he'd seen the man before. Some distant memory stirred momentarily, but then he turned to watch the frightened faces of the Africans as they were loaded into the six-oared longboats and ordered to squat in the center of the boats. He wondered if these unfortunate men and women would be any better off in the hands of the British in the muddy, malaria-filled streets of Freetown. He spotted the frightened face of the young African with Blackwood's sundial compass. He had his treasure firmly clenched in his hand. His gaze shifted to the Royal Navy ship where the British sailors were hanging over the bulwarks as they awaited the return of their captain. For a fleeting second he thought he saw a familiar face. One of the men looked a little like Hiram. He grabbed the spyglass and held it up to his eye, scanning the line of sailors now preparing for the arrival of the longboats. There was nothing. He shook his head as he realized how tired he was. He knew he needed rest.

Four days later, with a burning sun beating down on the ship, they passed the dreaded northern coast of Africa with its barren, treeless coastline, sandy hills, and remote mountains in the distance. To the north, Morgan could barely make out the hazy outline of the nearly mile-high peak on Gomera Island in the Canaries. He estimated that they were now 1,600 miles to the south of England. Morgan stood by the weather rail lost in thought about that bronze sundial compass. He wondered what his young wife would do when she reached England. He decided that the first thing he must do besides seeing to the repair of the ship's spars and rigging was to buy a new piano for the *Philadelphia.*

PART VIII

And the mother at home says, "Hark!
For his voice I listen and yearn;
It is growing late and dark,
And my boy does not return!"

—Henry Wadsworth Longfellow,
"The Fiftieth Birthday of Agassiz"

20

1835

In the gray light of predawn, Morgan pulled his coat more tightly around him. A chilly late September breeze had blown away the last of the summer winds. He'd been on deck standing by Icelander at the helm for several hours now, so he was hungry and getting tired. They'd been at sea for twenty-five days. The only noticeable sounds to be heard were the occasional mournful cries of seagulls. He watched as a figure emerged from the companionway and a big smile lit his face. It was Eliza, bringing him the first early morning brew of Lowery's hot coffee and some of the cook's freshly baked johnnycake.

She looked refreshed and wide awake, neatly dressed as always. She wore a woolen shawl over a loose-fitting cotton petticoat and a drawn bonnet of gingham to keep her hair in place. Lately she had taken to tying her hair back in a tightly wound bun, a look that made him notice her attractive, thin neck. He smiled at her, then scolded her in a gentle teasing way for not coming sooner. She made a funny scowling face at him, and then, placing her hands on her hips, asked about their current location. He told her he thought they were somewhere off the Georges Bank bearing down on Cape Cod. He watched her stride across the quarterdeck with confidence and disappear down the companionway. He had to admit she had earned her sea legs after making five ocean passages with him. He was happy, but he knew that this wouldn't last forever.

His mind wandered back to a year ago. When they arrived at St. Katherine's Docks after that first fateful voyage as a married couple, her tough reserve had evaporated like boiling water from a kettle. She had collapsed in tears in their cabin. He had held her in his arms, trying to comfort her. Sobbing, she confessed to him how terrified she'd been during the storm. She spoke of the recurring nightmares she was having, and how she was not looking forward to the rough passage back to New York. He bought a new ship's piano made with rosewood veneer, mahogany, and a finely scalloped ivory keyboard to replace the one that had been thrown overboard. That had helped her mood, but he could tell that she was anxious and unhappy.

He often thought that if it hadn't been for the Leslies and their kind hospitality, she would not still be making these passages across the Atlantic with him. Certainly the unexpected and welcome invitation of the Leslies had changed things for the better. At first, Eliza didn't want to go. She said she didn't feel like socializing, but he had insisted. They had taken a hackney cab from the docks, clip-clopping their way along the banks of the Thames, sightseeing and gawking at the mansions along Piccadilly, passing Hyde Park and the Duke of Wellington's stately mansion at Apsley House. The first sight of Edgware Road, with its sweet-smelling hayfields, the hedgerows, and the long line of oak trees, had been a delight. As they stepped out of their cab, they'd encountered the tall, amiable figure of Leslie just coming in from his afternoon walk with a handful of honeysuckle and roses, smiling and waving at them. Eliza was at first apprehensive around this older English couple, but she relaxed when she saw the three children, nine-year-old Robert and his two little sisters, Harriet and Mary.

At lunch that day, Morgan had looked over at her. She and Harriet Leslie were chatting away like sisters or old friends. They talked about gardens and recipes, laughing at the antics of young Robert, who was pretending a bootjack was a vicious dog. He overheard the two women comparing notes about life aboard an American packet ship. They were chuckling as they traded stories, announcing that the lack of fresh bathwater was the most serious of the many privations women were expected to endure on board ship, but that lack of privacy was a close second.

After lunch, Leslie showed the Morgans around his small cramped studio, where he hung paintings from some of his friends, including John Constable and J. M. W. Turner. Tea, hot muffins, and crumpets were served in the small garden. Charles Leslie told them the latest social gossip he had collected from some of his wealthy patrons, while Morgan recounted the details of their harrowing voyage. Both Leslies showered Eliza with much praise for her courage to be sailing with her husband.

That same day, as late afternoon tea drifted into presupper drinks, they met some of Leslie's artist friends, most of whom Morgan had met earlier at the Sketching Club meeting. Eliza had played some Bach and Mozart on the Leslies' piano. The ever-smiling Clarkson Stanfield with his wiry, muttonchop whiskers, bulldog face, and wide girth reminisced about his time at sea as a boy. Morgan told some amusing sea tales, including the story of an American ship captain by the name of Preserved Fish who was almost arrested by a government tax collector because he claimed to be carrying a cargo of pickled fish on board his ship, *Flying Fish*. Leslie's friends stared at him with disbelief. "Yes, gentlemen, this was his real, God-given name. That revenue man couldn't believe it either. He had to make an apology to Captain Fish." The small group at the Leslie house roared their approval at this tale and demanded more "Down East" stories from the American captain. Morgan warmed to his appreciative audience and the sea tales he'd heard in the fo'c'sle for years began pouring out.

"There was an old ship captain on the China run by the name of Grimshaw. He always seemed to know when a storm was brewing so the other captains would try to anchor next to his ship. They knew he would start making preparations a day or so before a storm would roll in. 'Close to Grimshaw was close to God,' they used to say. No one knew his secret until he retired from the sea. He became knarled and crippled. Every day he began shouting, 'Weigh anchor, typhoon's comin'!' No one could figure it out. There weren't any storms. That's when they discovered Captain Grimshaw's secret."

"What was it?" cried Stanfield.

"It was his arthritis."

Leslie's friends roared with laughter. The evening had ended with another round of charades and some drunken refrains from the sad sea chantey called "Tom Bowling" in honor of Leslie's new friend from the sea.

Over the next year, the Morgans were invited several times to Pine Apple Place, as the Leslies' house was called. They were introduced to more of his artist friends, including Constable and Turner. Morgan remembered how Leslie whispered to him in confidence that Constable was his best friend, but Turner was the greatest painter he had ever known. He thought of that first visit to Turner's Queen Anne studio with Leslie. They had walked into the dusty, dilapidated studio and there in the far corner of the room was the gray-haired Turner with his well-worn beaver hat perched on his head. He was standing by his easel and canvas, his brush and palate in one hand, hair askew, dressed in an overcoat and baggy trousers covered with paint. He had immediately wanted Morgan's opinion about one of the misty seascapes he was working on. Morgan had invited Turner to visit him on the *Philadelphia*.

He laughed to himself as he remembered the short, stout Turner walking the decks of the *Philadelphia*, duck footed, talking to himself distractedly like a drunken fisherman. The man had been so taken with the details of the rigging Morgan invited him to come with them on the voyage back to New York.

"Sometime you must come with us, at least as far as Portsmouth," Morgan said. "We'll give you a sea cruise."

To his surprise, just prior to embarking on this voyage, Turner had showed up at St. Katherine's Docks, asking for a berth. They had taken on a load of flannels, velvet, and carpeting in the upper hold so there were no steerage passengers to distract the painter. Turner had the ship's deck to himself, and he wandered back and forth from bow to stern. On the river journey, he continued showing interest in the sails and the rigging. Eliza bragged that she had been up the ratlines and seen the views from the topmast. The painter was so intrigued that after they dropped the pilot off at Gravesend and were approaching Margate, he insisted he be allowed to climb the ratlines as far as the main topmast so he could feel the sway and roll of the ship just as Mrs. Morgan had done. Two sailors had to pull the barrel-shaped Englishman around the futtock shrouds because he was too large to fit through the narrow lubber's hole. They actually tied a rope around him and used a block and tackle to get him up to the topmast.

After they reached the rolling North Sea, Turner insisted he be left there, tied to the mast. He stayed that way for several hours, oftentimes closing his eyes, his mind turned inward and from time to time looking up toward the sun like some sort of mystical man of the cloth. After they had safely lowered him to the deck, he spent the rest of the voyage to Portsmouth immersed in his watercolors and sketchbook. While Turner was scratching and painting away in his book Eliza gave Morgan the first hint that change was in the air in their relationship. She had turned to him, her face thoughtful and pensive, and said how sorry she was to leave London.

"Do you ever wonder, Ely, what it would be like to have a home of our own like the Leslies?"

He had looked at her with surprise. The comforts of the Leslie villa had been a welcome palliative for Eliza after each passage. When in London, she could always look forward to a crackling fireplace, a warm meal at a dining room table, and the sound of the Leslies' laughing children. Now it seemed those simple rewards of domestic life had taken root and Eliza's nesting instincts had sprouted. He had sighed, "I don't know, Eliza. We'll have to see."

☸

Eliza hadn't raised the topic of a house since they left the English Channel, but he knew that she would soon bring it up again. As the skies lightened with dawn, the wind veered to the northwest. Morgan could see powerful crosscurrents swirling off to the starboard, signaling a possible shoaly area. He ordered the helmsman to steer a few points to the south. He guessed that they were not far from a shallow area of sandbars fanning southeast from Nantucket Island that extended more than forty miles.

He was thinking once again about his wife's request and what his response should be. It had caught him by surprise. A home in New York would certainly change things. He knew what it would mean. She would want children, and she would make fewer and fewer trips with him. He thought about their time together this past year. Having her on board had proved to be an unexpected asset in the packet-polite world of the cabin passengers. She catered to their many demands with a woman's gentler touch. She had become the perfect hostess, working closely with Lowery and Scuttles to prepare the menus. She had made sure that his table manners improved and given him useful tips about initiating polite conversation. He had become used to her glowering at him whenever he tried to take too large a bite of food. Her skills on the piano were also much admired. Several of the passengers on this voyage had complimented him on his wife's soft touch with the ivories, particularly with Bach's keyboard *Partitas* and Schubert's *Impromptus*. He thought to himself that he'd never been happier. But he knew change was in the air. Eliza was a woman who was ready to have a home that didn't move under her feet.

His thoughts were interrupted by a loud trumpet blast. A thick bank of cold fog now enveloped them, robbing them of good visibility. Several sailors on the foredeck began yelling, "Fall off! Fall off!"

The fog trumpet blew and blew again. Morgan climbed up the ratlines so he could better see over the fog-shrouded bow of the ship. Before he could even react, the big packet flew by a cod fisherman in a large, open dory. A stooped older man and two young boys dressed in oilskins were pulling in long lines loaded with cod into their open boat. That sight of what looked like a father and two sons working together caused him to swallow hard. He thought of his old family home. Last year's planned visit to introduce his parents to Eliza had not come to pass because of the pressing needs of the shipping line.

It was more than just demands from the shipping company that had kept him from taking time off last year. He'd almost lost his job. He'd had a fiery altercation with Mr. Griswold and some of the other owners as soon as he got back to New York. They'd already heard the news about the storm and they had taken him to task for jettisoning most of the cargo, most particularly the valuable mahogany clock cases. They had grumbled at their losses. "Why couldn't you have thrown out something of less value," Mr. Griswold had asked brusquely in the business meeting. The others, Jacob Westervelt, Christian Bergh, and Robert Carnley, all wealthy shipbuilders and part owners of the *Philadelphia*, had nodded in agreement. Morgan's mind had shot back to the high seas crashing over the ship, the sight of Eliza's fear-stricken eyes, and his own near-death experience. Something clicked. He exploded and told them all to sail the ship themselves. "I wish you gentlemen would try your hand at ocean sailing. See how you do in a hurricane."

He had stormed out of the meeting. His request for family time was denied. At first he'd been disappointed about not going home, then relieved. Now with the passing of several months, tempers had cooled. At last the company was granting him extensive shore leave. He and Eliza were planning to travel to Lyme over the Thanksgiving holidays. His family would meet his new wife, and after thirteen years of being away from home, he would return to the Connecticut River like a wandering salmon finally coming in from the ocean.

The thought of seeing his father again made him anxious. Eliza had not stopped asking questions about his family. She wanted to know all about his sisters and his brother Josiah, and what life had been like growing up in Lyme. Without telling her about the conflict-ridden relationship he'd had with his father, he'd tried to let her know that his return home would not be without its emotional complications. He had told her about his search for Abraham and how disappointing it had been. He thought how little he really knew about what had happened to Abraham. So many years of searching for his brother and all he had were more suspicions of foul play. Josiah would certainly want to hear about any new information. What could he tell him? He didn't even know what had happened to John Taylor. He had searched for the man over the years, mentioning Taylor's name at some of the New York boarding houses more commonly frequented by sailors, but there was no trace of him. He supposed that the sickly man had most likely died in some hidden alleyway, his dark secrets forever lost.

The breakfast bell interrupted his thoughts. Lowery was just going below with the milk pail. Eliza now reemerged on deck, taking a look at the misty gray world that they were sailing through. Visibility was less than half a mile. He could see from her furrowed expression as she looked toward the bow of the ship that she was hoping to catch a glimpse of land.

When the *Philadelphia* arrived in New York after twenty-seven days at sea, Eliza rushed off to see her parents while Morgan oversaw the unloading of the cargo of fine woolens and cottons and assorted farm tools and hardware. The night before they arrived, when the ship was off Long

Island, she had asked him again about establishing a residence in New York, and sensing that he had no choice, he had agreed.

"I'll still be sailing with you," she had reassured him, "just not on all the passages." Then she repeated again, "It would mean so much for me if we have our own home, just like the Leslies."

The thought of sailing without her made him sad, but Morgan chose not to think about that. While the dockworkers loaded up the wagons, he walked over to inspect one of the Black X Line's newest ships built by Bergh & Company that spring. She was called the *Toronto*. He now held ownership shares in this 630-ton ship, as well as in the *Philadelphia* and one other. As soon as this new ship set sail, and he received his share of the earnings, he told himself, it would mean that he and Eliza could begin looking for a residence ashore. It also would mean he would now be viewed by some of the other owners as not just a ship captain, but as an important investor in the Black X Line. They would have to see him as one of them.

It was later that week, after a late-night meeting with Mr. Griswold and some shipping agents at a local tavern, that he saw a shadowy, solitary figure on the other side of the street. The man had a southwester cap over his head and a sailor's pea jacket. He was standing at the corner of South William Street underneath a street lantern looking directly at him. Morgan noticed him when he walked into the tavern where they were meeting and then later at ten o'clock when he came out. At first he paid little attention. Just another drunk, he thought, but then some instinct told him he should be careful. At night, the wharf area around South Street, with its many alleyways and dark corners, was thick with thieves. He looked back over his shoulder and then quickened his pace. He thought the man was following him.

Morgan walked toward Wall Street and then turned down toward Coenties Alley, where he hoped he would lose the man in the crowds. He stayed mostly in the shadows, avoiding the streetlights. The horse-drawn wagons were already arriving to unload the ships on the piers, so the streets adjacent to the docks were filled with noisy activity. He slipped behind a wagon being pulled by a large mule, ducked underneath another, and came out on the other side of the street. He hunched over as he walked beside a horse, turning onto a small alley, which took him to Cherry Street. He kept looking back. Perhaps he was just imagining this man following him. After all, the streets were filled with people. He looked again. There was nothing, but he quickened his pace all the same.

On the corner of Fulton and Water Streets the noise of scraping fiddles, strumming banjos, and screeching parrots spilled out of a brightly painted building with the name Jolly Tar hanging from the doorway. A man holding a drunken woman under his arm, muttering senseless gibberish, passed close by him. He kept his distance and walked even faster, pulling his hat down more firmly over his head. He passed a brick house known for some of the more popular blood sports at the time, dogfighting and rat baiting. He could hear the shouts and yelling of wagers inside.

Just then, he saw a quick glimpse of the man's cap. Perhaps he was mistaken, but another look back and he knew he was right. The man was walking across the street, his face turned in his direction. It was too dark to see any of his features. The shape of his thin body, hunched shoulders, southwester cap, and blue pea jacket convinced him this was the same man he'd first seen off South William Street. Morgan became concerned. His well-tailored clothes made him a possible target. He was dressed like a ship's merchant with a long-skirted blue coat, top hat, and Wellington boots. Still, whoever was following him must have more than money on his mind. Why else would he stalk him so intently through so many different crowded streets? No, he said to himself, this was personal. Someone was targeting him and he began to think of Blackwood.

When he saw wagons moving toward Peck's Slip, he followed them as far as South Street. He hadn't brought his pistols and felt vulnerable. He did have his sheath knife, which he always carried when he came ashore, and he fingered the handle with his right hand for reassurance. He was thinking of stopping and turning to confront his pursuer head-on when he heard a nervous, slightly hesitant voice behind him call out his name.

"Captain Morgan? Would that be you, Captain Morgan, brother of Abraham?"

Morgan quickly turned, knife in hand, and looked to the other side of the narrow street, but all he could see was a silhouetted figure.

"Who's there?" Morgan asked, a slight tremor in his voice.

"It's John Taylor, Captain."

"John Taylor?" Morgan asked in astonishment, stammering. He paused for a second as he tried to think how to react. "The John Taylor who sailed with my brother Abraham?"

"That would be me, Captain Morgan, the man you saved from a watery graveyard all those years ago, the one who wrote your mother about William and Abraham."

Morgan could hardly believe his ears. He walked over to this voice in the semidarkness, still somewhat suspicious.

"I thought it were you because of the way you walked," said the shadowy figure with the southwester cap. "I knew you were here."

Morgan stopped. "Why didn't you just approach me?"

"You were walking so fast, I almost lost you several times."

Morgan could now recognize the man under the dim light of a street lantern. He remembered his unmistakable thin, hollow cheeks and his weak jaw that fell inward toward his neck. He walked closer until he could see the weather-beaten face in front of him. Somehow the man with his droopy shoulders seemed even more thin and frail than he had been years earlier. His eyelids were red. He was dressed in a torn, battered pea jacket caked with mud, which told Morgan the man had either passed out or was sleeping in the street. The lines in his thin face and sadness in his eyes told the story of his troubled life.

"I'll be dammed if I ever thought I'd see you again, Taylor," Morgan said finally. "I thought you would be dead by now."

Taylor gave a slight start, but he said nothing, his features frozen, his taciturn face showing little emotion. He kept glancing backward nervously, and then looking back at Morgan and staring at some point beyond him. Morgan turned around quickly. A row of houses on the other side of the street was empty and dark, but in the distance the faint light of a grog shop revealed human shapes.

"What's wrong, Taylor? Is someone following you?"

"I thought I saw Big Red," he replied in a hoarse whisper.

"Big Red?"

"The mate who sailed with Abraham and me. Tom Edgars. He is the one who has been chasing me all these years, he and Blackwood. They was recruitin' sailors in some of the grog shops down on Cherry Street, but they been looking for me, making inquiries down at the docks. I been hiding and sleeping in the stinking wet gutters because they been trailing me."

"But why were you following me?"

Taylor made no reply, the tips of his fingers on his lips as he looked down at the cobblestones on the street. Morgan suddenly clenched his teeth as he felt his patience wane. He stepped forward to grab the man, coming close enough to his face to smell his rummy breath and a foul, vinegar-like smell that seemed to be seeping from every pore of his saturated body. The man's hollow cheeks were ashy white, his eyes bloodshot. The crushing memory of going back to see Taylor in the boarding house where he had brought him so many years ago, and finding his room empty, descended on him. As he stared into John Taylor's twitching eyes, which seemed to be lost in some other world, he remembered the man's cryptic remarks about Blackwood, the blood boat, and the foul dealings.

"Pull yourself together," Morgan said in an urgent tone. "What's done is done. You can't undo it. Now for Lord's sakes, tell me what you want. Do you have information about my brother?"

It was then that Morgan noticed Taylor was carrying a satchel. The man remained silent, but he now transferred his stare from the street to Morgan's face, extending his arms, his trembling hands holding out a package as if it were some priceless treasure.

"Captain Morgan, take this. I cannot have it near me anymore."

"What is it?" asked Morgan in a somber voice.

"Take it and leave me be, Captain. Your brother gave it to me after they locked him up. You and your family should have this."

"What is it, damn ye! Stop talking in riddles!"

"I am unable to tell the story about Abraham, Captain, even though it lives with me every waking hour. I have much to atone for. I am trying to forget all those scenes of violence."

Morgan took the satchel even as he sensed the man's desperation and loneliness. He looked straight into Taylor's haunted eyes and enlarged pupils that seemed to stare into nowhere.

Morgan thought Taylor was about to tell him more when a noisy group of drunken sailors came around the street corner, surrounding them. They wanted the captain to buy them a drink. Two of them draped their arms around Morgan. By the time he threw them off and looked around, Taylor was gone. He ran to the street corner, but there was no sign of anyone.

He called out his name frantically even though he recognized the futility of finding this man in the alleyways off South Street.

He walked back toward Wall Street and dropped into a small quiet tavern a few blocks from Broadway. There in a dark corner surrounded by white walls smudged with dirt and covered with chalk marks, Morgan sat alone, a decanter filled with rum on the table. He slowly opened the satchel. He wasn't sure he wanted to. He pulled out a well-worn book with yellowing pages and began leafing through its water-stained contents. Most of the writing was smudged, the ink splotched, but much of the first section was readable.

> We bin left here in Bridge Town with no ship for days now. Taylor and I bin swilling rum, I spied a man eyeing us pretty close today. He come up and fell into discourse with us.

Morgan was almost certain it was his brother's handwriting because of the way he curled his capital letters. He quickly read on.

> The man sounded us out, he did. Said he belonged to a beautiful topsail clipper named the *Charon* just come into Bridge Town harbor. He wanted to know if we were lookin' for a berth.

Just the mention of the *Charon* made Morgan's heart beat faster. He thumbed through the journal, gingerly turning the crumpled and wrinkled pages so as not to damage them. He read on.

> We woke up from a stupor as the ship sailed out of the harbor, the wind blowing from eastward. Our heads hurt something fierce. They started on us again. They beat Taylor and I fairly regul'r these past few days.

Then more writing smudged from the water stains. It was clear Abraham did not know what cargo his ship was carrying or their final destination. The ship picked up some passengers in Havana who only spoke Spanish. Abraham called them the Dons.

> The Dons stay back in the quarterdeck. No one speaks much to Taylor and me up in the foredeck, no one except that Bucko mate they call Big Red, and he just wants an excuse to pummel us. Am still in pain from

the beating I gut. The men on board are as ill tempered and as foul a set of rascals as I've ever come across.

They stopped in Cape Verde, where the ship's name was changed to something in Portuguese. Morgan slowly turned page after page of the small book, trying to decipher the smudged writing on the yellowed pages. It was hard to believe his brother had written these words some twenty years ago. He would have been just sixteen years old. In the middle of the book, he described landing in a remote place with rivers and lagoons filled with palm trees. There was a vivid description of going up some river in the ship's gig. They had been told to search for coconuts and hunt for wild pig. They grounded on a dark, sandy beach. The bush was swampy and impenetrable and filled with crocodiles. They came upon a creek and had spotted a schooner run ashore alongside a bank. There was nothing to identify her, no number, no name. Inside they found the dried-up bones and skulls of the crew, picked over by wild animals who had been there before them.

The pages after this passage were mostly unreadable. Morgan touched the creased and worn paper carefully, almost reverently. Most certainly, these were his brother's last words written in his hand. He could tell from the poor handwriting and the bad spelling. He held the open book tightly and felt like Abraham was sitting there next to him. It was not until the very end that he found a section that had somehow managed to remain dry. The writing was different, almost a child's scrawl, and it soon became apparent why. Abraham described himself as a prisoner in a dimly lit hold with only one porthole that let in light.

Day after day in this dark hole, I am blest with dry biscuit and cup of water. The disease is ragin'. Many of the crew are blind, lie helpless on the deck. I can hear their moaning. My eyes are very bad. I am all down to the foot of the hill and I don't suppose I shall soon git better.

More smudges and smears of ink. Morgan held the book closer as he read a legible paragraph on another page.

We had a very heavy gale of wind two nights ago. I fear the ship has lost its rudder and no hand is at the helm as the ship lunges with little

> purpose. We are like a phantom ship now on the ocean. We are truly at God's mercy. Who knows what will happen to us. Below me, I can hear the cries of despair and the wailing of the sick. I no longer have the strength to tolerate this cruelty. This is truly the Devil's own ship from hell. . . . So many have died already. I wish that I could be at home. I fear the trials I soon shall have to pass through. The flogging and beating I received was nothing. May we ever remember, whether in pain or suffering, prosperity or adversity that we all have to die.

The next page was made days later. Morgan read on.

> I slept none all night. I woke with a bad case of the fidgets and hysterics. There is no help for it. I don't know if John Taylor is still unaffected by this cursed disease. I will give him this journal the next time he comes to see me. I hope he will bring it to my mother if I am never to leave this place and he is to survive.

At that point the writing stopped. The next page was blank. Morgan poured himself another glass of rum. His eyes began to tear up as he pictured his brother in the dark hold of that ship. "Poor Abraham," he moaned. "Oh, my God, my poor brother." He held his head down between his hands. He felt a wall of grief overwhelm him as he began to feel the thin strand of hope that had maintained him all these years slip away.

21

The steamboat's whistle was deafening. As the old Connecticut River side-wheeler, the *Water Witch*, approached the landing area, Morgan scanned the docks where a small crowd was waiting. Only a few brown leaves were clinging to the branches of the oak trees scattered around the riverbanks. The temperatures seemed to be dropping, not surprising for late November. He could see the square-bowed sailing barge crossing the river ahead of them with a full load of livestock. He told Eliza that the Whittlesey family had been running that ferry service for well over one hundred years. He buttoned his coat tightly and put his arm around her, pulling her close. He'd been away for so long, he wondered if Lyme would seem like a foreign place. No one would recognize him. It had been thirteen years since he'd left.

His brother had written him that they were all eagerly awaiting his arrival over Thanksgiving. Some of his sisters might be there. He was looking forward to seeing them, but then he thought of his father and his emotions deadened, and he braced himself. Soon he would have to confront him and face that critical stare filled with disapproval. His guilt over abandoning the family farm so many years ago suddenly swept over him like a fast-moving wave. The thought of that coming encounter made him want to turn around and go back to New York. It was Eliza's smiling face that restored his sense of optimism.

The steamboat's crew hurled the docking lines onto the wharf, and some of the locals fastened the thick strands of heavy rope to the posts. Morgan spotted his brother in the crowd. It was an emotional moment for him. Josiah was standing atop the family's wagon scanning the crowd on deck and waving his handkerchief. Next to him was a woman dressed in a long cotton dress with a calico bonnet. Morgan pointed them out to Eliza.

"Look, there's my brother. That must be his wife, Amanda."

Both of them waved back, and upon seeing them Josiah immediately turned to another woman in a gingham bonnet, who looked up at the steamship for several seconds and then also began waving her white handkerchief enthusiastically. He almost hadn't recognized her because of her silver hair, and how much she had aged.

"My mother!" he told Eliza excitedly. With a mixture of disappointment and relief, he added, "I don't see anyone else."

There were scores of people waiting to pick up family members returning from New York or to load much-needed supplies onto their wagons. The arrival of the steamboat was a major event. He and Eliza picked their way through the crowd. When his mother caught sight of him, her hands went up to her mouth and she ran toward him. She hugged him for what seemed like an eternity before she turned to Eliza, holding her daughter-in-law's hands tightly as she welcomed her to the Connecticut River Valley. She then turned back to Ely, her hands touching his weathered rough cheeks and said, "Now let me look at you long and hard to make sure this is not a dream. My son, a packet shipmaster of a London liner, home at last!"

She sighed, long and deep, as she looked into his eyes.

"I have waited for this moment for such a long time."

Behind her, Morgan spotted his brother, who was holding the reins of the horse. Quietly they embraced, conveying to each other what words could not express.

"Where is father?" Morgan asked his mother, as they walked away from the noisy crowded docks.

"Your father is at home, Ely. The doctor is seeing him now. He has not been well for several months. I know that Josiah has written you that your father and I are now living with him and Amanda at their farm on Low Point north of here, near Hamburg Cove. Josiah built a separate wing onto the main house, which is where we are living."

Morgan nodded slowly while studying his mother. She was much changed since he'd seen her last. Her thin face had sagged considerably with lines and wrinkles. Her hair was now almost all silver, pulled back tightly into a bun. There was a sadness in her eyes, a toughness as well. He realized she was sixty-seven years old now. "I'm sorry to hear about father," he finally said. "What ails him?"

"He's just not himself," she replied. "He is faint and has difficulty breathing. The doctor says it's all just part of getting old. You know he's going to be seventy-nine this year."

Morgan had not kept track of his father's age that closely. Somehow he'd just assumed he would stay much the same as when he had last seen him. It was Sally Morgan who suggested that Ely sit up front with Josiah so the women could sit in the backseat of the wagon and talk. He guessed that his mother wanted to take serious measure of this new addition to the family. Morgan took the reins from his brother. It had been a long time since he'd held the reins of a horse, and he was amazed to find out that this bay filly was a granddaughter of the chestnut mare the family used to own. So much time had passed. They stopped to pick up some supplies at the village store. This took them through the center of Lyme, where Morgan realized his return to the river was a well-publicized event. As they trotted down the main street, he could see the tall spire of the church in the distance. People stopped and waved, many of whom he didn't even recognize.

"Welcome home, Captain!" they shouted. He could see people whispering and pointing in his direction. He hadn't realized it, but news of his career was followed on both sides of the river. A packet captain in the London line was viewed as a position of great prestige. His success as one of the elect of the seagoing community had been touted by some of the older captains like Daniel Chadwick of the Red Swallowtail Line and Henry Champlin of the Black X Line. Morgan had to rely on Josiah to tell him who many of these strangers were. He'd forgotten so many of the names.

The farm that Josiah bought with his help two years earlier was every bit as well situated as Ely had imagined. Part of it sat up on Low Point Hill where it commanded an excellent view of the river. The land was several hundred acres, but only a fraction of it was under cultivation with buckwheat, rye, corn, tobacco, and hay. The old country road wound its way past a pasture where a small herd of milking cows lazily chewed their cuds under the shade of a large oak tree. Off to the side, several horses were grazing. In the distance, he could hear a confused rooster crowing. The farmhouse soon came into view. The two-storied wooden house was originally built early in the previous century, and most of the beams had been hand hewn with an adze. The floorboards were wide pine planks stained a dark brown. When they walked into the kitchen, his father was seated by the large fireplace reading the Bible. The old man looked up, his face stern and rigid, his eyes locking onto him like a hawk spotting its prey. The bushy eyebrows, once stormy black, were now snowy white, as was his once thick, curly head of hair. Morgan stood there silently until his father broke the awkward moment.

"Finally decided to come home, eh?"

Morgan choked back his anger at this brusque remark but said nothing.

"I was wondering if your mother and I would ever lay eyes on you again."

Morgan felt a knot in his throat move down into his chest.

"We had to sell the old farm, you know," he said. "It was too much for your mother and me."

Morgan remained silent.

"We might have kept it if you'd stayed on." His voice now had a slight edge to it. "But I reckon you had other aspirations."

Morgan's fists closed as he fought back his anger.

"I reckon what happened was for the best, father. That was your farm, not mine. We were never meant to work together. You know that. Let's leave the past behind us."

Abraham Morgan scowled at his son but said nothing. Fortunately for both men, Eliza bounced through the door at that moment with a broad smile and a light step. The old man's face seemed to soften. "Tell me, young lady, how you came to become a member of this family."

That first evening home for Morgan was a blur of emotions. His father, whose hawklike stare and stern countenance used to terrify him as a boy, now seemed to be somehow diminished. His back was hunched over, his body frail and thin, his face gaunt. He sat up rigid in the high-backed chair. He was an old man now. The chilly reception when they first greeted each other soon gave way to more conviviality. Morgan sat down next to his father by the fire and began to tell him about their journey from New York on board the steamship. He seemed so different. Some of the anger and the bitterness appeared to have gone out of him like a sudden gust of wind in the summer, which fills the sails and then leaves them limp. Even the old man's voice seemed different. His thunderous shout was replaced with a softer, more balanced tone of voice. His strident manner also seemed quieter and more relaxed.

To his surprise, the vitriolic hatred Abraham Morgan used to have toward all sailors and the seagoing community seemed to have been replaced by an interest, even a curiosity, in hearing about his son's adventures. He wanted to know about London, the packet trade, and the stormy weather in the Atlantic. In turn, Morgan asked him about Josiah's new farm, the changes along the river, and all of his brothers and sisters, most of whom were now married. Maria Louisa and Jesse were the holdouts. They lived on the farm and helped with the many errands and chores. His father told him proudly about his many grandchildren. All three of Morgan's older sisters, Sarah, Asenath, and Nancy, had married deacons in various Congregational meetinghouses in the valley, and all but Nancy had a handful of children now.

His father clearly thought highly of his sons-in-law. Asenath's Deacon Talcott, Sarah's Deacon Lord, and Nancy's Deacon Bushnell were all prominent figures in their communities. Abraham Morgan's face filled with boyish joy as he talked about Asenath's and Sarah's pack of boys along with Josiah's two children, all of whom he liked to take on hayrides in the summer. Morgan could see that his father was now quite a different person to his grandchildren than he had been with his sons. He even smiled and laughed at their games, which was something he'd never seen him do before.

As Morgan watched his father rub noses and make faces with Josiah's youngest child, Walter, talking to the little boy about pony rides and cherry pie, he marveled that this was the same man who had raised him. It was almost as if his father was making amends for the cruelty and anger he'd demonstrated toward his own sons in their youth. All that rage seemed to have been silenced. Morgan became aware that his eyes were moist. He wiped them dry with the back of his hand and walked outside onto the porch to breathe in some fresh air. Two of Asenath's young sons, Will and Sam, ran after him, pulling at the tails of his long coat. "Uncle Ely! Uncle Ely!" they both cried out. He jumped in surprise. He'd never been called that before. He looked down at these two freckle-faced boys, his nephews, and for a moment he saw Abraham and himself years ago. For a moment, he was transported back in time. He and his brother were sitting on the rough-hewn wooden floor of the Lyme country store listening to an old tar tell his adventurous sea tales. Abraham had leaned over, his face flushed with excitement, and whispered that one day he would be a deep-water man just like that sailor.

"Tell us about crossing the ocean! Tell us about pirates and sea monsters."

Morgan's gaze lingered on the smiling faces of his two nephews. He held up his hand to his chin to show that he was giving their request some serious thought.

"Have you boys heard about the old ship merchant who felt he was cursed?" Morgan asked with a flourish.

"No, no, we haven't heard that one. Tell us that story, Uncle Ely!"

Morgan sat down on the rocking chair outside on the porch and motioned for the two boys to share a nearby bench.

"You see there was a proud, rich old gentleman ship merchant who was having his troubles. None of his ships was coming in on time. He was convinced that Satan held a grudge against him. His ships were always running into strong headwinds. So this clever old merchant devised a plan to trick the Devil."

Morgan raised his eyebrows and contorted his face so that he looked like he was a clever merchant plotting against the Devil. He rubbed his hands together as he continued to play the part of the scheming merchant. His voice now turned into a hushed whisper. "The old gentleman devised a strategy where four of his homeward bound ships would sail simultaneously from the four quarters of the compass. He thought the Devil couldn't possibly harm him now. At least one of his ships would be in luck and get favorable winds. That's what the shipping merchant reckoned. He went out and celebrated his clever plan, telling all his fellow merchants he'd outsmarted the Devil."

"Did it work?" asked the two boys, their eyes wide with wonder.

"That old gentleman may have been too clever by half because for the next six weeks, there was no wind. There was a dead calm across the entire ocean. Not even a slight breeze. His four ships floated along with their sails limp and lifeless, and he was forced to cancel all his contracts.

He went to church the next day and told the minister he never should have tried to outwit the Devil."

Morgan laughed at the sight of the puzzled faces of the two boys. They ran off to tell their cousins about this story from the sea they had just heard from their Uncle Ely.

On a cold Thanksgiving Day morning, Morgan and Eliza accompanied his parents and Josiah and Amanda with their two children to the service at the meetinghouse in Lyme. The tall, square building with its steeple stood on a small triangle of land and dominated the town's Common. The clanging of the steeple bell brought Morgan back to when he was a boy. The whole town had turned out to see the new bell arrive in town on the back of an ox cart, which had come all the way from Boston. He and Abraham had run alongside the cart to try to be the first ones to touch the new bell.

"Going to meeting" also reminded him of sailing amidst a field of icebergs. He could already feel the cold, chilly draft as they sat down in the long pews with the rest of his family. The soaring thirty-two-foot-high ceilings had much to do with the bitter cold temperatures. Eliza was shivering, her teeth chattering as she knelt to say her prayers. When they stood up with the rest of the congregation to begin singing the opening hymn, Morgan whispered, "You know why you're so cold, don't you?"

Eliza looked up at him with a quizzical look.

"You are supposed to be cold. It was the intent of the builders."

He gazed up at the high ceiling. Eliza again looked at him in puzzlement. He leaned closer and breathed into her ear.

"They wanted to test the resolve of the truly devoted."

Eliza almost laughed, but quickly controlled herself by shooting him a baleful, disapproving glare.

The service went on from eleven in the morning to two in the afternoon, and the church was crowded. His mother told him there were lots of new members thanks to the new young pastor. Some of the other seafaring families were there, the Chadwicks, the Pratts, the Tinkers, and the Lords. Reverend Erdix Tenny, who was around Morgan's age, spoke from a pulpit reached by a winding stairway with a lofty view of the entire congregation. The sermon was long and the meetinghouse increasingly cold, but the singing of some of the hymns with the accompaniment of the big bass viol and the flute brought back childhood memories for Morgan. The congregation belted out the rousing words of the "Missionary Hymn" and he felt a reassuring warmth inside of him at the sound of these familiar lyrics. It wasn't that he felt overly religious. It was more a moment of remembering the past. He thought to himself that this choir music was all his family had ever listened to, so different from the refined world in London he was now being exposed to.

After the meeting Abraham Morgan, despite his frail condition, was intent on introducing his packet shipmaster son to all the deacons and their wives. Morgan felt like he was being shown off like a prize bull at the annual fair. He may have softened somewhat, he thought to himself, but his father was still as proud and stubborn as ever. Still as he made the rounds amongst Abraham Morgan's friends and watched his father's face, he began to understand a bit more about the man he had once feared, a man devoted to his church. He could see the pride in his father's face, a man so conscious of his image and his standing in the community. That pride in the way others perceived him was all-important to Abraham Morgan. He had been ashamed of having his sons become sailors, fearful they would return home as penniless drunks, and concerned this would bring dishonor to the family name. And when the family received the tragic news in that letter, old Abraham had seen it as a message from God, a punishment from the heavens. His family had been marked as sinners.

When Morgan ran away from home, it was as if the Devil himself had been mocking him for his inability to control the wayward behavior of his own sons. Now that the rebellious younger one had at last returned, miraculously not as a drunken sailor, but as a successful packet ship captain and a part owner of several of the line's newest ships, he wanted to bask in some of that prestige. To him his son's success was a sign that God now approved. The shame had gone and the pride had returned. Shame and pride, Morgan thought to himself as he watched his smiling father shake hands with some of the deacons' wives. They are close cousins indeed, flip sides of the same coin.

It was only later when he was helping his mother in the kitchen by bringing in more firewood that he heard the reason for his father's metamorphosis. It was the sale of the farm, she explained. At first, he had been depressed, but then he gradually came to enjoy his free time. He still mostly read the Bible, but he was also reading some poetry by Cowper and some of the frontier novels of Cooper. They had moved in with Josiah and because of his shortness of breath, he was forced to stay in the house. That confinement had meant he spent more time with grandchildren.

"It seems like your father has finally discovered the magic of children, Ely. I am sorry for the way he treated you. Perhaps in his own way, he is too. I am sure he has his many regrets, but I am afraid his stubborn pride will keep him from ever sharing them with you."

Then she stopped and smiled, adding, "Even though your father can't express it, I know he's proud of you. And I'm so proud of you, Ely, for finding such a fine girl to marry. She must love you if she is willing to go to sea with you."

The Thanksgiving meal was a happy occasion. All of Morgan's older sisters and their husbands arrived in buggies. Their children screamed and laughed as they ran around the farm, playing hide-and-seek in the tobacco shed. The adults put the small ones on horseback and led them around the apple orchard. The older children pretended they were Indians and began stalking and scaring the younger ones. All the women clustered together in the big kitchen around the stove, chopping and cutting the potatoes and onions on the kitchen table, stuffing the turkey, rolling out the dough for the mince, pumpkin, and cherry pies, and basting the roast pig. Eliza was soon made to feel that she was part of a large, welcoming family. Morgan had never felt happier as his family sat down for the Thanksgiving supper, their heads bowed as Asenath's husband, Deacon Talcott said grace, giving thanks for the plentiful food and the return of those in peril on the sea. He looked at Morgan and Eliza as he said this, and then closed his eyes, and bowed his head. "And finally, O Lord, let us give thanks for the happiness that comes with reuniting a family." A resounding amen echoed around the dining room table.

After dinner, Morgan looked over at his mother, who was knitting by the fire, her wooden needles clacking and clicking in a slow, soothing rhythm, the soft yarn spilling to the floor. She was seemingly lost in the simple soothing repetition of one stitch, one purl, and then the same task all over again. Her gaze downward at her knitting appeared profound, meditative, and beyond his reach. He decided to say nothing as he watched her engage in the simple rhythmic process of knitting that he also found strangely calming. The small children were being read to by their mothers, while the men talked about the people they'd seen and spoken to at the meeting, the new hymns they sang, and Reverend Tenny's simple, but stirring words about driving temptation away.

No one noticed as he and Josiah walked out of the house toward Low Point to smoke cigars as dusk set in. It was there, overlooking the river, that Morgan shared Abraham's journal with his brother. He told him about John Taylor and how the man had run off as quickly and as mysteriously as he had surfaced. They read the journal together. Josiah remained quiet for a long time after that. Morgan watched him hold the journal, gingerly turning the pages, his face disturbed and intent. He could see that his brother was lost in the words. He turned away to give him time to recover his emotions. He walked to the overlook to gaze down at the river. Two men in a flat bottom pole boat carrying some livestock were navigating the serpentine shallows.

He finished his cigar and then walked back to find Josiah with his head down and the journal clasped tightly in his hands. Morgan asked his brother whether or not they should show it to their parents.

Josiah pondered that thought for a moment, and finally said, "Mother is not as strong as she might seem, Ely. She spends most of her time clacking away with those wooden needles. It's her way to forget her troubles, forget the past."

He paused to remove the cigar from his mouth.

"Do you think there be any chance that Abraham is still with the living, Ely?"

Morgan looked at Josiah for several seconds before he answered.

"I can't say. My mind tells me one thing. My heart tells me another. I suppose that after all these years you would have to say no. It has been too long. What do you think, Josiah?"

"I would have agreed with you all these years, Ely. Ever since we got that letter, I never expected to see him again. But just last month something pretty strange happened. A man introduced himself to me just outside the general store in Lyme. Big fellow, beet-red hair. Had a patch over one eye and kept looking at me strange with that one eye. Asked if I was Josiah Morgan. He sounded like an Englishman. Something about him made me shy of trusting him from the first so I asked what business did he have. He wasn't going to gull me any sooner than he could catch a weasel asleep. He asked if I had seen my brother Abraham recently, and as you might imagine, I thought it was a bad joke. I told him no, that Abraham had gone to sea a good many years ago and never come home. Then this Englishman looked at me real funny with that uneasy eye and said if for some reason he does come home I should tell him that one of his old mates is looking for him."

Morgan was dumbstruck by this news. It was both encouraging and unsettling. Who was this man?

"He walked away, but then all of a sudden he turned around and smiled, not kindly either, and said how he'd been here on the Connecticut River once long ago when the town of Essex was called Potapoug."

A slight chill went down Morgan's back as he pondered that cryptic clue. An English sailor who knew the name Potapoug, he thought to himself. That was strange. The words of John Taylor came to mind. "Big Red," he'd said. "A man by the name of Big Red had been pursuing him."

"You should keep the journal, Josiah. I will leave it up to you whether or not you share this with our mother, but I'm guessing you'll decide to keep it private for now. No one wants father to start raging again. Until we find out more about what happened to Abraham all those years ago, maybe it is best to stay silent."

PART IX

I have learned early to understand that wherever there is an Englishman in the question, it behooves an American to be reserved, punctilious, and sometimes stubborn.

—James Fenimore Cooper, *Gleanings in Europe*

22

1843

Morgan pulled himself out of his cabin berth, walked over to a small looking glass hanging from the bulkhead, and stared at his face. In the glass he saw a still-youthful man, although he was thirty-seven years old. Not in bad shape, after more than twenty years on the North Atlantic. No gray hairs on his head, a brown, weathered, clean-shaven face framed by well-trimmed whiskers, a few furrows above his nose, but a mostly smooth forehead. As he soaped and lathered his face with the hog-bristle brush to begin shaving, he could hear the creaking of the horse carts carrying hundreds of workers into St. Katherine's Docks. A chorus of stern dockmasters began shouting out orders for more men. The docks would soon be filled with the familiar squeal of rope and tackle as the men began the labor of loading and unloading cargo. It would be another hot August day on the docks.

As he scraped the straight razor across his soapy cheeks, his thoughts turned to Abraham. After all these years, the horrifying words in his brother's journal still shocked him. There hadn't been any further clues. The mysterious Englishman who had approached Josiah in Lyme had not resurfaced. Morgan had concluded that the man must have been either misdirected or misinformed. There had been no sign of John Taylor despite his repeated inquiries in the New York boarding houses frequented by sailors. He had almost given up hope. He had spent the last twenty years of his life on the North Atlantic, trying to solve the mystery of his brother's disappearance. It still sickened him to think that Hiram Smith was probably dead, all because of his quest. Yet he had continued with his mission, uncertain about his destination, drawn ever forward by some unseen, unknown force.

As a boy, he had always told himself he would find Abraham for his mother's sake, but she had died in March of last year with the snow still on the ground. His father was also gone. He had passed away in 1839 at the age of eighty-three. He thought of his mother's quiet, melancholy face. He knew that his decision to go to sea had caused her much worry and sadness. He and Josiah had never shared with her what they knew about Abraham. They both felt it would cause her too much anguish. He still wondered if they had done the right thing.

Then Josiah had written that when they discovered her body in the morning they found the old letter from John Taylor clutched firmly in her hand. He remembered how he had cried that day. She had never given up hope. Maybe that stubborn determination was what was still driving him.

He stared at himself steadily in the looking glass, not so much out of vanity as out of self-examination. His features may not have changed that much, but as he looked into his own eyes, he wondered if he was looking at a stranger. As often happened when he was alone, his thoughts turned to Eliza. They had two children now. The eldest, William, was five years old. Ruth was two. With the children to take care of, Eliza was no longer accompanying him across the Atlantic. The turning point for her came with the sudden death of her father in March of 1837. Morgan had tried to console her, but she would often sink into somber moods and worry about her mother.

After the arrival of William a year later she had told him that she was staying ashore in their home on East 22nd Street. The thought of Eliza brought back the painful memory of their parting before this last voyage. The vision of her tears, and their two small children's mournful eyes, had stayed with him. She was now pregnant with their third child. He had promised he would be back in time even though he wasn't sure he would be. She had pleaded with him to stay, but he had refused, saying the shipping line needed him. These first voyages of his new ship were too important, he told her. The truth was he often sailed with a heavy heart, feeling guilt for having left and lost in dark thoughts about himself. He wasn't sure what he wanted anymore. He was a man who was drawn to the sea. But he was also a father and a husband.

Morgan finished washing up and dressed quickly after brushing his hair and smoothing his coat. His thoughts turned to his business life as he sat down in his chair where a pool of sunlight had gathered. His life had certainly changed beyond his wildest imagination. He was a top packet ship captain, well known and well respected in both New York and London. He picked up the copy of the *Illustrated London News* from earlier that month. The August 12 article had referred to his new ship, which had made its first passage in April, as a "magnificent vessel" and a "superb work of structure and design." The lavish Saturday luncheon on the ship's quarterdeck had been well attended by leading English nobility, including the Duke of Sutherland, Lord Blantyre, several members of the *corps diplomatique* from the continent, as well as the American minister, Edward Everett. The event had been a great success and the newspaper reporter had given his new ship a rave review.

Morgan sat quietly and allowed his mind to wander back in time. So much had changed since the arrival of the ocean steamships in 1838, when the *Sirius* and the *Great Western* had steamed into New York harbor. Two years later the steamships of Samuel Cunard, financed by the British government, inaugurated service from Liverpool to Halifax and Boston. A new era had begun. The ocean's horizons were now filled with the funnels of steamships belching out black, coal-fired smoke. The mails now mostly came by steamship, and the cabin passengers were increasingly lured away from the sailing packet lines by the promise and hope of the quickest way across. Paddle wheelers, particularly the British Cunarders, were often beating the American sailing packets. The steamships could keep up a steady speed and travel in a straight line. They weren't dependent on the wind.

He thought again how fortunate it had been for him to meet Charles Leslie all those years ago. That friendship had changed his life. This past May after the opening of the annual Royal Academy exhibition, Morgan had been surprised as all his artist friends in the London Sketching Club had voted unanimously to make him an honorary member of their club. It was a heartfelt gesture. He sensed he had won their friendship and their trust, which had touched him. This was the only time in the exclusive London Sketching Club's forty-year history that, not only had a nonartist been chosen, but an American. He remembered Leslie's kind words when he made the announcement with all the club members present in his studio.

"Fellow members, we have in our midst a cousin from across the Atlantic who is from another England, a New England."

"Hear, hear!" they had shouted.

"Although it is not our club's custom to admit foreigners or nonartists, I believe we should break our rule and admit our own ship captain into this fine family of artists. Are there any objections?"

"Nay. Nay."

"Then with no objections, I hereby welcome Captain Morgan into the distinguished ranks of the London Sketching Club."

"Hear, hear! Drinks all around!"

He'd been invited to dinner later that week at Clarkson Stanfield's house at 49 Mornington Place along with several of the other artists in the Sketching Club. Leslie's friends from *Punch*, Tom Taylor and William Thackeray, had come as well, as had the prickly but witty Sydney Smith, who was then railing about money he'd lost by investing it in Pennsylvania bonds. He had appeased Smith by bringing him a barrel of Connecticut-grown apples and assuring him that, unlike Pennsylvania, these New England apples were from a solvent state. The imposing, hawklike Duke of Wellington was there. So was the jolly Lord Nanvers, who had recently been commissioning work from some of the club's artists.

Charles Dickens, who was a good friend of Stanfield's, had shown up unexpectedly. Dickens was in high spirits as his *American Notes* had won huge acclaim on this side of the Atlantic, and he was just finishing a new Christmas story. His keen blue eyes darted about the room until they landed unexpectedly on Morgan. He remembered how Dickens had started walking toward him, catching him off guard. Here was the man who had just written so critically of Americans, questioning their character, their morals, and their manners in his latest book. Many thin-skinned Americans had taken serious offense at his biting commentary, particularly on the topic of American equality. Here he was coming to introduce himself.

"You must be Leslie's good friend, the American captain?"

Morgan nodded. "Indeed, I am." He held out his hand. "Captain Elisha Ely Morgan of the Black X Line at your service."

Dickens extended his hand with a sardonic smile spreading across his face. "Pleased to meet you. Charles Dickens of the Royal Stinkpot Line."

Morgan was at first taken aback, but when he looked at Dickens's grinning face, he realized that the man was being facetious.

"You must excuse me, Captain. I have been wallowing in delightful sarcasm as I am in the midst of writing my American novel, *Martin Chuzzlewit*. I find it hard to restrain myself sometimes. Steamships are not my favorite vessels. I traveled on the Cunard liner to America and I was never happier to come back by sail."

"So I understand, Mr. Dickens. I read your lively account in *American Notes* of your stormy passage on the steamer, the *Britannia*, with great amusement. I am heartened by the brisk sales of your book as your descriptions of the dangers of traveling by steamship will no doubt mean more business for my shipping line."

"Indeed," Dickens exclaimed delightedly, his eyebrows arching upward. "With all the vitriol I have received of late from your countrymen, it is welcome to hear a rare endorsement from an American. My good friend Stanny has told me all about you, naturally only good things. I had expected you to have a mahogany face with a red bandanna on your head and rum-and-water teardrops in your eyes."

"Don't worry, Mr. Dickens, I hardly ever spit tobacco on the floor."

The author laughed.

"You seem to have won a place in this small club of theirs, Captain Morgan. Everyone has told me that I must meet you. They all say you are quite the salty storyteller."

Morgan nodded. "Maybe so, but in that case, Mr. Dickens, you must have considerably more brine in you than I do."

Dickens laughed again. "I'll take that as a compliment, Captain."

"You must come with us on a cruise down the Thames, Mr. Dickens. Leslie has already done this, and he says his friend Thackeray is eager as well. Uwins, the Chalon brothers, and Stanfield have all said they'll come with me. We will drop you off at Gravesend. Even old Turner may come."

"Did I hear the name of Turner? What is that madman painting now?"

Slightly startled by this sudden interruption, Morgan and Dickens turned to face the stout-chested Lord Nanvers, who introduced himself to Dickens even as he nodded to Morgan.

"In *The Slave Ship* you can barely see the vessel. Everything is a blur. Do you know that painting by Turner, Captain? I must say I far prefer the realistic maritime scenes of our host, Clarkson Stanfield. What about you, Mr. Dickens? Do you ever understand what Turner is depicting?"

"I would say that paintings are somewhat like human beings," replied Dickens with the faintest of smiles. "They're not always what they seem."

The sound of oak barrels being rolled up the gangway interrupted Morgan's reverie. He noticed that the pool of sunlight had shifted from his chair to an old chessboard he kept on a small table. He picked up one of the ivory pieces and began squeezing the smooth surface. The worn ivory board had been one of the many gifts he had received from Joseph Bonaparte, the former King of Spain, who had chartered his ship to cross the Atlantic three times. The chessboard had been used by Bonaparte's brother, Napoleon Bonaparte, during the fallen emperor's imprisonment on St. Helena. Morgan prized this possession. He often touched these ivory pieces with a certain awe as he tried to imagine the figures being moved around the chessboard by the man who had once conquered Europe. He put the bishop down and picked up the king, and his mind flashed back to the last trip with old Joseph

Bonaparte on the *Philadelphia* in the fall of 1839. That's when he had heard about the French slaver *Le Rodeur*, a story that had troubling similarities with the last snippets of information he had read in Abraham's journal.

On that September passage, the *Philadelphia*'s cargo hold had been loaded to capacity with crates and boxes of Bonaparte's treasured art, works from some of the great European masters like Titian, Murillo, Poussin, and Salvator Rosa. Bonaparte was leaving Point Breeze, his estate on the Delaware River, for good. He had fled to America in 1815 when he made his escape from Europe, and now he was returning. They had favorable westerly winds across the Atlantic and the *Philadelphia*'s saloon had been filled with memorable discussions about America. De Tocqueville's *De la Démocratie en Amerique* had recently been published in English under the title *Democracy in America.* Morgan pointed out how the book's optimistic views about the country differed sharply from Frances Trollope's merciless descriptions of America.

Bonaparte had shrugged off the English criticism and said something in French Morgan couldn't understand: "Il faut faire le dos rond et laisser la pluie tomber." Morgan asked Bonaparte's personal secretary, Monsieur Louis Mailliard, what that meant. "It means, Captain Morgan, that sometimes you have to resign yourself to take criticism. Literally in French, you have to round your back and let the rain fall."

Morgan had smiled at this image.

"That's one I should remember, Monsieur Mailliard."

He recalled that night well. His first mate was tending to the ship. Lowery had just served an entire meal in French, showing off his New Orleans roots. They had *potage de tortue, côtelettes de veau, quenelles de brochet avec une sauce de crème et de caviar Américain*, and a distinctively American dessert, apple fritters with maple syrup. The moody Bonaparte had retired early after losing several games of backgammon, but Morgan had stayed up with Mailliard to continue their discussion and finish off a decanter of sherry from Spain. They were talking about whether the French would soon abolish slavery. Under Louis Philippe, the French government had recently made the slave trade a crime, but they had not freed their slaves despite a growing clamor to do so in the Chamber of Deputies. That was when Mailliard brought up the horrors of the infamous French slaving ship *Le Rodeur*. He explained how the dramatic story of that ship's voyage had been a rallying cry of French abolitionists for years.

"Ecoutez-moi, Capitan Morgan, c'est une histoire triste. Le voyage commençait à Le Havre en 1819. *Le Rodeur* picked up a full load of 160 Africans on the Calabar River in West Africa and set sail for Guadeloupe. Somewhere in the middle of the Atlantic, the slaves in the cargo hold started to go blind. Imaginez l'horreur! Even though the crew was lowering food down to the Africans in slings, the mysterious disease began to quickly spread. The men's weepy eyes burned and crusted over, swelling shut. The captain and his mate soon became stone blind, as did most of the sailors. The slaves were left below, writhing in misery in a dark world. They were all infected with ophthalmia."

The similarity with his brother's journal was uncanny.

"What happened to that ship?" Morgan had asked as he poured himself and Monsieur Mailliard another glass of sherry.

"*Le Rodeur* arrived in Guadeloupe, but most all of the slaves and their captors were either blind or partially so. Had you never heard this story before, Captain?"

Morgan shook his head, but then added, "I have heard a similar story about a different ship in 1816, but I don't know what happened to it."

The Frenchman nodded soberly before speaking again.

"It is stories like *Le Rodeur* that j'espère, I hope, may one day persuade the French to finally end this horrible practice of human bondage."

☸

Morgan rubbed the ivory figure in his right hand as he looked at the same pool of sunlight that had now shifted to his mahogany desk. He thought again of his brother, and the troubling words in his journal. The story of *Le Rodeur* had given him a faint hope that Abraham might still be alive. The *Charon*, a British ship, had been a slave trader. That was clear. His brother had been infected with ophthalmia, but that didn't mean that he had gone blind like some of the others. He knew that John Taylor had not; nor had Blackwood. Maybe there was hope. He put the ivory figure of the king down and got up out of his chair to look at himself again in the small mirror. He heard the mate's voice pierce the early morning air, and he knew he would soon be needed on deck. His important visitor would be arriving soon. He straightened his cravat and told himself that today he needed to look his best.

23

Hours later, Morgan stood nervously on the ship's quarterdeck, scanning the docks. All the preparations had been made. He had been told that his special guest would arrive in her own closed carriage at eleven o'clock. The church bells in the distance had just struck the hour. He looked up above him at the ship's masts. All the sailors were dressed in their red shirts and were standing erect in the yards. Then he heard the scraping of the heavy metal gates open. He spotted an ornate black and yellow carriage drawn by a handsome pair of grays glide through the gates at St. Katherine's. Moments later, another carriage, pulled by two high-stepping bays, followed. The horses clip-clopped their way toward his ship. Morgan had never been so nervous. He could just make out a young woman's face inside the carriage, peering out at the ships. Seated next to her was a man in a high-collared black coat. Within moments, the two carriages had drawn up adjacent to his ship.

He had been told that this would be an informal visit with little fanfare, but the crowds within the docks began cheering loudly as soon as the small woman dressed in a white ruffled dress was helped out of her carriage. The man with the high-collared coat followed closely behind her. Morgan was surprised at how young she seemed, but then he reminded himself that she was only twenty-four years old. It was hard for him to fathom that the Queen of England, the sovereign of the world's richest and most powerful country, had come to visit his ship, which bore her name.

Morgan was waiting to receive the queen and the crown prince in the center of the *Victoria*'s quarterdeck. His mouth was dry, and his stomach churned. The royal couple seemed relaxed as they made their way across the quarterdeck, smiling and joking with each other. As he watched the small queen come down the companionway stairs, Morgan looked more closely at this illustrious young woman. Her high forehead and long brown hair, parted in the middle and partially tied up in a bun, reminded him somewhat of Eliza. Her lower face and small mouth narrowed and seemed pinched, giving the impression of a stubborn, independent young woman, but her lively laugh suggested a fun-loving personality. She wore a large diamond that dangled down low on her pale open neck, but it was her eyes that caught his attention. Her blue, oval-shaped eyes seemed to sparkle with life.

At her side was Prince Albert, his chestnut hair slicked back on his head, his small moustache slightly waxed. Even Morgan had to admit he cut a striking figure. He carried himself like a well-trained military man on parade with a protruding chin and a stiff carriage, but like her he seemed to reveal a slightly more informal side as they emerged in the satinwood-paneled saloon with its zebrawood trim and he scanned his new surroundings.

"Tell me about your new ship, Captain," Prince Albert asked. "How big is she?"

"The Victoria is almost 1,000 tons, 156 feet in length, and 36 feet in width," Morgan proudly explained to the royal couple as he led them around the saloon. The stewards had decorated the small tables with vases of clove-scented Sweet Williams, and Lowery had placed a large gilded cake in the shape of a crown in the center of the dining table.

"She can carry almost an acre of canvas," Morgan continued. "It took twenty-four tons of hemp to make her rigging. And from the royals to the keelson, the main mast is 155 feet high."

The crown prince politely nodded his head.

"How many passengers can she carry, Captain?"

"We have twenty-two first-class cabin suites here in the saloon, each with two berths, and a new second-class cabin amidships for another thirty passengers."

Prince Albert again nodded with interest even as Queen Victoria peered into one of the open staterooms. He escorted the royal party into the carpeted ladies cabin with its white and gold ceiling, where Queen Victoria was seated on a light blue and white silk damask-upholstered couch facing a white marble table. Her face lit up with pleasure at the sight of the ground glass windowpanes decorated with views of Windsor Castle and Buckingham Palace. As Lowery passed around a tray of cool drinks, she began to question Morgan about the Sketching Club. She wanted to hear how an American ship captain had fallen in with these well-known English artists.

"It is through Mr. Leslie and Mr. Landseer that I heard about your fine ship! I am quite familiar with the London Sketching Club. I have many of those artists' sketches. Several of the men in your club taught me watercolors over the years. In fact, many of them, including your good friend Mr. Leslie, have executed portraits of myself and the crown prince which we are quite fond of. One evening at one of their meetings I was even invited to give them themes for their sketches."

"Really! I wasn't aware of that, Your Majesty. What were the topics?"

"'Danger' was one. 'Elevation' the other," she replied enthusiastically.

"I can think of several places right here on the *Victoria*, Your Majesty, where you might find both, particularly out on the Atlantic highway."

The queen smiled. "Perhaps you can point those out, Captain, but from the safety of the deck." They both laughed.

"Are you an artist as well, Captain? I don't detect any trace of oil and varnish on you."

"No, Your Majesty, I can't say that I am. Although Mr. Leslie once told me that sailing a packet ship with its many sails is like a painter with brushes and colors in hand."

"Indeed," she replied. "Then Edwin Landseer should make a good sailor. Did you know, Captain, he has the ability to paint with both hands at the same time? He is a particular favorite of mine. He taught Albert and me how to do etchings."

It was while Lowery and the new steward, Sam Junkett, were serving cucumber sandwiches to the royal entourage that the Duke of Newcastle smugly asked the captain why he had never called one of his ships after Her Majesty before.

"After all, Captain, Her Majesty has been on the throne for nearly six years. Why have you been so slow to recognize and honor the queen?"

Morgan was smart enough to know that the old duke, who was known as an outspoken conservative, was trying to trip him up. All conversation came to a stop at the table. Even the stewards stopped passing the platter of tea sandwiches. Morgan's mind was working quickly. He could either apologize, and say something embarrassing about his own shipping line, or he could say something the English would interpret as demeaning to their queen and to England. After a few seconds pause, he looked back at the smiling face of the duke and responded smoothly: "Because, Your Lordship, we never built a ship before that was worthy of Her Majesty."

Queen Victoria's face beamed with pleasure. As if on cue everyone surrounding the royal couple began smiling as well. The duke was quite aware he was now on the defensive.

"Well, quite right, Captain," he responded. "It is indeed a fine ship and most worthy of Her Majesty."

He then abruptly changed the topic.

"If I may be so bold to ask, Captain, how fast have you made it across on the difficult westbound passage?"

Morgan paused for a second before answering.

"Twenty days, Your Lordship, I believe is my fastest crossing on the run westbound to New York."

"If I am not mistaken, Captain, the Great Western and the English Cunard Line paddle steamers are considerably faster. They can make it over in fourteen days, no matter that they are traveling east or west. Is that not so?"

Morgan's head dropped as he felt the sting of the Englishman's comment, but then he recovered.

"I readily admit, Your Lordship, a steamer is oftentimes faster, particularly on the westward passage, but most nautical experts acknowledge the risks are greater. You would have to ask yourself which you prefer, fourteen days of danger at sea on a sooty steamship or twenty days of relative safety on board a sailing packet. We in the packet shipping business think that there is room for both steam and sail on the Atlantic."

That ended the conversation. Even two years after the dramatic sinking of the British steamship the *President*, where 136 people perished, among them the popular Irish comedian Tyrone Power, the safety of traveling the Atlantic by paddle wheeler was still questioned by many travelers. The duke turned his attention elsewhere.

When the luncheon and tour were over and the carriages had left the docks, Morgan went below to congratulate Lowery and his new assistant, Sam Junkett, and then in the privacy of his own cabin savored the moment. He let out a deep breath. The afternoon sun had warmed his cabin, so he opened one of the portholes. He scanned the captain's quarters, and without thinking picked up one of the ivory figures on the chessboard and rubbed it with his fingers. This time it was the queen. The touch of the ivory figure at first was reassuring, but then it triggered an unexpected measure of unease. His mind drifted back to the British raid on the Connecticut River when he and Abraham were two frightened boys rowing for their lives. They'd raced away from certain death at the hands of the British redcoats. Now here he was so many years later entertaining the British queen whose grandfather was King George III. Had he forgotten who he was and where he came from? His mind wandered back to his days on the foredeck and he thought of his old friend Hiram. No doubt his old shipmate would have viewed his elevated status with disdain. He might have called him a "frothy lady's captain." That was the way he used to refer to Henry Champlin, when the captain spent all of his time below entertaining his guests rather than tending to the sailing of the ship.

Morgan put the figure of the queen back down on the chessboard and picked up one of the small pawns, holding it in his hand, squeezing it as hard as he could. The feelings of guilt that now enveloped him shifted to memories of Abraham. He felt a wave of self-doubt sweep over him. He squeezed the ivory pawn again. Then he shook his head and told himself he needed to look ahead. He had his own family to think of. He sat down at his desk to write a letter to Eliza to tell her all about Queen Victoria's visit. He thought of the chubby faces of his two children and he smiled. Then he thought of Eliza's condition. He wrote that he would do his best to be back by early November for the due date and that he would be spending Thanksgiving at home this year. He continued writing:

> *It made me feel bad when I left you with Ruth crying and William teary eyed. You must tell the children that they must keep up good courage, and you, my dear, must keep up a strong heart. Give them all a kiss for me. I have bought Ruth a doll, and a storybook for William. Tell them that I will be coming home as soon as my ship comes back. I will have a story for them about their Papa meeting the Queen. Tell them I will try to stay longer this time.*

24

1845

With the late afternoon summer sun shining directly in his eyes, Morgan struggled to make out who was in this incoming lugger. He was standing on the large quarterdeck of the *Victoria* with a spyglass held to his left eye. Beyond the small boat, he could just make out the glistening tips of the masts of Nelson's old ship, *Victory*, from the Battle of Trafalgar, barely visible over some of the roofs in Portsmouth. The harbor was full of Royal Navy ships, everything from corvettes and sloops of war to frigates and three-deckers. He'd seen the fleet come in earlier, their translucent sails extending across the Solent like a giant white curtain. He had stood there on deck powerless as they bore down on the anchored *Victoria*, veering off at the last minute. They had come so close he could see the barrels of the cannons and the leering faces of the British sailors. At the sound of a cannon, dozens of sails dropped simultaneously in a perfect display of naval discipline, the ships' anchors dropping into the water with a rumbling crescendo that resembled thunder. Morgan had stood silently, his eyes scanning the variety of ships until his gaze stopped at one in particular. It was a three-masted sloop of war, one of those fast ballyhoos that had run him down off the coast of Africa years ago. It looked like the same ship, but he couldn't be sure.

He now turned his attention back to the small one-masted boat. It was definitely sailing in the direction of the *Victoria*. His cabin passengers weren't due to arrive until the following morning, so he was puzzled as to whom this could be. The one passenger was wearing a pea jacket with the collar pulled up over his face. A wide-brimmed white hat was pulled down low over his ears, a strap fastened under his chin. His first thought was that the stewards were taking on a fresh supply of meat and vegetables, but a check with Mr. Lowery discounted that possibility. He then thought that perhaps this was one of Portsmouth's police officers, who was preparing to search the packet in pursuit of criminals in steerage. But as he looked through his spyglass at this passenger, it seemed unlikely that this hunched-over figure was a policeman. He looked more like a sailor.

As the small lugger neared the *Victoria*'s anchorage near the sloping shore of the Isle of Wight, he could see the spray splatter on the man's face as the lee rail dived in the water. Suddenly, the mystery passenger moved over to the windward side of the boat, and Morgan got a good look at his profile for the first time. "My Lord," he breathed out slowly. He couldn't believe what he saw. He had to look several times before he acknowledged that his first impression was right. The man coming to see him had changed a great deal. The full beard was gone. His round face was now framed by bushy whiskers that extended down to his jaw. He was wearing a white duck frock, and blue pants typical of some Royal Navy sailors. As the boat got closer and closer there was no doubt that it was his old friend, Hiram Smith, alive and to all appearances well.

With the practice of hundreds of boardings, the waterman at the tiller luffed the small lugger into the wind, the single sail flapping and banging, and before the two ships touched, Hiram grabbed the rope ladder with the firm grip of a sailor and began climbing up the fifteen-foot-high sides of the packet. Morgan was there with an outstretched hand to pull his friend over the bulwarks and onto the deck. He couldn't believe his old bunkmate in the fo'c'sle was alive.

"I'll be dammed if I ever thought I'd set eyes on you again, Hiram," Morgan stammered with a slight quiver in his voice.

"I'm greatly pleased to see you, Ely," Hiram said, before correcting himself, "or Captain Morgan, I should say."

The two of them gave each other a prolonged bear hug and then stood apart looking at each other. Morgan silently stared at his old friend unable to speak. Conflicting emotions swept over him. So many years had passed. Hiram had changed. There were flecks of gray in his temples and his brown, weathered face was now lined and creased with wrinkles. He was still the same man with his stocky torso and muscular, tattooed arms, the round, snub-nosed face and dimpled chin, but the deep furrows on his forehead and the dark bags under his eyes told the story of a hard life.

Morgan suddenly was overwhelmed with guilt.

"How many years has it been, Hiram?"

"Near on seventeen I would say."

"Way too long. I can't believe it," Morgan said with a smile, looking at his old friend quizzically, shaking his head in disbelief. His eyes had that droopy, rum-filled look he'd seen on many veteran sailors.

"Hiram, I want you to know I never meant for you to be in harm's way."

"That was long ago, Ely. It wasn't your fault."

"But it was my decision to go into that tavern, Hiram. I have blamed myself for whatever happened to you there."

Before Hiram could answer, he was surrounded by some of his old shipmates. A small group clustered around him, slapping him on his back, pushing and shoving him playfully. There was much joking when they discovered he was now sailing British. There weren't that many of the old crew who had sailed with him on board the *Hudson*. Old Scuttles was still there, but on the foredeck, the only veterans who had sailed with him were Icelander, the Spaniard, and Whipple. Dan Stark, the first mate, and Josiah Lord, the second mate, both from the Connecticut River, were new arrivals.

After Hiram caught up with some of his old mates, Morgan invited him down into his cabin. Hiram was looking all around as he stepped inside. Morgan studied his old friend. He seemed nervous and edgy. There was a bitter, sad smile on his lips that Morgan didn't recognize, a look of faded hopes, perhaps. Morgan motioned to him to sit down in the armchair on the other side of the cabin, but he ignored that offer and continued to walk around, his gaze wandering from cabin sole to the overhead skylight. Morgan pulled out his box of Havana cigars and offered one to Hiram before taking one himself.

"Sit yourself down and tell me your story. Why don't you start by telling me what happened all those years ago when they grabbed you in the White Bull."

Hiram's gaze seemed disconnected. He scratched his head and pulled at his side-whiskers before he responded.

"When the fighting started, Ely, all I remember is the sharp pain in my head and then everything went dark. They must have drugged me. When I woke up I was in a cold, dark fo'c'sle on a British Indiaman headed for Canton."

"What about Blackwood? Did you meet him?" asked Morgan incredulously.

Hiram shook his head.

"Never saw who it was that crimped me."

There was an awkward silence as Morgan studied his old friend, observing how his eyes wandered around the cabin as if he was purposely trying to avoid looking at him closely. Morgan felt a pang of guilt as he thought about Hiram's life of roaming. He imagined the hardships he had suffered, and he held himself responsible. Hiram would probably still be with the Black X Line if it weren't for him. He felt sympathetic as he looked at his changed old friend.

Finally Hiram stopped his nervous pacing around the cabin and looked out the porthole. He rolled a cigar in his fingers and lit it.

"Did you ever find out what happened to your brother, Ely?" he asked dispassionately. "Or have you given up that search?"

Morgan explained about the journal that Taylor had given him, and how he now knew that Abraham had been shanghaied onto a slaving ship. He described the accounts of the storm in the diary, saying he assumed this was probably the last he would hear about his brother.

Hiram listened restlessly but didn't seem overly curious.

"You got any rum, Ely?" he asked bluntly, while smiling in a gratuitous way. "I have a sudden hankering for some grog."

Morgan poured him a generous drink and watched his friend grab the glass.

"A man's not a sailor without his rum."

In one thirsty motion he gulped it down, wiping his chin with his trembling hands.

"Of course, you being a shipmaster now you might have changed?"

"I reckon we all have changed, Hiram."

"Not me, Ely. I'm a foredeck sailor, always been one. I wouldn't have it any other way."

He held out his mug. "Just a bit more, what do you say?"

Morgan poured him another drink.

"Why don't you tell me how you come to be sailing British in the Royal Navy of all places."

Hiram now seemed more relaxed after the rum began to numb his brain.

"It's a long story, Ely. I ended up staying with that British merchantman. Wasn't too bad. Then did the opium smuggling trade for many years. Wandered around the West Indies on trading schooners. I been with the Royal Navy's West Africa Squadron now for a spell, currently on a ship called the H.M.S. *Resolve*, one of them fast Bermuda-built sloops of war they call ballyhoos. We've been chasing down blackbirders these last few years from the Gulf of Guinea down to the south of the West African coast toward Benguela."

"I know that ship," Morgan exclaimed excitedly.

"How so?"

Morgan volunteered his own story about his encounter with the H.M.S. *Resolve* so many years ago. He told Hiram how Captain James Stryker had run down the old *Philadelphia* with the rescued African slaves on the deck.

"He fired cannon at us to make us square our yards. He thought our ship was a blackbirder."

Hiram didn't comment. An awkward silence filled the cabin.

"How is it that you are here in Portsmouth now?" Morgan asked.

"We are on maneuvers," Hiram replied, "part of the Royal Navy's Experimental Squadron." He puffed on his cigar and then smiled suddenly, his voice becoming more energetic.

"Man alive, it is sure good to see you, Ely! I was looking for you once a few years back when I came to New York. You wasn't there, but that's when they told me you'd gone and made shipmaster. I also heard you've gotten hitched and now have a fine comely missus."

They both laughed, and after congratulating him on "getting hitched," Hiram continued his story. Morgan thought he saw a glimpse of the old friend he had known and trusted. He looked expectantly at him. Hiram paused and started to say something. His face turned more somber, but when he took another drink he seemed to retreat back into some other private place. Morgan again tried to encourage him to talk. He thought about the group waiting for him in the saloon. Some of the Sketching Club artists and their friends had accompanied him on the two-day passage from London to Portsmouth. Leslie, Stanfield, Landseer, the Chalon brothers, Stumps, and Uwins were on board. So were Thackeray and Lord Nanvers. Dickens, who had just returned from Italy, had been too busy "trodding the boards" with his amateur theater group.

"I have a group of English friends waiting for me in the saloon who I know would want to hear your story, Hiram. They are fervent in their antislavery zeal. What do you say? How about a few words about the West Africa Squadron and the British crusade against slavery?"

Hiram looked dubious, in fact somewhat fearful, but Morgan was insistent so he reluctantly agreed to follow him into the saloon. The main course was just arriving at the table as they walked in. Lowery was carrying in a large platter of roasted English grouse cooked whole, heads and all, even as Sam Junkett was removing the bowls of cold potato soup. Landseer was expounding on the famine in Ireland, and how he felt the ungrateful Irish cats deserved their misery and hardship. Leslie was expressing his concerns over the growing tensions between England and America over the Oregon Territory. He asked Thackeray about the saber-rattling salvos in *Punch*. The writers had warned that if America dared to seize the Oregon Territory, the English would arm the slaves. At that point, Lord Nanvers jumped in.

"Arm the slaves! Those are fighting words, wouldn't you say, Mr. Thackeray? Imagine England arming America's slaves. I must say that's a terrible thought."

The conversation stopped as Morgan and Hiram entered the saloon. Hiram looked around at the well-dressed men seated at the table. He didn't say anything, his gaze traveling from face to face, and then he sat down. Morgan again could see the discomfort and suspicion in Hiram's smeary, rum-soaked eyes. He could also see the surprise in the faces of his English friends, who were clearly not expecting a common sailor to come into their midst.

Lord Nanvers, whose appetite seemed to be stimulated by the sight of the roasted grouse, had already speared one of the tiny bird's heads with his fork and was crunching and chewing in contentment. Morgan raised his glass to toast the end of the voyage for his passengers, praising them for braving the discomforts of the North Sea, and then he introduced his old friend.

"Gentlemen, this is Hiram Smith. He and I started sailing together when we were boys. We came in through the hawse holes as they say. We've slushed masts and been slushed ourselves by some bucko mates. We've slid down the forestays and swung out on the yards more times than we care to remember. We've seen our share of ice fields and Atlantic storms. Hiram saved my life at least once when I almost fell from a yard, and I did the same for him when we fought off some scuffle hunters on the Thames. He may be sailing British, but he's a Yankee tar from down Penobscot way as they say back home. Anyway, we haven't seen each other for quite a long time. It has been more than fifteen years since we last sailed together, hasn't it, Hiram?"

"Yup, I suppose that's about right."

"The reason I brought Hiram down to the saloon is that he has come here tonight to tell you about the gallant mission of the famous British cruisers that patrol the Guinea coastline to try to end the slave trade. He is a sailor on one of the Royal Navy sloops of war in the harbor."

"Hear, hear!" they shouted, raising their glasses in unison. "Truer words were never spoken."

The stewards then arrived with the next course of boiled potatoes and creamed peas and onions. Lord Nanvers directed his attention to the incoming dishes, sniffing appreciatively and giving them careful scrutiny before raising his glass to Morgan.

"To you, sir, Captain Morgan. This certainly is a most excellent meal and it promises to be a most provocative dinner topic. I am most intrigued to hear about England's war on slavery, as there is much ongoing debate in Parliament about its effectiveness. Let us hear what your salty friend has to say."

Hiram paused for a moment as he swallowed some rum from the bottle he was given by Lowery. He bit off a plug of tobacco, and began chewing it with obvious relish as he started telling his story about how he came to be sailing on a British sloop of war.

"I reckon my story should begin when I was picked up in Havana by a ship captain who offered me forty dollars a month, more money than I had ever made before."

Morgan watched the intent, eager faces all around the table, a receptive audience.

"Wa'al, she was fast, that ship was, all legs and wings. We sailed out that narrow entrance under the fortified walls of Moro Castle like a bird coming out of a cage with our staysails set, our kites flying. With the wind abeam she would do fourteen knots. The men on board were a swarthy set of rascals. Most of them were Spanish anyway, at least that's the language they spoke. We had a group of passengers from Brazil who I soon learned were the agents."

Hiram paused for another drink of rum, smacking his lips before he resumed his story.

"I gradually gained the confidence of the first mate, he was the only American, a fellow from New Bedford. Turns out he sold the ship to them Portuguese and Spaniards. He told me we were headed for Whydah in the Gulf of Guinea. That's when I guessed I had gotten myself on a slaver. I knew I had made a mistake."

Morgan winced at this unexpected twist. At the mention of slave ships, the English artists now crowded a little closer so as not to miss a word spoken. To them, Hiram was an example of the type of man with whom they never came into contact, a wandering, hard-drinking sailor who had more adventures than they could ever dream about. There wasn't a sound in the dark saloon, not even a rustle of clothes or the scraping of a chair. Hiram's blue eyes looked around the room and studied the intent faces surrounding him.

"I jumped ship the first opportunity I could in Porto Praya. They sent out their men to try to find me, but I hid out until they finally gave up and left. A few days later, an English frigate, a sloop of war, and one of them fast three-masted Bermuda boats, came into port. Turns out they were looking for sailors. I told them I was British from Halifax and they took me on."

"What was the name of your ship?" Leslie asked.

"The H.M.S. *Resolve*. The captain's name is Stryker, Captain James Stryker, one of the Royal Navy's best slave catchers. He is something of a hero, being as he rescued some British marines who were being held by Portuguese slavers a while back."

Out of the corner of his eye, Morgan thought he saw Lord Nanvers twitch suddenly, but it could have simply been a piece of the grouse's head stuck in his throat. He wasn't sure.

The story continued.

"Anyhow that's how I came to be sailing British. I signed on with Stryker and the *Resolve*. That was back in 1836, a couple of years after all them slaves were freed in the British islands."

Hiram turned toward Morgan, shaking his head.

"Ely, I've seen sights that would move the hardiest human heart. During a chase, I've seen them toss the slaves overboard. They'd throw their human cargo overboard a few at a time, hoping we would give up the chase and stop and pick them up."

"Do you?" asked Lord Nanvers. "Do you stop?"

"Captain Stryker, he won't stop," Hiram responded matter-of-factly. "He says what is important is to bring an end to the slave trade, and if he stops to rescue every drowning African, the slave traffickers escape. Naturally he would prefer to capture a full ship. That way he and all of us in the crew get our share of the prize money. Head money, we call it."

Morgan watched Nanvers as he looked at Hiram with a stony gaze.

"But you've had great success, have you not?" asked Stanfield.

Hiram stared at his empty glass in glum resignation. Finally, Lowery complied, refilling his glass, and Hiram continued.

"Wa'al, I would say chasing these slavers is like catching fish with your hands. For every one you snare, another hundred get away. I've heard tell that some ten to twenty thousand slaves are landed in Cuba each year, and that's with thirty Royal Navy warships patrolling the African coastline trying to stop 'em."

There was a heavy silence in the cabin interrupted finally by Clarkson Stanfield.

"But you are winning the freedom of many African slaves, are you not?"

Hiram let out a snort.

"As far as the slaves we rescue, we sometimes land them in Freetown, but oftentimes we send them on British merchant ships to the islands to work as emigrant laborers on the English sugar plantations. We call that freedom, but I am not sure those Africans do, once they get to the islands and see what's in store for them."

Hiram gave a half chuckle at what he thought was a clever remark, but one look at the serious faces around the table told Morgan that his English friends didn't see any humor. At that moment, he used a sudden noise up on deck to excuse himself, taking Hiram along with him. Once they reached the quarterdeck, Morgan pulled out a Havana, rolling it in his hand as he spoke to his old friend in a concerned voice. The two of them walked back to a dark corner at the stern of the ship. Morgan lit his cigar and blew the white smoke into the night.

"Given your generous criticism of the West Africa Squadron, I reckon you probably have something to tell me?"

Hiram laughed nervously, coughed and sputtered a bit, and then nodded.

"Yup, I was meaning to tell you earlier. I need your help. You see, I'm not on shore leave."

"What brings you here then?"

"I've jumped ship."

Morgan's eyes grew wider. He knew Hiram was capable of some bad decisions, but even he wasn't expecting this news from his old friend.

"Desertion is no small offense in the British Navy, Hiram. Are you aware of the consequences?"

"I had to jump ship, Ely."

"Why?"

"If I hadn't, I might soon be fighting my own countrymen."

"What do you mean?" Morgan asked incredulously. "How so? Why would you be fighting Americans?"

"I've overheard plans, you see. I was outside the captain's cabin and I listened in. I heard Captain Stryker tell another captain that this assembled war fleet here in Portsmouth is prepared to set sail. As soon as they're given the word, their orders are to sail westward and blockade New York and Boston, the whole east coast in fact. Stryker says they aim to teach Brother Jonathan a lesson."

Morgan gasped. "Is this over the Oregon dispute?"

Hiram nodded.

Morgan looked at him. He was stunned by this news. He blew out a mouthful of smoke as he turned away from Hiram and looked up into the night sky.

Hiram pleaded his case.

"Ely, I have no option. They've probably got marines looking for me right now. I am afraid they'll kill me with a flogging, a hundred lashes or more. That is the penalty for desertion. I need your help. Can you give me a berth? Aren't you sailing with the tides early tomorrow?"

Morgan didn't say anything as he looked at the glowing tip of his cigar. "I will give it some thought, Hiram."

He had a sense Hiram was still not telling him everything. Still, he owed him. For old times' sake, if for nothing else, he knew that he must help Hiram.

Shortly afterward, the sound of a steamer chugging and clanking nearby broke the silence of the night. The small steam ferry had come to take the artists ashore. They were all a little drunk and they were reminiscing about the late Sydney Smith, who had died earlier that year. Leslie said how much his witty remarks would be missed. Thackeray, with his deep melodious voice, decided to pay homage to Smith by reciting the first few lines of his famous recipe for potato salad.

> "Two large potatoes passed through the kitchen sieve
> Unwonted softness to the salad give."

Laughing good humoredly, Leslie quickly joined in.

> "Of mordant mustard, add a single spoon:
> Distrust the condiment which bites so soon."

When the steamer bumped alongside the *Victoria*, Morgan accompanied his friends up on deck and bid them farewell, even as he made plans for a quick getaway the next morning.

25

As the first rays of sunlight crept above the horizon, Morgan had already sent his boat ashore to notify the incoming cabin passengers that the packet ship would be leaving earlier than expected. The skies were clear with westerly winds. Morgan wiped the sweat off his brow. It was only June, but the summer heat had arrived. He told Mr. Lowery privately to hide Hiram in the barrel filled with potatoes in the dark, dimly lit storeroom beside the galley.

"Make sure it has a false bottom, Lowery. I know you've used one before to fool the inspectors at the docks. Put Hiram underneath that. Mark my words, we are likely to have a Royal Navy boarding. Tell no one that Hiram is aboard ship."

"Yes, sir, Cap'n."

"Mr. Stark, make ready for lifting the anchor as soon as the passengers come aboard."

"Aye, aye, sir."

"And Mr. Stark."

"Yes, Cap'n."

"Make sure that all the sailors on board know that our guest last night, Mr. Smith, has left the ship."

The first mate looked puzzled for a moment and then nodded. There was nothing to be read from the laconic expression on his face, but Morgan trusted him. He was a young man from the river who showed great promise.

"Stand by with buntlines!" he yelled up to the men high in the yards.

Even before the cabin passengers arrived from the docks at Portsmouth, Morgan spied the Admiralty sloop of war headed his way. It was the same ship he had seen years ago, an unusual sight in British waters. Sleek, raked-back masts with no square-rigged sails, and a fore and aft rig, which he knew from experience could overtake him on a windward passage. He looked through his telescope and was not surprised at what he saw. There was Captain Stryker standing erect by the gangway, his face now weathered after years of sailing in African waters, his hair graying at the temples. The shiny epaulettes on either shoulder of his blue coat glittered in the early morning sun. The three-masted sloop of war came up fast, rounding up into the wind with her sails flapping in the light early morning breeze.

The English captain held a trumpet and identified himself formally as if they'd never met. Morgan grabbed his trumpet from his first mate and stepped to the rail.

"As you can see we have a full ship and our cabin passengers are due shortly. We are anxious to be off with the tide. What is your business?"

"I am sorry to inform you, Captain, that we must ask you to stand by until we can board and search your ship."

"Might I ask why?"

"You are suspected of harboring a British Navy deserter."

Morgan grudgingly gave his assent. There was not much he could do with his ship anchored just off Portsmouth. Within five minutes, the English sloop of war had luffed off to the eastward and dropped anchor. A quarter boat was lowered and shortly thereafter the English commander and his men climbed the *Victoria*'s ladder. Morgan was again surprised that this captain had chosen to come himself, breaking with normal Royal Navy protocol. Up close Captain James Stryker had changed little over the past decade, the same well-defined, handsomely chiseled face, his black hair and whiskers now dusted with gray. Even Morgan had to admit the man was trim looking, a picture of strict naval discipline with his dark-blue-buttoned naval coat and its shiny epaulettes. He noticed he was wearing a silver-handled sword hanging from his belt, a reminder he had come armed.

"I believe I have the honor of having met you before, Captain," Morgan said as he extended his hand.

"Yes, Captain Morgan," he replied with a brusque voice. "I recall our past meeting."

"As do I," replied Morgan quickly with a note of sarcasm in his voice. "Did you ever find those slavers?"

"No, I am afraid we did not. They proved to be too elusive."

Stryker did not even feign the slightest hint of pleasantry. He glanced over at the forward section of the ship where the emigrants were clustered together, looking in their direction. Youthful faces, bearded faces, faces weathered by years of labor and sacrifice, all were looking at them worriedly. The English captain waved his hand contemptuously in the direction of his own countrymen.

"I see you have plenty of human cargo, Captain. The usual motley assortment of villains headed for the promised land of America, or should I say the promised land of disappointment?"

Morgan restrained himself as he felt a sudden impulsive urge to hit this man. Instead he bit his lip and pulled out one of his cigars. Again he felt a strange sense of foreboding that he had seen this man's face once before long ago.

"We're taking only people who want to leave your country, Captain. If there are thieves aboard, I reckon they've learned their trade well here in England. As for deserters, I regret to inform you that we have no British Royal Navy sailor on board."

Morgan stood silently by as he watched the armed British sailors scurry off to all corners of the ship, the forecastle, the lower cargo holds, the steerage, the bilge, the anchor chain locker in the bow, all dark, shadowy places where a man could hide. Quietly he was fuming at the insult of having his ship searched and his men questioned, but he took particular delight in his denial of harboring a British Navy sailor. After all, he hadn't told a lie, he said to himself. Hiram was an American even if he had masqueraded as a British sailor.

Morgan escorted the English captain to the saloon and sat him down at the long dining table, calling on Lowery to bring in a tray with coffee. He took stock of the man in front of him, proud, arrogant, distrustful, but also clearly concerned. Hiram must be important to him, he thought. Perhaps there is some truth to what he had told him about the Royal Navy's plans to blockade New York and Boston? Morgan wondered why Stryker seemed so sure that Hiram was on board the *Victoria*. Perhaps someone in Portsmouth had given him the information. Perhaps it was another sailor. It could have been the waterman who had ferried Hiram out to the *Victoria*. It could have been one of the wharf rats the British used as informants. He didn't like to think of the other alternative, but he knew it could have been one of his passengers. They were his friends, but they were English. They would not have refused giving information to a Royal Navy captain, particularly if they were told this was information vital to the queen's interest.

As Lowery poured the coffee, Morgan turned to Stryker, speaking with a controlled voice, hiding the contempt he felt for the man.

"Captain Stryker, I reckon it must be a most unpleasant duty for a British commander to be forced to board an American packet ship and look for a runaway sailor."

Stryker's face was tense and rigid as he took a sip of coffee.

"I'm sure this doesn't happen often, Captain, does it?" Morgan asked.

Stryker angrily dropped his coffee cup on the table, pushed it away, and stood up.

"Let's start with your personal quarters, Captain," Stryker said with a controlled businesslike voice as he glanced at the closed doors of the staterooms on all sides.

Morgan showed the English captain his own cabin, and then gave him a tour of the staterooms, making sure he mentioned the room that Queen Victoria and Prince Albert had visited. He did not hesitate to go over every detail, adopting the tone he used when he was welcoming his first-class passengers. His primary purpose was to avoid too many inquiries.

"Over there is the sleeping quarters for the cook and the stewards. And now we'll have a look at the galley," Morgan said as he walked ahead of Stryker, gesturing with his hands. "This is my steward, Mr. Lowery, his assistant, Mr. Junkett, and the cook, Mr. Scuttles."

Stryker nodded with disinterest as he walked by the three colored men and stepped into the ship's galley area. Lowery seemed to be trying to tell him something, but Morgan couldn't comprehend his facial gestures. Stryker's eyes roamed from one door to the next. He looked closely at Lowery with obvious distrust. Morgan invited the captain to have a look around and then walked intentionally with undue heavy steps beside the dark section of the pantry where the potatoes were kept and where Hiram was hidden.

"Very spacious, don't you agree?" Morgan continued, reaching over to the storeroom door and opening it with a flourish. There were dozens of barrels inside the storeroom with everything from apples and turnips, carrots and peas, to onions and potatoes. Stryker took another oblique step, lifting up the tops of some of the barrels. He held his nose at the sight and smell of the oily, greasy slush in one barrel. Lowery, who was standing behind Stryker, was now madly jerking his head up and down and rolling his eyes. Morgan looked at him with a puzzled face as he quickly turned back to attend to Stryker, who was opening each and every container.

The English captain poked his head into the onion barrel, and then unexpectedly withdrew his sword from his belt and began sticking it into the onions with small jabs and then thrusting it downward. He did the same with a barrel of apples and finally he reached the potatoes. Morgan almost called out a warning, but then quickly stifled it. Stryker raised his sword high above his head and thrust it down into the potatoes, all the way to the hilt. Morgan choked back a gasp as he waited for a noise, any noise, coming from inside the barrel, but there was none, just a prolonged silence. He imagined Hiram curled up inside, bleeding, writhing in pain. After a weighty pause, he asked if Stryker was satisfied with his tour of the first-class cabin area and would he now care to tour the more basic second-class area.

An hour later with the search over, Morgan showed the disappointed English captain out onto the quarterdeck and Stryker turned to him with a stony face, the backs of his hands resting on his hips.

"It may be we were given bad information, Captain. We were told by a very reliable source that the deserter was seen boarding your ship. If you find the man, Captain Morgan, I would ask you to arrest him and hand him over to the authorities in the nearest English port. I am sure you realize that failure to do so would have serious consequences for yourself and your ship."

"Thank you for that sober advice, Commander. It's been our pleasure to accommodate your search, but remember, when this ship leaves port, the next stop will be New York."

Morgan's boldness had the desired result. Stryker's face grew red with anger and disgust.

"Your disrespect for the Crown does not go unnoticed, Captain."

At the ladder the disgruntled English captain lingered.

"We will investigate this matter further, and if we find anything that implicates you or your ship, rest assured we will pursue you."

Stryker then turned his back to Morgan and left as quickly as he came without even a farewell. As the British sailors bent their shoulders into pulling the oars of their quarter boat, the *Victoria*'s cabin passengers were arriving on a small steamer. Soon the quarterdeck of the packet ship was swarming with top hats, swallowtail coats, billowy ankle-length dresses, ruffling petticoats, and brightly colored bonnets.

Morgan wiped the sweat off his brow. He wasted no time in getting the packet ship underway.

As the first mate, Mr. Stark yelled, "Anchor aweigh," Morgan rushed below and confronted Lowery.

"Is he dead?"

"No sir. He's alive."

"How is that possible? The man drove his sword to the bottom of the barrel, right to the hilt."

"He ain't in the potatoes, Cap'n. He's in here."

Lowery pointed to another barrel adjacent to the potatoes that was filled with beets.

"Is that what you were trying to signal me?"

"Yes, sir."

Morgan heard some banging and pounding. Scuttles opened the barrel, and pulled out a false bottom only two feet from the top, revealing a brown head of hair, the smiling, whiskery face of Hiram Smith quickly emerging amidst the beets.

"That was a close call, Ely."

"A narrow escape indeed, Hiram."

"Keep him out of sight, Lowery. He's our secret passenger."

With an ebb tide carrying them swiftly out of the Solent and a steady northwesterly wind, the *Victoria*'s bow cut through the water with ease. The packet had as much canvas as she could bear and was moving along at about twelve knots. Morgan had Icelander set a course for the northwestern tip of France. If they stayed off the wind and hugged the eastern side of the English Channel, passing close to Alderney, he thought to himself, they might be able to stay out of sight and elude any ship that pursued them.

PART X

Concerning the manner of your brother's death, it may be that I have some information to give you; though it may not be, for I am far from sure. Can we have a little talk alone?

—Charles Dickens, "A Message from the Sea,"
All the Year Round

26

1850

From his dimly lit cabin inside the packet ship, a quiet, reflective Morgan paused and listened to the late-night noises on the docks in New York. The hearty, full-throated laughs of drunken sailors returning from the taverns mixed in with the loud, gruff voices of angry ships' officers. It was well past midnight. The night was balmy for early June. The South Street docks would soon quiet down to the more gentle hum and murmur of a small village. He had been in New York for more than a week due to the pressing needs of the shipping line. He had received a cryptic note from Hiram Smith written a few weeks earlier. He hadn't heard a word from his old friend since he helped him escape from the clutches of the Royal Navy and dropped him off at Peck's Slip in New York. That was five years ago. "I have much to tell you, Ely," he had written. "I have new information about Abraham. I hope to be at the South Street docks before your June departure unless Stryker's men find me. I know they are looking for me." That was all he'd written.

Morgan looked at the short letter in his hand and shook his head in puzzlement. There was no indication where it had been sent from. It sounded like Hiram knew something important. Morgan had waited all week, but there was no sign of Hiram and there had been no new letter. Most of the crew members were now off ship. Only the stewards, Lowery and Junkett, were there with him in the cabin. Old Whipple was in the forecastle. Nearby he could hear the creaking oarlocks of a passing dory and in the distance the forlorn sound of a fiddle trading sorrowful notes with a slow-picked banjo.

He had tried to sleep but couldn't. He looked down at his desk at some of the financial correspondence he needed to attend to. His mind drifted to business matters and a wave of confidence and optimism swept over him. The threat of war with England over the Oregon dispute fortunately had been averted. He liked to think that the mutual benefits of trans-atlantic trade had won the day. Now the wharves of South Street were overflowing with cargo. Shovels, pick axes, pans, and other supplies, all brought from England, were emptied out of the packet ships and loaded onto clipper ships bound for the gold fields of California. Out of those same ships came a human river of hopeful emigrants also headed for the El Dorado. His new ship, the 1,299-ton *Southampton*, was the biggest of the London liners at 181 feet in length, far bigger than the *American Eagle* or the *Margaret Evans*, which had been built for the Black X Line a few years earlier. It was also about seven feet longer than the firm's speedy *Devonshire*, which the New York papers had called "almost a steamboat of speed."

Morgan felt that the *Southampton* was the fastest ship he had ever sailed on, capable of sustaining a speed of fourteen knots under full sail, just like the clippers now breaking all records on their way to the goldfields of California. Ironically, even as the sailing packets got bigger and faster, the Cunard steamers continued to steal away more and more travelers. The new larger and more elegant Collins steamships were also attracting the more affluent. Notwithstanding the *Herald*'s James Gordon Bennett's estimate a few years earlier that the New York ocean packets were still carrying over half of the cabin passengers, it was clear that the sailing ships were no longer the preferred way to cross the Atlantic. Even Morgan could no longer deny this. His writer friend Caroline Kirkland had written him in October 1848, "As to going home with you, you may be sure going in the steamer is none of my plan." She would have come, she wrote him, but her traveling companion wanted to try one of the new steamers.

As he sat there at his desk, he thought of Eliza and how she had been able to join him on the ship these last few years. It had been like old times, the two of them sailing together. She had kept the saloon filled with melodious sonatas of Mozart, Bach, and Chopin. In London, she had happily reacquainted herself with the Leslies and many of the other artists, including old Turner. Eliza also met Thackeray for the first time and was charmed by this witty man with his owl-like spectacles and his melodious voice. They'd traveled by carriage to Hampstead to see Stanfield's new house, whirling by the rolling green hills and trim hedgerows in that picturesque village. Then they had taken the train to Brighton to meet Morgan's new friend, Charles Dickens, who was vacationing there with his wife and some of his children. Eliza had been pleased that the author's eldest son, Charles, and her son, William, had gotten along famously, as he also did with Dickens's two daughters, who were just a couple of years older than her Ruth and Mary Frances.

The gentle lap of the water against the ship's wooden hull made him think of their new home. With four children now, the Morgans had moved out of New York to a house on the Connecticut River in Saybrook on the corner of Main Street and the Boston Road, not too far from the New York ferry landing. It was a gracious two-story home with an expansive rooftop terrace, ideal for views of the river, that was large enough for Eliza's mother to move in with them. He wondered how much longer he could keep up as a packet shipmaster. He was forty-four years old and he was well aware that his four children were growing up quickly, mostly without a father. Most packet ship captains did not last on the job for even five years. Only a dozen or so had retained command for fifteen years. Yet he had been a packet ship captain now for nearly twenty. He had crossed the Atlantic well over one hundred times. He thought of his old first mate, Dan Stark, who had been lost at sea six months ago on a cold winter voyage aboard the *Mediator*, his first command. He knew it could easily have been him. In the back of his mind he wondered how long his good fortune would last. Morgan's late-night reverie was again interrupted by the sound of creaking oarlocks from a small boat. The sound of the water slapping up against the ship's hull increased in intensity. He wondered to himself who could be rowing around his ship at this time of night.

The methodical sound of oars splashing the surface of the water soon faded, and Morgan went back to his task of writing letters. Just as he was finishing up sealing and addressing the last of the small letters, he thought he heard the sounds of muffled footsteps and the creaking of deck boards over his head, but then there was silence. He dismissed these noises as his imagination and he retired to his berth and fell asleep.

A sudden banging on his door jolted him awake. Morgan sat upright as Whipple stumbled into his quarters carrying a lantern. The man's shirt-tails were hanging loose, his pants unbuttoned, and he was barefoot. His face was flushed.

"Lord sakes, what is it, Whipple?"

"An intruder, Captain! Someone's inside the ship!"

"What? Where?"

"The chain locker. I heard lots of noises. The kind of scurrying and shuffling that could only come from a human crittur, Cap'n."

Morgan told Whipple to go rouse the two stewards just forward of the main cabin. Then he quickly put on some clothes and grabbed his two pistols. The four men met up on deck. Lowery and Junkett had thrown on their stewards' jackets over their bare chests, and each of them had a kitchen cleaver in their hands.

Whipple led this small group down the stairs from the upper hold into the lower cargo hold, swinging his lantern high in a wide circle and holding his knife out with his other hand. They were now deep in the belly of the ship below the water line. It was like descending underground into some large coffin, cold and damp, the stale air ripe from the heavy anchor hawsers. Morgan clutched his two pistols, keeping them high and ready. They were surrounded by a dark, shadowy maze of crates, bags, and barrels filled with flour and clover seed, as well as bales of tobacco and hogsheads of turpentine. He could hear the tiny claws of rats scurrying around. The big deck timbers below creaked as they tried to walk quietly through the lower hold. Whipple stopped suddenly and motioned for them to listen. The noises were coming from the center of the ship down in the bilge area below them.

They approached the hatch that led down to the bilge. Morgan could hear a scraping, and a grinding as metal carved through wood. The two stewards clutched their cleavers holding them in front of them. Morgan motioned Whipple to extinguish his lantern and with the sudden blackness now extending over them, they could see a dim light emerging through a hole in the lower deck. There definitely was someone in the bowels of the ship, deep in the bilge.

Morgan went first, delicately and slowly opening the hatch. The stench of the rank decay from muddy water dredged up from the river bottoms filled his nostrils. He felt his way down the narrow ladder. The reek of the bilges was so strong he had to breathe through his mouth, trying not to cough. The others followed, touching each other in the dark so as not to get disoriented. They could now hear a louder scraping of metal and a man's labored, heavy breathing. The bilge area had so little headroom they had to crouch. There they remained for a few minutes, not daring to move. Morgan held out his cocked pistols toward a faint hint of light that glimmered behind one of the ship's knees amidships.

"Who's there? Show yourself or I'll fire!" he yelled out.

The noise abruptly stopped. The faint light disappeared. There was no answer. For what seemed like an eternity to Morgan there was total silence. He wondered if he should fire. Suddenly, they heard the sound of fleeing footsteps, heavy breathing, and the frantic scratching and banging of someone running on all fours. Whipple lit his lantern and held it up high, straining to see down the narrow gloom of the inner cavity of the ship. Now they could hear crashes and curses as the intruder ran and stumbled to the stern of the ship away from them. The four of them gave pursuit, running and scrambling like hunchbacks as they followed the thudding footsteps ahead of them.

They stopped to catch their breath and Morgan yelled out again, "Stop or I will fire! There is nowhere for you to run!"

Suddenly out of the darkness came a scream. A black figure ran toward them. Morgan fired and then fired again. The others shouted in confusion. The figure continued hurtling toward them. He was carrying something like a spear extended out in front of him. He was screaming like a madman. Morgan prepared for the end when the unknown assailant fell to the ground with a crash.

"I got his foot, Cap'n!" yelled Lowery.

The man was growling and struggling like a wild animal caught in a trap as Whipple held the lantern up high and put a knife to the intruder's throat. Morgan put his pistols away and rolled the man over so he could see his face.

"Who are you? What are you doing on my ship?"

Whipple brought the light closer so they could now see who it was. The man's eyes were deeply sunk into his hollow, gaunt face. His hair was wild and ragged. Whiskers sprouted from his chin like bristles on a hog's back.

Morgan was shocked as he suddenly realized who he was looking at.

"Do you recognize him, Cap'n?" asked Whipple, who hadn't removed his knife from the man's throat.

"It's John Taylor," gasped Morgan as he looked intently at the fearful eyes now staring back at him. He turned to his stewards and told them to tie him up with some of the hawse lines that were scattered around the bilge area.

Whipple began swinging his lantern in a circle until he found the man's weapon.

"Here's what he was trying to kill you with, Cap'n. Looks to be an augur, a big one at that." Whipple held out a large unwieldy tool into the light with a nearly two-foot-long metal drilling bit some two inches in diameter. Morgan had an awful feeling as he tried to imagine what Taylor would be doing in the bottom of his ship with a deadly weapon.

"What were you doing here, Taylor?"

Morgan reached for the man's throat.

"Tell me!"

Morgan wasn't waiting for an answer.

"Quick Whipple, check the area he was in. I think he must have been trying to scuttle us."

The old ship's carpenter ran back to the center of the bilge near the keel area and began crawling around on all fours, keeping the lantern on the planking.

"There are about a dozen two-inch-wide holes in the thick outer planking of the ship about eight feet from the keel, Cap'n."

"Is water coming in?"

"There is some weeping, but I don't see no leaks."

"Check them through and through, Whipple."

"Looks like he may have gotten close, Cap'n, but he didn't get all the way through the copper sheathing."

Morgan told the two stewards to take the man up above into the lower cargo area. He then examined the holes closely. It looked as if Taylor had drilled a hole all the way through the outer planking and pricked the copper sheathing. With that little protection, the first heavy beating they encountered during the Atlantic crossing would have caused the ship to spring several major leaks.

"He was trying to sink us, Cap'n," Whipple said matter-of-factly.

"Plug up the holes with trenails and caulking, Mr. Whipple. I will be asking our visitor some questions."

Morgan found Taylor tied up in a chair, a lantern swinging over his head. He ran a critical eye over the man. Taylor was a pitiful sight. His thin, pointed face, covered with sweat and grime from the bilge, was unshaven and his hair was dirty. His eyes were sunk into their sockets with dark shadow underneath them. His mouth and teeth were black from smoking an opium pipe. Taylor looked up at him with dull, dead eyes.

Brandishing the augur in his hand, Morgan asked, "Why did you do this?"

"I ain't talking. He'll kill me if I say anything."

"Who?"

"No matter what you do to me, I got nothing to tell you."

Morgan turned to Lowery.

"Mr. Junkett, I am sure Scuttles has some rancid slush in his bucket in the galley. Bring that. I hear tell Mr. Taylor has a love of rats."

Taylor's eyes bulged out with horror and fear. Morgan then turned to Lowery.

"Blindfold him, gag him with a cloth, and get me a hog-bristle brush."

An hour later, Morgan watched as Lowery and Junkett coated Taylor's face and body with a thick coat of the slobbery mess. The man was squirming and struggling in his chair as the two stewards spread thick gobs over his face and hair. The smell of rancid grease filled the cargo hold, and it wasn't long before the rustle and scurrying of small feet could be heard in the dark corners of the hold. Along with that came the high-pitched squeals of hungry rats.

"Do you hear that, Taylor? They're starting to squeak with pleasure in anticipation of their feast. They can smell the grease. I reckon there are scores of rats in this ship. We're going to leave you here now, alone, so you can meet your new friends."

The blindfolded man struggled spasmodically to get free of the rope that bound him to the chair. Even with the gag, he was making terrible sounds as he tried to scream. Within minutes, a dozen rats appeared and began crawling over his body, starting at his feet and working their way up to his face, squeaking and snarling as they gorged themselves. Their bodies and tails wiggled and twisted as they happily bit into the man's slushy face, his head, and open neck. Taylor's body was in convulsions. He grunted and heaved, struggling to breathe as he tried to shake off his attackers.

Soon the man's face and arms were covered with squirming and squeaking rodents, hungrily nipping and tearing into the exposed flesh. After five minutes of listening to his muffled screams, Morgan reappeared, swatting away the rodents, kicking the persistent ones that were reluctant to leave their feast. He pulled off the man's gag. Taylor screamed, loud and long, his body still twitching with terror.

"Mercy. Have mercy," he gasped. "It was Blackwood. He told me to do it," cried out the still-blindfolded man. "For the love of God, set me free."

At the mention of Blackwood's name, Morgan was silent. He still made no move to untie the man or remove the blindfold.

"Is he the one giving you opium?"

"He promised me if I did this one job for him I could spend my days chasing the dragon."

Morgan glared at Taylor.

"Why? Why are you doing this?"

"Have mercy, Captain. The pipe is the only thing that helps me. Liquor was my salvation at first, but then I fell into the terrors and I began having horrible visions. Then I heard voices. They wouldn't stop. The pipe gave me a way to forget. When I smoke the voices go away."

"Where is Blackwood?" Morgan asked sharply. He pulled off the blindfold. Taylor's eyes blinked rapidly as he tried to adjust to his surroundings.

"I don't know. He finds me. I don't find him."

Morgan slowly took a Havana cigar out of his pocket, rolling it in his mouth. He picked up the lantern and lit it. After the first puff, he began speaking in a more strident voice.

"Well, Taylor, you are not leaving this ship until you tell me what you alone know. What happened to my brother all those years ago? He was your friend and you betrayed him. I already know that the *Charon* was a slave ship. Most of the crew were blind and the captain was losing his eyesight. Abraham was put in the hold. Why? Did he die there?"

Taylor looked shocked, but said nothing, lowering his head at first as if refusing to speak. His hands were noticeably trembling as he began speaking slowly with great hesitation.

"We were in the middle of the Atlantic. The captain ordered the hatches battened down. Those Africans in the lower hold got no air, only a little bit of hard biscuit thrown down at them. No one wanted to go down into that dark cavern. It reeked of sickness and death. Blackwood and his mate, Tom Edgars, we called him Big Red, they were having a discussion about what to do. Blackwood ordered us to get those sick Negroes up on deck. He kept telling Abraham and me that we Yankee seal pups needed to get to know the ship's cargo. He would laugh and tell us, 'Learn the trade, boys. Ye 'ave to learn the skill of handlin' black ebony.'"

Taylor paused as he gulped several times and pulled nervously at his stringy, dirty hair.

"It was too awful a sight to look at. Most of them Africans were infected, their eyes already crusty and closed. They were diseased. They couldn't see. The women were moaning and shrieking. Blackwood took a whip to them, prodding the noisy ones in their privates. 'That's 'ow ye make 'em respect yer,' he said. They were all manacled together, chains clanking away on their ankles and their wrists. He separated the healthier ones, but kept them up on deck. He summoned Abraham over and told him to shackle all two hundred slaves who were going blind to the anchor hawse line."

"He did what?" Morgan asked, his voice shocked and horrified.

"Abraham refused. Blackwood grabbed him and picked him up by the neck. 'Ye follow orders ye Yankee pig-dog,' he said. Those were his very words, Captain. Then it got worse."

Taylor looked up at Morgan with pleading eyes.

"Go on," said Morgan coldly as he braced himself for gruesome details he knew he didn't want to hear.

"He threw your brother down on the deck and drew his clenched fist back and slammed it into his face, telling him to crawl on his knees like an animal. 'Filthy Guinea lover,' he called him. Abraham struggled, but Blackwood kicked him and then brought out a rope with a knot at the end of it and started to beat and thrash him until he passed out. He fell flat on the deck. Blackwood ordered two of the men to take Abraham below deck and lock him in the hold."

Morgan said nothing, too astonished to react. His knuckles tightened on the augur he was still holding.

As if he was recounting a bad dream, Taylor continued, his eyes now becoming moist. He began speaking faster, his voice strained.

"Blackwood then turned on me and ordered me to do it. All the men were crowded around. They wanted to see what I would do. All those eyes were looking at me, Captain. I was so frightened. I tied that hawse line around the chains on the first slave and then ran it back through the long line of Africans, finally attaching the end to the kedge anchor. The slaves were moaning and wailing. Blackwood then ordered me to throw the anchor overboard, and 'make the sharks 'appy.' That's what he said."

"Make the sharks happy?" Morgan repeated in disbelief. "What kind of animal . . . ?" He shook his head in amazement at this tale of human brutality. "What did you do?"

"I told him I wouldn't do it, but he came at me with his rope, laughing like a madman." Taylor's face was now moist with perspiration. His body trembled and shook. He started weeping. His voice cracked.

"To my eternal shame, I did what he asked."

"Lord sakes" was all Morgan could say.

"The anchor fell like a boulder with a loud splash. I watched spellbound as those slaves, screaming and wailing, were pulled over the bulwarks, their eyes white with fear. I watched as one by one, all two hundred of them fell to their death, the splash of each body hitting the water, the sharks swarming around the ship turning the sea red, and then finally silence."

"Did the other slaves see this?"

Taylor nodded slowly.

"I have never forgotten the way they looked at me as they shuffled by, their chains clanking on the deck, their eyes piercing into my soul like sharp daggers. I can still hear the women sobbing and moaning."

He paused before continuing.

"I tried to tell you before, but I couldn't bring myself to confess."

Taylor looked over at Morgan, his eyes seeming to plead for forgiveness. Despite his revulsion of this pitiful, broken man, Morgan began to feel sorry for him. He took the cigar out of his mouth, and looked down at its glowing tip. His voice softened somewhat.

"What happened next?" he asked.

Taylor looked down at his hands, which were shaking uncontrollably, and continued with his story.

"That foul disease spread all over the ship. We were cursed. Soon enough, it was mostly Blackwood and me sailing the ship along with a few other men."

"How did you avoid getting it?"

"I drenched my hands and face with rum and put tarred mittens on my hands."

"What about Abraham?"

"I gave him food and water in the hold each day. Most of the other sailors were lying on the deck with bandannas around their eyes. Even Big Red, the mate, was of little use. Blackwood told me where to steer. Toward the end, he was losing his eyesight, which made me all the more important to him."

"What about the storm? Where were you when it struck?"

"We thought we were somewhere to the north of Puerto Rico when it started blowing hard. I was clutching onto the wheel as tight as a barnacle on a whale's back. The wind was howling and the waves rolling across the ship. They were like mountains. Must have been twenty feet high. We sailed westerly under one topsail, we thought, toward Jamaica, the winds coming in hard from the north. I spotted Cape Mole and I could barely see the mountains of Haiti as we laid a course through the Windward Passage. All the time, I could hear the moaning down below decks. That was the last time I ever saw Abraham. I gave him some hard biscuit that morning and he handed me his journal, making me swear I would give it to his mother."

Taylor paused, stumbled, and then lowered his eyes.

"Go on," Morgan said impatiently.

"It was in the middle of the night when we felt the first jolt. The ship reared up like a horse, and then came crashing down. That was when we heard the breakers. Blackwood told me to bear off. I did as he asked, but it was too late. The ship drove right onto the reef, the keel lodging itself in between rocks and coral. I could hear the cracking and splintering of wood and the cries of desperation from inside the ship. We were slanted over like a sloping hillside due to the force of the waves and Blackwood told me to lower the quarter boat. He grabbed Big Red and a couple of the other sailors who could still see and told me to load them up. We left behind most of the blind sailors on deck, crawling on all fours pleading for help, clutching any rope they could find. All the time I could hear the wailing from the belly of the ship. It was like the ship itself was crying out."

"What about Abraham?" Morgan asked slowly, as he tried to control his emotions.

"Blackwood had a pistol to my head. I had no choice but to row away. I am sorry, Captain. That was how your brother died. We left him trapped inside the hold along with all those Africans and the blind sailors with the ship taking on water. I am sorry. Not a day passes that I don't hear those cries for help and imagine those eyes staring at me in fear and hatred. Not a day passes that I don't imagine Abraham lying there in that wet holding locker, blind and unable to move with the water rising."

Morgan felt a sudden helplessness sweep over him. So that was it. He was glad his mother had never found out the truth. It had been better she had died with the faint hope that one of her two sons lost at sea was still alive.

"Did you make it ashore?"

"We survived the waves that stormy night. When daybreak came, we saw these huge mountains off to the west and we rode the breakers onto the beach near a place called Morant Bay. It turned out we were on the southeastern shore of Jamaica in the parish of St. Thomas. As soon as I got ashore, I ran away and kept running ever since."

"You never got the eye disease?"

"No. Blackwood and Big Red weren't so lucky. By the time we got to land, Blackwood's eyes were infected. To this day he bears those scars and Big Red lost one eye to that disease."

"Where did you hide out all these years, Taylor?"

"Many places. For many years it was the White Goose Tavern down on Water Street, you know where the blood sports pit is located. That was my hideaway. O'Leary, the Rat Man, put me to work collecting rats down at the wharf. I would come in at night with a fresh supply in a bag. Weasel bait we called it. One night I was about to make my delivery when I thought I saw Big Red. He had a patch on his eye. I ducked out of sight, but I think he spotted me then."

"When did they catch you?"

"It was only a few months ago that Blackwood tracked me down in the Blow-Hole Tavern over on Cherry Street."

Taylor reached into his pocket and pulled out a letter.

"Before I forget, Captain, Blackwood said I was to leave this by your cabin door before I left. You were supposed to find it in the morning."

Morgan took it from the man. The letter was addressed simply to Captain Morgan, the *Southampton*. It had no return address. He opened it and began reading a card. The handwriting was small, but clearly came from an educated hand. It was from Captain James Stryker on the H.M.S. *Hydra*, one of the paddle-wheel steam frigates of the Royal Navy.

27

Morgan straightened up as he stood beside the giant form of Icelander at the helm. It was pitch dark, just shy of midnight. The *Southampton* had cleared the markers outside the protected waters of Sandy Hook, and the force of the wind now filled the ship's sails. The Black X packet had a full load of first-class passengers. There was a sense of urgency on board. Morgan had informed the crew that the ship would be pushed to its limits. To reassure himself he was making the right decision, he pulled out the letter he had received from Stryker and read it again under the lantern light by the binnacle.

Dear Captain Morgan,

I am writing you from across the Hudson River in New Jersey at the Cunard Docks. It gives me great satisfaction to inform you that we have in our custody the runaway sailor and deserter Hiram Smith. We apprehended him in the West Indies. He is now a prisoner of the Royal Navy. He will be brought to justice before the Admiralty when we get back to England. The charges will be desertion from one of Her Majesty's ships, and espionage. I am thoroughly confident that he will receive the full taste of English justice which a foreign spy so richly deserves. After recoaling, we leave for England at first light.

Most sincerely,
Captain James Stryker, R.N.
H.M.S. Hydra

After reading it again, Morgan remained as astonished as he was the first time he read it. Stryker had nabbed Hiram. He was arresting him not only as a deserter, but as a spy, presumably because he had posed as a British sailor. It would mean a hanging, almost certainly. Morgan was determined he would try to get to England as soon as possible, perhaps even before the British Navy steamship. His idea was to try to enlist support from some of Leslie's influential friends in the nobility. He thought of Lord Nanvers. Nanvers had met Hiram. Perhaps the English Lord would try to help sway the Admiralty judges to be lenient.

Morgan had decided to take the far northern route across the roof of the Atlantic as sailors called it. This was slightly further to the north than the packet ship's normal route on the eastward passage. It was the shortest and most direct way to cross the Atlantic, a distance of approximately 2,800 miles. This route would take him north of the Grand Banks into possible ice fields, but he was quite familiar with the hazards.

He knew the steamer would choose the standard shipping lane along the southern route. It was considered the safer path, and most of the steamers chose this track because they would travel far away from the dangers of the shallow waters off the North American coast, and well south of the foul weather and ice to the north. But it was longer, roughly 3,100 miles. He calculated that if the steamer left at first light, it had a twelve-hour head start. He knew these paddle wheelers could only steam along at eleven to twelve knots, so with the right winds he thought the *Southampton* might be able to even overtake the H.M.S. *Hydra* before they reached the English Channel. He knew what was important was to get to London as soon as possible.

Morgan folded the letter and put it into his pocket. The *Southampton*'s bow rose to meet the ocean swells. He barked out orders for more canvas.

"Aloft there some of you and loose all sails."

"Aye, aye, sir. Royals and skysails as well?"

"Yes, and loose all head sails."

The new first mate, Richard Moore, joined in.

"You men over there, look alive! Take in those clewlines at the main. Clap a watch tackle on the starboard topsail sheet and rouse her home. Sheet home the topsails. Look alive there!"

The ship's large prominent bowsprit rose to meet the dark, oncoming waves like a steeplechase horse leaping over a looming fence. Morgan faced forward into the night and gazed at the bright tip of his glowing cigar. His mind shifted to Taylor's startling revelations. He was still stunned. He knew now what had happened to his brother, yet along with Taylor's grisly story had come so many questions, so many puzzling mysteries. Taylor had said Blackwood had given him Stryker's letter. It didn't make any sense. He couldn't grasp what would have brought Blackwood and Stryker together. A committed Royal Navy captain in the West African Squadron and a man he should be pursuing were an unlikely pair. He shook his head as he walked toward the main mast at the center of the ship and gazed out into the deep blackness of the night.

By the morning of June 14, the *Southampton* had cleared the Grand Banks, having been at sea for five and a half days. Ominously, as the sun slowly slipped down below the western horizon, Morgan looked ahead and saw a frozen expanse. Against the now dark and overcast sky, the blue ocean had suddenly disappeared into a sea of white. One vast ice field lay before them. It was a frightening but thrilling sight. The thick hull of the *Southampton* shuddered as it hit the thin crust of ice head on and began plowing through it. The hideous sound of the ice crackling and crunching exploded on either side of the ship. Soon they were well into the ice field as night descended on them. The ship was trembling like a frozen twig in a winter storm, the wooden beams and planks moaning under the stress.

A shout arose from below.

"Water in the hold. Man the pumps!"

Whipple went down below to assess the damage. Water was beginning to seep up into the lower cargo hold. A quick inspection showed some of the trenails he'd hammered in the day before had given way, but he soon discovered an even bigger problem. The ship was taking in water on the port side. The water level was already knee deep in parts of the bilge. Morgan set the crew to work pumping and jettisoning cargo as he reassured his passengers that the leak was nothing to worry about. This went on for nearly an hour as the ship continued to plow its way through the expansive field, peeling back and breaking off large, thin shards of ice.

Whipple waded into the freezing water at the bottom of the ship and began looking for cracks or breaks in the planking. He soon discovered the problem. Besides the holes near the keel, Taylor had perforated the ship's hull on the port side directly under the waterline, holes which Whipple had not detected. The friction from the ice had compromised the thin veneer of wood Taylor left in the planking. Water was pouring in. Whipple stuffed towels and rags into the holes. As the crew continued to pump and throw more cargo overboard to further lighten the ship, the water level slowly receded, allowing Whipple to plug the holes more permanently with large makeshift trenails, oakum, and tar.

With the winds still strong, the *Southampton* powered its way out of the ice pack. It took two hours to do so. Morgan squared the yards. He saw several black-and-white shearwaters dancing across the surface of the water, gliding and dipping over the waves, a sign that Ireland might be as close as two days away. The birds made him think of Old Jeremiah, and he remembered how that old superstitious tar had labeled John Taylor a Jonah. Maybe he was right. Taylor was cursed. He had almost succeeded in sinking the ship. In a moment of sympathy before departing, he had thought of bringing him on board, but now after this close call, he was glad to have left the opium addict behind to lose himself in the streets of New York. John Taylor needed to face his own demons now, but not on board the *Southampton.*

Over the next few days, the winds of the North Atlantic favored the packet ship and they were able to make up for lost time. The breeze stayed constant, eventually settling in from the southwest. The weather conditions were excellent, with cloudless skies and cool air. The tributaries of the Gulf Stream, moving at half a knot, were also helping to pull them eastward. With every possible sail set, the packet ticked off the miles as she sped eastward toward the continent at fourteen knots. It was about one hundred miles from the southwestern edge of Ireland that the cry came out from the lookout on the mainmast.

"Smoke on the horizon!"

Morgan grabbed his spyglass and sure enough he could see a trail of black smoke hanging over the far eastern horizon. A steamship was no more than ten miles ahead of them. The sun was just setting to the west, ominously coloring the skies a brilliant red.

The next morning Morgan could barely make out the Royal Navy flag flying off the steamship's mizzenmast. The first mate held the spyglass to his eye, and then turned toward him.

"Something strange there, Cap'n," he whispered. "That steamship. It almost seems like she slowed down overnight. Might be she's having engine trouble?"

A seed of doubt crept into Morgan's mind. If this steamship ahead of them was Stryker's ship, the *Hydra*, he couldn't possibly hope to accomplish anything by coming closer. His instincts told him to raise even more sails and give the steamship a wide berth, but some force he didn't understand wanted to see if this was Stryker's ship. Anger, pride, revenge, friendship, and loyalty were all bubbling inside of him. He reached into his pocket with his left hand and felt his brother's old pennywhistle, and in that moment he put his doubts aside. Like a sudden strong wind taking control of the sails, he felt unable to resist where he was being pulled. At that moment, it was Abraham, not Hiram, who was on the Royal Navy steamer ahead of him.

"Let's swing closer, Mr. Moore."

Within a few hours, they had moved to the windward of the paddle wheeler, still trailing by a mile. Morgan calculated that the steamer was moving along at about nine knots, slower than usual. The two ships were almost at the western edge of Ireland now. In the distance he could see the breakers crashing onto the rocky shoreline of the islands near Dunmore Head, with the bright green edge of the cliffs and mountains in the distance. The *Southampton* had left New York slightly more than eleven and a half days earlier. It was not just a fast passage. It had the makings of a record passage.

Morgan could see the individual paddles churning in the water and hear the roar and thumping of the engine arising from the guts of the steam frigate. With the spyglass, he could just make out the name of the ship on its transom. It was the *Hydra*. At the sight of the packet outracing the bigger 208-foot-long steamship, the delighted American passengers on board the *Southampton* were now singing "Yankee Doodle" and waving their white handkerchiefs triumphantly to signal that they would soon be saying good-bye to the smoky steamship.

The packet ship came even with the steamship's paddle wheels on the windward side. The two big ships were now just three hundred yards apart. If Morgan hadn't come that close, it's possible he might not have seen the scuffle on deck. A man dressed in a simple work shirt with blue dungarees was swinging an oar he'd picked up from one of the lifeboats. The man was surrounded by the frigate's officers, who were ducking and weaving.

"Bring us closer, Icelander. There's something strange happening on the deck of the Navy ship."

Morgan held the spyglass firmly to his left eye and tried to follow the action occurring at the stern of the *Hydra*. It took him several attempts to steady the glass, but he was finally able to focus on the man who was causing so much trouble. His face and arms were black with soot, and he was wielding the oar like a sailor who had rowed many a dory in a rough sea. He'd already knocked down two men. The ghostly vision of Abraham faded as Morgan looked more closely. It was definitely Hiram. He had grown a full beard since he'd seen him last.

At that moment, he saw the image of Stryker appear in his bouncing lens. The man's face was livid with rage. Next to him was another man he knew. His large head and body and his small, black eyes hidden beneath fleshy eyelids made him unmistakable. It was the same man who had led the attempted mutiny against him on the *Philadelphia* years ago. He breathed out slowly even as he felt a chill go down his spine. "Blackwood." The man's black hair was now streaked with silver, but otherwise he was unchanged. Standing next to him was a man with beet-red hair and an eye patch. "Big Red," he whispered.

"What did you say, Cap'n?" asked the mate.

"Nothing, Mr. Moore. Nothing. Steady on."

He kept his eye to the spyglass. Blackwood and Big Red were both armed with clubs and were trying to get close to the sooty-faced, bearded sailor. Just as they appeared to be cornering him, he watched in astonishment as the man either jumped off or fell overboard into the ocean. Morgan didn't hesitate. He immediately ordered the first mate to back the yards, and then signaled for the lifeboats to be lowered on either side of the ship. In water below forty degrees, a man could be dead within fifteen minutes of striking the water of the North Atlantic. Sailors called the paralyzing freezing water the "cold locker." Fortunately, in June the water temperatures were not anywhere near as cold as forty degrees, but the temperatures were frigid enough to make someone lose consciousness if they were not rescued quickly.

Soon the *Southampton*'s lifeboats were afloat, the men rowing vigorously through the waves back to where the man had jumped. Morgan followed the action with his spyglass and watched as they approached an unmoving figure afloat, slumped across a barely visible oar. For a moment he looked up to see what was happening with the steamship. The *Hydra* had slowed momentarily, altering its course, and appeared to be in the process of turning around. The *Southampton*'s lifeboats rescued the trembling man. Morgan couldn't believe his eyes as he watched a shivering, bedraggled Hiram lifted aboard the packet ship.

He quickly turned his attention back to the ship and the helmsman. The Royal Navy frigate had turned around and was steaming its way toward the packet ship, raising her sails to add power to the large paddlewheels churning up the water. Morgan quickly gave the order to get underway.

"Mr. Moore. Belay the headsails port side. Sheets and braces, men."

"Shouldn't we hove to, Cap'n?"

"Steady on, Mr. Moore. Signal the Royal Navy frigate that we will be turning this man over to the proper authorities in Falmouth."

"But Cap'n, I don't . . ."

"A Yankee liner stays on schedule, Mr. Moore, and our next stop is Falmouth."

"Aye, aye, Captain," replied the first mate, even as his frowning face clearly revealed his doubts.

With the backed headsails slowly turning the ship's bow, and the topsails high up the mast flapping and then filling with wind, the packet slid through the water, resuming its easterly direction. The *Southampton*'s wide yards were braced to the wind; the main, the topsails, the topgallants, and the royals were now stretched and straining with the force of the strengthening breeze. Morgan noticed that the sailors on board the *Hydra* were frantically raising the ship's flags.

"What are they signaling, Mr. Moore?" asked Morgan.

"They are informing us that we will be boarded in Falmouth where they will take custody of the sailor. How should we respond, Cap'n?"

"Tell them we intend to fully comply," Morgan replied simply. He wanted to avoid any possible incident with the warship, but he also wanted to buy time until he could figure out what to do with Hiram.

The two ships sailed in tandem all day, never too far apart, the steamship following close behind the fast packet. Off to the port side was the rugged coast of Ireland surrounded by gray, overcast skies. Squall bands were moving in, promising a stormy night. They passed the tiny islands of the Bull and the Cow at the tip of Dursey Head. It was growing dark by the time they passed Mizen Head and Fastnet Rock, headed for the Scilly Islands. The next morning brought more dark skies and steep, confused seas with the crests of the waves crashing into each other. The winds were now picking up sharply, and Morgan charted a course keeping Round Island and the outer edge of the Scillies off to starboard and Wolf Rock ahead of them to port. He was familiar with the course and knew he would get through, but he was hoping coming this close to the cliffs of Land's End would force the larger Navy ship to bear off. The stormy weather had now given him an idea. His plan was to get Hiram off the ship in Falmouth before the *Hydra* could anchor. He could claim Hiram had escaped. All he needed to do was to beat the Navy steamer into port. With these heavy winds he thought he might be able to do that.

Down below, a pathetic Hiram began to tell his story. He'd been picked up by Stryker's men when he was in Jamaica. That's where he had been in hiding. He was trying to get a berth to New York when they found him.

"Stryker sent me a letter in New York informing me that he had arrested you," Morgan told Hiram.

Hiram shook his head. He hadn't known that.

"It was like he was challenging me to pursue him," Morgan said in a puzzled voice. "And then when we sighted your smokestack near the coast of Ireland, we noticed that the steamer had slowed down. It seemed almost as if he was waiting for us."

Morgan was fishing for any information Hiram might have, but his old friend scratched his head and pulled at his beard.

"I don't know, Ely. All I know is I was shoveling coal in the furnace room when they told me they were giving me some fresh air. They took my foot manacles off, and led me up on deck."

"Had they done this before?"

"No, never."

"Did they say anything?"

"No, nothing. When I stepped out into the sunlight, my eyes were at first blinded. Then I spied your ship right alongside us and spotted the red pennant and the Black X streaked across the topgallants. I knew it was your packet, and I grabbed one of the quarter boat's oars that was stored on deck and started swinging and then jumped overboard."

A horrible thought passed through Morgan's mind. What if they wanted Hiram to jump because they knew Morgan would rescue him? Stryker could be toying with him for the pleasure of the chase. He wondered if by picking up Hiram he had just fallen into an elaborate trap. Stryker could simply tell any Navy tribunal that Morgan was Hiram's accomplice. He was well aware that Hiram Smith was being brought to England to face trial for desertion and espionage. If he didn't turn Hiram over, he could be charged and his ship might be seized. The dark thought in the back of his mind was still the vision of Blackwood and Big Red on the deck of that Royal Navy frigate.

☸

Hours later, the *Southampton* was running before a strengthening southwest gale at the speed of fourteen knots. The *Hydra* was trailing a half mile back, its tall funnel spewing out black smoke and black embers. Morgan could barely see the solitary figure of the blue-coated captain standing on the top of the half moon-shaped paddle-wheel box. The weather was so rough the ship could only stand double-reefed topgallants and single-reefed main topsails with the mainsail furled.

Visibility was getting worse and Morgan decided to bear off, charting a course over to France on the other side of the English Channel. This was the safest way for him to avoid the treacherous rocks of Lizard Point, which guarded the entrance to Falmouth. He also calculated that by crossing over toward France, he would be able to tack back across the channel and sail directly into Falmouth. With the strong winds on their back, the *Southampton* was now running at fifteen knots, and the steamship could not keep up. Soon they lost sight of the steamer frigate even though they could hear the faint, churning drone of the paddle wheeler in the distance.

They continued on toward France that stormy night, headed toward the island of Ouessant, the eastern edge of the English Channel. Morgan was quite aware that these were dangerous waters filled with powerful crosscurrents, deadly tides, and underwater ledges. Amongst sailors, the islands of Ouessant and Molène were known as a ship's graveyard. "He who sees Ouessant sees his blood" was the old saying. Morgan took careful measure to estimate his speed and distance across the Channel. He had a man stationed at the tip of the bowsprit listening for the roaring of the sea lashing against rocks just in case he had miscalculated, but to be cautious, he gave the order to tack back toward England well before they got to the westward edge of Ouessant.

With the Black X packet now sailing hard to the wind back across the English Channel, Morgan heard the steamship passing them off to port a half mile away, still holding her course. He told Lowery to douse the lights below decks, and told the bow lookout to shutter the lantern on the bowsprit. He could just make out the faint sparks of coal embers rising up from the ship's tall funnel. He could hear the British sailors' agitated voices shouting through the stormy night, causing him to travel back in time. Suddenly he was a terror-stricken boy again, immobilized, lying flat on the wet floorboards of the rowboat, waiting for the lead bullets to tear through his skin. The hushed voice of the first mate, asking him for the course, snapped him back to the present.

"North-northwest," he whispered back. "Full sail to Falmouth."

He was expecting the Royal Navy ship to change course, but the paddle wheels kept moving in the same direction. Amazingly, they hadn't spotted them. For the longest time, he stood at the stern of the ship listening to the churn of the paddles fading away into the dark gloom of the night. Finally, there was silence. Morgan wondered if Stryker was confused at his exact position. He knew well enough if the Royal Navy ship did not change her course, she would run ashore on the deadly rocks off Ouessant and Molène.

28

At first light, Morgan scanned the horizon off to the east for any sign of smoke, but there was nothing, only a few coastal schooners working their way up and down the English Channel. The storm had cleared and the sky was clear. A few hours later, the *Southampton* finally coasted into Falmouth harbor. The passengers were celebrating with a chorus of hip-hip-hoorays. The sailors threw their hats in the air. The stewards banged pots and pans and waved their white serving jackets over their heads. It was not just a fast passage, but a transatlantic record for a sailing ship. Captain Morgan had crossed the Atlantic, going from New York to England, in thirteen days, twelve hours. Despite all the problems in the voyage, the *Southampton* could claim to be the fastest of the transatlantic wind packets, at least for the moment.

But Morgan had little time to celebrate. He was worried the Navy ship would soon surface on the horizon. He told his first mate, Mr. Moore, to keep his spyglass focused on the English Channel and notify him if he saw any signs of smoke on the horizon. With all the singing and laughter going on in the quarterdeck and the center of the ship, Morgan lost no time in pulling Hiram aside. They both walked over to the wheelhouse, where they found a quiet corner by the stern rail.

Morgan looked at him expectantly.

"Time is short, Hiram. That Navy ship will be here before you know it. What do you have to tell me?"

Hiram fidgeted back and forth, stroking his beard. He shuffled his feet as he seemed to be thinking how to respond. Morgan tapped his finger impatiently on the rail.

"They are still looking for Abraham."

"What?" Morgan gave a start of disbelief. "Who do you mean?"

"Blackwood. Blackwood and Stryker. When they were searching for me in Jamaica, my mates in the taverns told me their men were also making inquiries about Abraham."

Morgan stared at Hiram with a perplexed, incomprehensive look.

"How is that possible, Hiram? Abraham's dead. John Taylor told me what happened."

Hiram seemed genuinely surprised.

"Are you sure?" he asked. "I thought maybe . . ."

"No, he's dead. That's what Taylor said. My brother was trapped in that cursed ship along with those slaves. There was no way out. He drowned."

Hiram pulled at his beard, giving Morgan an uneasy stare.

"I am sorry. I am sorry, Ely."

Hiram coughed into his fist in clear discomfort.

"Is there something you need to tell me?" Morgan asked.

"I wanted to . . ."

Hiram looked at him, and gave a nervous shrug.

"This is hard for me. Don't get riled, Ely." His voice became hushed. "When they captured me at the White Bull that night all those many years ago, I met Blackwood."

Morgan's eyebrows shot up in surprise.

"He wanted to know what you knew about his operation. I told him you didn't know much of anything, but he said I had to come with him. I wish I hadn't but I did."

"You sailed with Blackwood?" Morgan asked in a state of incomprehension. He looked at his friend and shook his head in dismay.

"You were on a slaver?"

"No, no, not exactly. He put me on Stryker's ship, the H.M.S. *Resolve*. You see, they were in it together. They still are."

Morgan shook his head in amazement.

"How can that be, Hiram? I don't understand."

"I swear, in the beginning I didn't know what I was doing. All that blackbird chasing we did on the *Resolve* was a cover. We all would have been hanged if the admirals had discovered what we were really doing."

"Which was . . . ?"

Hiram could not bring himself to meet Morgan's stern gaze. Instead, he looked beyond him as he continued his startling confession.

"Every three months or so we would rendezvous on the African coastline with one specific slave ship. This meeting was as regular as the comings and goings of one of your packets. Stryker seemed to know where to sail the *Resolve*. We would find the slave ship, somewhere between Lopez and Benguela in a hidden lagoon or up some river. The Bonny River area with all its many hideaways was a common destination."

"Was it Blackwood?" asked Morgan.

"It was. The ship always had a Portuguese name, but it was the same ship with a snake figurehead under the bowsprit."

"Was that the *Charon* we spotted years ago in the West India Docks, only with a changed name? Do you remember, Hiram?"

"I can't say for sure. I suspect there were many slave ships that were all made to look the same. They were all topsail schooners built in Baltimore. We would watch as canoe loads of guinea slaves were loaded onto that ship like human cattle, the overseer's whip cracking through the humid air, that whistling sound always followed by human cries. Blackwood was usually there on the deck, examining the walking cargo like a farmer examining his livestock."

Just then Morgan heard shouts coming from the quarterdeck. He looked nervously over his shoulder, shading his eyes with his hands, expecting to see a Royal Navy paddle wheeler steaming their way. Instead, he saw Lowery and Junkett passing out more champagne to the passengers. He shouted out to Mr. Moore.

"Any sign of that steamship?"

"No, sir, not as yet."

Morgan turned back to find Hiram looking forlornly down at his feet.

"Go ahead," Morgan said as he stepped up to stand closer to Hiram at the rail. Hiram squirted a mouthful of tobacco juice over the side.

"Once we set sail we would chase this ship, or I should say escort it, all the way to the West Indies. When any other Royal Navy cruiser patrolling the Caribbean would come close, we would flag them off, pretending like we were on a chase. In the early years, we would drop off our cargo in Jamaica, secretly at night. But once the English abolished all slavery, our destination was always the same, one of them bays between Cienfuegos and Trinidad on the south coast of Cuba. We would come in at night and stand watch as that slave ship would unload its human cargo. Nothing was said to those of us in the crew, but days later, all of us would get a special compensation in gold coins and Stryker would tell us to stow our blabbers."

"How many of these passages did you make?" asked Morgan, stunned that his friend had been part of a slaving operation for so many years. Hiram seemed to be his own worst enemy with the decisions he made and the company he kept.

"Two to three passages a year, sometimes as many as six hundred crammed into a ship half the size of the *Southampton*. Word was that most of them would end up on American plantations in the South going through New Orleans. Sometimes to avoid suspicion we would on occasion hand over that slave ship to the Royal Navy authorities in Jamaica with a story about all the slaves drowning and the blackbirders killed. It helped polish Stryker's record and reputation as a successful slave catcher. Then Blackwood would show up months later with a new ship."

Morgan was silent, troubled by what he was hearing. Where was Hiram's conscience? Where was his moral compass? It seemed like trouble was the man's constant companion, and bad luck was his lot in life.

"So why did you desert, Hiram? Was that story about an English blockade all a pack of lies?"

Hiram seemed almost relieved to answer this question.

"No, I had heard that rumor, but it was only that, hearsay."

"So what was the real reason?"

"I knew too much. They didn't trust me I suppose. I'd seen Stryker's eyes, cold and dark, looking at me. I knew I was in trouble if I didn't get away. I had seen names and dates, information that made me a potential threat to the operation."

"Who else was involved?"

Hiram squirted another gob of tobacco juice over the side as he looked toward the shoreline, and then finally, awkwardly turned to face Morgan.

"Stryker sent me down to his cabin one day to fetch the chronometer, and that's where I spied the shipping papers and the contracts he kept on his desk along with his ledger book. As you know I am not much of a book learner, but I did look them over. I suspected he was cheating us tars. Stryker had a record of all the trips we had made and the number of Africans dropped off. There were lots of signatures, including those of some American plantation owners from Mississippi and Georgia, some Spanish or Portuguese names. I couldn't make much of them numbers and fancy words except that all of the papers referred to the business as Ophion Trading Partners. I knew that Blackwood was supplying manufactured goods from Britain to barter for the slaves, but what I didn't know was how big a network it was. There was a list of all the people involved, the Portuguese agents in Cape Verde and Africa, Cuban customs officials, even manufacturers in England, the ship captains and the crew, and the money. The records went all the way back for decades. All the names were there. I opened the ledger with the company's name on it and it looked like the same ship took weapons, textiles, and brass hardware from Liverpool to West Africa, then slaves to Cuba, and then sugar and tobacco back to England. Here is the surprising part. The ledger showed the financing came from England. This whole devil's plan is operating under the noses of the Foreign Office and the Admiralty."

"Did Stryker find out you read these papers?"

"He barged in his cabin door, all scary looking and mad. I reckon he must have just remembered he had left all those papers on the desk. Fortunately, I wasn't reading nothing when he walked in, but he looked me up and down real suspiciously. Sometimes I wonder if he wouldn't have killed me then and there if it weren't for a cry for all hands on deck right at that moment. I think he always wondered how much I knew about his partners and this company. He was downright hostile to me after that."

"Is that when you decided to jump ship in Portsmouth?" asked Morgan frowning.

"That's right, Ely," he said with a sigh.

"Why didn't you tell any of this to me before?"

"I couldn't, Ely. I just couldn't. I was too scared to tell you about the slaving."

"That sounds like pickled nonsense to me," Morgan said tartly, his eyes narrowing in suspicion.

"I'm sorry. I knew you might not have helped me if you knew about my slaving. That's why I couldn't tell you before. I needed your help. If I had told you, you would have refused to take me."

Silent and brooding, Morgan began walking around. He was getting a clearer picture. This was not just a small operation. This was a slaving syndicate with international connections. If Hiram had talked, he was a threat to their business. Maybe that was why they were after him too. He suddenly realized he was a target now. Hiram had seen too much, and now he had all the same information.

Hiram looked at Morgan for a moment, his face revealing some regret. He raised an eyebrow and then began examining the thick calluses on his hands, picking at them nervously before continuing.

"Before I go, I should tell you something else. Blackwood made a prediction. He told me I would hang and he said you would die in Neptune's locker. He laughed at me. I asked him why he was laughing and he told me, ''Yer friend Morgan don't even know. One of 'is fine acquaintances in London is the one who 'as ordered 'im dead.'"

"Acquaintance of mine? What did he mean by that?"

"That's all he said, Ely, before that varmint devil handed me over to Stryker, and they shoved me down into the coal furnace of that steamship."

Morgan was silent. Some of the anger and indignation he felt began to surface as he slapped the packet's stern rail.

"I know you didn't have any choice in the beginning, Hiram, but why did you continue slaving?"

"I don't know why, Ely. It seemed like a good idea at the time. It was good money, but I wouldn't go back to it. Doesn't that speak in my favor? I am truly on the bench of repentance now and intend to overhaul my life."

"Look Hiram, I'm not going to turn you in. You are a wanted man. My ship is going to be boarded as soon as that steamer arrives. I can ill afford to protect you. My advice to you is to hightail it out of here and get yourself on the first boat you can out of England."

Hiram's shoulders seemed to sag and wilt. His face was forlorn and he seemed older.

"Let us hope I can find out who is behind this Ophion Trading Partners before they find me."

"I am sorry, Ely."

Squinting his eyes at the sparkling sunlight on the water, Hiram looked toward the harbor and took a deep breath.

"What will you tell Stryker?" he asked.

"I will simply tell the truth, or I should say, something close to the truth. You were being rowed away to shore to be handed over to the authorities when you escaped."

Hiram smiled. For a brief moment, it felt like they were friends again as they shook hands uneasily. They both knew it was probably for the last time. Morgan reached into his coat pocket and brought out six gold sovereign coins.

"Take it. You may need it. Good luck."

Morgan watched as Hiram climbed over the side and jumped into one of the quarter boats. His eyes followed him as Icelander and two others pulled their oars through the waves, carrying Hiram Smith to shore. He kept on looking until the sunlight shining on the water blinded him and he lost sight of the boat.

Morgan looked over at the quarterdeck. The celebrations on board were still going on. A noisy squadron of seagulls was hovering and squawking overhead. There were calls for more champagne and a speech from the captain, but Morgan politely declined and went back to his cabin to think about what his next step should be.

As he tried to distill all the information he'd just heard, Hiram's conversation with Blackwood kept coming back to him. One of his friends had ordered Blackwood to kill him. This was too shocking, too amazing, to even comprehend. He wondered how much he could believe of Hiram's story. It made no sense. Surely this was a fabrication. It just didn't seem feasible that a thug like Blackwood would know any of his London acquaintances.

He stopped to think of all his friends in the Sketching Club. They were gentle spirits incapable of harming anyone. Thackeray and Dickens were both so witty and socially adept at traveling the London social world. They were all sympathetic to the abolitionist cause and hated the slave trade, or at least that's what they professed. Of course, over the years he had met dozens of other acquaintances in London, many of whom were high up in the social order, or influential in politics. Some were unsavory shipping contacts. He remembered that repellent stockjobber named Fleming who had tried to charter the *Philadelphia* as a slave ship. He wondered if there were other acquaintances of his who shared Fleming's views about the acceptability of slavery.

Just then he heard a shout from his first mate.

"Steamer ho!"

A plume of black smoke billowing up from a ship signaled trouble. A steamer flying the British colors headed straight for them, her bow covered with armed British sailors. Morgan picked up his spyglass, fearing the worst. He looked for the faces of Stryker and Blackwood on the ship's deck, but he couldn't find them. The ship steamed into the harbor at close to her full speed. Morgan could now see the figure of the ship's captain standing up on the arched paddle wheel, the smoking funnel directly behind him. He expected the steamship to come alongside, but instead the frigate steamed by, hardly noticing them. It wasn't Stryker's ship, the *Hydra*. It was another Royal Navy paddle-wheel frigate built to the same specifications. Once all the passengers were brought to shore, Morgan wasted no time in calling for the *Southampton*'s anchor to be raised.

29

Morgan arrived at Pine Apple Place just as his friend Charles Leslie was coming in from the garden. After a three-day-long passage from Falmouth, he had docked the *Southampton* at St. Katherine's that morning, and had decided to consult with Leslie about the events in this last horrendous passage to London. The cheery, beaming face of Leslie greeted him at the front gate. He had a basket of fresh lettuce and tomatoes from his garden under his arm. The artist was busy painting a scene from *Much Ado About Nothing*, one of several Shakespearean-inspired paintings he had been commissioned to work on that year. Leslie showed him the almost completed portrait of the Morgan family and promised him that it would be done when he returned in the fall. Leslie was eager to hear the captain's news about his record-breaking passage. He said they would throw him a party to celebrate his accomplishment. But it was Leslie's news that filled most of their conversation. Had Morgan heard about the shipwreck of a Royal Navy steam paddle-wheel frigate off the coast of France?

"It was the H.M.S. *Hydra*, just returning from a tour of duty in the West Indies," exclaimed Leslie. "She crashed onto the rocky shore of the French island of Ushant. I think the French call it Ouessant!"

"What!" Morgan exclaimed. "Are you sure? What happened?"

Leslie's eyes glistened with the excitement of this horrific story.

"Some local people standing on the southwestern edge of the island said they saw men being swept off the decks by crashing waves that engulfed the entire ship."

"Were there survivors?" Morgan asked, his voice quavering.

"The local fishermen couldn't help them. They were afraid the high waves battering the coastline would sweep them away."

"Were there any survivors?" Morgan asked again more emphatically. Leslie quickly found that day's copy of the *Times* and read it to him.

"It says here 'no survivors, but amazingly the ship's hull remained intact. The Admiralty has sent a special team to investigate, and see what they can recover.'"

Leslie dropped the paper and looked directly at the captain.

"Can you imagine that, Morgan, watching all of those people die?"

"Oh, my Lord!" Morgan gasped.

"Did you see that ship by chance on your way up the Channel?"

Morgan winced slightly. "We did see a ship steam up from the south as we entered the Channel," he said cautiously, tugging at his earlobe. "It followed us past the Scillies and Wolf Rock. Then it disappeared."

Leslie nodded soberly as he continued to look at the newspaper.

"It says here that this ship was in Bermuda and had been newly assigned to the West Africa Squadron. It had gone to New York to refuel at the coaling station over in New Jersey."

Morgan kept his feelings to himself, not wanting to reveal too much, even to Leslie. He was reeling with the horror of the news. He felt so badly for all those sailors. His mind was awash with contradictory emotions of shock and sadness, mixed with relief and triumph. He imagined all those men being swept off the decks into the churning water. He felt a wave of nausea, but then he saw the faces of Blackwood, Big Red, and Stryker, and he felt no empathy, only a strange sense of freedom. He decided to change the topic. Soon they were talking about the Royal Academy and how Leslie's son Robert had exhibited at the academy this year with a painting called *A Sailor's Yarn* inspired by one of his passages across the Atlantic with Morgan.

"It was one of the few contemporary paintings at this year's exhibit," the artist rattled on.

Morgan nodded with only moderate interest. He was used to Leslie chattering on for hours about the London art world. He was reading the newspaper's account of the shipwreck, wondering what information about his own complicated life and the dangers he faced he could share with Leslie.

"One of the academy's best patrons has just asked me to do a painting from a Greek myth. I am not sure whether I want to do it or not. As you know, I really prefer scenes from classic works like Cervantes and Molière."

Morgan looked up with a distracted expression. He hadn't been listening.

"The commission, Morgan. Should I take it? It is a Greek creation myth, the story of Eurynome and Ophion."

Morgan's eyes grew wide.

"What was that you said, Leslie?" he asked cautiously. "Did you say Ophion?"

"Yes, Ophion," replied the artist nonchalantly. "No reason you should know that name. Ophion is not one of the better-known figures in Greek mythology. Why, have you heard of it?"

"No, or, maybe I have. I'm not sure. Please go on," Morgan replied.

Leslie got up to walk around his studio to a bookshelf where he pulled out a large book on the gods of ancient Greece. He opened it to a page with an illustration of a serpent wrapped around a mermaid's arm and handed it to Morgan.

"Look at the first chapter. Ophion was at the very center of the ancient Greek creation myth. This was at the dawn of time when Eurynome, the goddess of all things, held sway on Olympus. As the myth goes, Eurynome rose up from chaos and divided the sea from the sky. She created a giant snake called Ophion and together they ruled the universe until he became unruly. Then she banished the serpent into the underworld."

Morgan was stroking his chin as he pondered the connection of this myth, if any, to Ophion Trading Partners. "Reminds me a little of Queen Victoria banishing the serpent of slavery from England and creating a new era. It was Queen Victoria who presided over the final act of freeing the slaves when the apprenticeship program ended in 1838. Isn't that right, Leslie?"

The artist's face lit up with excitement, and he grabbed the book from Morgan, slapping the illustration of Ophion and Eurynome with the back of his hand.

"That's brilliant, Morgan! I never thought of that before. That could be the answer. I could paint Her Majesty in her coronation robes, seated on the throne with her scepter, banishing a vile-looking serpent into the ground. I will have to suggest that to my patron. The comparison is perfect. It will transform the Ophion myth into a contemporary topic."

"Who is commissioning the painting, if I may ask?" queried Morgan.

"Well, I usually don't divulge for whom I am painting unless, of course, it is a portrait, but I am sure it is all right to tell you as he is an old acquaintance of yours as well. It is none other than our friend Lord Nanvers."

Morgan felt the air being sucked out of his lungs, and almost unconsciously he breathed out the name, "Nanvers."

"Yes, it is Nanvers."

"Why do you think Lord Nanvers wants a painting of the Ophion myth?" Morgan asked quietly.

"I wondered that as well," replied Leslie. "I think he is becoming more reflective. He is sixty years old now, even though he doesn't seem it. His family crest is a coiled serpent, you know."

"Oh yes, I remember," replied Morgan. "Nanvers has a ring with a serpent's design, quite distinctive."

"Yes, I think he is proud of his family heritage. He has always been an avid admirer of the sculpture of ancient Greece."

"I don't know much about Lord Nanvers's family heritage, or business, Leslie. What can you tell me?"

Eager to show his familiarity with the Nanvers name, Leslie volunteered more information.

"As you know, Morgan, Lord Nanvers is George Wilberton, the third Earl of Nanvers." His voice changed in tone as he began speaking in a whisper. "Nanvers is what they call in London's finer circles 'a West Indian.' Did you know that?"

"A West Indian?" Morgan replied with a puzzled voice. "What do you mean?"

"Just a generation ago, the Wilbertons were looked down upon by some of the more established members of the landed aristocracy. I believe they were treated quite poorly because their family fortune came from the West Indies. New money, if you know what I mean. But now that the family is so ensconced in the landed aristocracy, that has changed. The transformation really began with Nanvers's father. He tried to distance the family name from the original source of their wealth, and now I would say our good friend Nanvers has succeeded in being accepted even among some of the more snobbish aristocrats here in London."

"Does the family still have financial interests in the West Indies?" Morgan asked in a barely restrained voice.

"I believe so. At one point, the Wilberton family had more than five working plantations in Jamaica, Nevis, and Barbados with thousands of slaves. They owned these properties for more than a century. Naturally the family owned their own ships, and were involved in transporting not only sugar but rum to England. Of course, once slavery was abolished all that changed. The family was generously compensated by the Crown for all their slaves, and as I understand it, they reduced their landholdings in the West Indies. Since then I believe they have diversified substantially, even with interests in manufacturing."

"I didn't know any of that," Morgan replied with feigned disinterest, even though a stream of new, random thoughts were tumbling through his mind.

"But enough of that, Morgan," Leslie said with a big smile on his face. "You look far too serious. Suffice to say, Lord Nanvers is a very wealthy man and very generous to those of us in the arts. He is always praising you. Just the other day he asked me about that sailor friend of yours who was sailing with the West Africa Squadron. What was his name, Horace? Henry? Remember, he came to speak to us in the cabin of your ship."

"Hiram, Hiram Smith," replied Morgan.

"Right," said Leslie. "Well, he wanted to know how that sailor had fared and whether you had heard from him recently."

"Nice of him to show such interest in a simple sailor," Morgan said, trying to hide the sarcasm in his voice as well as the concern.

"Is he still sailing with the West Africa Squadron?"

"No, I believe he's left the Royal Navy. I think he's looking for another ship."

"Oh," replied Leslie simply, his mind already shifting to another topic. "Say, I have an idea, Morgan." Leslie looked at him expectantly, his face beaming with pleasure. "Why don't you come with me to Nanvers's estate? He's just back today from a long hunting trip in Scotland. He took Landseer with him to do some sketches of the hunt. I heard all about it.

Landseer says Nanvers is now anxious to be back in the whirl and mix of London activities. I was due to visit him shortly anyway to discuss this project, but now that you have given me this brilliant idea, I will travel there this afternoon. Nanvers House is just north of London in the rolling hills of Hertfordshire. Why don't you come?"

A few hours later Leslie and Morgan were escorted into Nanvers House by the footman and told to wait at the front entrance. It was a stone house built in the eighteenth century with the vast sugar fortune of Nanvers's father, Edmund Wilberton, the second Earl of Nanvers. The front entrance was framed by several Greek statues amidst a colorful mixture of white lilies, roses, and miniature box bushes. Morgan had a chance to look around the front hallway. The walls were old walnut wainscoting covered with large hunting tapestries that reached as high as the ornate white ceilings. The floors were covered with thick Indian rugs and life-size paintings of the Wilberton ancestors, who looked down at them from the walls with condescending stares.

Nanvers appeared suddenly, entering the room in a leisurely and autocratic manner. "Why, Leslie, what a wonderful surprise," he exclaimed. "Welcome, welcome. Do come in. As you know I am just back from the highlands and I have been miserably out of touch. I have not even glimpsed at a newspaper in days. You will have to tell me what's happening in London."

Just then he spotted the captain. For a fleeting moment Morgan thought he caught a glimpse of a dark side, but then an impassive mask with a tepid smile once again seemed to emerge on the English lord's face.

"Captain Morgan," Nanvers said with a surprised tone in his voice. "What are you doing here in London so soon? I thought you would still be at sea on your packet ship. I am honored."

Nanvers ushered them into his library with its floor-to-ceiling mahogany bookcases, amply cushioned leather chairs and sofas, and a lovely writing desk that looked out onto terraced gardens outside. A large oil painting of his father standing beside two greyhounds in a forest setting hung over the mantle. Nanvers offered them sherry and motioned for them to sit down in the leather chairs. Leslie excitedly told him about the idea to transform the Greek creation myth project into a symbolic painting of Queen Victoria.

"What do you think, Lord Nanvers? Her Majesty would love the symbolism. I think she would be pleased to be depicted as the Greek Mother Goddess who banished the unruly serpent into the underworld. Do you agree? As the *Punch* reviewers wrote recently, 'If art is vital, it needs to find food among living events.'"

Nanvers didn't comment immediately, but then rose from his chair and said in a deliberate voice, "I like your creative thoughts, Leslie."

"It was actually Morgan's idea," Leslie persisted eagerly. "The captain even came up with the brilliant thought that Ophion becomes a convenient symbol of slavery and Queen Victoria, the heroic figure of emancipation. What do you think, Lord Nanvers? Ophion, the serpent?"

Morgan had been watching the English lord in thoughtful silence, but when Leslie stated Nanvers's name followed by Ophion, the serpent, he saw him flinch, his mouth twisting to one side as if he had a toothache. Nanvers turned toward the captain and stared at him, his hardened face lingering. Instead of answering Leslie, he got up and paced around the library. After several minutes, which seemed like hours to Morgan, their host finally spoke.

"Leslie, I am not thinking clearly. I have a great many business obligations to catch up with. Would you excuse me? Don't rush off. Please finish your sherry and make yourself at home here in the library."

He turned to leave, but then, as if he had abruptly changed his mind, he walked back toward Leslie and Morgan, his eyes now cold and businesslike.

"Oh, Captain Morgan, I wondered if you wouldn't mind giving me just a few minutes of your time before you leave. I would greatly value your advice. I need to consult with you on a business matter. Leslie, would you mind terribly if I take Morgan away for just a short time."

"Not at all, your Lordship."

"Good man!" said Lord Nanvers, patting the artist on his back.

Nanvers led Morgan into a small room across the hallway from the library, which he clearly used as an office. A large mahogany desk occupied most of the room with just a few straight-backed wooden chairs. On the walls, hung a painting of a sugar windmill on a hilltop with bare-breasted slave women walking alongside a donkey cart amidst some palm trees, an old map of Africa and the West Indies, and an oil painting, presumably by Landseer, of a pack of hunting dogs surrounding the carcass of a recently killed elk. Nanvers closed the door behind them and turned to Morgan with that same cold stare.

His menacing eyes bore into Morgan's face.

"Enough pleasantries! What is your game, Captain?" Nanvers hissed fiercely, his eyebrows rising.

"I'm not sure what you mean, Lord Nanvers," replied Morgan defensively.

"We have always understood each other well, Captain. It appears we both share something. Why don't you tell me what you think you know about Ophion."

Steeling himself for a confrontation, Morgan answered in a calm tone with a sharp edge to it.

"I have only suspicions and questions, Lord Nanvers. That is all."

"I like questions," exclaimed Nanvers with a dry, haughty laugh. "But as for suspicions, Captain . . ."

Nanvers paused as he walked around the room. Morgan thought about what he should do. He wondered about excusing himself and backing away from this confrontation. He considered staying silent, refusing to reveal what he knew. But his curiosity, anger, and a certain mindless courage combined in convincing him to take a risk. He cleared his throat.

"Do you deny, Lord Nanvers, that you have been pursuing certain illegal opportunities right under the nose of the Royal Navy's admirals?"

"What kind of opportunities are you referring to?" Nanvers replied, his mouth twisting to one side. "What exactly are you suggesting?"

The chilly, arrogant tone in the man's voice was too much for Morgan. He felt an unknown force boil up inside of him. He threw all caution aside. Despite his emotional state, he spoke evenly and clearly, as if he had been rehearsing this moment for most of his life. His eyes never wavered as they locked on to Lord Nanvers's face.

"What I have surmised is that you are the head of a well-established slaving syndicate called Ophion Trading Partners, and you have used at least one of Her Majesty's warships stationed off of Africa to promote your illegal business dealings in the slave trade. Your associates are responsible for murdering hundreds of Africans and no doubt countless numbers of sailors, including Abraham Morgan. That would be my brother, who as you well know, I have been looking for . . ."

Nanvers cut him off. His face had grown red. "Slaving syndicate," he snorted. "What utter nonsense, Morgan. You are such an innocent, like some of these Wilberforce reformers here in London. Why do you object, Captain, to something the world needs? Cheaper sugar. Cheaper clothing. You should know that is what everyone wants in today's world. To do that you need cheap labor, and there is no more efficient way to provide that largesse than with slavery. Who else will do that work but the Africans? At least America is doing that right. Your country is indeed the land of the free, Morgan . . . free labor, that is."

Nanvers laughed and resumed his walk around the room, his jowly face more serious. He stopped to pick up his walking cane and began slapping his palm with the gilded handle. Morgan noticed it was a serpent's head. Nanvers suddenly whirled around and turned to Morgan, speaking in a subdued, hushed tone.

"What if I am running a slave syndicate, Morgan? Isn't that what the hypocritical world wants? Even some of these navy admirals you speak of, they know it is useless to stop slaving. They can try, but it can't be done. It is as simple as the laws of supply and demand, Morgan. As a ship captain, you should know those laws."

Morgan hardly dared to breathe as he listened to this startling confession from a man he thought he knew.

"Aren't you bothered by so flagrantly breaking your own country's laws?" Morgan asked. "You, sir, are betraying England!"

"How dare you suggest such a thing, Morgan!" Nanvers replied explosively as he slammed the palm of his hand on his desk, then pointed a trembling forefinger at him. "How dare you suggest that I am betraying England! My forefathers endured hardship. They left England to build plantations in those pestilent islands well over a century ago. They sacrificed to give England what she needed. And now, look at how we have been repaid all these decades later. The compensation money we received was a pittance. We cared for our slaves, and look at how we have been repaid by an ungrateful Parliament in the hands of liberal reformers and those meddling missionaries and self-righteous women in the Anti-Slavery Society. They have banned slavery, but not the import of slave-grown sugar. When the duties on foreign sugar were repealed a few years ago, all in the name of free trade, I knew we planters in the English islands were doomed. Parliament ruined us, even as those sanctimonious fools have no scruples or qualms about allowing England to swallow slave-grown sugar from Cuba. As for the Africans, I would say that they are better off away from that indecent continent where they can be civilized properly. As a Christian nation, we in England should take care of these black heathen. We can give them religion. We need to teach them about the sanctity of marriage and the teachings of the Bible. That is what my family has done for well over a century. We cared for our African slaves. We did it all for the good of England."

Nanvers paused for a second as he collected his thoughts. He walked over to Morgan and leaned toward him, pointing the head of his cane at his face.

"You listen to me, Morgan. I don't think you should be so moralizing on the subject of slavery, particularly as you are American born. You American merchants have been shipping slave-grown cotton to us for years. It has been your lifeblood, so do not put on a morally righteous air with me. No, Captain Morgan. I have no regrets about my human trade. Simply put, I cannot run a sugar plantation with indentured laborers. I plan to move my investments and operations to Cuba. With nearly half a million slaves, and more arriving every week, Cuba is already becoming England's new sugar provider. It is the future, a place where sugar can be produced affordably and profits made. Why don't you be realistic and join my operation? I could use an experienced ship captain like you."

"Now it's my turn to be offended, Lord Nanvers," Morgan exclaimed as he stood up abruptly, his face coming just inches away from Nanvers's nose. He gestured at Landseer's painting. "You had me fooled all these years. I thought you were a lover of the arts. I never suspected you to be the murderous scoundrel you are. No, I have no interest in trafficking in the human trade. Whips and manacles are not to my liking either."

"I am sorry you feel that way. I have always liked you, Morgan," Nanvers said in a more hospitable voice as he twirled his cane.

The captain's eyes flashed with anger.

"Is that why your man Blackwood sent his opium-addicted lacky to drill holes into my ship?" Morgan asked tartly, making no effort to stifle his disgust. "In fact, you were there years ago during the mutiny on the *Philadelphia*. That vermin Blackwood and his fellow rodents wanted to sink us then too. What was your plan, Nanvers? Join the mutineers had they succeeded?"

The effort to keep his voice under control was causing Morgan to clench his fists. He stormed around the room to try to calm himself down. Nanvers opened a box on his desk and pulled out a cigar, slamming the lid shut with a bang. He didn't offer one to Morgan. With a small silver knife he pulled from his vest pocket, he snipped off the tip, and then struck one of the new, highly flammable Euperion matches. He held the bright flame up to the tip of his cigar, and began puffing vigorously.

"Do not think of me as an evil creature, Captain. I regret Mr. Blackwood's impulsivity. He has always been hard to control. He wanted to kill you from the beginning. He sent that pretty toffer in the East End to spy on you and find out why you were looking for him. He knew he could be hanged, so of course he wanted you dead. He kept telling me you were going to be trouble. I decided to find out for myself just how compromised our operation was so I booked a passage on your ship. A fine ship indeed, the *Philadelphia*. I greatly enjoyed the voyage. Blackwood was instructed to wait for a signal from me, but he was too impatient. We had our words after that. He was angry, but he agreed to leave you alone. I told him I would keep my eyes on you. We both wanted to make sure you didn't find out anything about our operation. I became a loyal patron of the Sketching Club artists so I could find out if you knew anything about our operation. That was working well. You were left alone all those many years until we realized your old shipmate, Hiram Smith, was trying to fly out of his gilded cage. I learned with alarm from Stryker that he could possibly know every detail of our operation. He was to be disposed of, but when he escaped on your ship in Portsmouth. . . . Well, that complicated matters. I began to see you would eventually find out about our operation. Still, I held off."

Morgan listened to this confession with silent, rapt attention. He allowed the silence to fill the room. Nanvers blew out a cloud of smoke that billowed around his head as he fondled the snake's head on his cane.

"Let me be candid, Captain Morgan," he exclaimed in a weary but autocratic tone. "You are either with us or against us."

"That sounds more like a threat than a proposal to me."

"Interpret it as you will, Captain. We are in the process of silencing those that can harm us. I have received word that your friend Hiram

Smith has been captured. He will face the stern hand of English justice shortly, I have no doubt. Now you, Morgan! What shall we do with you? Blackwood and Stryker are due here shortly. Unlike Smith, you have a choice. I need a good captain."

Morgan breathed in sharply. He quickly averted his gaze down to the floor to try to conceal his surprise that Nanvers had not yet heard about the shipwreck. He then smiled calmly, and looked up engagingly at the man.

"How did you meet, Blackwood, Edgars, and Stryker?"

The English lord seemed surprised at this question at first, but then responded.

"William Blackwood," he said with a huge sigh. "He was trouble for me from the beginning, ever since he was a boy. I should tell you the story, Captain, as I know it would interest you. Blackwood is more than just an employee or business associate. He is my son. Yes, my son, an illegitimate son, but still my son. His mother was a Creole whom I had intimate relations with when I was just sixteen years old. Not black, mind you. She was a mulatto, a shapely one I might add, who worked as my mother's house slave at the plantation in Jamaica. I gave her some money each year, of course, to keep her from telling my mother, and I also persuaded my father to free the boy. Later, when William was nearly grown, she begged me to do something with him. It was about that time that the second war with America broke out. William looked white, so I found him a position on one of the Royal Navy ships patrolling Long Island Sound as part of the blockade. That's where he met James Stryker and Tom Edgars. They were all navy sailors."

Morgan's face twitched in sudden surprise. For a brief moment he was that frightened boy again hiding in the tree watching the British raiding party pull in to shore. He could see their faces. He suddenly remembered the name, Stryker. He was the one. The two men under the tree. Blackwood was there. Edgars too. They had fired on him and Abraham. They had all tried to kill them. Nanvers smiled sardonically and then continued to ramble on as Morgan's thoughts spun.

"During the war, I was based in Bermuda as a naval supplies administrator serving under Admiral Cochrane. You see, I was the younger son and was expected to have an occupation, but then my older brother, Richard, died unexpectedly, falling off a horse while jumping over a fence. As the only remaining son, I was now in line to inherit the Wilberton fortune and the title. When my father died shortly after my brother's fatal accident, I became the third Earl of Nanvers. Among my landholdings were the family's remaining plantations in Jamaica. Like many of the sugar estates on the island, they were in financial trouble, and I knew I would need money to keep them going. Because of my job, I was able to acquire one of the captured American privateers, and we renamed it the *Charon*. You see, I have always had a passion for Greek mythology. I met my son and his two friends in Hamilton after the war ended and I persuaded them to join a slaving operation. I could see William's two friends were looking for opportunities. We had a challenge as Mother England was strengthening her effort to stop slave trafficking, setting up a blockade. I devised a plan where Stryker stayed in the Royal Navy, rising to captain because he was ruthless and knew no fear. He was in dire need of money at the time so he was receptive to my proposal. He became the key to our success, helping us to get across with our shipments of human cargo on the speedy *Charon* and giving us information, which helped us elude Royal Navy ships. When the old *Charon* sank, we simply had another one built in Baltimore, and we gave the new ship the same name."

Nanvers paused as he puffed vigorously on his cigar.

"So you see, all of this was done with a great deal of thought. Oh, but I am boring you, Captain. Shall I continue?"

"Please, go ahead," Morgan replied. He had calmed down ever since he realized that Nanvers did not know about the shipwreck of the *Hydra*. "I would like to know when you first heard about my brother?"

Nanvers took a long drag on his cigar as he suddenly appeared more philosophical.

"When I think that all of your interest in my affairs, Morgan, began with your search for your brother . . . It is quite a coincidence, is it not? I was always touched by that story. Brother searching for brother. Just like Hiram Smith, your brother Abraham stumbled on some accounting papers he was not supposed to see. Blackwood caught him in his cabin. It was unfortunate. We couldn't let that stand. One way or the other, he had to be eliminated. For a good while we actually thought your brother might be alive. Stryker heard tales of a blind white man who was shipwrecked years earlier on the offshore reefs of Morant to the east of Jamaica. A missionary told him about it and even had the name of our ship. The rumor was that he lived with runaway slaves up in the rugged Cockpit Country. We looked, but there were no roads, only footpaths. We couldn't find him. We were worried that if it was Abraham, he might have gone to America. I actually sent Tom Edgars to your hometown of Lyme to inquire whether anyone had seen your brother. When we couldn't find him, we soon concluded that the story of the blind white man was some cockeyed missionary tale."

Morgan stared intently at Nanvers. "You actually thought my brother was alive, and that he survived the shipwreck?"

"We thought it highly unlikely, but we couldn't take the chance."

"Why was he so important? Surely there are others who knew your secrets."

"None who knew my name. Unfortunately, your brother Abraham stumbled on papers which mentioned my name as the purchaser of slave cargoes. No one else knew that or knows that today, not even our trading partners."

"Still, what harm could a blind man possibly have done to you, Lord Nanvers?"

"I am surprised that you don't know the answer to that, Morgan. It is very simple really. The answer is . . ." He paused as he slapped the head of his cane on the palm of his hand. "The answer, my dear Captain Morgan, is you."

Nanvers smiled at the confused look on Morgan's face. "If somehow Abraham were alive, we knew you might eventually find him and then we would have a problem. You would not have been content to keep a secret. Am I right, Captain?"

Morgan was silent.

"Now that I have been so candid with you, Captain, and divulged all of our secrets, I think you understand the seriousness of my proposal. You are a smart man, Morgan. You must realize you have no choice but to join our business syndicate. Am I being perfectly clear, Captain?"

Morgan was boiling inside. He looked up at Nanvers and said firmly, "It does sound like you are not aware, Lord Nanvers, that the *Hydra* was shipwrecked on the rocky shoreline of the French island of Ouessant. All on board are reported lost. That includes your son, William Blackwood, and your two business associates, Captain James Stryker and Tom Edgars. If you don't believe me, look in today's paper."

There was a deathly silence in the room as the two men stared at each other with long penetrating looks, each taking careful measure of the other. Morgan took some satisfaction in noticing that Lord Nanvers's lips were quivering and his hands were shaking.

30

Morgan caught a cab early in the morning for the docks. As was customary, he had stayed at the Queens Hotel, where many of the American packet ship captains lodged when they came ashore in London. The coolness of the morning air rejuvenated him, and he took off his black beaver top hat to feel the breeze on his head. The driver slapped the reins, and soon the clattering hooves of the horses and the already busy streets of London jolted him awake. More than two weeks had passed since his confrontation with Lord Nanvers. At first, he didn't think he would survive another day. He was sure he would be killed. He had said nothing about Nanvers's confession to Leslie. He knew he was in serious danger, but he had tried to put that fear out of his mind. He still felt guilty about the *Hydra*, sad for all the innocent sailors who had died. But he also felt relieved that there were fewer men who wanted him dead. With Stryker, Edgars, and Blackwood gone, he guessed Nanvers would be uncertain about his next move.

Today was departure day. He was looking forward to going home to see his family. It was becoming harder for him to be away. The children always plaintively asked their mother when their father would be home. He had invited the usual group for the daylong cruise down the Thames, everyone except Nanvers. A late breakfast with plenty of refreshments would be served on the quarterdeck. Only a handful of the Sketching Club artists could make it. Dickens wrote to Morgan that he would be bringing some artists he worked with, including Frank Stone and Hablot Browne. They were going to do sketches of the emigrants. Thackeray was also coming with the well-known illustrator Richard Doyle from *Punch* and his editor, Tom Taylor. Leslie had sent word he would be there even though he was busy with commissioned paintings. Morgan didn't have the courage to tell his old friend that this might well be one of his last regular journeys down the Thames as a packet ship captain. He was seriously thinking of accepting Griswold's offer to join him as a manager for the Black X shipping line. He would be coming ashore for the sake of Eliza and the children.

As his cab pulled up to his ship, Morgan was alarmed at the sight of Constable Pinkleton with his small battalion of police officers. They were ready to begin their inspection of what looked like a full shipload of emigrants. Pinkleton was already writing down a list of all the sailors and the emigrants. Morgan wondered if perhaps he was looking for Hiram. Worse still, he could be looking for him. To his surprise, he learned that Pinkleton seemed more interested in the whereabouts of Lord Nanvers than he was about the sailors and the emigrants. He asked why, but the policeman didn't answer. It was at this point Morgan became aware of a small man dressed formally in a long black coat, white shirt, and cravat who was clearly waiting to speak with him at the gangway.

"Captain Morgan, I presume?" he asked politely.

"Yes, indeed. What can I do for you, sir?"

Morgan noticed the man's hands, clasped together in front of him.

"My name is Reverend John Wall, and I am just back in London after many years of service as a Baptist missionary in the West Indies."

"Are you in need of a stateroom? We may still have availability."

"No, Captain, that is not why I am here. I have a story to tell you and a message to deliver. I know you are extremely busy, but could I have a few moments of your time, perhaps in your quarters?"

Morgan nodded brusquely and motioned him to come up the gangway and to follow him. He offered the man a chair in the seating area outside his cabin. The small man with thinning gray hair wasted no time in beginning his story.

"Captain, I am someone who has dedicated his life to baptizing and bringing the word of God to the unfortunate African laborers who were enslaved and brutally treated in the English islands. I worked with William Knibb, who once said that sugar is sweet, but the liberty of man is much more sweet. Those words have been my life's compass. My colleagues and I have opened scores of missions and churches in Jamaica alone, and helped to establish free Negro villages deep in the mountains where few white men go. Now these past few months I am back here in London to tell those interested about how the planters have established a new form of slavery with emigrant laborers. The fight for liberty and justice is far from over."

Morgan nodded impatiently. He had a ship to prepare for departure and he was uncertain as to how any of this pertained to him. The man seemed unaware of Morgan's restlessness as he continued speaking.

"I was addressing the London Ladies' Anti-Slavery Society a week ago, and I mentioned several touching human stories of courage and defiance against the institution of slavery. One story in particular about a blind man caused considerable interest. A woman who was introduced to me as Harriet Leslie approached me and suggested I contact you right away."

The mention of Harriet Leslie caused Morgan to put his growing impatience in check, but it was the detail about the blind man that triggered his curiosity.

"What did he look like, this blind man?"

The minister paused, and looked at Morgan intently.

"A man about your height, stockier, bearded face, hair thinning and gray, a good-looking man I would say, with a straight forehead and a strong chin. You can't see his eyes. His eyelids are closed shut. Why do you ask?"

Morgan shook his head.

"It's probably nothing, just a notion I had. Please go on."

"I should give you a little bit of background, Captain. My missionary work began in Jamaica at the time just before emancipation, just after the bloody Sharpe Rebellion where hundreds were killed. One of the areas the runaway slaves fled to was a remote mountainous region in the western end of the island called the Land of Look Behind. It was named long ago for the soldiers who rode two in the saddle, back to back, to make sure they could see any possible attackers from all directions. Now it is more commonly called Cockpit Country because of the pockmarked terrain riddled with sinkholes reminiscent of cockfighting pits. Maybe you have heard of this part of Jamaica, Captain?"

Morgan didn't say anything. He shook his head.

"This is an uncharted place with no roads, only narrow footpaths that wind their way up steep forested slopes. Believe me, it is rugged terrain, an easy place to get lost in or to elude your hunters. There are dozens of hidden caverns and sinkholes filled with water, lush forests, and waterfalls. It is a veritable Garden of Eden, Captain. Birds you have never seen before, and yes, many poisonous snakes. The frightful fer-de-lance is actually prevalent there. The people who have lived there for centuries are called Maroons, the descendants of runaway slaves who first defied the Spanish and then the English."

Wall paused as Lowery brought in some coffee.

"It was here in this lost land that I found the blind man, his eyelids sealed over his eyes. He was a white man living amidst these African souls in one of the thatch huts in the village. These settlements are so well hidden in the forest that you can walk right by them and not know they are there. I found this white man, his skin bronzed and leathery from years in the sun, seated on a small stool weaving a hammock. He was talking with a group of barefoot children. He spoke the patois that these people speak, a rich stew of English mixed with some Spanish and African words, all spoken in a lilting voice."

Morgan pulled out one of his Havanas, his first of the day, and lit it with the lantern on the table.

"I went over to this man and spoke to him. He seemed surprised to hear my English voice, and once I explained who I was he began to speak in a halting way. His accent was American. I asked him where he was from, and he just shook his head and said he had no memory of the past. I offered to take him with me to the nearest Baptist mission, but he seemed disinterested. I sat and read the Bible with him, and I knew he came from a Christian home because he seemed familiar with many of the scriptures I read. Before I left, I asked the village elder about the white man and he told me he had come to them with a group of African slaves who had been shipwrecked off the coast of Jamaica. This was many years ago, he said. He pointed to a tall black woman who was talking with several other women who were weaving baskets. He told me she was his wife. Her name was Adeola. She was a Yoruba princess from somewhere north of the Kingdom of Dahomey."

"What was his name?" Morgan whispered."

"In the village they called him Enitan," the man replied. "I was told that in the Yoruba dialect that means a person with an important story."

Morgan sat transfixed as the tale unraveled. Reverend Wall looked up at one of the glass skylights above him, and then turned his glance back to the captain's face.

"Please continue, Reverend. I am most interested in your story."

The man clasped his hands together and placed them on his lap.

"I went over to the woman named Adeola and attempted to talk with her, but she only spoke her African dialect mixed with the Jamaican patois and I couldn't understand exactly what she said. All I could decipher was that they were in a shipwreck and had escaped from a slave ship. They lived on some uninhabited sandy islands off the eastern end of Jamaica until they built a raft from the wreckage and paddled their way to the big island. They walked up into the mountains and wound their way up the footpaths until they came to where they are now. She pointed to the blind man and indicated that at that time he could still see, and she pointed to her own eyes, which were partially closed. It was clear to me they had been stricken with some kind of eye disease, Captain. Strangely enough, she remembered the name of the ship, something like the *Karen* or *Charon*."

At that point, Morgan jumped to attention.

"The *Charon*! When did this shipwreck occur?"

"As I said, the village elder told me it was many years before emancipation, possibly ten to fifteen years before I arrived in Jamaica."

"What was the blind man's Christian name?" Morgan asked breathlessly.

The Baptist minister smiled. "I do not know, but your reaction was exactly the same as the one I received when I first told this story to a Royal Navy captain. He was there visiting Jamaica as part of the West Africa Squadron. When he heard the ship's name he wanted to go to that village immediately. He said the blind man was a criminal, a slave trafficker, and needed to be arrested."

"Did you tell him where the man was?" Morgan asked with a note of urgency in his voice.

The minister shook his head.

"I was about to reveal the location of the village when I looked into this man's face and suddenly felt like I should not. He had a reckless look, dare I say it, a ruthless look, and the simple fact was I could not accept his assertion that the blind man had ever been a slaver. He seemed too gentle a man, and he was clearly familiar with Scripture. So may God forgive me, I lied, and told him I had put the blind man on a trading schooner leaving for America."

Morgan now suspected he knew the reason why Lord Nanvers had sent Edgars to Lyme to inquire about Abraham all those many years ago. Hope rose up deep inside of him like a sharp gust of wind filling a sail.

"Go on, please tell me more. Did you ever see this blind man again?"

"Years later, I went back to that same village. This was during the period before 1838 when slaves were desperate. They had been freed, but England had allowed a new form of slavery even worse than the old system. We abolitionists campaigned hard to have this fiction of apprenticeship repealed. Planters flogged slaves at random and put women on the treadmill, all in a desperate move to keep the slaves working. Scores of runaway slaves were leaving the plantations and seeking refuge in the caves and the forested hillsides of Cockpit Country. I saw him again then. He was still blind, but working in the fields. He seemed to understand many things about farming and how to till the land even though he was blind. He had several children then. His wife was pregnant with another. I asked him again if he remembered anything more about the past, but he just shook his head."

Morgan looked perplexed.

"Is the man still there?"

"I believe so," he replied. "And that is the reason why I am here telling you this story."

"Please go on," Morgan said.

"Before I left just a few months ago, I went back to that village and to my surprise I learned from one of the village elders that the blind man had recovered some parts of his memory. I rushed over to talk to him. I asked him what his Christian name was. He didn't respond, but he began to tell me about the harrowing voyage that had brought him to Jamaica so many years ago. He even remembered the year, 1816. It was an extraordinary story. He was young and had only been to sea for one year. He told me how he had been shanghaied by slavers, English slavers, to my shame, and that his entire ship had been infected by an eye disease."

Morgan was mesmerized at the story that was unfolding.

"We walked down to one of the nearby waterfalls not too far from the Quick Step Trail. It was familiar to him because he walked without fear, using a cane to make his way along the footpath. Several of the village boys followed along behind. It was lucky they did too. I have never forgotten that walk because he suddenly stopped, and whispered for me to stop as well. He talked to one of the boys in patois and pointed with his cane. I still hadn't seen anything. A brownish mottled snake about eight feet long slithered out onto the path, lifting its arrow-shaped head up as if to strike us. I had seen them before. It was a fer-de-lance, which I knew was deadly. The boys had picked up rocks and started throwing them at the snake. One of them produced a machete from the cane fields and he eventually cut its head off."

"How did he know where that snake was?" asked Morgan.

"I think because he was blind he must have developed especially keen hearing. That was the only explanation I could think of, but the boys clearly thought he was a magic man. 'Obeah,' they called him."

"Tell me more," said Morgan, now totally engaged in the minister's story.

"Shortly after we had killed the snake, Enitan continued recalling and recounting that fateful voyage so many years ago, how he had refused the captain's orders to drown some two hundred of the blind slaves. He was beaten and locked in a cell. A terrible storm came up and then one night he heard the wrenching noise of the ship slamming into a reef, the wooden hull splintering, water pouring in. He was freed by about a dozen of the slaves, who somehow had worked themselves free of their manacles. They all grabbed onto some of the spare yards and spars stored in the cargo holds and on deck and threw themselves into the sea. The next thing he remembered was the burning hot sun, the scalding sand, and a black woman's face looking down at him. He was on a small spit of land in the midst of reefs. He could barely see; his eyes were crusting over as the disease was progressing. In the distance, he could make out the blue mountains of what turned out to be Jamaica. They greeted him as a friend because they had seen him defy the captain and the mate. He helped the others build a raft and paddles from the remains of the ship, which had drifted ashore. They even found some canvas remnants of the sails, and they set out for the nearby mountainous island. With the prevailing trade winds now blowing behind them, they landed the next day on the southeastern coast of the island and started climbing."

"Did you ask him what his Christian name was?" Morgan asked again.

"I did, Captain, but unfortunately he wasn't certain, but he did tell me something, and that is why Mrs. Leslie thought I should come and see you. He said he thinks his name was Morgan, or something like that, and he sometimes dreams of a place by a big river called Lyme. When I mentioned this story to the ladies' group, and told them I was carrying a letter addressed to his family, Mrs. Leslie said I should contact you. You would know what to do."

It was hard to describe his sensations. Morgan's head was reeling. He had no sense of time or place.

"Here is the letter. See for yourself. It is addressed simply to 'A shipwrecked sailor's family, Lyme.' That is my handwriting. I helped him write it. I did not know how else to advise him."

Morgan picked up the letter, gingerly holding it as if it were the most valuable piece of jewelry in the world. He opened it slowly and began reading.

To Whomever May Read This Letter:

I am a shipwrecked sailor. I believe my last name is Morgan, or some name similar to that. My home was once on the banks alongside a wide river in a place called Lyme. I have given this letter to a good man who knows my story and how I came to be shipwrecked on an offshore reef near Jamaica in the summer of 1816. Sadly, I have lived all these years with a failed memory. I am blind, but I have learned to see in other ways. The sounds of the forest paint pictures for me. The birds speak to me with their songs, sometimes warning me, other times guiding me. I am told by the missionaries who come here that God will visit the earth in judgment of the many sins of the slave traders who brought me here against my will. I know the man of the cloth who is carrying this letter will explain that to you. If this should fall into the hands of my family, I want them to know I am safe here. My wife, Adeola, and I are blessed with four children. Beyond the painful memories of my voyage, I have no recollection of my early years.

My dear family, should you read this letter, and you recognize who I am, may the kind Providence bring us together again in this life.
Enitan

Morgan stood there for what seemed like an eternity rereading the letter over and over again after the Baptist minister had left. He was too emotional to even speak so he just nodded to himself, gulped, and bit his lip. Tears streamed down his face and he tried to wipe them away. His mind was lost as he tried to imagine this world of shadows the letter described, the sounds of the forest, the singing birds. Finally he heard his name being called out, and he surfaced on deck to the chorus of competing orders from the mates readying the ship. The dockmaster was loading last-minute cargo into the ship's hold. He scanned the hardworking faces of the emigrants on deck, their belongings all around them, infants crying and children screaming.

Morgan's mind was far away as he watched his well-dressed friends walk up the wooden gangway onto the quarterdeck. Landseer's silver-gray, bushy head bobbed up and down in the mix of people. Behind them came the large and rotund Clarkson Stanfield and the tall and slim Charles Leslie, followed by his lovely daughter, Harriet, who was now twenty-one years old and catching the attention of many roving eyes, including those of Mr. Dickens and Mr. Thackeray. He was sad to hear Leslie say that the old club might soon fade away. There were fewer members of the Sketching Club, and now many of the older members, including Leslie, often didn't attend. Old Turner was too ill now to even go to the Royal Academy. They were all getting older, and many of them were painting less.

He spotted Dickens, who was wearing a new top hat and had a jaunty look on his thin, angular face. His illustrator friends followed close behind, their expressions filled with amazement at the chaos on board the ship. The giant figure of Thackeray with his distinctive glasses also followed this group up the gangway.

"That'll do, Mr. Moore, with your 'ead line," yelled the garrulous dockmaster. "If you'll be good enough to 'aul yer stern line to port and 'ave those sailors tail on to that quarter line, we'll 'ave you cleared and ready for departure."

Minutes later, the *Southampton* gently moved out of the enclosed St. Katherine's Docks where two steamers were waiting. Morgan ordered some of the men high up in the yards to release the fore topsail with the large Black X on it, more for looks than anything else, as there was little wind. His guests were milling about the quarterdeck around Dickens and Thackeray, who were the center of the large group's attention.

The banks of the Thames were cloaked with mist and coal smoke, a gloomy, gray riverscape that Morgan thought had an odd beauty about it, much like one of Turner's paintings. From the forecastle, he could hear the men singing. A Creole bones player, Ben Sheets, clicked out a rhythm. He recognized the sound of Ochoa strumming and thumping on his guitar. A wailing fiddle and a pulsating accordion quickly joined in. He could hear Icelander and Whipple belt out a familiar chorus, their voices soaring and swooping like birds in flight.

"At St. Katherine's Dock I bade adieu
To Poll and Bet and lovely Sue,
The anchor's weighed, the sails unfurled
We're bound to plough the watery world
Don't you see we're homeward bound?"

He walked over to the group surrounding Dickens and Thackeray, who now had serious looks on their faces.

"No one seems to have seen him for days," Landseer said.

"Where could he have gone?" asked Dickens.

Richard Doyle from *Punch* then chimed in. "I have heard that the Admiralty is trying to question him, apparently something to do with the wreck of the *Hydra* off the coast of France. They found some suspicious papers on board that ship."

"You don't think Nanvers is in any trouble do you?" asked Leslie incredulously. "I was just there at his house two weeks ago. Captain Morgan was with me. What did he tell you when he met with you privately?"

Morgan pulled at one of his earlobes before answering as he thought about what he should say.

"Lord Nanvers had some business matters to discuss. He seemed to have some financial concerns and wondered if I could help him captain one of his ships. I thanked him, of course, but told him I had no interest in leaving the Black X Line. Why, what has happened to Nanvers?"

"He seems to have disappeared," replied Dickens, his eyebrows arching upward. "He hasn't been seen for days, and he left no word with his staff at the estate about any travel plans. I am sure he will show up in good time. It is not like Nanvers to miss one of your river cruises, Captain."

"It is strange though," remarked Leslie with a puzzled shake of his head. "Maybe he has been called away to one of his landholdings in Jamaica," he said in a hopeful tone.

Lowery was making his rounds with glass decanters of sherry and claret. Sam Junkett followed behind with glasses of Leslie's favorite punch, an old recipe from Philadelphia called Fish House Punch, a powerful concoction of peach brandy, cognac, and dark rum. As he sipped appreciably on his punch, Dickens turned to Morgan with a mischievous sparkle in his eye.

"Is it fair to say, Captain, that I have once again stepped onto American soil?"

Morgan paused a moment and laughed.

"Yes sir, Mr. Dickens. I suppose you have."

"Does that make me subject to the laws of your United States?"

Packet-polite as always, Morgan responded diplomatically.

"I am not a legal scholar, Mr. Dickens, but I would say as master of this American flagged vessel you can consider yourself free to express your opinion, whatever that may be."

The two men laughed. They had become fast friends over the past few years. Morgan pulled out a cigar and offered one to Dickens. The English author beamed as he rolled the cigar in his wide mouth. Soon the pungent smell of Havanas enveloped the quarterdeck, the wispy clouds of smoke drifting out over the Thames.

Dickens didn't say anything at first as he puffed appreciably on his cigar, but then turned to the captain.

"Captain Morgan, this is a good cigar indeed. On a more serious note, a good cigar requires a good yarn. You know I have always enjoyed your stories. I hope you don't mind that I have repeated them on several occasions, sometimes to great effect. The one about the 'wet lovers and the dry one' is a personal favorite. Have you another for me?"

"How much time do you have, Mr. Dickens?" Morgan asked. "The tale I am thinking of is a long one."

"Indeed, Captain Morgan." Dickens took another pleasurable puff on his cigar. His expressive eyebrows inched upward. "Does the story have a happy ending?"

"I believe so," Morgan replied as he felt the smooth surface of the lead pennywhistle in his coat pocket. A broad smile broke across his face like the sun emerging from behind a dark cloud. "Yes, I believe it does."

"What is it about?"

"The search for a sailor feared to be lost at sea."

"How does it begin?"

"It begins with a letter from another sailor."

"A message from the sea," mused Dickens. "I like the sound of that."

Epilogue

Captain E. E. Morgan retired as an active packet ship captain in 1851 to take over the running of the Black X Line. He had been at sea for nearly thirty years. He died at his New York residence on April 19, 1864, at the age of fifty-eight. As manager of the Black X Line and a member of the Chamber of Commerce of the State of New York, he was considered to be one of the state's most prominent merchants. In his obituary, the *New York Tribune* wrote, "he was a bluff, honest sailor, a strictly upright merchant, and a thorough Union man." The *New York World* praised him for his work to promote the welfare of sailors and his service to the city as a pilot and a harbor commissioner. He died a year before the end of the Civil War, but he never doubted that the North would prevail. He expressed that opinion to a skeptical Charles Dickens and some of his other English friends. Months before he died, Morgan signed a proclamation with other leading figures in New York urging that Abraham Lincoln be reelected. Ever the optimist, during the height of the Civil War, he had the Westervelt shipyard in New York build what would be one of the last of the big sailing packets. She was called the *Hudson II*, and she was 205 feet in length, almost twice the size of the original *Hudson*. The Black X Line, or the Morgan Line as it came to be known, ceased its regularly scheduled passages across the Atlantic in 1868. The last sailing packet ship to cross the Atlantic was the three-decker *Ne Plus Ultra* of Grinnell & Minturn's Red Swallowtail Line. She arrived in New York on May 18, 1881.

Acknowledgments

I have many people to thank for helping me with this book. First and foremost, I should mention my grandmother, Elizabeth Babcock. By passing on the portrait of Elisha Ely Morgan to me in her will, she inadvertently may have set me on this journey years ago. I would like to thank my distant cousin, Gerald Morgan Jr., who kindly allowed me to read an old family scrapbook filled with letters to Elisha Ely Morgan from some of his English friends as well as his own research on the Morgan family. It is a great sadness that he did not live to see the book, but he did enjoy hearing and reading about some of my research. Thanks as well to Annette and Philip Rulon for permission to use the Thomas Dutton colored lithograph of the *Victoria* on the cover.

I want to give my deepest thanks to my wife, Tamara, for her ongoing perseverance. She was a stalwart support in this book from the beginning, patiently reading all the early versions of the manuscript and giving me much appreciated and valuable feedback. Her encouragement and constructive suggestions over these past few years helped to keep me going. Special thanks are due to my editor, Alexandra Shelley. I couldn't have done this book without her professional oversight, guidance, suggestions, and detailed criticism. She encouraged me to take risks and push myself as a writer into new uncharted territories.

I am tremendously grateful to maritime historian Renny Stackpole for sharing some of his detailed expertise on the rigging and layout of tall ships, and for kindly reading an early version of the story. Another maritime historian to whom I owe considerable gratitude is Tom Wareham. His knowledge of the Thames, the docklands of London, and the merchant and naval ships of the time period is truly extraordinary. I would like to express gratitude to the appropriate staff at Mystic Seaport Museum and the Connecticut River Museum in Essex. In particular, I want to thank Brenda Milkofsky, the museum's former senior curator. Her detailed knowledge about the history of Essex and Lyme is truly impressive.

Special thanks are due as well to Polly Saltonstall, longtime trustee of Maine's Penobscot Marine Museum, and John K. Hanson Jr., publisher of the boating magazine *Maine Boats, Homes & Harbors*. They both were so kind to read the manuscript at an unfinished stage in its evolution and offer important suggestions. I also want to thank my daughter, Marisa Lloyd, for reading an early version of the manuscript with a meticulous, constructive eye for detail. Thanks to other researchers and specialists: John Weedy helped me with newspaper research in London on the *Victoria*; James Ward, a genealogist, found details about the Robinson family in New York and Virginia; Ruby Bell-Gam, the African studies librarian at UCLA, helped me with my usage of the Igbo language. Charles Weldon of the Saybrook Historical Society helped me with research on Morgan family genealogy, as did my aunt, Betsy Moulton, and Rev. Edward Morgan III, a distant cousin. Thanks also to the town of Essex's much-respected historian Don Malcarne, who sadly passed away while I was still researching this book. He helped me with the early history of the Black X Line. Stacey Warner of Warner Graphics was a tireless ally on the printing front. Finally, I would also like to thank Hillel Black, Nira Hyman, and Dana Lee, who tightened up all the loose editorial strings at the end of this long journey, and Donald Street, who read a final version of the manuscript with a nautical eye.

Author's Note

When I started my research on Elisha Ely Morgan four years ago, I wasn't thinking about writing a novel. I was merely trying to get more basic information about Morgan and his collection of important friends in London. I had inherited a short letter from Dickens to the captain as well as several letters from Dickens to the captain's son, William. They implied a close friendship between Dickens and the Morgan family, and I wanted to find out how this happened. I knew nothing about Morgan's seafaring life. I didn't even know what packet ships were, and I certainly had never heard of the Black X Line. I began gathering information by reading well-known books on the early American merchant marine and the packet ship era by Carl Cutler, Arthur Clark, Robert Albion, Richard McKay, Basil Lubbock, and William Fairburn, with his multivolume *Merchant Sail.* Of those books, *South Street* by Richard McKay and *The Western Ocean Packets* by Basil Lubbock were the most helpful in giving me a broad-brush understanding of the ships and the era. Albion's well-researched and informative book *Square Riggers on Schedule* became a constant companion, providing me with most of the specific information on the world of packet ships. Most of these books make mention of E. E. Morgan because of his connections in England, and the fact that he eventually became the manager of the Black X shipping line. This was an unusual transition for a packet ship captain. I was intrigued.

This led to my reading several ship captains' memoirs: *From the Forecastle to the Cabin* by Captain Samuel Samuels, Captain Hervey Townshend's *Self-Portrait of an American Packet Ship Sailor*, and *Before the Wind* by Captain Charles Tyng, all from the packet ship era. I then discovered Melville's *Redburn* and Cooper's *Homeward Bound*, both fictional works reputed to be based on these authors' respective experiences at sea. Cooper's *Ned Myers* was also helpful in capturing the voice of the sailors. As I continued my research, I came across an excellent source on the packet ship era in a little-known book by H. Hobart Holly on New York ships and ship captains, called *The Vessels of Robert Carnley*.

When Morgan was mentioned in these historical books about the packet ship era, he was frequently described as a ship captain who was considered a social lion in London. He had entertained Queen Victoria on board one of his ships, and had carried Joseph Bonaparte, the exiled brother of Napoleon Bonaparte, across the Atlantic on three occasions. Much of the information about Morgan seemed to come from one article written in October 1877 for *Scribner's Monthly* by an M. F. Armstrong. It was entitled, "A Yankee Tar and His Friends," and I soon realized maritime historical writers had been quoting portions of this article for decades.

This endearing, informative article mentioned a few details about Bonaparte's voyages with Morgan and quoted tantalizing portions of short notes and letters to Morgan from Dickens, Thackeray, Turner, Landseer, Sydney Smith, C. R. Leslie, and others. It was clear he had entertained many of these men of the London literary and arts scene on board ship when he sailed from London, down the Thames to Gravesend, and then on to Portsmouth, where they landed and took the train or carriage back to London. Morgan was given the unusual distinction of being selected as an honorary member of the London Sketching Club, and it was clear that he socialized with a far different group than most American ship captains while in London. The writer described Morgan as "charming, witty, and with an immense heartiness of nature, wherein seems to have lain the attraction which drew to him men so different from himself."

The *Scribner's* article and my other readings did provide me with a solid base of information and some important clues about Morgan's time in London. Early on in his career as a ship captain, Morgan had carried over to America in the passenger cabin the English artist Charles Robert

Leslie, his wife Harriet, and their small family, and then six months later he brought them back to London. Charles Robert Leslie's autobiography and letters, *Autobiographical Recollections of Charles Robert Leslie*, enlightened me on how Morgan had become one of the artist's close friends.

Leslie's eldest son, Robert, proved to be one of the best sources of information about Morgan. Robert Leslie wrote three books about his love of ships, and in those he described some details about the voyages he made with Morgan. These books, *A Waterbiography*, *Old Sea Wings and Words*, and *A Sea Painter's Log*, gave me more insight into Morgan's character as a confirmed optimist who seemed "to consider it a duty to always be cheerful." It was from Robert Leslie that I got a description of Morgan as a colorful raconteur of sea stories who was calm under pressure and who preferred friendly persuasion over conflict on a ship's deck. I also got some of Morgan's folksy sayings from Leslie's recollections.

An article written by Robert Leslie in a March 1896 issue of the London magazine *Temple Bar* also helped give insight into Morgan's life ashore. The article focused on Leslie's memories of the London Sketching Club, and among those recollections was an account of how Captain Morgan fit in. Leslie wrote, "It mattered little what might be the rank of those about him, Morgan was sure to hold his own, and become the animating spirit of the party." That same article provided me with much historical detail about the London Sketching Club's activities, including the quirks and traits of some of its members, as well as some brief descriptions of Morgan's first meeting with Turner.

In that same article, Leslie quotes a letter from his father, written to the captain after he has decided to retire from a life at sea: "My Dear Captain: We hear you talk of retiring into private life; of course, you cannot do this without the consent of your friends in England. . . . Everybody wants to see you. I sat next to Dickens at a dinner-party lately, and he would talk of no one else. We say no one ever sees you without feeling happier for the rest of their life."

I soon understood that the Leslie connection provided the key to understanding how Morgan came to know all of these important people in London. Turner, Constable, Sydney Smith, Landseer, Thackeray, Dickens, even Queen Victoria and countless lords and ladies, including the Duke of Wellington, all were friendly with Charles Leslie. These friendships between Morgan and this group of renowned Englishmen were all the more remarkable because of the ongoing cultural friction between America and England during these early decades of the nineteenth century.

The *Scribner's Monthly* article contained wonderfully personal details about Morgan, including some of the stories he told. This caused me to wonder who the writer was. How did he or she get access to these personal letters? M. F. Armstrong described Morgan's early life as typical of many New England boys of his generation. He was born on "a rocky New England farm, received his education at the common school," and was described as having "a keen brain and a generous soul." His sense of humor "was of the dry Yankee type," the author wrote, "and his jokes and stories, of which he had an unfailing supply, had always a flavor of the keen New England air." The article was written thirteen years after Morgan's death, and I was intrigued by the writer's mention of letters and personal papers of Morgan's. If I could find these letters, I thought to myself, I might find a diary or a journal.

While reading a published collection of Dickens's letters, I came across several letters the author wrote to Morgan after he had retired from the sea. In one letter written in January 1861, Dickens mentions the fictional story he had just written about the captain in his Christmas publication, *All the Year Round.* It was called "A Message from the Sea," and it depicts the arrival of an American ship captain by the name of Jorgan in a picturesque fishing village in Devonshire on the southwestern coast of England. The captain carries a mysterious letter. With the help of a distinguished English club called the Arthurians, he solves a troubling mystery that removes a cloud of suspicion from one of the families in the town, saving their reputation. In the short story, Dickens describes his seagoing hero as "American born . . . a citizen of the world and a combination of most of the best qualities of most of its best countries." In Dickens's folksy, cheery description of this captain, I got a better understanding of how the English author may have perceived Elisha Morgan, as a problem solver "with a sagacious weather-beaten face," who was witty and clever and had a healthy sense of humor and an open nature. In that same letter, Dickens mischievously describes to Morgan how his sea captain hero has "a touch or two of remembrance of Somebody you know." The "Somebody" was Morgan.

What I still was searching for most diligently were any journals, diaries, or letters that might still be in existence. I contacted the South Street

Museum in New York, the Mystic Seaport Museum, and the Connecticut River Museum. From those institutions, I received good, useful facts on Morgan and the ships he sailed on, as well as a good background on life in the Connecticut River Valley at the time. The Connecticut River Museum was most helpful in providing me with detailed primary material on the English raid on the town of Potapoug, and information about Henry Champlin. One excellent source that helped me depict Morgan's life as a young boy was a small book published by the Connecticut River Museum titled *Recollections of John Howard Redfield.* A compilation of letters between Charles Chadwick and his wife, Mary, titled *Dear and Affectionate Wife* were also revealing about life in Lyme in the early to mid-nineteenth century, and the colloquial language used at the time.

Still, no letters or journals from the Morgan family had been given to any of these museums. I went to the Library of Congress and also found nothing on Morgan, except for the *Scribner's Monthly* article on microfilm. Finally, through calling members of the larger Morgan family, I came across what were the remnants of the letters and papers that the *Scribner's Monthly* writer, M. F. Armstrong, had come across back in 1877. They were in the possession of one of the captain's direct descendants, Gerald Morgan Jr., a great-grandson. They had been placed in an old scrapbook, which was now quite tattered and frayed, and appeared to date back to the nineteenth century. It wasn't the complete collection that was mentioned in the article, but there were enough letters to get an appreciation for how the captain used his ships as a way to return the hospitality he received in London.

It was through this distant cousin of mine and the family records he provided me that I came to realize who M. F. Armstrong was. She was none other than the captain's youngest daughter, Mary Frances. Her married name was Armstrong. She had written that article for *Scribner's Monthly* shortly after her mother, Eliza Morgan, had died, and the family was cleaning out the house in Saybrook. The captain had died thirteen years prior to that. Once I discovered who she was, I soon found an 1862 letter from Dickens to her and her sister, Ruth, thanking them both for delivering a gift of a box of cigars from their father. They were visiting in London and had gone to see Dickens at one of his readings. The captain's eldest son, William Morgan, was the company's shipping representative in London at the time, and he was a constant visitor at Dickens's house at Gad's Hill. Now the small handful of friendly letters from Dickens to William Morgan that I had inherited from my grandmother made sense. Dickens was friendly not just with the captain and Eliza, but with the Morgan children as well.

From the family records, I did get a list of the captain's siblings, his children, and the pertinent dates of death for his mother and father. The details about Eliza's father I uncovered with the help of a library researcher. When it came time to end my research and write something about Morgan, I first tried to put together a history, but I realized that there weren't enough details about his more than one hundred trips across the Atlantic, all over a nearly thirty-year period. The only way to tell his story as a sailor and a ship captain was through fiction. Similarly, the only way to convey his character, his personal life with his family, and to depict his relationship with his London friends was again through fiction. Thus I became a reluctant novelist. This freedom allowed me to write about his early life before he became a captain, about which there is absolutely no record. Because I knew he was a young seaman on the *Hudson* when James Fenimore Cooper traveled across the Atlantic on this same ship with his family in 1826, it allowed me to create a scene between Morgan, the young sailor, and Cooper. There's no record that it happened, but then who's to say it didn't? That general philosophy guided me in how to weave together the fiction with the known facts about the captain's life at sea to create this novel. My goal became to fill in the blanks of all those many voyages with a compelling fictional story that would capture the man, the era, and the ships he sailed on.

Another example of this approach was my curiosity about how Morgan met Eliza. I could find no details about this. Given his itinerant lifestyle and her background, I thought it probable that they might have met at sea on the *Philadelphia*. From the family records, I knew the date of their marriage, the name of the church, Trinity Church, and the unusual early morning hour of six o'clock as the time of the wedding. This was reportedly written into a family Bible that I never saw. As there were no details about their life together, I took a funny story mentioned in the *Scribner's Monthly* article that Morgan had told to an appreciative Dickens. This was the story of "the wet lovers and the dry one." This endearing tale inspired me to write this much expanded, fictional version in the novel about how Eliza and Captain Morgan first met. Morgan's luncheon meeting with Queen Victoria, the Crown Prince, and their entourage on the *Victoria* is mentioned in several of the maritime books. The quote from the Duke of Newcastle asking Morgan why a ship named for the queen had not been built earlier is part of that factual story, along with Morgan's response.

As for Morgan's meetings with the Sketching Club, the year when he became a member is accurate, but there are no other details. J. M. W. Turner did visit the *Philadelphia*, according to Robert Leslie, but there is no record of what he did on board ship or how often he traveled with Captain Morgan. The family letters I perused contained one letter to Morgan from Turner written in August of 1846. In it, Turner describes that a storm has damaged his Queen Anne studio: "Have the goodness to ask Mrs. Morgan to allow all the time available before you sail for America for the said broken lights to be repaired by the glaziers." Turner goes on to thank Morgan for the "kind offer of a trip to Portsmouth." This was typical of many of the short letters contained in the scrapbook.

As part of my research on the ships, I read journals and letters, published and nonpublished, of the cabin passengers describing their long journeys across the Atlantic. Naturally, the famous authors were some of the more interesting; Longfellow, Emerson, Washington Irving, Cooper, Hawthorne, and Melville were just some of the American writers who crossed the Atlantic. Basil Hall, Martineau, Fanny Trollope, Marryat, Dickens, and later Thackeray were some of the English authors who wrote about their transatlantic passages, as well as their impressions about America either through fiction or in travelogues. Fanny Trollope's book *Domestic Manners of the Americans*, along with Frederick Marryat's *A Diary in America* and Charles Dickens's *American Notes*, are all important reading to understanding the British mindset about America.

It was in reading these observations about early America by these English writers and others that I realized how central the issue of slavery was in the cultural debate between England and America at that time. The harrowing tale of the slave ship *Le Rodeur* came from a little-known book by Isidor Paiewonsky titled *Eyewitness Accounts of Slavery in the Danish West Indies*. Some of the grim details about the world of African slavers came from a memoir by a former slave ship captain by the name of Theodore Canot, *Captain Canot, Twenty Years of an African Slaver*. The background information about slavery in the West Indies and the

British emancipation of the slaves came from a book by Elizabeth Abbott titled *Sugar: A Bittersweet History*. The idea for the entirely fictional Lord Nanvers character also came from reading the descriptions in this book of the great West Indian fortunes, and their gradual decline in London society after the emancipation of the slaves.

The inspiration for the slaving syndicate partially came from an account of a Liverpool ship called the *Douro*, allegedly wrecked and sunk at Round Rock in the Scilly Islands in 1843. It was said to be carrying textiles and munitions, but divers who searched the wreck site reportedly discovered a cargo of glass beads, manillas, and bronze trading tokens, which were items used to trade for slaves in West Africa. This raised questions about whether or not the *Douro* was involved in illegal slaving decades after English ships were banned from the trade. Other historical accounts I read about the evolution of slave trading in the second quarter of the nineteenth century suggested the possibility that British investment money was used in financing some slave voyages long after the Emancipation Act was passed. However, the entire depiction of the slaving syndicate, Ophion Trading Partners, Lord Nanvers, and his ties with the Royal Navy captain Stryker are not based on any real life historical figures or events.

From the Morgan family records I read, one startling fact stood out about Morgan's early life. His two older brothers had gone off to sea, and in 1816 the family received a letter from a sailor that related the death of William Morgan, and then a few more cryptic sentences about Abraham's fate. The original handwritten letter was not part of these records, but a typewritten copy was provided to me. On the page was the date, place, and the name of the writer, John Taylor. The verbatim of that letter, including the unusual erratic lettering with randomly capitalized letters, has been reproduced in this novel. Anecdotal information gleaned from an old family letter indicates that Elisha Ely Morgan ran away from home to go to sea around the age of fifteen, some six years after his parents learned of the probable death at sea of their two eldest sons. The novel evolved from there.

Robin Lloyd
January 13, 2013